NKN · AF

07/21

Please return or renew this item by the last date
shown.

Libraries Line and Renewals: **020 7361 3010**

Web Renewals: www.rbkc.gov.uk/renewyourbooks

KENSINGTON AND CHE

The Forgotten Life of Arthur Pettinger

Suzanne Fortin

HEAD
ZEUS

An Aria Book

This edition first published in the United Kingdom in 2021 by Aria,
an imprint of Head of Zeus Ltd

A CIP catalogue record for this book is available
from the British Library.

ISBN (E): 9781800243750
ISBN (PBO): 9781800243767

Cover design © Leah Jacobs-Gordan

Typeset by Siliconchips Services Ltd UK

Printed and bound in Great Britain by
CPI Group (UK) Ltd, Croydon CR0 4YY

Aria
c/o Head of Zeus
5–8 Hardwick Street
London EC1R 4RG
WWW.ARIAFICTION.COM

To my dear Dad and our long goodbye. xx

'The best and most beautiful things in the world cannot be seen or even touched. They must be felt with the heart.'

– *Helen Keller*

Part 1

I

He knew his name was Arthur Pettinger and he was ninety-six years old. He also knew he was in his bedroom because on the door was a picture of himself with his name written underneath. Tomorrow, he might not know any of this. Yesterday, he was twenty years old and loading bales of hay onto the back of his father's tractor.

'Gramps, what are you doing?' came the impatient voice of a young woman... Heather? Hazel? Helen? He wasn't sure. He thought it began with H.

Here she came, stomping up the stairs. He didn't like her much when she was like this. She was a proper moaning Minnie. He would tell her and she would get cross or ignore him. Sometimes, he didn't know if he was saying the words out loud or in his head. Sometimes, he couldn't find the words but he could feel them. He could feel the dislike but didn't know how to say it. The words were lost somewhere between feeling and thought.

'Gramps, you've got your slippers on the wrong feet.'

Moaning Minnie was in his room now with her little dog bringing up the rear. Gramps liked the animal. It would come and sit next to him and allow him to stroke it. Gramps liked the feel of the soft black coat; it was like stroking a silk scarf and it made Gramps feel relaxed. The owner was standing in front of him scowling and her hands were on her hips. 'Sit down,' she said, with a big huff.

Sit down. Arthur thought about the words. He recognised the words but he couldn't remember what they meant. He thought hard. Sit down. He looked around his room and then back at Moaning Minnie.

'For God's sake,' she grumbled, before taking his arm and guiding him to the bed. 'Sit here.'

Arthur finally understood the words. It was like they were far off in the distance, words he could only just hear, but wasn't quite sure of their meaning and, frustratingly, he knew he should understand them. It was just taking a while to penetrate this fog in his brain. There were pathways the words needed to travel but not all the pathways were open anymore or they were partially blocked and the words couldn't always get through or they would get lost in their pursuit of meaning and context.

This time, the words found their way through the labyrinth of his mind and Arthur sat down.

'At least I won't have to do this for much longer,' muttered Helen. Or was it Hazel?

Unceremoniously, she pulled off his slippers. Arthur looked down as she put his slippers back on. Why was she taking them off and putting them on again?

'Slippers,' he heard himself say.

'Yes, slippers, Gramps. You had them on the wrong feet.' She looked up at him with pity. 'I'd be lying if I said I was going to miss you.' She stood up and looked at her watch. 'Now don't go peeing your pants before she gets here.'

The fog began to lift and the pathways cleared enough for

Arthur to feel the coldness in her words like an unwelcome winter's frost. 'Who's coming?'

'Maddy. Maddy's coming. Your other granddaughter. She's coming to look after you now. She's bringing Esther with her.'

'Oh, Maddy. That will be nice,' said Arthur, an image of his granddaughter presenting itself clearly at the front of his mind. He hadn't seen Maddy for a long time. He was very fond of her – she smiled a lot. He looked at Hazel, yes that was her name, and was sad to see the tiredness in her face. 'Why don't you make yourself a cup of tea? You look worn out.'

Hazel gave him a look he couldn't quite read. A meaning that was just out of his grasp.

'Poor old sod,' she muttered as she turned and left him sitting in his chair. 'Fifi! Come on, girl. Do you want to go out?' The little black dog trotted out of the room after her mistress.

Arthur fumbled in his pocket for his handkerchief to dab at his watery eye. It wasn't much fun getting old as his body and mind gradually surrendered to the inevitable. He opened his handkerchief, his thumb brushing across the embroidered letter M in the corner and his heart bumped at the long-held memory this dislodged. He looked at his hands, suntanned from years of exposure, age-spotted, bulging veins and bony fingers. He didn't recognise the hands. They belonged to an old man.

2

Maddy looked at the email once again. She was nervous, unsure as to the reception she was going to receive from her half-sister, Hazel.

To: Maddy1990
From: Hazelnuttree
Subject: Enough! I've had enough!
Date: 7 June 2019

Maddy, I was going to start by saying I'm sorry, but actually I'm not. I'm so tired and can't do this anymore. Gramps is driving me mad – no pun intended. I need to have some time away. I don't know how long but I'm going away and you need to come and look after him. Or have him at your place. I don't care what you do, but you've got to look after him. I know you've been going through shit of your own but that's life and it's your turn to step up now. There's no one else to ask.

Anyway, I'm leaving in three weeks' time. If you can't get here to look after him, then you need to make some alternative arrangements for his care. I've attached a file with all the names of his care workers, social workers, doctor, bank, etc.

From Hazel

PS. Don't leave the dog food out otherwise Gramps will eat it.

It was a typically blunt email from Hazel who had inherited their mother's direct approach, whereas Maddy was more like her father, or so everyone said. Maddy's father had died when she was five years old, not long after divorcing from her mother, who had remarried and gone on to have Hazel, only to divorce a second time – all within the space of a few years. As kids, despite being different characters with different interests, they'd rubbed along together, but there had never been a tightness between them, no sisterly bond that Maddy had heard her friends often talk about. When she was younger, it hadn't bothered her but as she'd got older, she'd often wished it was different while, at the same time, realistic enough to appreciate if it was going to happen, it would have done so a long time ago.

Maddy pulled up on the driveway of the detached Georgian house – The Old Rectory in Hemingford Grey where her grandfather had moved to after giving up Holly Tree Farm a few years after the war and fulfilled his ambition of opening up a camera shop and photography studio. It had been six months since she was last here and the guilt that had been sitting on her shoulder, poking her on a regular basis, stabbed at her again. She had been so wrapped up in her own problems of ending a two-year relationship with her now ex-partner, together with trying to deal with Esther's father and his lack of parental responsibility, that she hadn't taken the time to visit Gramps, since Hazel had moved in to care for him. If she was being totally honest, the few months leading up to that had been fraught with anxiety as she was made redundant from her graphic design job and was forced to go freelance. Somehow and quite unforgivably, she hadn't noticed her grandfather's decline as Alzheimer's tightened its grip. If it hadn't been for his friend, Sheila, contacting the family, and expressing her concern, then goodness knows what would have happened. Maddy was just grateful her half-sister had offered to step in and care for Gramps and, being so immersed in her own problems, Maddy had been happy to agree and allowed Hazel to shoulder the responsibility.

'We're here!' Esther's eager voice broke her thoughts.

'Hooray!' Maddy joined in with the excitement.

They got out of the car and Maddy took a moment to look up at the imposing eighteenth-century red brick building with its black front door in the centre, the hardware tarnished now. Maddy loved the symmetry of the house – the two large Georgian paned windows either side of the front door, the three running across the front on the first floor and the four attic windows in the roof. Wisteria grew from the left corner. Maddy remembered Gramps training it further along the building each year and the magnificent purple flowers in the early summer, which hung like raindrops. He said it reminded him of a house he stayed at during the war and it was one of the reasons he'd bought The Old Rectory.

'It's been ages since I was last here,' said Esther as they approached the door.

'I know. Too long,' replied Maddy.

'I can't wait to go out in the garden,' Esther continued. 'Do you think the swing will still be here?'

'I should imagine so.'

When Maddy was about six or seven, Gramps had made her a wooden swing, which he'd tied to the bough of the oak tree at the end of the garden. She'd helped him paint it pillar-box red. 'Just think, you'll have all that garden to play in. A bit different to the park around the corner from the flat.'

'I can't wait.'

'You can play out as much as you like and even go to the shop.' They were standing on the black and white tiled doorstep now.

'On my own?'

'Yes, on your own. It's only a few minutes' walk down the road.'

'Cool.' Esther's face lit up further and Maddy was reassured once again that this was a good move for her daughter. Esther would be going into secondary school in September and Maddy was aware she'd probably been a bit too protective but living in a city Maddy hadn't been prepared to give her daughter the freedom to venture out on her own. It was something she hoped the move would rectify.

Maddy took a deep breath and as she raised her hand to press the white doorbell sitting in a circular brass holder, the door opened.

'You came, then?' Hazel stood in the entrance porch, eyeing her half-sister up and down. She glanced at Esther and gave a quick smile.

'Of course we came,' said Maddy. 'That was the arrangement.'

'You'd better come in. Nice to see you, anyway.' Hazel opened the door wide and stepped back to allow them into the large porched area, where they hung their jackets.

'Apart from the obvious, how are you?' asked Maddy.

'I've been all right. You?' Hazel closed the door behind them.

'You know... not so bad,' said Maddy, matching the blandness of Hazel's reply. They'd kept in touch via email over the last couple of years, infrequently mostly, until more recently when it had been to discuss Gramps, and roughly knew how the land lay with each other but not the detail. It was the way their relationship worked – more of a polite interest than a deep concern.

'To be honest, I thought you might bail at the last minute.' Hazel raised her eyebrows.

Maddy didn't misread the gesture and slightly mocking tone. 'And if I had?'

Hazel shrugged. 'Like I said, I've got plans. It's too much for me.'

'You were really going to leave him?'

'It's irrelevant anyway; you're here now.' Hazel turned and walked through the main door into the hallway.

Maddy and Esther followed her in. The hallway was more like a reception room, square in shape, parquet flooring and a table in the middle with a wooden bowl that looked to be where Hazel kept all the keys. At the back was a staircase that led to the first floor. Standing at the foot of the stairs was a large suitcase and a smaller one next to it.

The sound of scampering came down the hallway as a small but solid-looking dog came running to greet them. Immediately Esther crouched down and began to make a fuss of the animal.

'Oh, she's lovely,' cooed Esther, hugging the dog.

'That's Fifi. She's a French bulldog and as of today, she's all yours,' said Hazel.

'Really? I love her! Oh, Mum, look isn't she adorable?'

'The dog? I didn't think you were leaving her,' said Maddy to Hazel. 'You only got her last year.'

'I can't very well take her with me.'

Maddy sighed, knowing she had already lost the battle as she watched Esther continue to fuss over the dog. She went to give Fifi a pat, but the dog turned her back on her.

'Oh, don't mind her, she's a bit fussy with who she likes and who she doesn't,' said Hazel.

'Where's Gramps?' asked Maddy, deciding the dog wasn't a priority right now anyway.

'In his room. Upstairs. I'll take you up to see him in a minute.'

'How is he?'

Hazel gave a snort. 'Exactly how I've been telling you for the last few months. One minute he's talking sense, the next he's off with the bloody fairies.'

'Does he know you're leaving?' Maddy followed Hazel through to the kitchen at the back of the house.

'I've told him but who knows if he remembers. Now, I've made this folder up of everything to do with him.' Hazel flipped open a blue ring-binder. 'Daily routine. Important numbers like the doctor, meals on wheels, chiropodists, all that sort of stuff... Here, it's his medication. Can you believe they're still giving him tablets for his memory? Ridiculous if you ask me.'

'Have you queried it with the doctor?' Maddy stood beside her half-sister, looking at the folder on the kitchen table.

'Waste of time talking to them. They're not interested. Once your seven minutes are up, they're shoving you out the door.'

'Why are there labels on everything?' Esther piped up.

'Oh, that was the social worker's idea. Label everything up so Gramps can find stuff.'

'Does it work?' asked Maddy, looking around at the stickers – plates, cups, bread, cutlery, table, chair.

'Sort of but to be honest, I do it myself. It's easier than trying to get him to do it.'

'But can he still do things like make a cup of tea?'

'Who knows. I haven't let him try.'

'If you don't let people try then they'll never be able to do anything,' said Esther.

'Well, who pulled your chain?' Hazel folded her arms and looked down at Esther. 'Rather precocious, aren't you? I remember your mum being like that.'

'What?' Maddy wasn't sure what surprised her more: Hazel goading Esther or mocking her.

'I think I know Gramps better than Esther does,' said Hazel. 'What does an eleven-year-old know about a ninety-six-year-old with Alzheimer's?'

Maddy could see her daughter about to answer and spoke first. 'Quite a lot as it happens. Anyway, let's not worry about that now. I'm going up to see Gramps. Come on, Esther.'

Maddy stood outside her grandfather's room and looked at the picture on the door. It had been taken a couple of years ago, when he was out at lunch with her grandmother, Joan. She was sitting next to him at the table. Maddy remembered taking this photo herself. It had been a lovely afternoon but at the same time as bringing a smile to her face, it brought with it the sadness of what was to follow that week when she'd broken up from a long-term relationship. It hadn't been her first or her last break-up of a relationship, but it was the one that hurt the most – still did if she was honest. She shooed away the memory of Joe Finch, annoyed that with another broken relationship under her belt, which she was collecting like military honours, it was still able to have that effect on her.

'Are we going in?' Esther nodded towards the room.

Maddy smiled and knocked on the door before opening it. 'Gramps? Are you there? It's me, Maddy.' She stepped into the room. Her grandfather was lying on his bed, his eyes closed. He was fully dressed and a walking stick was alongside him on the bed. Although Maddy hadn't seen him for a while, she hadn't remembered him looking so frail and so... so old. He was in his nineties, she reminded herself, but all the same.

His eyes flickered open. 'Who's that?'

'It's me, Maddy.' She moved to the side of the bed as her grandfather sat up and on lopsided arms, due to an injury he'd picked up in the war. He shuffled himself further up the bed. Maddy smiled, making eye contact with him. 'How are you, Gramps?'

'Maddy.' He looked at her, his once bright blue eyes now paler with a hint of grey. 'Maddy.' He reached out a hand and took hers. Maddy thought she could see a glimmer of recognition from him.

'Yes, it's me, Gramps.' She gave his hand a little pat. 'This is Esther. You haven't seen her for a while.'

'A year and a half to be exact. I didn't come the last time you did,' cut in Esther. 'Hello, Gramps.'

'Well, this is lovely,' said Arthur. 'I'm delighted to see you both.'

Maddy leaned over and gave her grandfather a kiss on the cheek and a brief hug. 'We're coming to stay with you for a while.'

'Jolly good. That will be nice.' He sat up further and waved a hand in Esther's direction, beckoning her to come nearer. 'Ah, that's better. You look very serious, young lady.' Gramps opened his bedside drawer and after a moment fumbling with the tin inside, he opened the lid and offered the box to her.

Maddy looked on as her daughter tentatively chose a red boiled sweet in a cellophane wrapper.

Gramps leaned forward and spoke in a loud whisper. 'You ever want one, you come and help yourself but...' he tapped the side of his nose '...don't tell the grown-ups. They'll say it's bad for your teeth.' With that he jutted out his jaw and pushed his false teeth forward.

Esther let out a whoop of laughter and Gramps winked at her before sucking them back in and then looking innocently at Maddy.

Maddy couldn't help giggling herself. She remembered how her grandfather had always done this when she was a child. 'I see I'm going to have to keep my eye on you two.' She put the tin back in the drawer. 'Would you like a cup of tea, Gramps?'

He looked at her with a blank expression for a few seconds before replying. 'Tea? Yes, that will be nice.' A frown creased his forehead. 'Do I like tea?'

Maddy felt her heart drop a little. She crouched down in front of him. 'You love tea. You have two sugars and a dash of milk.'

'Tea. Two sugars. Dash of milk.' His hands fidgeted together in his lap. 'Tea. Two sugars. Dash of milk.'

Maddy put her hand under his arm, encouraging him to stand and passed his walking stick to him. 'Come on, let's go downstairs. Esther, you go the other side to help Gramps. Hold his arm to help steady him.'

Her grandfather looked at his left arm and tutted. 'Not what it used to be.'

They made their way downstairs and into the living room, where Maddy settled Gramps in the winged-back chair by the bay window. She was surprised how steady Gramps was on his feet once he got his balance.

Hazel hovered behind them. 'Good luck with that,' she said, her arms folded. 'You'll never get him out of there now. He'll be trying to switch the TV over all the time with the telephone. He likes to hide the remote control in his pocket.'

'I'm sure he's not hiding it on purpose,' said Maddy, trying to conceal her irritation.

Hazel gave a snort. 'You'll soon get fed up with it all.'

Maddy chose to ignore Hazel and went about settling her grandfather into the chair. She put the TV on and found a programme about rural life. 'Gramps was brought up on a farm,' she said to Esther. 'He used to drive the tractor and herd the cows.'

Esther sat on the sofa and began watching the TV too. 'Look at all those cows,' she said.

'Cows. I used to have cows. Lots of them. Very stupid animals. And smelly.' Arthur looked over at Esther and they exchanged a grin.

Maddy turned to Hazel and motioned to her to come out into the hall. 'I just want to say thank you,' began Maddy. 'And I really mean it. You've looked after Gramps all this time and I know I haven't been much use.'

'Any use,' corrected Hazel.

Maddy gave an apologetic smile. 'Yeah. I know. I am sorry.'

'Look, Maddy, I don't want to fall out with you or anything,' said Hazel, her tone softening for the first time since Maddy had arrived. 'I know you've had a lot on your plate, but I have too and I didn't think it would be so hard looking after Gramps. I'm not cut out for this sort of stuff.' She returned Maddy's earlier gesture of a smile. 'I'm a bit too much like Mum, I suppose.'

That was spot on. Both Hazel and their mother, Carol, had a lack of empathy or perhaps being less generous, a larger than average streak of selfishness. Maddy could understand it in her mother, to a certain extent, and although it pained her to admit it, there had been a certain amount of selfishness in the way she hadn't helped Hazel in the last six months.

'I think we're all a bit selfish at times,' said Maddy.

'Oh, meant to say,' said Hazel, slinging her bag over her shoulder, the conversation seemingly over, 'the Wi-Fi code is in the back of that blue folder in the kitchen. I've made loads of notes and reminders for you so you know what you're doing.'

'What's the Wi-Fi like here?' asked Maddy, conscious that the one thing she needed to carry on working from home was good internet. 'Only I do most of my work online.'

'It's OK. You might want to upgrade if it's for work. You still doing that drawing stuff?'

'Drawing stuff? If you mean graphic design, then yes.'

Hazel gave a laugh. 'Still so easy to get a rise from you. Well, I'll be off now.'

'OK. Have a nice time wherever you're going,' said Maddy, realising that she didn't know what Hazel's plans were.

'I'm going on holiday for a fortnight and then I'm going to see what I fancy doing next.' Hazel moved into the room. 'Bye, then, Gramps.' She tapped his arm. 'I'm off now. Maddy is looking after you.'

'OK. Bye. See you soon,' replied Gramps.

Maddy could have sworn her grandfather muttered 'not too soon though' as Hazel turned to go. She caught him and Esther exchanging another conspiratorial look.

Standing on the doorstep, she watched Hazel climb into her car and drive away, giving a toot of the car horn as she disappeared through the gates.

'Goodbye, Hazel,' Maddy said softly, certain she wouldn't see Hazel again for a long time. The thought didn't upset her especially. They'd long since lived their separate lives, and she genuinely wished Hazel well but she did acknowledge the small pang of sadness that their relationship had never quite hit the right spot. Something Maddy was far too familiar with and was reminded of the dating app her friend had insisted she download. Maddy had obliged but had not done a thing with it since then. It was the last thing on her mind, considering her track record. Besides, she had Esther and Gramps to put first as they all had the challenge of adjusting to life together.

She went back inside to find Gramps standing over the radio, fiddling with the dial. He was muttering to himself. 'Got to find the right channel. Important news.' He looked up as she came over. 'Do you know how to work this thing?'

'I'll give it a go,' replied Maddy, switching off the TV. She remembered Gramps had always liked listening to the radio and it didn't take long to find the Days Gone By station. 'Here we go, some nice old songs for you.'

Gramps settled back in this chair. 'Thank you, duck.'

3

September 1939

The grave tones of Neville Chamberlain and the crackle of the radio filled the sitting room.

'...and that consequently, this country is at war with Germany.'

'Bloody hell,' said Arthur. 'Chamberlain has only gone and done it.'

'Do not use such language, Arthur,' scolded Helena Pettinger, her French accent always stronger when she was cross. She raised her eyebrows in reproach at her son.

'Oh, come on, love, he's sixteen years old next month,' said Reg.

'I do not care how old he is, I will not have that language in my house. War or no war.' Helena gave her husband an even harder glare.

'What's going to happen now?' asked Arthur, to defuse the confrontation. No one wanted to rile his mother. She may have left her native France at the age of eighteen to live and work in England, but her Gallic temperament had most definitely come with her. 'What about John?'

Reg Pettinger returned to polishing his shoe. 'Nothing probably. It's all bluff. Brinkmanship. You mark my words;

it will all be over this time next week. John will be all right. Besides, it's his job.'

Arthur couldn't help feeling a little disappointed at his father's prediction. His older brother John was already serving in the army and from what John had said during his last trip home, it sounded like it was going to be a bit more than just a petty argument. John had told his younger brother all about how they had been preparing for war in the regiment and what they would have to do.

To Arthur, it sounded exciting. Much better than being stuck on the farm, ploughing the fields, stacking hay bales, feeding the cows, blah, blah, blah. How many times had he sat on that tractor and wished he was doing what his brother was doing? And it pissed him off that he had been left helping his folks on the farm. He didn't want to be a farmer but last in line to the throne at Holly Tree Farm had meant the honours had fallen to him. If only he'd been born the eldest, then he'd be the one dressed in that smart uniform, marching with his regiment, preparing for war, preparing for excitement.

'I can't wait until I'm old enough to join,' said Arthur. 'Did you hear that Pip Nelson is going to refuse to sign up. Conscientious objector.'

'He should be ashamed of himself,' said Reg. 'Anyway, he'll end up going to a tribunal and I'll bet a week's wages, they'll overrule it and he'll still have to go or face a stint behind bars.'

'Of course, if there were medical grounds…' began Helena.

Her husband cut her off. 'Don't go putting such ideas into the lad's head. There's nothing wrong with Arthur.'

Helena looked down at the tea towel in her hands and fiddled with the corner. Arthur could feel the angst she was holding in. She'd been distraught enough when John had joined the army before war was even on the cards, so Arthur was well aware of her feelings about him joining now war was a certainty.

'Don't worry, Mum,' said Arthur in an attempt to reassure her. 'I'll be all right.'

Helena threw the tea towel she was holding onto the table. 'How can you say that? You do not know that. It is bad enough with one son out there. I do not want two sons gone and no one to help on the farm.' Helena flounced back to the worktop and resumed kneading the dough, this time with much more gusto than before.

Reg rose from the table and hooked his jacket from the back of the chair. 'Come on, lad,' he said, motioning towards the door. 'We've got work to do.'

Arthur followed his father out of the house, giving a final look over his shoulder at his mother, but she remained head bowed, pushing and pulling at the dough.

'She'll be OK,' said Reg. 'She just needs some time to come to terms with everything.'

'I'm going to sign up as soon as I'm old enough,' said Arthur.

His father placed a hand on his shoulder. 'I know you are, lad. And I'll be proud of you and, no matter what she says, your mother will be too. But with any luck nothing will come of it or it will be all over by the time you're old enough.'

4

Well, that was a turn-up for the books. Moaning Minnie had gone and the smiley one was staying. Maddy, that was her name; he was sure of it. Maddy. Arthur repeated the name several times out loud. He wanted to remember her.

Maddy Pettinger. Of course, dear, sweet Maddy – his granddaughter. He could see her when she was a small child, maybe about five or six. She was wearing a blue pinafore dress and her hair was in bunches with blue ribbon. A warmth filled his heart as he could see the man holding Maddy's hand. It's his own son, Charles. Charles in his late twenties, a grown man, and he was so proud of Maddy and rightly so; she was such a delightful child.

There was a memory he couldn't quite see clearly. It was all fuzzy, like the horizon on a road in the height of summer when the heat made everything blurry. The memory was there but it wasn't clear. Arthur frowned as he tried to look through the heat waves. Slowly the mental image became sharper and Arthur's heart hurt.

Charles, his dear son – he was no longer with him. He was with Joan. He shouldn't be with Joan yet. Charles was too young. He was emerging from the blur, standing beyond Arthur's reach.

Arthur could see himself, looking down, and Maddy was with him, standing at the end of that long road, looking at the man they both loved so dearly.

'Hello.'

A voice from the doorway made Arthur look up. For a moment he thought it was Maddy, but then he realised it was the girl who came with her. Arthur smiled. 'Hello, young lady.'

She gave an uncertain smile, which turned into a frown as she looked at his feet. 'Your slippers are on the wrong feet.'

Wrong feet. Wrong feet. Arthur blew out a frustrated breath. Wrong feet? What was wrong with his feet? He looked down at them. Slippers? 'Hmm,' he said. 'Wrong feet.'

The girl stepped into the room and crouched down in front of him. She reached for his foot and cupped the heel with her hand. She paused and looked up. Arthur wasn't quite sure what she wanted him to do, but he lifted his foot and watched as she removed his slipper. She repeated the process with the other foot and then put the slippers back on his feet.

'That's better,' she said, standing up.

Arthur nodded. 'Thank you.' He wasn't quite sure what he was thanking her for, but it seemed the right thing to say. He remembered his sweets in the drawer and reaching out, he removed the tin and offered it to the child. 'Would you like a sweet... err... young lady?' He wished he could remember her name.

The child hesitated before poking around in the tin, examining the sweets, finally settling on a pink one. She unwrapped it and popped it into her mouth. 'Esther. My name's Esther.'

'Esther. Esther, Esther, Esther.' Arthur tapped his head as he repeated the name. He wanted it to stick. 'Well then, Esther, what are you doing today?'

'I've made a YouTube video.'

Arthur was baffled. He had no idea what one of them was, but she looked pleased about it. 'Is that right? Good for you.'

'I have one hundred and fifty subscribers.'

Again, she looked immensely proud of this but alas Arthur was clueless. He nodded and smiled all the same. 'One hundred and fifty, eh? That sounds a lot.'

Her smile dropped and she gave a shrug. 'Not really. Some people have thousands.'

'Quality not quantity. Happiness should be measured in quality.'

She gave him an odd look, before wandering over to the bookcase. 'You have lots of books.'

'Books. I like books.' Arthur pushed himself off the bed and with his stick to help his balance, he shuffled over to stand beside the child. He couldn't remember her name. He knew she'd told him, but it didn't have time to get a foothold in his mind. He cursed himself for being a silly old fool and wished he wasn't like this. He spotted a dark green hardback book on the bottom shelf and tapped it with the rubber stopper on his walking stick. 'My favourite. Go on, get it.'

Esther knelt down and pulled out the bulky book. Arthur made his way to the chair in the corner of his room and, holding on to the arms, he let himself drop into the soft plush cushions. The child brought the book to him and placed it on his lap, before perching on the side of the chair next to him.

'What's the book about?' she asked.

'It's my special book. I made it.'

'You wrote a book? You're an author?'

Arthur nodded and opened the cover. The pages were an off-white colour with the texture of watercolour paper. This was the book of his life. He knew it said his name on the first page.

Arthur Reginald Pettinger
DOB 5 May 1923
Born Holly Tree Farm, near Hemingford Grey
Parents Reginald and Helena Pettinger

There was a faded sepia photograph stuck in the centre of the page of a boy of about two. The boy was sitting on a cushion, wearing a hand-knitted jumper, shorts and buckle-up shoes, looking solemnly at the camera.

'Is that you?'

Arthur tapped the photograph. 'Cheeky chappy.'

The child turned the next page and there were more photographs of the same boy but this time a little older. In one picture he was sitting on a tractor with an older man, presumably his father, behind him. The sun was shining making them squint their eyes as they smiled at the camera.

'Arthur and Reg, Holly Tree Farm, Summer 1926.' The child read the words written below.

'Holly Tree Farm – that was my farm,' said Arthur. 'I lived there for a long time.'

'Did you like living on the farm?'

Arthur looked at the child and mulled over her question, paying particular attention to the words *Holly Tree Farm* as they triggered deep-buried memories. 'It was boring, but don't tell anyone I said that.' He mimed zipping his mouth closed.

An unbidden image flashed to the fore of his mind. He could see his mother on the doorstep of Holly Tree Farm. She was trying very hard not to cry. He was walking away, waving to her. He could feel the sadness and there was also excitement but, for the life of him, Arthur had no idea what it represented. Another memory locked away where no one could access it. Damn his mind.

5

June 1941

Arthur's mother was standing at the door, wiping her hands with a tea towel. She was smiling but her eyes were full of sadness. He realised she wasn't drying her hands on the cloth at all, she was wringing her hands to try to hide her nerves.

His father was alongside her and was smiling too, but there was a look of pride in his father's eyes. 'So, this is it, lad,' said Reg Pettinger. 'Time for your big adventure.'

'Do not call it an adventure,' scolded Helena. She went to say something else but the look from Reg quietened her.

'No more of that, love,' he said, gently leading her out of the doorway. 'We're to send Arthur off with no worries. We don't want him fretting about us here. He needs to have a clear head so he can concentrate on doing his job.'

Helena nodded and extended her smile. 'Of course.' She stood in front of Arthur and needlessly straightened the collar on his jacket. 'You look very smart.' She brushed non-existent dust from his shoulders. 'I am so proud of you.' Her voice gave way at the end and she pressed her lips tightly together, swallowed hard and then forced the smile to return. 'Very proud.'

Arthur pulled his mum into a hug. 'It will be OK, Mum, I promise.' Her shoulders jolted and she stifled a sob deep in her throat. Then nodding in agreement, she stepped back, her eyes looking down as she blinked away tears.

'You make sure you write to me, now,' she said, having regained a degree of composure.

'I will. I promise.'

'Only when you can though, lad,' interjected Reg. 'Now come on, we need to get down to the village. The bus will be along soon.'

Arthur had to admit, leaving his parents wasn't quite as easy as he thought it would be. He knew they were both putting on a brave face for him, his father being the more successful of the two, but when it came to saying goodbye to his dad, the hug they shared had been fierce. The depth of the emotion inhabited Arthur's heart long after the bus had drawn away and he'd watched from the rear window the figure of his father grow smaller and smaller until the bus rounded the corner and he was out of sight.

For all his talk about excitement and adventure, the realisation that this was it, he was leaving home to join the army to fight Hitler, began to dawn on him. This was for real. He acknowledged that he might never see his parents again and the notion blindsided him, giving him the clarity of appreciating how his mother felt. It was hard to imagine how it must be for a parent to think it was possibly the last time they'd see their son.

By the time his second bus had arrived at the barracks, he had managed to shake off the sobering thoughts of leaving home. He refocused on all the reasons he'd wanted to sign up for the last two years. Arthur knew it wouldn't be good to dwell on what was now his old life – if he was going to be any good at this soldiering lark and have any chance of coming back home in one piece, or at all, then he needed to concentrate on the job in hand.

Arthur could barely believe the number of men lining up waiting to have their sign-up papers checked and to be welcomed into the British Army. The war, which his father had doubted would happen, showed no sign of letting up and only two months earlier Germany had invaded both Greece and Yugoslavia, although Arthur couldn't claim to know where the latter of the two countries was exactly.

He shuffled forward in the queue until it was his turn.

The sergeant at the desk took his papers without looking up and flipped through them, ticking off boxes on the sheet in front of him. He paused and took a closer look at the sheet, before looking up at Arthur.

'Pettinger.'

'Yes, sir.' Arthur fixed his gaze straight ahead and stood tall.

'It says here you speak French. Is that right?'

'Yes, sir.'

'Fluently?'

'Yes, sir. My mother is French.' Arthur allowed his eyes to meet those of the sergeant.

'Any other languages?'

'A bit of Italian and some German,' replied Arthur. 'Been learning it at home. Thought it might come in handy.'

'Indeed,' replied the sergeant. 'Indeed.' He passed Arthur's papers back to him and then pointed to the opposite side of the room to where most of the recruits were being sent. 'You go over there and see Sergeant Hadley. He's looking for linguists.'

A ripple of excitement ran through Arthur. He congratulated

himself on taking the initiative and teaching himself Italian and German. His Latin master at school had always sung his praises, saying he had a knack for picking up languages – turned out he was right. Admittedly, the Italian had been the easier of the two – derived from Latin, as was French. German, however, was proving a little more challenging.

He joined the back of the queue at Sergeant Hadley's desk.

The man in front of him turned and gave a nod of acknowledgement. 'You get picked out for speaking another lingo?' He spoke in a broad cockney accent.

'Yeah. French, Italian and a bit of German.'

'Ooh, three languages.'

'You?' asked Arthur.

'French and German.' The man looked a bit older than Arthur, maybe in his early twenties.

'Have you only just been called up?' asked Arthur.

'I was exempt. I'm a baker but there's plenty of women to do the jobs now. My Ivy's taken over from me so I can come and do my bit.'

'Whatever that bit is,' said Arthur. 'My brother's in North Africa somewhere. He sent me a letter saying he'd not seen or done anything he wouldn't see or do again.'

'My guess is they've something planned for us lot once we get through our basic training.' He nodded to the line of men waiting at Sergeant Hadley's desk. 'What branch are you in?'

'REME,' replied Arthur.

'Same 'ere. Royal Electrical and Mechanical Engineers. Thank God they shortened it, bit of a mouthful otherwise,' said the man with a grin. He held out his hand. 'Freddie Travers.' Arthur shook hands and introduced himself. Freddie grinned at him. 'Well, Arthur Pettinger, it looks like we're going to be seeing a lot of each other.'

6

It had been a long day and more tiring than Maddy had imagined. Gramps had eaten his tea without any complaint, despite what Hazel had put in the book.

Fussy bugger. Takes a long time to eat his food. Don't give him peas – they go all over the floor and you'll be on your hands and knees trying to clean them up.

Well, Maddy had given Gramps peas and, yes, quite a few had ended up on the carpet but for the most part, he had managed them successfully. In fact, he had eaten everything on his plate. She had given him a child-sized portion, the same size as she'd given Esther. The three of them had sat at the table together and eaten their meal. Maddy had deemed it a success.

It was a shame the dog wasn't such an easy resident. Any time Maddy went near the French bulldog, the animal either turned her back on Maddy or got up and walked out of the room. When Maddy had put the dog's food down, Fifi had sniffed at it and then sat down refusing to look at either Maddy or the food. In the end, Esther had picked the bowl up and taken it over to the dog, who after a little coaxing had eagerly gulped down the food.

'Well, Fifi likes you,' Maddy said with a sigh.

'We're best friends already,' announced Esther, stroking the dog's head. She had remained sitting next to Fifi until all the food was eaten and then the two of them had gone out into the garden. Maddy had looked on from the kitchen window. It gladdened her heart to see Esther laughing and squealing in delight as Fifi tore around the garden after a tennis ball.

As Maddy now sat at the kitchen table alone, flicking through the pages of the handbook Hazel had left her, she absentmindedly picked up a pen. It was a big fat black marker pen. Perfect! With a certain amount of satisfaction, Maddy scored through Hazel's comment about Gramps being a fussy eater. She popped the lid back on the pen and sat back, admiring the heavy bold line.

'Not a fussy eater,' she said out loud.

She wondered what else she would find to cross out in the book. Most of them read like warnings of what chaos Gramps would cause if she didn't stop him from doing things. Maddy was yet to come across anything positive in the folder.

- *Watch Gramps in the garden. He'll start digging the soil with his bare hands. He'll get soil stuck in his nails, which will be a bugger to clean.*
- *Keep the biscuits hidden otherwise Gramps will find them and eat them all in one go or hide them. You'll be finding broken bits of biscuits all over the place. He likes to put them in the toaster or hide them in his shoes.*
- *Don't let Gramps go to the bathroom on his own or at least check after he's been. He leaves the taps running with the plug in!*

And so the list went on. Maddy gave another sigh and closed the folder. Was it really as bad as Hazel was making out?

The rest of the day passed smoothly, although Maddy did notice Gramps becoming anxious as the day drew to a close. Something that was entirely normal, according to the Alzheimer's website, and Maddy patiently explained countless times that she and Esther were staying with him and, yes, she had locked up properly and no, the dog didn't need a walk.

As she climbed into bed that evening, Maddy thought of the practical things she'd need to do tomorrow. She'd purposely blocked the next two weeks out for work so she could give herself time to settle in and get everything sorted out with Gramps's care before she threw her workload into the mix. She'd had Power of Attorney jointly with Hazel for the past six months, ever since her mother Carol had washed her hands of caring for Gramps by relocating to Spain with her very own Mr Spain. Or the Spanish restaurant owner at any rate. Raul was nearly twelve years her mother's junior and neither Hazel nor Maddy had been entirely sure it was only their mother's sense of fun that Raul had been interested in.

Thinking back to Gramps, Maddy wished they had seen the signs of the dementia earlier; they might have been able to get some treatment for him to at least slow the advancement of the disease. Again, she felt more guilt that she hadn't even considered this might be happening to her grandfather. They had all brushed over the forgetfulness, passed it off as normal, not thinking for a minute it could be the start of something more sinister.

A bubble of sadness rolled inside her. Not for herself – she didn't mind being here; in fact, she wanted to look after

Gramps, but the sadness was for Gramps himself. He was gradually slipping away from them, so slowly that it had been hard to see at first, but now the journey was gathering pace and only leaving heartbreak in its wake.

Maddy must have eventually drifted off to sleep but she was disturbed sometime later by movement somewhere within the house. She lay still, tuning her hearing in to the noise. It was a sliding sound, accompanied by a rhythmic thud.

She sat up in bed, fully alert now, and listened to the sound again as it grew louder, as if passing her door before fading and then coming back. Finally, she recognised what she was hearing. It was shuffling footsteps and the clomp of Gramps's walking stick. For some reason he was pacing, as much as he could, up and down the landing.

Maddy hopped out of bed and pulled on her dressing gown, before going over to the door. She could hear him now muttering to himself; she couldn't make out what he was saying, but he sounded upset about something.

Not wanting to scare him, Maddy eased open the door and softly called his name. He looked up at her and came to a halt. Maddy went out to him.

'You OK, Gramps?'

He was dressed in his pyjama trousers and slippers but on his top half he was wearing a shirt, wrongly buttoned, and his suit jacket over the top with his tie fastened in some elaborate-looking knot halfway down his chest. He frowned at her as she approached him. 'Joan. Joan. Where is it? Have you moved it? I can't find it anywhere and I'm going to be late.'

It was unusual to hear the impatience in his voice, something Maddy struggled to associate with her grandfather. She smiled reassuringly at him. 'Hi, Gramps. It's me, Maddy.

You know it's late at night. Shall we get you back to bed?'

'But I don't know where it is. What have you done with it? I'm hungry.' He thumped the floor with his walking stick as if to underline his frustrations and then turned away from her to continue his shuffle along the landing.

'Gramps, this way. Let's see if it's in your room.' Maddy had no idea what Gramps was looking for and she thought it was probably not the best time to question him. Whatever it was, it was real to him right now and trying to get him to explain might only make his frustration worse. As he turned to begin his return leg, Maddy put her hand through his arm and encouraged him back towards his room.

'I just wish she'd leave it alone. Always moving it.' Gramps continued to mutter as they made their way along the landing. 'I'm going to be late for work at this rate.'

'Here we go, Gramps. Back into your room. It's night-time, let's get you back in bed.'

He thumped his walking stick on the floor again. 'Where is it?' he demanded. 'Where has it gone?'

Despite trying her hardest to keep the noise down, they must have woken Esther as she appeared at her bedroom door.

'What's going on?' asked Esther, pushing her hair from her face.

'Have you got it?' asked Gramps before Maddy had time to reply. 'Has she got it?'

'Got what?' asked Esther.

Maddy shook her head at her daughter. 'Don't worry about it now. Gramps has lost something but we're going to look for it in the morning.' She saw Esther eye Gramps and take in what he was wearing. 'Don't say anything,' said

Maddy pre-empting her daughter's question. 'We just need to get Gramps back to bed.'

'What has he lost?' asked Esther.

'Not now,' said Maddy. She wanted to avoid the question of what Gramps was looking for; she remembered reading that it had potential to add to the dementia sufferer's confusion.

Esther moved around Maddy and went over to Gramps. 'Have you got any sweets? You know the ones in your drawer? Can I have one, please?'

'Sweets? Why I think I do,' said Gramps, his face lighting up.

Maddy said a silent prayer of thanks that Esther had thought of a distraction. 'What a good idea. I think we should all have some sweets.'

In no time, the three of them were in Gramps's bedroom where Gramps was sitting on the edge of the bed, retrieving the packet of sweets from his drawer.

Gramps cooperated with Maddy's suggestions of getting his jacket, shirt and tie off and putting his top back on. 'Don't I need this?' he asked holding up the tie by the thin end. 'I should wear it for work.'

'You don't need it right now,' said Maddy, buttoning up his pyjama top. 'You can put it on in the morning. For now, I'm going to hang it back up in the wardrobe.'

'But I need it for work.'

'In the morning, Gramps. You need to go back to sleep now.'

'I do?'

'Yes, that's right.' Maddy helped lift his legs onto the bed and settled him back on the pillows.

'Have you found it? Ask Joan where it is,' he said. 'Is it in there?' He pointed to the bedside table. 'Or under here?'

Gramps then began fumbling under his pillow, pulling out several tissues.

Maddy got up and went over to the dressing table. After opening the top drawer, she took out a clean white handkerchief. She remembered her grandfather always had proper handkerchiefs, rather than tissues. Maybe Hazel had got fed up with washing them? 'Here you go, Gramps.'

He took the handkerchief and opened it out, inspecting each corner as he did so. He must have gone around the edge of the fabric at least three times. 'It's not here,' he said and resumed rummaging under his pillow.

Esther was on the other side of the bed and lifted up her side of the pillow, pulling out a cotton handkerchief. 'Is this it?'

Gramps took it from her and, as before, began inspecting the corners. On the third corner with the cloth between his finger and thumb, he stopped at the embroidered letter M. 'You found it.'

'It was under your pillow,' said Esther.

'*Elle me l'avait donné. Merci. C'est bien gentil. Maryse, merci beaucoup. Maryse. Maryse,*' said Gramps, folding the handkerchief into quarters. 'I have this with me all the time.' He unfolded it and repeated the process of refolding it. 'Must have it with me.'

Esther looked at her mother. 'He's speaking French,' said Maddy, suddenly feeling a pang of regret that she never continued speaking the language with Esther after she'd started nursery. Any grasp Esther had at the tender age of three was soon lost. She turned her attention back to Gramps. 'Put it in your pocket and then you can settle down.' For a moment, Maddy thought Gramps was going to get out of bed again but she gently rested her hand on his shoulder. 'Lie back, Gramps. It's late. You need to go to sleep.'

'It's night-time, is it?'

'Yes. Stay there now, Gramps. It's late and we all need to go to sleep,' said Esther. She pulled the duvet up under his chin and tucked him in as if he were a small child. 'Night, night.'

Maddy felt a heart swell of pride at Esther. She was only eleven but she already understood how to help Gramps in the most caring way. There was a deeper level of understanding than Maddy had perhaps given her credit for.

They both crept out of the room and Maddy was relieved to hear the steady breathing of her grandfather before she even closed the door. She hoped he'd stay asleep for the rest of the night.

'Thank you,' she said to Esther as she went back into her daughter's room.

'For what?' asked Esther.

'For being so helpful and grown up about Gramps.'

'You know, I read about it,' said Esther. 'I googled it. They said people with dementia find it most difficult at the end of the day and it's worse at night times. It's called "sundowning".'

Maddy couldn't help but give an impressed look. 'That's right. I didn't know you knew that.'

Esther shrugged as she lay down in her bed. 'And when they get cross or upset, it's because they don't understand. It would be like me trying to convince you it was daytime now.'

'You're very wise for someone so young,' said Maddy. 'And I think we should talk about this more. It will help us understand what Gramps is going through, just not tonight though as it's the middle of the night.'

'Do you think Gramps was just looking for that

handkerchief all along?' asked Esther sleepily. 'And why has it got the letter M on it?'

'I've no idea. He mentioned Joan, who was my grandmother, so maybe it was an old memory.'

'He said Mary or *maman* – something like that too. Who's she? Maybe that's what the M is for.' Esther sounded more alert suddenly.

'I don't know. He's probably confusing his memories.' Maddy brushed her daughter's hair from her face. 'Try to go back to sleep now.'

'It must be a bit like a tangle of wool. One memory string is pulled, but it brings with it a knot of other memories and it's such a mess, there's no hope of untangling it all.'

Esther had summed it up in the perfect way. 'Yes, I imagine it is like that,' she said, giving her daughter a hug.

'I wish we could untangle it.'

'Me too.'

7

Arthur sipped his cup of tea that Maddy had brought him. He wasn't quite sure how long it had been sitting on the side table next to his chair, but it was tepid now. He liked his tea hot usually but didn't want to appear needy or be a nuisance. The poor girl had looked very tired that morning.

Arthur looked out of the living room window. The sun was out and it was a bright day. He liked days like this; they made him feel alive and aware of things around him.

'Hello, Gramps.'

Arthur looked back and the child was standing in the doorway. He smiled and reached out his hand, beckoning her into the room. 'Come in, child.' He noticed she was holding something in her hand. A fluffy teddy bear, perhaps? 'What have you got there?'

The child came over and stood in front of him. 'It's my pencil case. I've got my pencils, gel pens and writing pens.' She unzipped it and pulled open the fabric.

Arthur looked in at the array of colours. 'A rainbow,' he said. The child said nothing but gave him a quizzical look. Arthur saw something else in her hand. He pointed to it. 'What's that?'

'It's my diary.'

'Is it full of secrets?' He smiled and somewhere at the back of his mind a memory was dislodged.

Secrets. It was to do with secrets. He felt a sense of both danger and love attached to the memory but it wasn't clear. It was like looking through distorted glass. His memories were merely shapes and silhouettes, outlines, blurred as they merged with each other and he couldn't identify anything. He could feel though. His heart jumped and a rush of adrenaline shot through him. He wished he could pin those memories down. He wished the window to his past was clear.

'I'm writing a story,' announced the child.

Arthur looked at her. 'A story? That's good. What sort of story? Can I look?'

The child opened the notebook. He tried hard to remember her name but his mind wasn't cooperating right now. Blasted thing. He realised he was frowning and made a conscious effort to smile. He didn't want to frighten her.

'It's about a girl who moves away to a new home but hasn't got any friends,' explained the child.

'Oh, that's sad,' said Arthur. 'Why hasn't she got any friends? What about the other children at her new school?'

'She hasn't started school yet because it's the summer holidays.' She looked down at her notebook and Arthur felt a tug on his heartstrings. There was a sense of sadness about her. He didn't want her to be sad. Children should be happy. Children should enjoy their childhood – the best days of their lives.

'Isn't there anyone?' he asked. 'A sister? A brother?'

The child shook her head. 'No.'

'Who else lives in the house?'

'Her mother and great-grandfather.'

A small silence settled in the room and Arthur thought

about the child's story. He wished he could remember her name. It had gone. Had he ever had it? Bugger his brain. He looked at the child. Where did she come from? What was she doing here? He frowned as he tried to think. Ah, yes. She came with... not the miserable one... with... with Maddy. He smiled, pleased he had remembered. Maddy. She was his granddaughter. The child came with Maddy. She was Maddy's daughter. That must mean she belonged to him too. Poor child. Her eyes looked so sad. The same sadness he'd seen in Maddy's eyes.

Arthur looked at the words on the page of the book the child was holding. He could identify some of them but he wasn't sure about all the words. He used to read a lot when he was younger but he didn't have the eyesight or the mind for it these days. He tapped the page with his finger. 'The girl in the book needs a friend. I think the grandfather can be her friend.'

He smiled and gave the child a wink. She returned the smile and took the notebook, before settling herself at the end of the sofa near him. She spent some time writing. Arthur couldn't say how long and he might even have dozed off for a while but as he looked over again, she closed her book. 'The girl and the great-grandfather are friends. He's now telling her stories of when he was young.' She rattled the pen between her teeth before speaking again. 'Will you tell me a story about you now? From your scrapbook?'

'Fetch it here, then,' said Arthur. He waited while the child went out of the room and upstairs, returning a few minutes later, carrying the green book.

Arthur took the book and laid it on his lap. His hands clasped each side and he took a moment to admire it, to feel the leather cover as he caressed it with his thumbs. He couldn't remember exactly what was in it, but the book gave him a sense of calm. It felt familiar in a way he didn't always these days. He felt connected with this book. It was part of him. He knew that. He couldn't explain it, but he felt it. He looked at the child and smiled as he opened the cover.

'Which page are you going to read?' she asked snuggling up against the chair so she could look at the book with him.

'Oh, I don't know. What page would you like?'

She leaned over and turned the pages. 'Is that you?' she asked pointing at a black and white photograph of a man in military uniform, standing to attention.

Arthur peered closely. He tapped the photograph with his finger. 'That's my regiment.'

'But is it you?'

'I do believe it is,' said Arthur as an image from the past blasted by him. He tried to grab it as it went. 'Army. War. Yes, that's right. It is me. Just before I went to France.' Suddenly the memories flooded his mind with a clarity he hadn't experienced for some time. 'We had to take a train. I'm not sure when but there were lots of other young men my age on the train. We were all in uniform with our bags in the luggage rail overhead. Most of us were laughing and joking. We smoked cigarettes. We all looked like we were going on holiday to the seaside. None of us knew what lay ahead. Underneath all that bravado we were frightened but none of us wanted to admit it. We were men. We were going to war.'

'How long were you away for?'

Arthur frowned. How long was he away for? He couldn't remember. 'A long time,' he said, in answer to her question. 'Too long.'

The child turned the page of the scrapbook. There was another photograph held in place with card holders, one at each corner. This photograph was of a long house, surrounded by a stone wall. 'Is this your house?'

Arthur's heart thudded a little harder as he looked at the farmhouse. It was a black and white photo but the longer he looked, the more colour appeared as he remembered the beautiful lilac wisteria that crawled its way across the stone building. The oak door that creaked as it was opened. The wooden slatted shutters, a deep red, flanking each window of the house.

Arthur reached out and ran his finger across the photograph. He could remember the grittiness of the stone on his fingertips. How cool it was despite the hot French sun.

'This was where they lived,' he said, his voice almost a whisper.

'Who? Who lived there?'

'Maryse. The children came to play,' he said out loud and as he did, his heart thundered so hard against his chest, he thought it was going to burst out. 'Dearest Maryse.'

'Was she your friend? What does she look like?'

Arthur rubbed at his shoulder and winced. Did it still hurt or was he wincing from the memory? His other hand stayed resting on the page. He didn't know why, but he found himself sliding his finger down the edge of the photograph, lifting it a fraction before popping one of the corners from the tab. He did this with the opposite corner and took the photograph from the book. Again, with no conscious decision or thought, Arthur turned the photograph over. On the back was stuck a smaller photograph of a woman.

She was standing outside the house. Her dark curls piled on her head and held in place by a headscarf. She was wearing a pretty floral-print dress with an apron tied around her waist. She was smiling broadly at the camera and the beauty was more than skin deep. It shone from her eyes, radiated from her mouth and surrounded her body like a celestial glow.

He lifted the photograph to his lips, his hand shaking as he did so. Dearest Maryse. Beautiful Maryse. Brave Maryse. How he missed her. He could feel her in his heart, like it was yesterday. Tears swamped his eyes and he let them fill and then fall.

'Gramps,' came a small voice. 'Do you want a tissue?' A white tissue was stuffed in his hand. 'Don't cry.'

Arthur held the photograph to his heart and his mind was flooded once again with images from the past. Her black curls falling on her bare shoulders, her smooth skin against his rough five o'clock shadow, the touch of her hand as she ran her fingers through his hair. He could even smell her. A delicate rose-like fragrance.

'Gramps.'

Arthur opened his eyes and looked down at his hand, where the child had stuffed the tissue. He wiped his eyes. 'Sorry.' He shouldn't cry like this in front of the child. He shouldn't upset her, but he couldn't help it.

She plucked another tissue and she wiped his eyes. 'Don't cry, Gramps. Don't cry. I'm sorry.'

'You don't have to be sorry,' said Arthur. He looked at the photograph still in his hand. 'I'm the one who should be sorry. Everything went so wrong. From the start. Terrible... it was terrible.'

8

April 1944

'So, Pettinger, is that all clear?' asked General Smithers.

'Yes, sir,' replied Arthur with confidence. He was also secretly delighted after being briefed on his next mission that he and Freddie Travers were going to be laying the ground for the D-Day landings in two months' time. Vital and dangerous work, the general had stressed. Not to mention top secret, hence them being told in strict confidence at a command centre tucked away in the Cambridgeshire countryside.

Arthur gave a sideways look to Freddie who confirmed his understanding too. Arthur had also been pleased to see Travers turn up last week at the 'waiting house' in Peterborough, neither with any knowledge as to what lay ahead of them. They hadn't seen each other for about eighteen months as both had been on different missions behind enemy lines.

Shortly after signing up when Arthur had first met Freddie, hand-picked for their bilingual skills, they'd both been taken under the wing of the Special Operations Executive and to date undertaken secret missions in the south of France. This was the first time they would be working together though.

'Right, well, I need to speak to you before you go,

Pettinger,' said General Smithers. He nodded towards Freddie. 'That will be all, Travers. Good luck.'

'Thank you, sir.' Freddie rose to his feet, saluted and marched out of the office double-quick time.

The general sat back in his chair and eyed the newly promoted staff sergeant, before taking a small but noticeable breath. Arthur kept his hands on his knees and retained eye contact, internally bracing himself for something that obviously gave the general a certain amount of concern.

'There's no easy way to tell you this,' Smithers began, 'but I've had news today that your brother, John, has been killed in action. I suppose it's all right for you to know now, but your brother was working for the SOE too because, of course, he was fluent in French as well.'

Arthur's heart stopped for at least two beats and he swallowed down a lump the size of a tennis ball in his throat. The palms of his hands broke out into a sweat and he gripped the knees of his uniform trousers. 'Sir,' he somehow managed to say in acknowledgement of the news. He summoned every ounce of training he'd undertaken to remain composed in a moment of utter blackness.

'He was killed while trying to blow up a communication line. Shot. He died instantly.'

Arthur nodded, struggling to take in the news. 'Has my mother been informed?'

'She should hear tomorrow,' said Smithers. 'Now, I understand this is a shock and devastating news, so I need to ask you whether you want to withdraw from the mission. Being perfectly blunt, we need you focused. If you can't give one hundred per cent to the task in hand, then I'm going to have to withdraw you.'

Arthur jumped to his feet and stood to attention. 'I don't

need replacing, sir.' He couldn't think about his brother. He couldn't let it get to him.

'Very well, if you're sure,' replied Smithers.

'Yes, General. I'm absolutely certain.' The reply was tight in his throat but it came out clear, nonetheless.

The general dismissed him and Arthur took his leave. Out in the corridor he felt his knees weaken. Suddenly he had an overwhelming need to vomit. He dashed into the lavs at the end of the hall and threw up in the toilet bowl.

John was dead. No. That couldn't be true. Not his brother. Jesus Christ. He knew it was true. Arthur spat into the bowl and pulled the overhead chain, before slumping back in the cubicle, ramming the heels of his hands into his eye sockets. If he blocked the tears, he could block the emotion.

He sat there for several minutes, refusing to give in to the battering waves of grief. He took long deep breaths. John would tell him to stop being a baby, to man up. On his last leave home, John had said how proud he was to be fighting for his country. Arthur wasn't going to let him down. His grief morphed into anger. Those bastards who killed John were going to pay for this. Arthur would make sure of that.

He got to his feet, his breathing ragged as he fought to regain control. Out at the washbasin he splashed cold water on his face and dried it with a paper towel. Straightening up to his full six feet, Arthur faced himself in the mirror.

Fuck the Germans. *Les Boches*. *Les doryphores*. The blight on France.

Invigorated by this new sense of anger and purpose, Arthur stood and puffed out his chest. He could sense John's presence within him. Arthur was going to make every second count and do his family proud.

He went back to the waiting house that night with Freddie

and although he had a feeling Freddie thought something was up, his oppo never asked any questions. You just didn't. Some things were too bad to talk about. It wasn't good for morale if Arthur broke down in front of Freddie or any of the other men.

Forty-eight hours later, Arthur and Freddie were sitting in the jump seats of an aircraft flying low over the Breton countryside. They were being dropped in 'blind' in that there was no welcoming party of the local resistance to guide the plane in by torchlight and no one to gather them up. Both men were dressed as Breton locals with every detail of their attire carefully considered and put together with genuine French utility clothing to ensure they looked like they had been born and bred in the Morbihan department. This also meant they were not given any weapons, provisions or vast sums of money in case they were stopped. On the downside, not being in uniform also meant that if they were captured, once interrogated, it would be certain execution on the grounds of spying.

Official papers had, of course, been provided and Arthur was now 'Christophe Martin' and Freddie was 'Guy Chapelle' and they were to call each other by these names at all times.

'Five minutes!' called the despatcher above the rattle of the aircraft and the noise of the engines.

Arthur was first in the jumping order and he shuffled his way to the open side of the plane as it began its descent under the patchy low-lying cloud, allowing just enough light to get through from the moon.

'Running in!' shouted the despatcher.

Arthur looked down as the treetops of the Breton countryside seemed to be rushing up to meet them. His feet were dangling in the night sky. He felt the despatcher's hand thump onto his shoulder.

'Go!'

Without hesitation, Arthur jumped from the plane and a few seconds after making sure he'd cleared the aircraft, his parachute opened. He glanced up to make sure the silk fabric ballooned out and caught a glimpse of Freddie several metres above and to his left.

The plane disappeared, leaving Arthur floating down to earth. This moment between leaving the plane and touching the ground always had a surreal feeling to it, but Arthur was also alert for sounds of gunfire in case they had been spotted by the Germans or the local Milice – to all intents and purposes, a militia set up by the Vichy government to assist the occupying German forces; in particular, hounding down the local resistance movements.

Seconds later, Arthur was on the ground and gathering up his chute, while simultaneously keeping an eye on where Freddie was landing – the next field along as it happened. Arthur had come down in a potato field. He also watched as another canister, ejected after Freddie by the despatcher, also landed in the other field.

Grappling with his parachute, Arthur ran across the potato field, hopped the ditch and met up with Freddie who had by now bundled up his parachute.

Next they collected the canister and headed towards the woodland to their east, which they had been briefed about. It took another ninety minutes to bury their chutes and the canister, which they would come back to later when it was safe to gather up the provisions and supplies they would need.

'Where to now?' asked Freddie, as they crouched down in the undergrowth. 'I don't like it here. Doesn't feel right.'

Arthur didn't feel in a position to argue. The night was far too quiet for his liking. Following their arrival, although in a field on farmland stretching out over one hundred acres, not so much as an owl had stirred.

'We need to head towards Sérent,' said Arthur, recalling the briefing meeting where they'd been given instructions on how to navigate from the forest to the village of Sérent some seven miles away.

Working their way through the forest was the easy part, but their journey would also require being on the road for several miles. Fortunately, the French farmers appeared to be keeping their ditches relatively clear and Arthur had already noted them as a potential hiding spot if any vehicles came along as, after all, they were out during the curfew so they'd have to explain what they were doing.

They were just reaching the edge of the forest when all of a sudden, from out of the shadows of the trees, four men stepped out about ten feet ahead, guns raised, blocking their path.

'What we got here?' muttered Freddie as both men halted. 'Welcoming committee?'

'I hope so,' replied Arthur. He raised his hands to shoulder height in surrender. They didn't have a lot of choice.

Three of the men were holding what Arthur recognised as Sten guns and the fourth was holding a pistol. They were dressed much the same as himself and Freddie, in civilian utility clothing.

'Who are you?' asked the pistol-holding Frenchman.

Arthur had to answer carefully. Although his initial thoughts were these were the local resistance, he couldn't be too sure. They could be the Milice or they could be local sympathisers who wouldn't hesitate turning them in to the Germans in return for extra rations. Food in occupied France was becoming something of a luxury and Arthur accepted they did what they had to in order to survive.

'Christophe Martin,' replied Arthur, applying his best French accent. 'We're on our way to my cousin in Sérent.'

The Frenchman who appeared to be leading this group nodded towards Freddie. 'You?'

'Guy Chapelle. I'm also going to Sérent. We're helping out on his cousin's farm.' Freddie also had his hands in the air at this point as he relayed their pre-agreed cover story.

'At this time of night?'

'We got waylaid at Malestroit,' said Arthur. 'Local hospitality of the female kind.' He gave a knowing look, hoping these men weren't from Malestroit themselves and didn't take offence at what he was implying.

The Frenchman gave a small snort. 'I hope it was worth it.' He motioned to the men behind him and two of them came over to Arthur and Freddie and searched them for what Arthur assumed was concealed weapons.

'You're nothing to do with the airplane that just flew over, then?' asked the leader.

Arthur gave a shrug. 'What aircraft?' He had to play this out, there was no point revealing who he and Freddie were too soon. The Milice could be luring them into a false sense of security.

'Who's your cousin?'

'Hugo Dupont,' Arthur replied without hesitation.

Before the conversation could go any further, there was a flurry of gunfire from somewhere in the forest, sending the group diving for cover in the undergrowth and behind trees.

Arthur could only assume it was German soldiers who had somehow managed to creep up on them unnoticed.

'*Allez! Allez!*' the Frenchman was shouting at them and beckoning from behind a nearby tree.

Arthur momentarily considered their options. Stay and try to convince the Germans they weren't anything to do with the resistance or go with the locals and hope they had a good escape plan. He turned to Freddie and was shocked to see his friend gripping his leg and blood oozing through his trousers at the calf.

'You go on,' said Freddie. 'I'll only slow you up.'

'Don't be so ridiculous,' said Arthur. 'You think you can make it over to those trees? Matey over there wants us to go with him.'

Freddie nodded, wincing as he crawled almost on his belly, dragging his wounded leg behind him, towards the Frenchman.

'*Vite! Vite!*' shouted one of the other Frenchmen, gabbling away in his mother tongue nearly as quickly as his machine gun was churning out bullets.

They made it to the tree. 'What do you reckon?' asked Arthur panting hard and trying to take in the situation.

'This lot or that?' grunted Freddie. 'Don't think we have a lot of choice.'

'That's what I thought. Here we go.' He hoisted Freddie up across his shoulders. 'If this all goes tits up, I apologise in advance.'

'Apology accepted in advance,' said Freddie, giving a groan as Arthur wedged his shoulder under his stomach, before breaking into something of a run and following the Frenchman as gunfire from the French contingent provided cover.

They ran twisting through trees, ducking around bushes, leaving the sound of the gunfire behind them. Arthur's progress gradually slowed as the burden of his mate began to take its toll.

'How much further?' he managed to puff out in French.

'Just through here.' The Frenchman stopped. 'Give him to me.'

Arthur hesitated, not sure if he should. 'Now's not the time to argue,' muttered Freddie. 'Let's just get out of here.'

Unceremoniously, Freddie was unloaded and loaded up onto the Frenchman, who made light work of carrying the smaller Englishman. 'My name is Louis,' the Frenchman said and Arthur took this as an act of comradeship between the three of them.

'Just as well it was me who copped the lead,' said Freddie. 'I would have broken my back trying to lift you. I don't think even old Louis here would have been able to carry you.' He gave a laugh and Arthur smiled at the gallows humour.

Five minutes later they were on the edge of what looked like a hamlet. Louis approached the first of the stone dwellings and without knocking, walked straight in.

'*Maman*, we have two guests for the night,' he said.

His mother who Arthur assessed to be in her mid-fifties, was sitting by the fireside, looked up and without so much as blinking, nodded to her son. She got up from the chair. 'I'll boil some water.'

Louis placed Freddie down on the sofa. His mother paused and regarded the blood-soaked trouser leg. She pulled it up, causing Freddie to give a small cry of pain. 'I'll bathe it in saltwater, but it will need proper medical attention.'

'We will sort that out tomorrow. They'll be gone at first light,' replied Louis.

'*Merci, madame*,' said Arthur, grateful for the hospitality. He didn't like the look of Freddie's leg, where the bullet appeared to be lodged in the calf muscle. 'It will be all right, mate. We'll get it sorted.'

Freddie put his head back and closed his eyes. 'Yes, mate. I know.'

Arthur sat down with a sigh, fully aware that neither of them were convinced by the narrative they were spinning.

9

Maddy listened as Esther and Gramps talked. It was a balm to her bruised heart to hear them chatting. She remembered when she was a youngster and she used to love sitting with Gramps as he read her stories from the big hardback book – tales from Hans Christian Andersen was one of her favourites. The thought triggered another long-forgotten memory. Gramps had another beautifully bound hardback book. She didn't know what it was called, but she could picture the dark brown cover with a gold border and pretty fairies on the front. Thinking about it now, it reminded her of old-fashioned postcards with glossy, brightly coloured images. The book was written in a foreign language so she'd never been able to read it but she had adored looking at the pictures inside. She wondered if Gramps still had the book. Maybe she would have a look for it on the shelf later. It might even stir some memories for him.

It was painful to see how much he had deteriorated in the last six months. The memory loss was more evident now and although he still had more moments than not of lucidity, those moments were so fragile, they could shatter at any moment.

How she wished she'd come sooner. It was a costly error and she intended to make up for it now.

Maddy flicked on the kettle and made Gramps a cup of tea, putting two digestive biscuits on a plate. He always loved a digestive with his cuppa, she remembered fondly. A wet splodge on her foot had Maddy looking down.

'Yuk! Fifi, you've dribbled on me.' Maddy grabbed a sheet of kitchen towel and wiped off the slobber. She noticed that for once Fifi hadn't turned her back on her and was making eye contact. 'You can't have a biscuit – they're not good for you.' Maddy rummaged around in the cupboard and found a box of dog treats. 'There you go,' she said, dropping a couple onto the floor.

Carrying the tray with the tea and biscuits, Maddy went into the living room. Fifi, having gobbled up the treats in an instant, was now hot in pursuit clearly in the hope of more spoiling.

'Ooh, biscuits,' said Arthur.

'Digestives. Your favourites,' said Maddy, placing the tray onto the coffee table and shooing Fifi away. She held the plate out to Gramps and watched as his eyes lit up.

'Thank you,' he said, before munching on the digestive. He took the second one and scoffed that with uncontained joy.

Maddy caught Esther's eye. Her daughter was looking on in amazement at the speed with which Gramps was shovelling in the biscuit, no doubt expecting Maddy to comment on his manners as she would if Esther had done such a thing.

'I don't think Gramps has had any biscuits in a while,' said Maddy, by way of explanation.

'Lovely,' said Gramps, licking a crumb from his lip. 'You can stay.'

'What have you two been looking at?' asked Maddy, removing the scrapbook from Gramps's lap in case he spilt any tea on it. She flicked through the pages. 'Oh, wow!

This is your scrapbook. I remember this from when I was a child.'

'Gramps was showing me the house in France where he stayed when he was in the war,' said Esther.

Maddy took the photograph Esther passed her. 'Oh, I remember this picture,' she said. 'I used to think it looked so pretty with the flowers around the front door. There's another photograph somewhere else in the book of the family who used to live there. Let me see if I can find it.'

Maddy turned the next couple of pages and sure enough, as she remembered, there was the photograph of the same house, taken from a different angle with four members of the family standing in a line outside.

Esther looked eagerly at the photograph. 'What are their names?' she asked Gramps.

Gramps looked at the page and ran his finger across the black and white photograph. 'I... err... I'm not sure.' His finger stilled on the image of the young woman. 'This... this is...'

'It's OK, Gramps, don't worry about their names,' said Maddy, in response to her grandfather's frown.

'That's Maryse!' exclaimed Esther.

Gramps's finger slid across to the man standing next to her. A young man in his early twenties. It was hard to see his features as the photograph was old and taken at a distance, but Maddy thought his eyes looked intense and serious, to match his unsmiling mouth. The young woman, on the other hand, was smiling radiantly at whoever was taking the photograph. Maddy wondered if Gramps had taken it. He'd always been a keen amateur photographer – documenting social history, as he'd often described his hobby.

Maddy looked at the woman standing on the other side

who she assumed was the mother. She had the same serious look on her face as the young man.

'Hugo,' said Gramps in a quiet voice and then again, but louder: 'Hugo.'

'This man?' asked Maddy. 'That's Hugo?' She felt a sense of pleasure that Gramps had managed to remember at least one of the names. She wondered if he had been friends with Hugo in the war. She wouldn't ever know, although Gramps did appear fairly lucid today. 'Do you know who this is?' She pointed at the older woman.

'Bread,' said Gramps. 'She made the tastiest bread. She put onions in it.'

'Sounds delicious.' Maddy smiled encouragingly at Gramps. 'And this lady, who's she?'

'It's Maryse,' said Esther. 'That lady is called Maryse. Isn't she, Gramps?'

Maddy looked at Gramps but the veil of confusion was beginning to fall across his face. She rested her hand on Esther's arm. 'Don't pester Gramps. It was a long time ago.'

'But he told me,' insisted Esther. 'He's got a photograph of her. Another photo. Haven't you, Gramps?' She turned the page back to the photograph of the house. 'It was here, behind this photograph.' The picture had been left in the crease of the book. Esther picked it up and turned it over but there was nothing else there. 'It was here just now. Gramps showed it to me.'

'Esther, please. Don't worry about it,' said Maddy, aware that Gramps's hands were fidgeting at his sides, tugging at the pockets of his trousers. She could see he was getting agitated. 'We'll look for the photograph later.' She closed the scrapbook and tucked it under her arm. 'Why don't you eat your biscuits now, Gramps,' she said, gesturing towards the plate.

'Biscuits?'

Gramps looked up at her. 'Oh, digestives, my favourite. You can stay.'

Maddy shot Esther a warning look. She was sure her daughter was about to remind Gramps that he had just said those exact words. If Esther was going to say it, the look clearly did its job, for she closed her mouth and pouted at her mother instead.

Maddy slid the scrapbook onto the shelf below the coffee table and switched on the TV, searching for the documentary channels. She was grateful that Hazel had installed satellite TV to feed her gluttony for the shopping channel. The cupboard in the single room that Esther was sleeping in was filled with packaging from mail-order companies.

Having found a documentary about old railways of the UK, which Maddy thought might feel more familiar to Gramps, she had just settled back into the sofa with her cup of tea when there was a knock at the door.

All three occupants of the living room looked at each other and after a moment's hesitation, Maddy got up to answer it.

She was met by a woman dressed in a long spectacularly coloured magenta dress, which tipped the top of her ankles. The spaghetti straps keeping the garment in place graced toned and tanned shoulders. Her fingernails were well manicured and Maddy couldn't help noticing how they matched the woman's toenails. She couldn't see how old the woman was, for a big floppy sun hat hid most of her face.

'Hello, you must be Maddy,' she said, her thin voice the only clue to her age. She extended a hand and Maddy automatically shook it. The bangles on the visitor's arm jangled in response. She tilted her head upwards so Maddy could now see her visitor. Fuchsia pink lips spread across her face. She was old, Maddy concluded but how old was hard to say. 'I'm Sheila,' she introduced herself. 'I'm a friend of Arthur's. We used to play Bridge together. Obviously we don't anymore – the poor darling hasn't got the mind for it – but I still like to call in to say hello.'

'Oh, right,' said Maddy, slightly taken aback. She didn't remember reading anywhere in Hazel's notes about a friend. She quickly regained her composure. 'Would you like to come in now?' She wasn't in the habit of inviting complete strangers into the house but a quick assessment of Sheila and Maddy was sure she wasn't a threat.

'Thank you so much,' said Sheila, stepping across the threshold with a confidence that indicated she had done so many times before. 'In the sitting room, is he?' She whipped off her sun hat with a flourish to reveal snow white hair, neatly arranged in a French pleat. She gave a glance over her shoulder. Her green eyes sparkled and her expression was one of kindness. She acknowledged Maddy's nod of the head and then strode through the door on the left. 'Arthur, darling. It's me, Sheila. How are you?'

Maddy watched from the doorway as Sheila gave Gramps a kiss on each side of his face. She wasn't sure but there might have been a small flicker of recognition in his expression.

'Hello, duck,' he said, holding Sheila's hand and patting it with the other. 'How are you?'

Perhaps he did know her or perhaps he was bluffing, being far too polite to say he didn't remember who she was when clearly she knew him, Maddy thought. 'Would you like a cup of tea?' she asked, as Sheila sat down in the chair next to him.

'That would be lovely, thank you, dear. Milk. No sugar,' came the reply and then noticing Esther for the first time: 'And who do we have here?'

'I'm Esther.'

'Hello. I'm Sheila.' Again Sheila proffered her hand, which Esther accepted. 'Very pleased to meet you. And I take it Maddy is your mother?'

Esther nodded. 'Yes.'

'Wonderful.' She looked at Gramps. 'So, Arthur, this is your great-granddaughter. How delightful. She has the same colour eyes as you.'

'Yes. Quite,' replied Gramps, beaming at her.

Maddy wasn't entirely convinced Gramps could place his visitor but he was happy and comfortable in her company so maybe there was something there. She decided reading his body language and facial expression, especially his eyes, was turning out to be a good indicator of his awareness.

When she came back into the room with a cup of tea for their guest, she was amazed to see Fifi sitting angelically in front of Sheila.

'Hello, Fifi,' said Sheila, reaching down to stroke the hound. 'How are you? It's so lovely to see you.'

Maddy looked on in amazement at Fifi's obvious affection for Sheila. Why wasn't the dog like that with her? 'She likes you,' said Maddy, as Fifi then rolled on her stomach and with her tongue lolling out, took obvious pleasure in the fuss being made of her.

'She's such a dear,' said Sheila. 'I wasn't expecting to see her. I assumed she'd be going with her mistress.'

'Hazel said she couldn't take the dog with her,' said Maddy. 'She's going abroad apparently. So, Fifi has been left with us. How do you get her to do that for you?'

'I've had dogs all my life, well, up until recently,' said Sheila. 'Poor Daisy passed away last year and I haven't been able to bring myself to replace her. Besides, I'm not getting any younger and dogs need a lot of exercise.'

'Hmmm,' agreed Maddy. 'You can say that again.'

'I like Fifi,' said Esther. 'I've always wanted a dog but we haven't been able to have one before because we lived in a flat.'

'Yes, of course, that wouldn't be fair at all,' replied Sheila. 'Now, Arthur, there's a tea dance at the village hall on Friday. I was wondering if you'd like to come with me?'

'Tea dance?' said Arthur. 'I don't know if I've been to one before.'

'Yes you have. You came with me. Vera Lynn was there. Well, not the real Vera of course but you know, a tribute singer or whatever it is they call themselves.' Sheila started to softly sing 'We'll Meet Again'.

Maddy watched as Gramps cocked his head to one side, seemingly concentrating on the song. And then he began to join in, rather erratically but there was a distinct series of notes that matched with what Sheila was singing. Gramps took Sheila's hand and made little movements back and forth in time with the words.

'Well done, Arthur,' said Sheila. 'Now, are you going to accompany me to the dance on Friday?'

'It would be my pleasure,' said Arthur. 'Shall we go now?'

'Not today. It's on Friday,' said Sheila. She turned to Maddy. 'I usually get a taxi there. It's only in the village but still a bit too far for your grandfather to walk.'

'I could drive you,' said Maddy. 'In fact, if you give me your address, I'll pick you up.'

'Oh, how lovely. That is kind of you. Did you hear that, Arthur? Your granddaughter is going to drive us.'

'Very good,' said Arthur. 'Shall I get my coat?'

'Not just yet, dear,' said Sheila. 'Finish your tea.' She passed him the cup.

'Thank you,' said Maddy, with a smile. 'You're very patient.'

'Of course, I am. Arthur is a dear friend of mine. And thank you for the offer of a lift. You know I used to be a driver in the army. A few years after the war had ended – but we were still mopping up the mess the war had left behind.'

'Really? What... cars? Like a chauffeur?'

'Sometimes cars, sometimes trucks and once I rode a motorbike. The car was out of action, couldn't be fixed, and the sergeant needed to attend an important meeting. So we hopped on the Triumph and shot off through the streets to the station. He wasn't going to hold on at first, but after hitting a few potholes he was clinging on for dear life. Poor chap, I think he was mighty relieved to get off in the end.'

'You can ride a motorbike?' said Esther, looking thoroughly impressed.

Sheila leant in towards Esther. 'Actually, between you and me, I can't. It was the first time I'd been on the damn thing and fortunately it was the last but hey-ho, we did what we had to do.'

Maddy marvelled at Sheila's story – it meant Sheila had to be around her grandfather's age. Maddy had thought the older woman was no more than eighty at the most. 'Well, it didn't do you any harm,' she said. 'You don't look old enough to be driving during the war.'

'As I said, it was a few years after the war ended but I was stationed in Hamburg and senior ranks still needed ferrying about.'

Maddy did the maths and by her reckoning Sheila must be

in her late eighties. 'Gramps was in the war,' she said. 'In fact, we were just looking at his scrapbook. Weren't we, Gramps?'

'What? Oh, the war... yes. Bad times. Sad times,' said Arthur. 'France. I didn't want to go. Didn't want to leave her. Had to take the children. Didn't have any choice.' He put a shaky hand to his mouth and blinked hard.

'Oh, Gramps, I'm sorry,' said Maddy in alarm. She looked at Sheila for help. 'Is this normal for him to get upset?'

'Sometimes,' confirmed Sheila. 'Come on, Arthur. No tears.' She spoke with a firm but kind tone as she rubbed his arm. 'Why don't you have another biscuit?'

'Who is Gramps talking about?' asked Esther.

'I don't know, but let's not talk about it anymore if it's upsetting him,' replied Maddy, still concerned about Gramps's reaction. Maybe it had all been too much for him and jogged far too many memories. She did know from the Alzheimer's webpage she'd looked at last night, that some people became more emotional, the more the disease took hold. She felt a spike of guilt in her heart. She shouldn't have carried on talking about the war. It was her fault. She hated to see Gramps so upset.

She made a mental note to put the scrapbook well out of the way when she could. Maybe hide it in the cupboard so even if Gramps or Esther thought about it, they wouldn't be able to find it. She didn't want Gramps getting upset again.

10

April 1944

Arthur had managed to get a bit of shut-eye that night but not much. He was tired physically but mentally his mind had other ideas. He was also concerned about Freddie. Louis's mother had dressed the wound but the consensus of opinion was that proper medical assistance was needed and that, apparently, would happen once they were at the Duponts' farm.

For the night they were staying in a storeroom at the rear of the property, lying on a makeshift mattress of straw with a blanket over it and another grey scratchy blanket over the top. Body heat was the only other source of warmth. Several strings of onions and garlic hung in the corner, together with bunches of dried lavender. There was shelving down one side with wooden crates filled with potatoes and other root vegetables. Arthur spied a box of apples and went to take one but hesitated. It wasn't right just to take without asking or being offered. These people had been kind enough and brave enough to take him and Freddie in for the night and he was well aware food was scarce in France. Their need was greater than his.

The room was cool and windowless and apart from the door, which led back into the kitchen, there was another door on the outside wall that Louis had unlocked for them in case they needed to make a hasty escape. It opened onto the rear garden and gave direct access to the fields and woodland beyond.

Arthur opened his eyes at the sound of deadened footsteps approaching the storeroom from the kitchen. The latch lifted and Louis appeared in the doorway in his socked feet.

Louis looked down at Freddie. 'How is he?'

Arthur, now sitting up, gave a shrug and exchanged a look with the Frenchman that said more than any words could. 'He needs a doctor,' Arthur added, just in case there needed any clarification.

'I know. There will be one waiting at the Duponts' for you.'

Arthur nodded. 'Good.'

'You need to be ready to move in thirty minutes, just before dawn. Andre, from the local farm, will pick you up in his truck. He has special travel permission to deliver milk, eggs and flour. You can travel up front with Andre but your friend will have to hide in the back. If you get stopped you won't be able to explain away a bullet wound.'

'Understood,' said Arthur, glad Louis was thinking logically and had a plan.

'He can hide in the back. There's a false wall. It's narrow so he will have to stand.' He gave Freddie a look. 'Good job he is on the thin side.'

Arthur smiled at Louis's attempt at humour and set about sorting himself and Freddie out.

Half an hour later, they had positioned Freddie behind the false wall at the back of the lorry where a broom and a pitchfork were also stored. Arthur assumed it was to claim it was a cupboard in case it was ever found. There were two roped loops at about shoulder height, which Freddie slipped his hands through to stop himself being thrown around while the lorry was moving.

'We will be there in twenty minutes,' said Andre as Arthur climbed in beside him. 'I have to make my usual rounds in the usual order so as not to arouse suspicion. So, I am giving you a lift to the Duponts' after you stayed with a friend last night. *Oui?*'

'*Oui. C'est ça,*' replied Arthur.

'*Bon chance. A tout a l'heure.*' Louis closed the truck door and gave a couple of thumps with the side of his fist so Freddie would brace for pulling away.

The journey to the Duponts went without any hitch. It was still early and not many people were about and even when they were stopped at a checkpoint just outside Sérent, the German soldiers just gave a cursory glance at the papers. They didn't even question what Arthur was doing in the cab. One of them had a quick look in the back of the truck but didn't want to climb in and inspect anything. Arthur remained impassive the whole time as if this was quite a normal event for him.

As they pulled away, Andre congratulated him. 'Good to see you can hold your nerve.'

'*Et toi,*' retorted Arthur. He hadn't been selected for SOE and gone through rigorous training, only to fall apart at the first sniff of the opposition. Neither was it his first time in France undercover. However, that didn't need explaining to Andre. Arthur acknowledged that the locals were entitled to be wary and not wholly trusting of newcomers. He'd have to earn their trust and respect.

Soon they were leaving Sérent and heading north, the signposts indicating Lizio was just a few miles ahead but as they climbed the hill, Andre took a left onto a smaller road and then after about another half a mile, turned off onto a dirt track.

The farm lay ahead at the top of a small incline, embraced in a horseshoe of trees, which stretched out into the forest beyond. Nice and secluded Arthur noted as they trundled through the gates and along the driveway, passing the sandstone farmhouse with Breton red shutters and matching front door, faded from the sun over the years. They came to a halt in the courtyard alongside a barn whose roof looked like it had seen better days.

'*Attendez*,' said Andre, ordering Arthur to stay where he was.

Arthur looked in the wing mirror of the truck as his driver left the cab and went around to talk to two men who had appeared from the farmhouse. One looked to be Arthur's age and the other a few years younger. He watched as the conversation took place, every now and then the older of the men looking towards the cab. A few minutes later he came over and pulled open Arthur's door.

'We weren't expecting you,' he said, clearly not impressed at the situation.

'We didn't want anyone to expect us,' replied Arthur, climbing out of the cab. He could feel the hostility and suspicion oozing from the man. 'I was told your mother is cooking goose for dinner.' He used the coded expression he'd be instructed to say on meeting with the local resistance.

'It's not goose, it's hog roast tonight,' came the expected reply.

'Hog roast doesn't suit my taste.' The final predetermined exchange. Arthur could see the tension in the man's face and body relax.

The man held out his hand. 'Hugo Dupont.'

Arthur accepted the greeting. 'Christophe Martin, your friend from Paris.' He shook hands with the younger man who introduced himself simply as Marcel, a friend of the Duponts. Arthur left it there. It didn't do to pry into backstories. He gestured towards the truck. 'My friend from Paris, Guy Chapelle, is here also. He needs to see a doctor.'

'So I understand. He's been called to a small emergency. He will be here at nine o'clock this morning,' replied Hugo. 'In the meantime, you can bed down in the guest house.' He gave a snort and once again, Arthur appreciated the dark humour.

They got Freddie out of the truck and Arthur and Hugo made a cradle with their arms and lifted him across the courtyard and into the barn. Getting up the loft ladder was more difficult, but Freddie found the strength from somewhere to manage it before collapsing on another makeshift straw and blanket mattress.

Sweat was pouring off Freddie and Arthur was growing more and more concerned.

'I'll get my sister, Maryse, to come over and dress the wound,' said Hugo, looking at the now blood-soaked trouser leg. 'Here's some bread and a pitcher of water.'

'*Merci*,' replied Arthur. 'We have supplies buried in the woodland where we landed. I need to get them today.'

'It's already being taken care of,' said Hugo. He must have noted Arthur's look of surprise. 'My men were watching you. They'll retrieve it for you.'

Arthur noted two things: the first was Hugo referring to the other resistance members as 'his men' and the second, which was unnerving, they had been watching Arthur and Freddie from the moment they landed. 'Watching us? Helping us sooner might have been better. Old Freddie here might not have had to take a bullet.'

Hugo smiled and lit a cigarette. 'They had to make sure you were on our side. No point helping the Milice.' He drew on his cigarette. 'They are upping their game and trying to find ways to infiltrate the resistance. My men were under orders not to take any chances.'

Arthur quelled his initial anger. He knew Hugo was right. 'I understand,' he forced himself to say. No point arguing over it now; they couldn't change anything and Hugo had every right to be cautious.

'I will be back when the doctor arrives,' said Hugo.

Arthur thanked both men and after they had descended the loft ladder, he went over to the gable end and watched from the small circular window as the two men had a brief conversation in the courtyard, shook hands, and then Andre climbed into the cab and the truck rattled its way across the cobbles, back through the stone archway to continue the deliveries.

'Here you go, mate,' Arthur said to Freddie, passing over the pitcher of water. 'Drink this.'

Arthur wasn't a medical man, but he thought Freddie's grey pallor was worrying. He lifted Freddie's head and tipped the pitcher to his lips.

'Thanks,' muttered Freddie. He took a few sips, but even that small action looked to tire him.

'Have some bread,' instructed Arthur. 'You need to eat to get your strength up. Then we can get out of here.'

There was a silence as Freddie didn't answer immediately. After a moment he spoke. 'I admire your optimism. Not sure I'm getting out of here at all.'

'We'll have none of that talk. The doc will be here in a few hours,' said Arthur, but his stomach lurched and his heart thumped hard. 'Of course you're getting out of here. You've got Ivy waiting at home for you and lovely little Vera. You're getting that leg put right and you'll be going home.'

'Yeah. Sure. I'm going home.' Freddie closed his eyes, his body going limp.

Arthur picked up the heel of bread, never more grateful to see a slightly stale end of a loaf than he was that morning. The water tasted refreshingly pure and he suspected it had been drawn from the well in the courtyard. He was sure it quenched his thirst like no other water had.

He sat upright at the sound of the barn door opening and then someone climbing the wooden loft ladder.

A dark head of hair appeared in the hatch and a young woman climbed up into the loft space. She looked a little uncertain but as she got to her feet, so did Arthur, brushing himself down. She paused and took in the clothes he was wearing, a small smile touching the corners of her mouth.

'Very authentic,' she said.

'Ah, yes,' replied Arthur, feeling self-conscious. 'We do our best.'

Her eyes flicked over to Freddie and the injured leg. 'That doesn't look good.' She went over and crouched by his side, before rolling up the trouser leg. She sucked in air between her teeth when she saw the injury. '*Merde!* A bullet wound?' She looked up at Arthur for confirmation.

Arthur knelt down on the other side of Freddie. 'It was

cleaned and dressed last night, but the bullet is still there.'

Tenderly, Maryse began to unwrap the makeshift bandage. Freddie groaned a few times in his sleep but he didn't wake until Maryse dabbed at the wound with some disinfected water, whereupon he let out a cry and thrashed his arms around.

'I'm sorry,' she said, as Arthur reassured Freddie and held him down.

Very soon the new bandage was on and Maryse was standing up again. 'The doctor won't be long.'

'*Merci*,' said Arthur, standing up too, noticing for the first time how green her eyes were.

She looked around and saw the half-eaten crust of bread. 'Sorry about that.'

'No, don't be sorry. We appreciate your kindness.'

'Good. In that case, I have more kindness for you,' she said, this time smiling openly as from her pocket she produced something wrapped in a checked cloth. Arthur hesitated but she pushed her offering towards him. 'Please,' she said in English.

Arthur took the gift. It was the size of a cigarette packet but when he unwrapped it, he was surprised to see a slab of cheese. 'For us?'

She nodded and gave a small smile. 'It was my dinner.'

'Oh, no. I couldn't possibly take it,' began Arthur, even though his mouth was watering. He couldn't contemplate taking this woman's own food.

She folded her arms. 'It is good manners not to refuse,' she said, giving a small raise of her eyebrows. 'You are our guests.'

She was adamant and he didn't want to offend her. 'Thank you. *Merci. Merci beaucoup.*'

'Your French is very good,' she remarked. 'Better than the last one.'

Arthur raised an eyebrow in question. 'The last one?'

'*Oui*. A pilot who'd been shot down came our way.'

Ah, of course, the pipeline as it was known – a safe route to repatriate Allied pilots via the Normandy coastline where they waited for a boat to pick them up and take them back to the UK. The Dupont farm was part of that underground system and it appeared Maryse was fully aware of what was happening. 'My mother is French,' Arthur replied to explain his fluency in the language. 'She met my father soon after the first war and went to live with him in England. She always said knowing French would come in useful, although I'm not sure she envisaged this scenario.'

'One day when the war is over, I want to visit England. It has been a dream of mine since I was a little girl.' Before Arthur could say anything else, a voice calling Maryse broke through the morning air. She tutted and gave a roll of her eyes. 'That is my brother. He is such a tyrant at times. I'd better see what he wants.'

Arthur nodded. 'Of course. Thank you for the cheese. *Merci pour la fromage.*'

'You're welcome,' she said again in English. 'My name's Maryse.' She held out her hand to him.

Arthur took it. 'Christophe,' he replied.

She turned and climbed onto the ladder. 'Of course, I know that's not your real name but you can tell me that when this war is over.'

Arthur watched her disappear down the ladder, not sure what to make of Maryse Dupont. She had an understated confidence and behind the no-nonsense facade he sensed someone with a sense of humour and fun. And there was the contradiction, for he could also see a deep sadness in her eyes. Perhaps it was the result of living under German occupation.

11

It was now a couple of weeks since they had come to live with Gramps and Maddy was starting to fall into a new routine. In the mornings, Gramps was usually already awake when she got up at seven. He was most disorientated in the early evenings when daylight was fading and often sought reassurances as to where he was, what time it was, whether he'd had tea and occasionally he mentioned his mother.

She was also getting used to hearing Gramps shuffling around at night. The first few nights she had got up to make sure he was OK and encourage him back to bed, but she soon realised this was futile. Gramps didn't sleep as much as she had expected and often spent the twilight hours moving around his room, reorganising his drawer in his dressing table and sometimes taking clothes out of his wardrobe and laying them on the chair ready for the following morning.

He wasn't distressed at these times and Maddy had decided as long as he wasn't coming to any harm, she would let him be.

Fifi was still giving Maddy the run-around and only being cooperative if Maddy had any food to bribe the dog with. Fortunately though, the dog had taken to Esther and liked to follow her around the house. Maddy often found both Esther and the dog cosied up in the living room with Gramps. The three of them were forming a heart-warming allegiance. It reminded her of the relationship she'd had with her grandfather as a child.

That morning, Maddy had a lot to get organised. She was taking Esther to have a look around her new secondary school that she would be attending from September and to have a chat with the head teacher. Sheila had offered to come and sit with Gramps while she was out.

She went into Gramps's room and was taken aback by the sight that met her – it looked like a jumble sale. Gramps had taken three pairs of trousers from his wardrobe, two shirts, five ties and what looked like a dozen pair of socks.

'Oh, Gramps, I don't think you need all of these,' she said, folding and putting back the obsolete garments. 'Here you go, put these on. Do you need any help today?'

Gramps took the pair of trousers from Maddy and studied the waistband, running it back and forth between his finger and thumb.

'Trousers,' he mumbled to himself. 'Trousers.' He folded them together and placed them on the bed beside him.

'You need to put them on, Gramps,' said Maddy.

Gramps picked them up again and repeated the process of running the waistband through his finger and thumb. He looked up at Maddy. 'Trousers. Yes. Trousers.'

'You need to take your pyjamas off first,' said Maddy. Should she help him? Did he want his granddaughter helping him dress? She moved towards him. 'Here, Gramps, let me help you.'

'Thank you, duck. That's very kind. You're a kind girl.' He patted her shoulder and then using the bedside table to hoist himself up, he inched down his pyjama bottoms, before sinking back onto the mattress.

'Wait a minute, Gramps, you need some pants,' said Maddy. Poor Gramps, he would be mortified if he knew she was finding this aspect of his care difficult; it wasn't his fault after all and she needed to get over herself. Quickly snatching a pair of underpants from the drawer, she deftly took off his pyjama trousers and negotiated his feet into the legs of the pants, pulling them up as far as she could. 'Now, stand up, Gramps and I'll pull them up for you.'

It was all done in a matter of seconds and with as much dignity as possible. She hated the thought that he would have a lucid moment and realise how she'd had to help him.

It wasn't long before Maddy had managed to dress her grandfather, pass him the flannel to wash his face, pop in his false teeth and give his face a quick once-over with the electric razor.

'There – all done,' she declared, smiling at him. This was how she liked to think of her grandfather. Dressed smartly, hair smooth, clean-shaven and smelling, well, smelling of Gramps – all soapy and clean.

Maddy could hear her mobile ringing from her bedroom. 'Wait there. I need to grab my phone.'

It was Sheila. 'Sorry, Maddy, I just heard on the radio that there's an accident on the main road. You'll need to go into town from the other side. You'll need to give yourself an extra fifteen minutes.'

'Oh, thank you.' Maddy checked her watch. 'Are you able to come over a bit earlier?'

'Yes, meant to say that but just wanted to give you enough time. I'll see you a bit later. Or sooner, should I say.'

Maddy couldn't help but consider herself lucky to have

such a considerate friend as Sheila. She stopped and smiled to herself at the thought of Sheila being her friend. It was a nice thought; she was a bit short on friends. Plenty of work colleagues, but not so many friends, as her life had taken a different path to her single friends. She still kept in touch over social media but bringing up a child on her own, as well as carving out a career in graphic design, didn't leave a great deal of time for going to the pub or night club with her contemporaries.

As she went back into Gramps's bedroom, she was horrified to see Gramps on his knees in the doorway to the en suite, wiping a bath towel around on the floor, trying to mop up the overflowing washbasin.

'Oh, Gramps! What's happened?' She hurried over and, squeezing past him, managed to turn off the cold tap and release the plug. She knew she hadn't left the tap on and could only assume Gramps had done it.

Helping him to his feet and back onto the bedroom chair, Maddy was dismayed to see his clean pressed trousers sodden with water from the knees down. His socks and slippers hadn't fared much better either.

'It's everywhere,' said Gramps, raising a bony finger in the direction of the en suite. 'I think we've got a leak.'

'You left the tap running,' said Maddy without thinking. She saw the look of confusion on her grandfather's face, which preceded a look of sorrow.

'Did I? Oh, why did I do that?'

Maddy wished she hadn't said anything. It only compounded the situation. 'It doesn't matter,' she said cheerily. 'I'll get you changed into some dry trousers and then I'll clean it up. It's only a drop of water.'

'I'm a silly old man,' said Gramps. He tapped his head with

the heel of his hand. 'Silly old man with a silly old brain.'

'Oh, Gramps, no you're not,' said Maddy, hugging him. 'You're not at all. Don't be saying such things. Come on, let's get you sorted.'

It didn't take too long to dress Gramps in fresh clothes and he waited patiently in his chair while she made quick work of the en suite. Fortunately, it had a tiled floor and apart from needing three full-sized bath sheets to mop and dry the floor, it didn't take five minutes to sort out. Maddy looked at the offending plug. It was one of those plunge plugs that released when you applied pressure. She unscrewed it and put it on top of the bathroom cabinet, that way Gramps wouldn't be able to let the basin overflow again but she'd know where it was when she helped him wash and shave in future.

'Are we ready?' asked Gramps as Maddy came out with the towels and dumped them in the laundry basket. She'd come back for that later once she'd got Gramps his breakfast.

'Yes, all ready. Let's go and get something to eat.' So much for leaving early; she was going to be late at this rate, but still, it couldn't be helped and, if necessary, she'd simply have to ring the school and let them know.

As they sat eating boiled eggs and toast cut up into soldiers, Maddy contemplated the day ahead. They were visiting the secondary school because the local primary school didn't have any places for Esther, because it was oversubscribed. As there were only a few weeks until the end of term, Maddy had already taken the decision not to send her in but to home-school her until September when she would start secondary school.

'What time are we going to the school?' asked Esther.

'At eleven o'clock,' replied Maddy. 'Are you looking forward to it?'

Esther studied her slice of toast and gave a shrug. 'Sort of.'

'It will be nice to see the teachers and the classrooms,' said Maddy.

'Do you think I'll make new friends?'

'Of course you will, darling,' said Maddy, with a reassuring smile.

Esther returned a weakened version of Maddy's smile. 'They'll want to know all about me, won't they?'

Maddy wasn't quite sure where Esther was going with this. 'Well, yes, that's usual but only in the same way you'll get to know more about them.'

'I wish I had a dad.' Esther dipped her head, studying the plate in front of her.

'But you do,' said Maddy.

'I mean one who lives with us.'

'Oh, darling,' said Maddy, moving from her chair to put her arm around her daughter. 'We'll be OK – me, you and Gramps.' She looked up at Gramps who was plastering his slice of toast with marmalade. She had to hold back her own emotions. Esther had no father, at least not in any practical terms, no grandfather and her great-grandfather wasn't aware enough to fill the role.

'Sorry, I've not been very good with picking men,' said Maddy.

'Joe was nice.' Esther didn't attempt to hide the sulk in her voice and Maddy couldn't exactly argue with her about Joe being nice.

Maddy had been in love with Joe, her only serious relationship other than the one with Esther's father, but Joe hadn't been into commitment. As for Esther's real dad, he'd made it perfectly clear where his priorities were and although he was supposed to see Esther every other weekend, it was a rare occurrence and was more out of duty than love. He'd been working in Cornwall for the last few months, where he hadn't seen Esther at all, and was currently on a trip Down Under. The fact that he was now talking about moving to Australia only served to confirm his laissez-faire attitude towards fatherhood.

Maddy might as well give up on men. She obviously made lousy choices. She dropped a kiss on her daughter's head. 'I'll always be here for you. I know it's not the same, but I'm always here.'

As she looked down to see if Esther was crying, she saw Gramps's aged hand extend across the table and cover both hers and Esther's. 'I'm here too, duck.'

Sheila arrived fifteen minutes early, like she said she would, and Maddy had somehow managed to make the time up so she and Esther were ready to go. As usual, Sheila had her face made up as if she was on a night out, her hair neatly compiled into what Maddy realised was her trademark French pleat. The floppy sun hat was missing this time as today was slightly overcast, but it didn't stop Sheila wearing a beautiful multicoloured coat and a long denim dress underneath.

'Hello, Arthur,' she said, kissing him on each cheek. 'How are we today?'

She gave Maddy a glance, who signalled with a discreet wobble of her open hand that Gramps was so-so and it could go either way.

'Gramps has had his breakfast and has just had a doze,' said Maddy, smiling at her grandfather. 'You were saying how you'd like a cup of tea.'

'Oh, let me make that,' said Sheila. 'You two get off.' She looked at Esther. 'Everything all right, dear?'

Esther plastered on a reluctant smile. 'Yes, thank you.'

'Looking forward to seeing your new school?'

'Mmm,' came the reply.

'That wasn't exactly convincing.' Sheila raised her eyebrows.

'She's just a little nervous,' explained Maddy. 'I'm sure it will be all fine once we're there.'

Maddy said her goodbyes and hurried Esther out of the door before either of them was questioned any further.

'Don't rush back! Your grandfather is fine with me,' called Sheila from the doorway, as she stooped to hold on to Fifi's collar. 'You go off and have a look around the town, get a cream cake or something.'

Maddy couldn't help thinking how thoughtful Sheila was. She wasn't quite sure how she'd manage without her. In the short space of time they'd been at Hemingford Grey, she was already calling in favours.

12

Arthur was happy his friend had come to visit him. He knew she was his friend because he could feel it. He couldn't remember how he knew her. How long he'd known her or where he knew her from, but he knew she was kind. She smiled a lot and laughed, not at him, but with him. It was a pretty laugh, which somehow made the room sparkle and made him feel happy.

Arthur could hear the music playing as they pulled up outside the village hall. He knew he liked coming here and knew he'd been here often with his friend. 'I like this place,' he said.

'I know. It's the local day centre for us oldies,' she said. 'We often come here. It's a special dementia day today. Come on, we don't want to miss out on tea and cake or a dance.'

He couldn't quite place the tune or who was singing but he found himself humming along to it.

'Oh, this is one of my favourites,' said his friend. 'I used to listen to Doris Day all the time. Come on, Arthur, let's go inside. Here, take my arm. That's it, put your bad arm in mine and hold on to your walking stick with the other hand.'

Slowly they made their way into the hall. It was filled with men and women his age, some of them were dancing in couples and some were sitting at the tables that surrounded the edge of the hall. They had cups of tea or coffee and there were sandwiches and cakes. Someone had strung pretty red, white and blue bunting across the hall. On the stage a lady, dressed in a white dress with red polka dots and wearing a matching red bow in her hair, was singing into a microphone. Everyone looked to be happy and enjoying themselves.

There was a familiar atmosphere, one that Arthur felt comfortable with, which reignited a deeply embedded memory.

'Hello, Arthur.' A woman dressed in a white tunic with blue trousers greeted them at the door. 'Hi, Sheila. It's lovely to see you both.'

Arthur smiled at... he didn't know her name but she was wearing a nurse's outfit, sort of anyway. 'Hello,' he replied out of manners.

The nurse took them over to a table where some other people were sitting and left with promises of returning with a cup of tea. Arthur hoped she'd bring the biscuits too – digestive ones, of course.

It was very pleasant in the hall and as Arthur listened to the music and watched people dancing, he felt a calmness wash over him. As he looked on, it was as if the years were rolling away and everyone was young again. Enjoying themselves in the village hall, pretending everything was all right in the world. For a short time, they could suspend reality.

'Are you OK, Arthur?'

It was his companion – Sheila! Yes, that was her name, he remembered now. He beamed at his recollection. 'Do you want to dance, Sheila?' he asked.

'I'd love to,' she said, rising to her feet.

Arthur followed suit. They made their way over to the

dance floor. Sheila placed one hand on his shoulder and rested her other hand over his on the walking stick. He put an arm around her waist and they swayed from side to side in time to the music. 'I'm afraid my feet aren't up to it these days, duck. They don't like to move the way they used to.'

'Don't you worry about that. I'm having a lovely time. This is perfectly acceptable.'

They continued to sway and make tiny little movements with their feet as the song ended and the singer launched straight into another number. Arthur closed his eyes and rested his head against Sheila's. He felt happy. He wasn't sure why, but he was certainly happy. An image of a man in uniform with his arms around a young woman came to mind. They were at some sort of dance, but they were outside and the music was filtering through from a distance. He couldn't see the faces of the couple, but they were holding each other close and were very much in a world of their own. They were obviously in love, Arthur thought. So nice to see people in love and yet so painful too. He wasn't sure where the pain came from but it struck him in the heart.

'Are you OK, Arthur? Perhaps we should sit down now and have another drink and something to eat.' Sheila moved out of his arms and, holding on to his elbow, guided him across the floor to one of the tables, where they were greeted by other guests. Arthur felt unsettled from his thoughts and tried to push them away and concentrate on what the woman sitting opposite him was saying. He couldn't make out the words. She was speaking fast and they all merged into one another.

He turned his attention back to the music. He liked listening to the lady sing.

When it was time to go, he was disappointed but the music

had finished and people were putting on their jackets and coats. He wished he could remember some of those songs. He knew them but he couldn't think what they were called. Damn it.

When they arrived back at Arthur's house, he was pleased to see Maddy and the child were home too. Immediately, he felt better. The child cheered him up no end – he couldn't deny that.

'Hello, Gramps, did you have a nice time?' asked Maddy. She was smiling at him and helping him off with his jacket.

'I did. Thank you,' he replied. He looked at his companion – what was her blasted name again? Oh, he was bloody useless at times. It was on the tip of his tongue. Sheila! There, he'd managed to dredge it up from his memory. Good for him. 'Me and... and...' Blast! It was gone again. 'We had a very nice time.' But as he said it, he wasn't sure if they had. He wasn't even sure where they'd been, but it had seemed the expected thing to say.

'That's good,' said Maddy. 'Did you dance?'

'Oh, yes, we danced,' said his companion. 'And very nice it was too.'

'What sort of dancing did you do?' asked the child. 'Was it like on the TV?'

'I don't think Gramps would have been skipping around the dance floor,' said Maddy, with a warm smile. She stroked the child's head as she spoke.

Dancing. That's what they had been doing. Yes. He remembered now. He was dancing. 'Doris Day was singing,' he said.

'Who's that?' asked the child.

'It was a lady from our era,' said his dance partner.

'Wow! Was she there?' The child looked impressed.

'Yes,' said Gramps. He remembered her on the stage. 'She was there.'

'What Gramps means is that a lady was there singing Doris Day songs. Not the real Doris Day. She's dead.'

The child nodded and Arthur frowned. Doris Day was dead? How could that be? She was there singing away. He'd heard her. He went to say as much, but Maddy was talking again. Thanking the other lady for looking after him and taking him out.

'How did you get on at the school?' she was now asking Maddy.

'We met the head teacher and she was nice, wasn't she, Esther?'

The child shrugged. 'I suppose so.'

Arthur couldn't keep up with the conversation but it was something to do with the child and teachers. 'I was once made to stand out in the yard by my teacher,' he said to the child.

She looked up at him. 'Why? And what's the yard?'

'Gramps means the playground,' said Maddy.

Arthur nodded. 'I didn't know the capital of India.'

'And they made you stand outside?' asked the child.

'I wasn't allowed in until I remembered it,' continued Arthur. He could see himself now, very clearly. A boy of about ten years old in grey shorts, a white shirt and a grey-coloured blazer with a red stripe running around the lapels. It had belonged to his brother John before him. It was too big for him but his mum said he'd grow into it and she didn't have the money to go buying a new one when John's old uniform still had wear in it.

'How long were you out there for?' asked the child.

'Until lunchtime,' said Arthur. 'I couldn't remember the capital of India but one of my friends passed me by and whispered it. When the teacher came out and asked me, I was able to tell him straight away. New Delhi. I was given a clip round the ear for not remembering it sooner and then allowed to go and have my dinner.'

'Your teacher hit you?' The child's eyes widened.

'Yep. I was lucky it wasn't the cane.'

'Fortunately, teachers aren't allowed to do that these days,' said Maddy.

'More's the pity,' muttered the other lady. 'Some of them would do well with a tanned backside.' She fished her purse from her bag and took out some coins, pressing them into the child's hand. 'Here, get some sweets.'

'Oh, no, you don't have to,' said Maddy.

'I know I don't but I want to and that's the difference,' came the reply.

The child looked up at the woman. 'Thank you.' The girl smiled. Arthur wished she would smile more often.

Later that day, Arthur was in the sitting room, dozing, when he had the sense that someone was watching him. He opened his right eye a fraction, whilst not moving a muscle anywhere in his body – an old army trick. There sitting on the sofa was the child. He opened both eyes and smiled at her.

She returned the smile. 'Hello, Gramps.'

'Well, hello, duck.' Arthur sat up in the chair and tugged at the cuffs of his shirt to make sure he was presentable – more old army habits. 'What have you got there?' He nodded to the rectangular black thing on her lap. He had no idea what it was.

'This? It's my tablet.'

'Tablet? Doesn't look like any tablet I know. How do you swallow that?'

She giggled and rocked back on the sofa. 'Not that sort of tablet!' She laughed again. He liked it when she laughed. 'This is like Mum's laptop, sort of.'

Gramps was still uncertain. 'What does it do?'

'I can go on the internet and upload my vlogs.'

Arthur had no idea what she was talking about. 'You'll have to show me.'

She fiddled with the tablet – strange sort of name for it, but if she said it was a tablet, then that's what it was – and then she tapped it and it lit up. She turned it to face him. It was a television! A little one at that, but definitely a television, Arthur decided.

'Look, this is my YouTube channel and this is me.' She tapped the screen with her finger and a programme came on.

Arthur tried to follow what was happening but it wasn't that easy. He could see that the young girl in the video was, in fact, the same girl sitting beside him. She was in a kitchen doing some sort of cooking. Apart from that Arthur wasn't sure what was going on. The child looked to be enjoying herself though. He stole a glance at her as she watched the little rectangular screen. She was smiling. Arthur smiled too.

'You like cooking?' he asked.

'Yes, I do. I can make you some cupcakes, if you like.' She looked enthusiastically at him. 'I can make them tomorrow.'

Arthur nodded. He wasn't sure what a cupcake was, but she was keen to do whatever it was she wanted to. 'That would be nice,' he said.

She turned her attention back to the screen on her lap and

tapped at it a few more times, before holding it up in front of them. 'Smile,' she said.

Arthur looked up at the screen. It was some sort of camera. He poked his tongue out. She laughed and then copied him. He pulled another face, this time making his eyes cross. She giggled. He made some more faces. He liked making her laugh. It was infectious. Soon he was laughing too.

Afterwards, she showed him the photographs on the screen. 'Look at our selfies,' she said.

They laughed all over again at them. The child had such an infectious laugh, one of pure innocence. He patted her hand as their laughing subsided. He loved to hear children laughing; it had always brought him such joy. A memory stirred, a gentle rumble and louder almost a clatter, like heels on cobbled stones. And then, as if the curtain was being raised on the stage, he could see them, running and laughing as they chased one another around.

13

April 1944

Arthur heard the gentle squeals of laughter coming from the courtyard. Definitely children, he thought and wondered whether they were younger siblings of Maryse. He got up from the straw bed, easing himself to his feet slowly so as not to disturb Freddie. The doctor had been out to him yesterday and with some crude surgery had managed to extract the bullet. However, the hole it left behind didn't look good and although the doctor had cleaned it up the best he could, he was concerned enough to warn them that the infection might have already set in. He'd given Freddie some knock-out tablets so he could rest and let his body fight the infection.

Arthur went over to the window in the gable end and peered out onto the courtyard. Sure enough, two children were there, playing a game of tag with Maryse. She looked to be having just as much fun as they were. He watched them for a few minutes and debated whether to go down and join in but ultimately decided against the idea. The fewer people, children included, who saw him, the better. Even though he was here with correct papers, it still was better not to draw attention to himself with the children. Loose lips and all that.

Maryse must have sensed his gaze on her, as she glanced up towards the window. She gave a small nod of acknowledgement and then returned her attention to the children, gathering them in a circle. After she talked to them, they skipped on ahead of her back towards the house. She stole a last look up towards the window as she ushered the children inside.

Arthur didn't see her again until later that afternoon when she and Hugo climbed up into the hayloft.

'We've let London know you've arrived safely,' said Hugo.

'Did you tell them about Guy?' asked Arthur remembering to use Freddie's alias.

'*Oui*. You're to carry on with the orders alone. They will try to arrange a pickup for your friend,' replied Hugo. 'I have spoken with my contact in Malestroit. They want to meet you in the café in Sérent this afternoon.'

Arthur was impressed at the speed with which the network was reacting to his presence. 'Good. What time?'

'In one hour. You shall go with my sister and me. We will meet in the café, have lunch – I will be introducing you as an acquaintance from Paris who has come to the countryside to help with the farm. Patrick, who we are meeting, may be interested in you working for him too. Understand?'

'Yes.' Arthur understood the plan perfectly so far and knew his backstory as if it were his own.

Thirty minutes later, they were heading in towards the village – Hugo driving the horse and cart with Maryse and Arthur sitting on the back, their legs swinging as the wheels bumped their way along the track.

'Who were the children you were with earlier?' asked Arthur, holding on to the edge of the cart as it sent him one way and then the other over a particularly patchy part of the track.

'The Rochelle children,' said Maryse. 'Their father is the headmaster of the village school. I've been helping look after them.'

'Where's their mother?'

'She was taken by the Gestapo last week. No one has seen her since.' There was anger as well as concern in Maryse's voice. 'She's Jewish.'

'I'm sorry,' said Arthur. He was well aware of the stance the Gestapo took with Jews and said a silent, yet probably futile prayer, for her safe return. 'If it's any consolation, you looked like you were doing a good job of cheering them up.'

'They don't need to know the truth yet,' she said with a sadness. 'Do you have children?'

Arthur gave a small laugh. 'No. I would like to one day, but not yet. When I'm older and wiser and this bloody war is over it would be nice. Assuming someone will have me, that is.'

'You don't have a girl waiting for you back home?'

Arthur shook his head. 'No. Can't say as I have. What about you?'

'There are more important things for me to worry about right now than the love of a man.' She turned her head away and looked out across the fields, the conversation clearly brought to a halt.

They arrived in the village of Sérent. Hopping off the rear of the cart, Maryse and Arthur brushed themselves down, taking a moment to surreptitiously scan the square to see who was about.

L'eglise Saint Pierre occupied the centre of the square, slightly elevated above the rest of the buildings. Its spire reached high above everything else, housing the bell on the inside and a clock face on the exterior.

A small market was set up on the north side of the square, selling local produce, and there were enough people milling around so that Arthur and Maryse did not stand out. There were two cafés on opposite sides of the square and a small group of German soldiers were sitting at the pavement tables enjoying a coffee, looking relaxed as they smoked and laughed amongst themselves.

The back of Arthur's throat dried as he watched them from under the brim of his hat.

'Please tell me we're not going to that café,' he said.

'No, we are going to this one. Albert will happily take their money and entertain them. He also listens to their conversations. It's amazing what they let slip after a few cognacs,' replied Maryse, linking her arm through his and steering him towards the more humble-looking of the two cafés. The paintwork was fading from the sun and the canopy above the front window was bleached out. It looked like it had seen better days. 'Come.'

They entered the café and Arthur was aware of the attention he was drawing.

'*Bonjour, Yvette,*' said Maryse, to the lady behind the counter as they took their seat at a table by the window. '*Deux cafés, s'il vous plaît.*'

The burr of the café conversation restarted and Arthur was pleased he was no longer the focus of attention. 'Where's Hugo?' he asked.

'He'll be along in a minute. Just leaving the horse and cart with someone he knows.'

'Do you have any vehicles yourselves?'

'*Oui*. We have a truck but we only use that if we have to. The fuel is being rationed even more. We might need it for something more important.'

Yvette brought over two coffees, which looked extremely strong to Arthur. It wasn't his favourite drink, he much preferred tea, but he could hardly ask for that whilst pretending to be a Frenchman.

'*Merci*, Yvette,' said Maryse. The older woman loitered, obviously waiting for an introduction. 'This is my friend, Christophe, from Paris. He's here to help on the farm and possibly work for Patrick Thomas.'

Arthur held out his hand. '*Enchanté, madame.*'

The older woman shook Arthur's hand, holding on to it a moment before letting go. 'He hasn't worked the land before.'

'*Non, madame. Pas dupis longtemps. Je suis professeur ou plutôt je l'étais.*' It wasn't exactly a lie. The part claiming he was a teacher, or at least used to be before the occupation, was a complete fabrication but the café owner didn't question, simply nodded her head sagely. Arthur wondered if she was part of the resistance network, which would also explain why he and Maryse were meeting Patrick here.

A few minutes later, Hugo joined them and then shortly afterwards another man who turned out to be Patrick sat with them. The conversation was informal and they talked about the farm and what needed to be done. The whole discussion was a complete ruse, designed to look like four friends meeting for a morning chat that would not draw attention to themselves by any local informants, plain-clothed Gestapo or Milice.

After an hour the charade came to a close and the four of them left the café, saying their final goodbyes very publicly in the street before going their separate ways.

'Where to now?' asked Arthur as once again Maryse slipped her hand into his arm.

'We're going to buy some fruit from the market first,' said Maryse. 'Just to make sure none of us have attracted unwanted attention.'

Maryse took her time picking over the fruit and selecting a bag of apples, before moving onto the next stall where she purchased a small jar of honey.

'All OK?' asked Arthur.

'*Oui*. This way.' They walked across the square and right by the Germans sitting outside the other café.

Arthur ensured he didn't make eye contact and as they rounded the corner, well out of sight of the soldiers, he turned to Maryse. 'Was that necessary? Walking straight by them?'

'No. It wasn't,' she replied. 'But I like doing it.'

'What?'

'They think they are so smug sitting there, drinking, smoking, taking what they want from who they want. It gives me a sense of power. They have no idea what I am doing behind their backs.'

'Parading me in front of them just for one of your power trips, isn't something I appreciate. You could jeopardise the whole operation. Not to mention my life.' Arthur could feel the anger welling up inside him. 'It's reckless. Don't do that again.'

They continued to walk along the path and he felt Maryse tighten her fingers around his arm. 'Don't you tell me what I can and cannot do. Unless you have lived here, day in, day out. Until you have had your life stolen from you. Until you have been left helpless. Until you have had your loved ones killed. Until then, you have no right to judge me. You can walk away from this. You will return to England and you will be safe. We do not have that luxury.'

Arthur didn't reply. What could he say? She was right, to a certain extent. There was every chance he would make it back to England at some point and he could indeed lead a relatively stress-free life while he was there but what was there for the people of France? He'd never be able to totally empathise with them but he would do everything in his power to help them, that he could guarantee.

'We're here,' said Maryse. She unhooked her hand and with a quick glance up and down the road, she pushed the bell in the wall. The door was opened within a few seconds and Maryse made a fuss of greeting the man, who showed them in.

Once inside, they trotted up the stairs and into a room in the attic of the building, where Hugo and Patrick were waiting.

'You weren't followed?' asked Patrick.

'No.'

'Positive?'

'Positive.'

The whole clandestine meeting took no longer than fifteen minutes as they swiftly discussed what was to happen next. Arthur had been briefed about finding a new landing strip for the Allied aircraft to drop supplies. They were looking to bolster up the resistance's weaponry in anticipation for the big event in June.

Up until this point, the local resistance had been relatively low-key, monitoring and reporting on German troop movement as they were shipped in and out of the region. Brittany was used as something of a recreation ground for German soldiers and a base for building up their supplies so they could send reinforcements further to the east where needed.

'So in a few weeks, we need to up the ante on sabotaging the railway lines out of the area,' Arthur explained. 'We need to stop reinforcements reaching the Normandy coastline. You've got someone on the inside at the station, I believe.'

There was a small silence in the room and the tension in the atmosphere increased. Arthur looked from one to the other. 'You have someone at the station?' he asked again, wondering if his French had somehow become so bad, he couldn't be understood. Maryse lowered her eyes.

It was Hugo who spoke. 'Not anymore. He was under suspicion.'

Arthur took in the information, swearing silently to himself. 'Is he still working there?'

'No.' The reply was stiff.

'He can't get reinstated at all? This is crucial information. We need it to know which trains to target.' Arthur shook his head. This was not the news he wanted to hear.

'No, he can't!' said Maryse suddenly, looking up at Arthur. Her eyes blazed with anger. 'He's dead. They arrested him. Interrogated him. Executed him. There, now do you understand?'

There was something in her voice, the way her eyes bored deep into him, like a knife burrowing into flesh, which told Arthur he had hit a nerve. Something that was raw and personal to Maryse.

14

The sky was a beautiful clear blue today and the sun's heat worthy of Mediterranean status, with only the softest of breezes. Maddy was glad she had persuaded Gramps to wear his hat. His thinning hair was no protection to his aged scalp. Esther was wearing a baseball cap and Maddy had found a straw sun hat for herself in the cupboard. Not quite up to Sheila's standards, but it did the trick. She assumed it was one that Hazel had left behind.

Thinking of Hazel, Maddy hadn't heard a word from her since she'd left. She realised she had no idea where Hazel was or what she was doing, and she'd have no way of knowing if she was OK. Maddy hadn't expected to hear from Hazel again, but her own curiosity was piqued as much as her desire to make sure everything was OK. Later Maddy decided she'd have a look at Facebook and see if Hazel had posted there. Maddy had a Facebook account but she rarely used it these days and more often than not forgot she even had it. Hopefully, she'd be able to remember her password.

She pushed the wheelchair into the park and followed the path as it meandered past the shrubs and bushes, through the trees and towards the duck pond.

'Can you see the ducks, Gramps?' she asked, coming

to crouch by the side of the wheelchair so she was at his eye level. She pointed towards the water. 'Over there. See them?'

'Oh, yes, I can, duck.'

Maddy caught Esther's eye and they both grinned. Bless him.

'Look, Gramps,' said Esther, taking a handful of bread-crumbs and throwing them into the water. The ducks came swimming over, quacking their gratitude.

'Ducks. I like ducks,' said Gramps. 'Especially with orange sauce.'

'Gramps!' exclaimed Maddy but couldn't help laughing. There was a mischievous twinkle in his eye. Sometimes, it was like he was reverting back to being a child himself. No wonder he and Esther got on so well.

That evening, Maddy was sitting in the living room, with Gramps in his chair and Esther sitting next to him as they watched a documentary about lions in Africa. It was a heart-warming sight to see them both so comfortable in each other's company. It reminded Maddy of when she was a child and used to come to stay with Gramps and Grandma. Those had been happy days. She remembered Grandma toasting thick slices of bread in front of the fire on a long toasting fork. Gramps would then coat the toast with lashings of thick butter, which would melt, and you had to be careful not to let it drip onto your lap. Happy days.

'Have you locked the doors?' asked Gramps, as the programme came to an end.

'Yes, all done,' said Maddy.

'The front door and the back door?' Gramps continued with

his questioning. It was something of a regular conversation they had most evenings.

'Front and back.'

'Here's another programme about penguins coming on,' said Esther, pointing the remote control at the TV.

'Penguins. They're nice to eat,' said Gramps.

'What!? You can't eat penguins!' cried Esther.

'He's teasing you,' said Maddy smiling at her daughter's look of alarm.

'Chocolate biscuit ones you can,' said Gramps with a wink.

Esther let out a groan at the joke. 'Hilarious,' she muttered, focusing back on the TV.

'Did you lock the doors?' asked Gramps.

Maddy reined in a sigh. It was going to be one of those nights where Gramps wouldn't be able to settle and would ask the same question over and over again. She knew it wasn't his fault but sometimes, when she was tired, it was hard work having to keep reassuring him. 'All locked,' she said, picking up her laptop.

'Front and back?'

'Yes, front and back. Look at the TV, Gramps. All those penguins there.'

Esther tapped at his arm. 'They're all huddled up together to keep warm.'

Maddy was grateful for Esther's attempt to distract him and while his attention was fixed on the wildlife show, she took the opportunity to log onto Facebook. There were numerous notifications but she ignored them and typed Hazel's name into the search bar.

However, her attempts at tracking Hazel down were thwarted as Gramps began his questioning about the locks again. This time though, he got to his feet and insisted on checking the doors himself.

'Can't be too careful,' he said as he moved down the hallway from the front door to the dining room at the rear of the house where the French doors leading out to the garden were. He tested the handle. 'Where's the… the thingy bob?'

'The key? I've put it away so we don't lose it,' said Maddy as she followed him into the room. 'Why don't you go back and sit with Esther. That penguin programme is really interesting.'

'The back door. Is the back door locked?' Gramps made his way out of the room and along to the kitchen. 'Got to make sure.'

'Gramps, please. It's locked. Let me make you a cup of Horlicks.'

'Is it locked? Must lock up at night.'

'Gramps!'

'I need to check the front door. Come on, you're in the way.' Gramps waved his walking stick as if shooing a fly. 'Move out the way.'

'Please, Gramps. Go and sit down.' Maddy hated feeling frustrated with him but some nights, she found this routine so exhausting.

'Out the way.' Gramps sounded more insistent.

Reluctantly, Maddy moved out of the way and watched from the doorway of the kitchen as her grandfather padded up the hall to the main door. Rather than fight what was going to be a losing battle tonight, Maddy resigned herself to watching him and simply making sure he was safe. It was nearly nine o'clock, only another hour and he would be going to bed.

It was in fact, nearly two hours before Maddy managed to get her grandfather settled, with the help of Esther. He was having one of his more challenging evenings but he'd taken his night-time medication without any fuss and was now settling down.

Maddy made a mental note to speak to her grandfather's GP tomorrow to see if there was anything they could do to help him have less disturbed evenings and nights. They all needed their sleep and if she was to look after him properly like she wanted to, then she couldn't survive on so little sleep. It was like having a new-born, except in reverse.

The thought made her sad and she couldn't help feeling alone as she said goodnight to Esther and went downstairs to tidy up for the night. As she went to close the living room door, she spied her laptop and remembered what she'd been attempting to do earlier – find Hazel.

Maddy took her laptop up to bed with her. Not something she advocated but now she'd started thinking about Hazel, she knew she wouldn't be able to settle until she'd checked up on her. She found her half-sister straight away and a quick look down Hazel's timeline gave Maddy all the reassurance she needed that there was nothing to worry about. It was filled with photographs of Hazel in Spain, sitting by the pool with their mother, Carol. If not by the pool, then on the beach, or on the terrace of the villa, or at a bar or at a restaurant. Hazel was having the time of her life. Begrudgingly, Maddy forced herself to admit that Hazel deserved the break. Whilst it was hard work looking after Gramps, Maddy was enjoying it – she wasn't sure Hazel would ever have used the word enjoyment to describe her experience. Oh well, at least Hazel was OK. And their mother looked well too.

It had been a long time since Maddy had missed her mother and seeing the most recent pictures did nothing to change that feeling either. Carol was fine and being Carol.

Or so she told herself.

From out of nowhere a sudden pang for a close relationship with her mother, the same one that Hazel had, hit Maddy hard. Why was that? She didn't even know this feeling existed anymore. There had been a time when she had craved her mother's love and she couldn't say Carol didn't love her – Maddy knew she did. It was just Carol didn't love her enough. Not in the same way she loved Hazel.

Maddy remembered saying something along similar lines to her grandfather one summer and he'd been clear about his feelings on it. He said that Carol had loved Maddy's father so much, that when he died, within six months, she had got rid of every personal item belonging to Charles and anything that reminded her of him. It had been far too painful for her to face. And it hadn't stopped at the physical things. Carol had pushed away anyone who had been friends with Charles; not only that, she had pushed away the family too. The only person she couldn't do that to was Maddy, not completely anyway. So over the years, Maddy – who looked so like her father – was another painful reminder and she too was slowly but surely pushed away. Maddy ended up spending most of her school holidays with Gramps and Grandma, while Carol continued to carve out a life with Hazel that didn't include Maddy.

Maddy had left home, gone to uni, graduated, got a job and rented a small one-bed flat and forged her own new life. She did visit Carol and Hazel but the bond between mother and daughter had disintegrated and Maddy had accepted that.

What gnarled her later was not the rejection by her mother, but the rejection of Esther. Maddy had hoped that having a baby would bring them all closer, but that hadn't happened either.

Maddy had long since accepted this status quo. It was her family; it was what had shaped and moulded her into the person she was today. Most of the time she could deal with that but every so often those painful memories of being rejected came back.

She needed to stop thinking about it. Sometimes, it was overwhelming and, coupled with the tiredness she felt, she didn't even have the energy to get under the covers. As she lay there with her eyes closed, she felt the dip of the mattress and the warm body of Esther snuggle up to her, pulling the duvet over the pair of them.

'Don't be sad, Mum,' whispered Esther. 'I love you.'

15

Arthur was sitting in his chair in the living room as usual. The radio was playing in the background and the sun was warm against his face as it shone through the window. Maddy had fiddled with the radio and put some sort of round shiny thing into it. She did say what it was, but he couldn't remember. It wasn't a record, but something like that. Anyway, whatever it was called, it played some of his favourite tunes. He put his head back against the chair and hummed along. He couldn't remember the words but some sort of humming that mildly resembled the tune did the trick. He smiled as he listened.

He was enjoying the music so much, he wasn't sure how long he had sat there but he was disappointed when it finally ended. He could hear chattering coming from the other room and after easing himself from the chair, using his walking stick for balance, he headed towards the voices.

'Hello, Gramps.' It was Maddy. She was getting pots and pans out of the cupboards. 'You OK?'

He nodded. 'Yes. What's going on here?' He rested his hand on top of the work surface and gave a minimal sweeping gesture with his walking stick.

'I'm making a vlog for my YouTube channel,' said the child.

Arthur raised his eyebrows. He had no idea what she was talking about. 'That's good,' he said, as it seemed the right thing to say. The child looked happy at whatever it was she was doing.

'I'm doing mini cheesecakes today,' she continued.

'Right, I think that's everything you need,' said Maddy. 'You all set?'

The child was standing behind the counter wearing an apron with various bowls of ingredients set out in front of her, together with wooden spoons.

'Gramps, we have to stay quiet now while Esther does her recording,' said Maddy. 'Shall I make you a fresh cup of tea quickly before she starts?'

'Tea. That would be nice. And biscuits?'

'Naturally,' said Maddy with a laugh. She patted his arm. 'Why don't you sit down here while I make it.'

Arthur looked at her and realised she was waiting for him to respond. After a moment, Maddy pulled out a dining chair and gently put her hand on his elbow. 'You want me there?' he asked.

'Yes, sit here, Gramps. I'm going to make you a cup of tea and a sandwich. That's it.'

The tea and ham sandwich were produced a few minutes later. 'I'll take Gramps into the other room so you can do your recording,' said Maddy. She stopped and cocked her head. 'Blast. I think that's my phone. It's upstairs.' She placed the cup of tea and sandwich on the table, together with a couple of biscuits. 'I won't be a minute.'

Arthur eyed the biscuits. Digestives. He couldn't resist. He picked one up and bit into it. He realised the child was watching him. 'Do you want one?'

'No, thank you.' She was still standing behind the counter, as if ready to do something, thought Arthur. He studied the cooking items on the counter. Yes, she was definitely going to bake something.

'Do you need any help?' he asked.

'No. Yes. Maybe.' She looked thoughtful for a moment before speaking again. 'I was going to wait for Mum but it sounds like she's talking on the phone. I'll start now.'

Arthur watched as she turned the rectangular screen around to face him and picked up some sort of remote control, before coming to stand next to him.

'Right, you ready?'

'Yes,' replied Arthur, although he wasn't sure what he was supposed to be ready for.

'OK. Here we go. Three. Two. One… Hi, guys! Thank you for tuning in. Today is starting a little bit different as I need your help. Listen up. You may notice that I'm in a different kitchen today. That's because we've moved house! I'm now living with my great-grandfather, or Gramps as we call him.' She put her arm around his shoulder. 'This is Gramps and he has an amazing story about someone he met in the war but has lost touch with.' She moved from the counter and picked up the TV screen thingamajig and came to sit next to Arthur, putting it on the table. From her pocket she took a photograph and held it up to the camera. 'This is Gramps's friend from the war. She looked after him. Her name is Maryse. I think she might have two children. If anyone knows where she is, can they leave a comment below? I want to reunite them as I know it will make Gramps happy.' She looked at Arthur. 'Won't it, Gramps? You would like to see Maryse again, wouldn't you?'

'Maryse,' repeated Arthur. His heart lurched this time and his stomach tumbled over on itself. 'Maryse. Oh, yes. My lovely Maryse.'

'So, if anyone knows how I can track her down, please leave a comment below. It would mean so much to us both.' She made some sort of heart sign with her hands towards the screen thing.

Arthur chuckled. He could see himself and the child. They were on the little TV screen. How funny. He waved at his own image. The child then went and turned the screen around and positioned herself back behind the counter. She pressed another button and started speaking again.

'So, that's Gramps and now it's time to make those delicious mini cheesecakes.'

Arthur watched her as she chatted away to the little TV screen and went about baking. She looked happy doing this which, in turn, made Arthur feel happy. He had a vague recollection of the child being sad but he wasn't sure why and when that was. He didn't like her being sad; it made everyone sad.

'So, that's how you make mini cheesecakes,' the child was saying.

'Thanks for tuning in again, guys. Don't forget to like and subscribe. Bye!' She waved earnestly at the screen and then switched it off. 'Well done, Gramps! You've just done your first YouTube video.'

'Oh, have I? That's good.'

'I'm going to play it back and then upload it.'

Arthur sat there as she fiddled around with the screen and after some time, she looked happy enough with it. 'That all looks good. I'll upload it now.'

Arthur stood up. He'd finished his cup of tea and eaten his biscuits. He would really like another, but he didn't know where they were. The chair he'd been sitting on was uncomfortable and he decided he'd like to sit in his usual chair. He shuffled his way back to the other room, settled himself into the chair and closed his eyes. He'd quite like forty winks now.

As he dozed, his mind wandered back in time, throwing up snapshots of his past and people he knew. It was a nice feeling. He could see Joan – dear, Joan. She was kneading bread at the kitchen table and then he could see his mother doing the same. Both women were smiling at him. He smiled back. He could feel the love between him and both these important women in his life. And then he was assaulted with images of guns, loud noises, explosions, men shouting, men crying. The sun was hot on his face. A rivulet of sweat wormed its way out from under his helmet and carved a path through his dust-coated skin.

And then it was quiet. So very quiet. He could see the trees above him, the blue sky filtering through the branches and the blur of the sun. Children running across the courtyard, laughing as they played a game of tag. And then, he could see her – Maryse. She was smiling at him. Her sparkly green eyes so full of... yes, love. He could feel that love. He really could.

A movement from somewhere to the side disturbed him. He tried to hang on to the images of his loved ones, but they were slipping back into the haze of the heat, becoming thinner and thinner. He didn't want them to go. He didn't want them to leave him but he had no way of making them stay.

There was the noise again. His body jolted. He opened his eyes and looked over.

'Hello, duck,' he said, looking at the child standing in the doorway. 'How are you?'

She held up the plate with his sandwich on. 'You forgot to eat your lunch.' She brought it over and placed it in his hands.

Arthur looked down at the sandwich and lifted the top slice to see what was inside. Ham. At least that's what he thought it was. He liked ham. He was sure of that. 'What are you doing now?' he asked squashing the bread back together.

She shrugged. 'I don't know. Mum's upstairs in her room. She's got a headache. She's having a sleep.'

'Oh dear.'

'Can we look at the scrapbook again?'

'Scrapbook? Hmmm, I don't know where it is.' Arthur looked around, unsure what he was looking for exactly. A book of some sort but he was having trouble bringing up the image.

'I know where it is,' said the child. 'Mum put it in the cupboard. I saw her the other night.' She went over to the cupboard at the side of the fireplace and retrieved a big green book.

'Oh yes. I see,' said Arthur, recognising the book. It had all his pictures in there. He put his half-eaten sandwich back on the plate.

The child settled herself next to him and opened the book. It was on the page of the cottage. France. That's where it was. He had a flash of recollection. The cottage was in Brittany. The child turned the page and there was another photograph of a young man standing next to a young woman in a floral dress. He had his arm around her shoulders and they were looking at each other and laughing. He smiled. It made him feel good.

'That's you,' said the child.

Arthur peered at the photograph. Arthur Pettinger. Yes, that's who it was and yes, that was him. '789776, REME, Twelfth Division.'

'REME? What does that mean?'

'Royal Electrical and Mechanical Engineers.' It came without hesitation and Arthur recognised the sense of pride that accompanied it.

'Who is the lady?'

'*Ma chérie*. My darling. *Je t'aime avec tout mon coeur*.'

The child looked wide-eyed at him. 'Wow. What language was that?'

'I'm sorry, *ma chérie*. I'm sorry.' A tear slipped from his eye. 'I miss you. I wish I could see you and the children again.'

He felt the child slip her hand into his. 'Don't cry, Gramps,' she said, glancing towards the door. 'Don't let Mum see you crying; she'll tell me off.'

He fumbled for a handkerchief from his pocket and dabbed at his eyes. He squeezed the child's hand. He didn't want her to worry about him. What was he like? He wasn't someone who cried. Certainly not in front of anyone, let alone a child. 'I'm sorry.' He took a deep breath. And again. There, that was better. He could feel a sense of calm coming again.

'Don't worry, Gramps,' said Esther. 'I've got a plan. I'm going to make everything better. Now eat your sandwich before Mum comes back down.'

'Sandwich? Oh yes.' He looked at the plate on his lap. It would be wrong to let good food go to waste.

16

April 1944

Later that evening after Arthur had finished the meal Madame Dupont had prepared, he tried to encourage Freddie to eat without much success. Freddie's leg had been cleaned and redressed, using the silk from the parachute to make bandages but sitting there tonight, Arthur had noticed the undeniable smell of rotting flesh. The infection was taking hold and no matter how much the wound was cleaned, it wasn't looking good.

'Try some water,' Arthur suggested when Freddie turned his head away from the food. 'At least have a drink.'

Freddie's lips were dry and cracking, but with the help of Arthur, he lifted his head and managed a few sips, before falling back into a sleep.

Arthur went outside. It was a warmer night than before, partly due to the cloud cover that had moved into the area that evening and spread a light drizzle over the ground. Arthur looked across the courtyard towards the farmhouse, where a small light was leaking out from beneath a shuttered window. He turned to his left and walked along the side of the barn towards the gate, which opened out onto some land that was currently being used as a vegetable patch and then further onto a small apple tree orchard before finally reaching the forest.

Arthur walked to the boundary of the farm where during the day he would be greeted with a view of Sérent nestling in the valley. Tonight, there was only blackness. Somewhere nearby he could hear running water, a gentle babble as it swept over rocks and stones.

Lighting his cigarette, he contemplated his strategy for the following day. He was to go with Hugo to search out a new drop zone and possible landing strip. Hugo knew of a farm about ten miles away that might be suitable but Arthur needed to see it for himself.

He also needed to meet with other leaders of the local resistance to plan some attacks on strategic buildings and bridges in the coming weeks. It was a damn shame the chap at the station had been caught. Vital information that was once at their fingertips was now no longer available.

A noise behind him had him spinning around. God, he wished he was armed.

'Sorry, I didn't mean to frighten you.'

It was Maryse. She was carrying a lantern and the small flame from the candle inside was just strong enough to light up her features as she held it up beside her head.

'Is everything OK?' asked Arthur wondering why she had sought him out.

'Yes. And no.'

'What's the yes part?'

'Your plans. Everything is OK with your reason for being here,' she replied, still standing a few feet away from him.

'So the part that isn't OK?'

'My conscience,' she replied, no longer the confident and brusque woman she'd been earlier. Arthur could hear the apprehension in her voice as she continued to speak. 'I owe you an apology.'

'You do?' Arthur ground out his cigarette and scuffed it away into the grass verge. Authentic French cigarettes were pretty awful.

'For the way I spoke to you this afternoon at the apartment,' said Maryse. 'It was rude of me and I'm sorry but I had my reasons.'

'Apology accepted.'

'The man at the station,' she began.

'Honestly, you don't have to explain,' said Arthur.

'I want to. It is not right to pretend something has never happened and never to speak of it.'

'Right-O. I'm listening.' Arthur felt the light drizzle of rain begin again, but he ignored it. Maryse had a shawl wrapped around her shoulders and was clutching it to her chest.

'The man at the station who provided us with copies of the manifests listing all the serviceable materials and men being moved by train to Rennes, Le Mans and Paris, he was my brother, Lucas.'

Arthur groaned inwardly as he took in the significance of this tiny bit of information. No wonder Maryse had reacted the way she had. 'I'm so sorry,' he said softly. He thought of his own brother, John. Something he hadn't allowed himself to do since he'd heard the news the other night. He pushed away the emotion that was threatening to swamp him. This wasn't about him. This was about Maryse and her loss. 'How old was he?' Arthur didn't know why he asked, but it was suddenly important to him that he knew more of this man, this brother, who had given his life fighting for the freedom of his country and to help Arthur do the job he had come here to do.

'He was twenty-two,' replied Maryse. 'He had been working there for the past twelve months. I don't know how the Germans found out what he was doing. We tried to warn him, but it was too late.'

Her voice broke and she let go of her shawl to wipe the tears from her face, which glistened like a moonlit stream in the light of the candle.

Arthur's natural reaction was to offer her some form of comfort, but he stopped himself, unsure whether his gesture would be taken the wrong way. It wouldn't do to upset the family who were harbouring him and Freddie.

'When did this happen?' he asked instead.

'We finally found out last month what had happened to him. They wouldn't tell us. No one could find anything out. The Gestapo came here. They interviewed us all.'

Arthur noted she used the word interviewed, rather than interrogated. 'Aren't you taking a huge risk having me and Guy here? Won't they be keeping a closer eye on you all?'

'Don't worry. You are not at risk.'

'I wasn't thinking so much of myself, as you and your family.'

'We know what we are doing. We cannot sit back and let the Germans take over. We have to at least feel we are doing something to resist. I don't want my brother to have died for nothing.' She had stopped crying now and her voice grew stronger. 'I don't suppose you understand though.'

'Maybe more than you think,' Arthur replied. He swallowed hard before continuing. 'I lost my brother too. I found out three days ago.'

'I did not know. I am sorry.'

'I had the opportunity not to come on this mission but, like you, I didn't want my brother's death to be for nothing. He was in the army and I know without a shadow of a doubt, he would want me to continue. My only regret is that I'm not there with my parents, my mother especially, who will be devastated.'

He could hear the emotion in his own voice. He wasn't as stoic as Maryse. He couldn't quite convert all that pain into anger. It hurt and it hurt deep.

They stood in silence for some time, each lost in thoughts of their own grief and the sacrifices their brothers had made and the pain their families were enduring in a bid to defeat the fascist Nazi regime.

'We have more in common than we knew,' said Maryse at last.

'This may not be my homeland, but it is my mother's and I feel a deep-rooted connection to it and a loyalty to the people of France,' replied Arthur. 'The liberation of France and of Europe means far more to me than you realise.'

Maryse reached out with her hand and placed it on Arthur's chest. 'Your mother would be so proud of you if she could hear you. I am sure.'

Arthur put his hand over hers. 'And I'm sure our brothers would be too.'

Arthur fixed his gaze on hers as a mutual understanding passed between them.

Maryse broke the deadlock first, sliding her hand away, with what Arthur felt was a reluctance. 'Thank you for listening to me.'

'Thank *you*,' insisted Arthur.

He stood there watching her departing figure, the glow of the candle in the lantern fading as she hurried back to the farmhouse.

Part 2

17

Joe took a last bite of his toast and washed it down with a gulp of coffee, while simultaneously ramming his arm into his jacket and then dumping his cup and bread board into the sink. He never saw the point of using a plate when the bread board was sufficient – it saved on the washing up for a start.

He grabbed his bag and was heading down the hallway when the doorbell rang. Through the glass he could see the silhouette of a man. He scooped up the post from the mat and opened the door. He was surprised to see Matt, his next-door neighbour standing there. 'Everything all right, mate?'

'Yeah, sorry to call so early,' began Matt, 'but Kay said I should come over sooner rather than later.'

Joe straightened his jacket and slid his tie up to his collar, fiddling with the top button. 'OK. That sounds ominous.'

Matt thrust an envelope into Joe's hand. 'Have a look at this when you get time today.'

Joe took the envelope, which was already open. He looked inside at the folded sheet of paper. 'What's this?'

'It's a letter from Esther. As in Esther Pettinger-Shaw.'

'What?' Joe looked down at the two folded sheets of paper and unfolded the top one.

'That's the one she sent to us, asking us to pass the other one on to you.'

Joe frowned as he read the short note from Esther.

Dear Kay and Matt

Please could you give this other letter to Joe who lives next door to you or if he has moved and you know where he lives now can you give it to him?

Thank you.

From Esther Pettinger-Shaw (Maddy's daughter. Maddy who used to be with Joe Finch who lives next door to you.)

Joe smiled at Esther's explanation of who she was although none of them were likely to forget Maddy and Esther. He looked at the other piece of paper, which had been folded into four. 'Did you read it?'

Matt looked embarrassed. 'Sorry, but we did. Kay didn't want to just give it to you in case it was bad news or something.'

'And is it?'

'No. It's intriguing more than anything. Read it later, yeah?'

'I take it Maddy doesn't know Esther's sent this, then.'

'Pretty sure she doesn't,' confirmed Matt. 'Look, Kay thinks it's something special. Read the letter and you'll understand. Let me know what you think later. Kay said, come round for tea tonight to talk about it.'

Joe hesitated for a minute. Matt was serious. He tucked the letter into his inside pocket. He'd have a read of it when he was on his own. It would give him time to think about whatever it was before being interrogated by Kay later, which he was certain would happen. 'What's for tea?'

'Homemade chilli.'

'How could I refuse?'

'That's what Kay said.'

'OK. I'll have a look later. Sorry, but I've got to get on.'

'Yeah, sure. See you tonight,' said Matt, already turning on his heel and cutting across the open-plan lawn to his own front door.

It was a busy morning at Sussex Private Investigators and Joe had been passed two new cases that morning. One was for an elderly lady who had died with no known family and HMRC were after the estate if no living relatives were found. The second was more covert where a local company wanted to find out if an employee was as incapacitated as he claimed to be.

'Any luck on finding more relatives for the Benson case?' called his boss, Peter Southerton, from the doorway of his office. 'We've got two brothers and a second cousin so far.'

Joe checked the computer screen for the up-to-date info. 'Nothing yet – we're still trying to track down the other brother. Apparently, he moved to New Zealand. I'm waiting for some info to come back from there.'

'We've only got until the end of the week and I heard on the grapevine that Taylors might take on the case if we don't come up with the goods. Haven't you got any other contacts you can call on?' Southerton pushed himself away from the doorframe and walked over to look at the computer screen. There was fierce competition between the two local firms of private investigators, which Peter took personally. 'Can't you call up one of your mates?'

'If I had any in New Zealand, I might be able to do that,' said Joe. 'Unfortunately, all my police work was done on home soil.'

'Friends of friends? Anyone? You must know someone?'

Joe shook his head. 'Nope but I'll phone around again.' He hoped this would be enough to keep his boss off his back. Southerton was good to work for most of the time but he thought because Joe had once been in the police force, he had contacts and sources all over the place. The truth was his days in uniform and later in CID were much less exciting than Southerton imagined.

It wasn't until Joe was making himself a coffee later that morning, that he had a chance to look at the letter from Esther. As he took it from his pocket, his phone buzzed through with a text message. It was Kay.

Hi Joe, Matt said he gave you Esther's letter. Sorry for reading it but I wanted to make sure it wasn't something bad or upsetting. Anyway, I don't know why but I really want to help her. Please say you can help too. Will love you forever. Will put extra chilli flakes in your chilli and I won't tell Matt. See you at 6. Xx

He smiled at Kay's message. She was a sweetheart. He sent a reply.

The extra chilli flakes swung it. See you later.

Going back to his desk with his coffee, he sat down and unfolded the letter.

Dear Joe

I'm sorry for braking breaking my promise not to contact you but this is important. I need your help. Me and Mum have moved in with Gramps as he isn't very

*well and Hazel can't look after him anymore. Gramps
showed me his scrapbook and in it was a picture of a
lady who Gramps wants to see again. He gets upset when
he talks about her and keeps saying he is sorry. I think
it would make him feel happy again if he could see her
and let her know how much he misses her and that he is
sorry. She's called Maryse and he met her when he was in
France in the war. She's French but he has a picture of her
and on the back is an address in Peterborough. I think
it must be her address. I've copied it at the end of the
letter. Can you find out Can you please find out if she's
there or where she is now? Gramps also talked about two
children and I think Maryse is their mum.*
    From Esther Pettinger-Shaw
    PS. Mum doesn't know I've sent this.

Joe read the letter for a second time. It was a sweet
idea from Esther but seriously the great-grandfather must be
well into his nineties and although possible, the chances of
Maryse still being alive were low. It was a French-sounding
name and there was mention of France, so it was a bit
confusing why there was an English address.

He folded the letter and replaced it in the envelope, unsure
why Kay was so excited about it. Clearly, she thought he
could find this woman but Joe was lacking the same sense of
enthusiasm.

However, right now, all that was the least of his concerns.
He couldn't ignore the fact that this was Maddy's daughter
contacting him and all the issues that came with that and how
he was going to handle it.

He inwardly winced at what Maddy would say when
she found out Esther had gone behind her back and he

winced further when he realised he'd be betraying Esther's confidence if he told Maddy about the letter. He couldn't win. In fact, it had potential to cause a complete shitstorm. Already, just the thought of Maddy was stirring up a morass of emotions – emotions he thought he'd well and truly shut away. He pinched the bridge of his nose and shut his eyes. No, he couldn't do this. There was no way he'd be able to help Esther. He'd have to get Kay to tell her and that way he wouldn't have to contact Esther or Maddy himself.

As he pushed the envelope back into his inside pocket, he ignored the taunt of his subconscious that this was the chicken way out.

'What do you mean it's like looking for a needle in a haystack?' exclaimed Kay as she served Joe his chilli con carne that evening. 'I thought that's what you did for a living – find the impossible.'

If Joe thought he was going to get some sort of moral support from Matt, he was mistaken. Matt shrugged in that way he did when he knew he was defeated by his wife.

'I'm merely being realistic,' said Joe. 'What have we got to go on? A letter from an eleven-year-old about someone her grandfather knew in the war who may or may not live in England.'

'Great-grandfather. He's her great-grandfather.'

'OK, but it doesn't change the facts.'

'And it's not some random eleven-year-old – it's Esther, it's her great-grandfather and Maddy's grandfather,' pressed Kay. 'You know, Maddy who you had a long-term relationship with for, let me see… three years.'

'That's irrelevant,' countered Joe. 'Inadmissible.'

'Inadmissible? You're joking, right?' Kay looked at Matt.

Matt gave an apologetic shrug in Joe's direction. 'Overruled. It's totally admissible.'

'Whose side are you on?' Joe shook his head and turned back to Kay. 'Look, Maddy made it perfectly clear that she didn't want anything to do with me when we broke up. She even told Esther she wasn't to contact me again after she sent me that letter telling me she missed me. It was over three years ago for God's sake. I can't undermine her.'

'You're scared, aren't you?' said Kay, putting her knife and fork down and taking a sip of her wine.

'I am not!'

'Yes you are.'

'Scared of what, exactly?' Joe demanded.

'Scared of Maddy. Well, not Maddy herself but scared of how you'll feel seeing her again.' Kay sat back in her seat with a look of satisfaction.

'Wait a minute, you're jumping ahead here,' said Joe. 'I've no intention of contacting Maddy but that's not because I'm scared of how I'll react...'

'Scared of how she'll react?' offered Matt.

'She hates me,' said Joe.

'She does not.' Kay clearly wasn't backing down.

Joe let out a sigh and paused to allow the tension that was building to diminish somewhat. 'Look, Kay, I can't do this for Esther. She's a lovely kid and all that, but Maddy would crucify me if I went behind her back and as for approaching Maddy directly, (a) that's dropping Esther in it and (b) Maddy doesn't want anything to do with me. She's moved on. She's got herself another fella. She doesn't want me upsetting the apple cart.'

'And that's where your argument falls down,' said Kay.

'Maddy is going to find out one way or another that Esther has written to you, whether that comes from me, Matt or you is irrelevant. As for Maddy – she's single. She's not with that bloke, what's his name?'

'Braden,' supplied Joe and then felt like kicking himself.

'Aha, so you know his name. You've obviously been checking up on Maddy,' said Kay. 'Which tells me you still think about her and that's also why you've never had another serious relationship since breaking up with her.'

Joe chose to ignore the summary. 'She's broken up with him?'

'I'm still friends with her on Facebook. We have mutual friends. We like each other's posts sometimes,' explained Kay. 'I've kept up with what she's doing.'

'I still don't think it's a good idea. Maybe I can recommend someone else help them.'

'Oh, come on, Joe, that's a cop-out. Esther has asked you directly. You can't let her down.'

There was an awkward pause at this remark and Joe was sure all three of them had silently added the word *again* to the end of that last sentence. 'I don't know...' he said eventually.

Kay sat forwards eagerly. 'Maddy's grandfather cries when he thinks of this woman. He says he's sorry. Esther wants to make him happy. She's worried enough to contact you, despite what Maddy said. Even this must penetrate that wall of steel you've built around your heart.' She gave him puppy-dog eyes.

Joe shook his head, unable to repress the smile. 'You're a romanticist.'

'Did you do any digging at all?' asked Kay. 'I googled the name but didn't find anything myself. Of course, you've got other ways open to you. I did, however, find this on Esther's YouTube channel.' She picked up her tablet from the side and turned it around to show Joe.

With a certain amount of reluctance, Joe took the tablet Kay had shoved under his nose. He watched as Esther appeared on the screen. She'd certainly grown up since he'd last seen her as an eight-year-old with her hair in bunches and a gap between her teeth where her baby tooth had fallen out. He watched as she spoke about her great-grandfather and then brought him into shot. Joe had met Arthur several times in the past and he was pleasantly surprised to see that despite his age, Arthur still looked well. He patiently watched it until the end, half expecting – or was that hoping? – Maddy would be part of the recording and he acknowledged the disappointment he felt at not getting the chance to see what she looked like now.

'It's all very sweet,' he said, passing the tablet back. 'But I'm still not convinced there's anything in it.'

'Oh, you're so heartless,' bemoaned Kay. 'Where's your compassion gone?' She pouted and then gave Matt a tap on the arm. 'Tell him, Matt. Tell him why he should help Esther.'

Matt looked slightly startled at the sudden call to support his wife's cause. He sat upright, looked from one to the other, before holding his hands out palms up. 'To stop Kay giving me earache. To help a friend out.'

'Never mind me, what about Esther and what about Arthur? You could really be helping them out. Have you seen how many "likes" the video is getting?' She held the tablet up to face Joe. 'Look, so far three hundred and ten.'

'I'm sure someone on there will be able to help her,' said Joe.

'I'm sure there will be people offering,' said Kay, clearly not taking no for an answer. 'But just think how many scammers there are, ready to take advantage of her plight? And you've got a legitimate reason to help her – you've got the letter. You've got the upper hand. This is your territory. It's your job to find people.'

'Oh, Kay, it's sweet that you want to help her, or rather you want me to help her, but I don't know what I can do. I'm busy at work at the moment.'

'You could do it evenings and weekends. And don't tell me you're busy then. For the past six months you've done nothing but mope around. You barely go out. You sit indoors most evenings watching Netflix and weekends you may wash your car or mow the lawn but that's about as exciting as it gets unless we take you out.' She looked at him sternly, daring him to contradict her.

The truth was, he couldn't. She was spot on. He'd had no inclination to do anything other than sup a few beers in the evenings and bury himself away. Even the excitement of a new date had deserted him lately and he'd begun to realise he was simply going through the motions with no intention of finding that special someone.

Joe looked at Matt. 'Help me out here.'

'Don't look at me,' replied his friend. 'Kay's not going to give up and, to be honest, I think it would do you some good.'

'Not you as well.'

'Just think about it,' said Kay. 'Please.'

Joe relented. It was easier than arguing that was for sure. 'OK. I'll have a think but I'm not making any promises.'

'Excellent!' said Kay. 'That's that sorted. I know you'll be able to help her, I just know it.'

'I haven't agreed to anything yet!' Joe reminded her.

'No. But you will do.' Kay said it with such certainty, that Joe wondered if he should give in there and then.

18

Later that evening when Joe had thanked Matt and Kay for dinner and returned home, he found himself thinking back to the letter. Kay had insisted he keep it and have another look at it. He wasn't sure there was anything more to look at; however, he had taken pity on Matt and conceded to think more about it.

It was still only ten o'clock, which in Joe's books was far too early to go to bed. He'd always been something of a night owl and living on his own made it easy to stay up late, either watching TV or sometimes bringing work home with him. He could do a reasonable amount of investigating on the laptop at home and it was better than doing nothing.

Not bothering to switch on the kitchen light, he took a beer from the fridge and opened it as he moved through the house to the living room. His house was a modest three-bedroom semi, which he'd bought at a bargain price due to the work it needed to bring it up to date. The avocado bathroom suite was a leftover from when it had been modernised back in the 60s. Joe had got as far as ripping out the old kitchen and installing a new one, but his DIY enthusiasm had waned and his avocado bathroom suite was in danger of becoming fashionably retro. He took a swig of his beer and slumped down into the sofa, before picking up the remote control and channel-hopping in the hope of finding something that would interest him.

In the end he settled on a documentary about the resistance and the Second World War. History had always been a favourite subject of his and it was half the reason why he found part of his job so interesting. He loved delving into the past, digging around in family history and putting long forgotten and misplaced pieces of a puzzle together. He especially loved it when his findings brought together families who had been estranged or didn't even know each other existed, or those who had gaps in their family history. He loved the sense that the past was being sewn back together so that it could be enjoyed by future generations, like an old patchwork quilt. He hated it most when people died and no living relatives were found. He felt an undeniable and genuine sadness that the person had died and along with them all their memories and their past. Gone. Just like that. No one to talk about them. No one to remember them. That part of history would never be told again.

He finished his beer and was debating whether to get another one and only half paying attention to the documentary, when some old black and white footage was shown of a young girl of about twelve or thirteen working out in the fields with a man Joe assumed was her grandfather. They were harvesting wheat, the girl using a pitchfork with admirable adeptness. It struck him that the father and the brothers were probably away fighting in the war.

He couldn't help likening it to the YouTube channel he had watched earlier of Esther and her great-grandfather. Different generations working together, enjoying each other's company.

Joe let out a sigh and muttered an expletive. It was no use

pretending anymore to himself that Esther's letter had not been at the forefront of his mind all day. And not only Esther, but Maddy too. There was no way he could ignore either of them.

Joe picked up his laptop and searched the internet for the clip Kay had shown him of Esther. Gramps didn't appear to understand what was going on, but this didn't perturb Esther. There was an invisible connection between the two family members.

Joe watched it one more time and then retrieved the letter from his pocket. He hated the thought of letting Esther down and imagined how disappointed she'd be that he hadn't been able to help her, hadn't been able to fix something for her. He'd failed her once before and had spent the last three years feeling a complete shit for it. Oh hell! What was he supposed to do? He had to admit, he was quite intrigued by this Maryse woman and what her connection to Arthur Pettinger was.

Logging onto his work's portal, Joe was able to gain access to other resources. For a start, he could easily look at the electoral register. He wanted to see if anyone by that name had lived at the address Esther had quoted. It would be easier with a surname but the Christian name was unusual enough. Unfortunately, he drew a blank with the name. The previous owners had lived in the house for twenty years and the ones before that had been there since the house had been built in the 1930s.

He knew a little about Maddy's family history from their time together but he wanted to get a clear idea of names and dates. He tapped in Arthur Pettinger's name and checking births, marriages and deaths, after a little digging found Arthur had married a Joan Newman in 1951 and they had one son, Charles – whom he knew was Maddy's father – two years later. There was no record of a Maryse anywhere so Joe could only conclude Arthur had never married this supposed love of his. A wartime love affair? It was a distinct possibility. It happened a lot, probably more so than anyone cared to admit.

Joe fetched his notebook from his bag and on a clean page, jotted down the brief family history of Arthur Pettinger. On the face of it, the man had lived a fairly typical and unremarkable life. Joe had been able to tap into the war records via his work's access codes and found that Arthur had served in the REMEs in the war and had been stationed in North Africa and then Italy for a short time, before being selected for a mission in France. Details of that were scant and Joe wondered if it had been some sort of secret mission. Possibly something to do with the Special Operations Executive, or SOE as it was abbreviated to and more importantly the French branch – SOE(F). Before the war had ended, Arthur was back in England on desk duty, stationed in East Anglia. Presumably preparing for D-Day and distracting the Germans. Joe made some more notes in his pad.

Joe hadn't as yet found a place for Maryse in the story though and this was the woman who Esther thought was important enough to make her great-grandfather happy. She'd also mentioned two children but there was little or no detail about who they were, not even a name, so for now he wouldn't worry about them. Finding the woman might lead to the children.

It was at this point Joe dropped the pen onto the pad and let out a long sigh. It was all starting to sound a bit far-fetched and romantic for his liking. This Maryse woman could be anyone, anywhere.

He sank back in the sofa and tried to refocus on the TV. The clock on the mantel showing it to be getting on for midnight now. Those two hours had certainly gone quick.

It was too early though for Joe to contemplate bed. His mind was refusing to stop ticking over and he found himself increasingly thinking of Maryse and Arthur Pettinger.

He must have eventually nodded off where he had been sitting, waking up to find himself sprawled across the sofa at around five o'clock in the morning. He groaned. It wasn't worth taking himself off up to bed now as he'd have to be getting up in an hour. Still, four or five hours' sleep was about average for him. He was good at running on empty, a throwback to his days in the police force.

However, it had been a disturbed sleep where images of Esther and Gramps pervaded, with Maddy at the centre. Random scenes that in typical dream fashion didn't make sense and couldn't be remembered in detail. The memory might not be there but the unmistakable and overriding feeling of sadness lingered, easing its way from subconscious to conscious.

He picked up the notebook from the floor where it must have slipped off the sofa at some point in the night and flicked through the pages to recap on his findings, pushing all thoughts of Maddy to one side. He wasn't quite ready to confront them just yet. The big question was who was Maryse? He definitely needed more info. He could feel the buzz of excitement that he often experienced when taking on a new case. It hadn't happened for a long time but there it was today, simmering in the background. Was that a sign? He didn't believe in fate and all that, but it surprised him that he had that old feeling for this case when he hadn't had it in… oh, let's think… a good six months. Unsurprisingly, that tied in with the break-up from Lisa, his last girlfriend. She'd have corrected him with the noun 'partner' but to Joe that indicated some kind of long-term relationship. He'd hardly call six months long term although to be fair, it had been the longest relationship he'd managed since Maddy.

Shit! There he was again, thinking about Maddy.

He closed his notebook and slipped it into his bag, along with the letter from Esther. He took a slow shower and, for once, had breakfast before he left for work, rather than grabbing something on the go.

As he went out his front door, from the corner of his eye he saw next door's shutter move. Kay was on the lookout. Sure enough, by the time he had checked his front door was locked, she was coming out onto her path.

'Morning!' she called. 'So, what's your answer?'

Joe turned slowly on his heel to face her. 'Did you even go to bed last night? Don't tell me you spent the whole night at the window so you didn't miss me.'

Matt appeared at the door. 'Don't jest,' he called over, with a raise of his hand in greeting. 'You don't know how close to the truth that is.'

Kay looked expectantly at him as she stood in her nurse's uniform, her hands together as if in prayer and a pleading look on her face.

Joe rolled his eyes. Oh, what the hell. 'OK. I'll do it,' he said.

'Yay! I knew you would!' exclaimed Kay.

'Don't get your hopes up though,' said Joe, giving Matt a look. 'It's all got to be done properly and I need to speak to Maddy first to see if she wants me to do this. And, of course, her grandfather. It's not simply a case of me ploughing ahead.'

'This is so exciting,' said Kay, seemingly oblivious to Joe's caution. 'What are you going to do? Phone her? You should phone her when we're there too. Or would that be too much?'

'See what you've started?' Matt gave a roll of his eyes.

'I think you started it, mate,' said Joe, blipping the remote locking on his car. 'I'll pop round tonight and we'll talk strategy.'

'Thank you, Joe! You're the best,' called Kay, blowing kisses as he reversed off his drive and headed down the road.

Shit. What had he got himself into? But the thought was lost as questions about who Maryse was and how he was going to find her took over.

19

April 1944

Arthur and Freddie had been at the farm on the hill for over a week now. Arthur had been out on a recce with Hugo and Patrick, locating a strip of farmland that would be suitable as a new drop zone and also landing strip. The farmer who owned the land was part of the resistance Patrick commanded and had been more than happy to co-operate. He owned over two hundred acres of farm and woodland and the field was nestled between the trees with no direct access from the road. It was perfect. Arthur had sent a message back to London with the co-ordinates the previous evening.

He hadn't seen much of Maryse over the past few days, except in the evenings when invariably she brought them their food and tended to Freddie's dressing.

She arrived as usual early evening just after dusk and instead of hurrying off, she stayed a little longer and walked down to the boundary of the farm with him. 'It's nice to have other company,' she explained. 'And company that is nice.'

They stood side by side in the dark, talking about Maryse's work at the school where she spent her days helping the headmaster to teach the children and generally giving them an escape from the harsh realities of living under the occupying forces.

'Any news of the headmaster's wife?' asked Arthur.

'No. I'm sure we won't see her again. The children have stopped asking about her. It's heart-breaking but it's also a reality we have to face.' She sighed deeply. 'Monsieur Rochelle is worried about the children.'

'In what way?'

'Because their mother is Jewish, by default, the Germans might view the children as such.'

'And what about Monsieur Rochelle? Is he Jewish?'

'No. But he is in danger too. Jewish sympathisers are not looked upon too fondly. He told me today he thinks he's being watched.'

'By the Gestapo?'

'Possibly. More like Milice. Plain-clothed.'

'Can he not leave?'

'He won't leave the other children at the school. He doesn't want to abandon them. For a precious few hours each day, we are their only escape.'

'What about you? Are you safe?' Arthur felt an unexpected protectiveness for Maryse.

'As safe as anyone else,' she replied. 'We don't know until it's too late.'

Arthur knew she must be thinking of her brother. Instinctively, he put an arm around her shoulder and gave a squeeze. He went to take his hand away, but she held it in place and leaned against his shoulder.

Arthur moved his other arm around her and brought her into his chest. He rested his chin on her head, the soft waves of her hair against his skin. The sweet rose scent of her hair was at odds with the sourness of the burden of grief and responsibility she carried. He could only admire her for her courage and compassion. She was doing everything she could to protect those children and to support them, but was anyone looking out for her?

The moment was broken as, in the distance, the night sky lit up in a bright red glow, followed by the muffled noise of an explosion.

They broke from their embrace to stare at the sight, the redness turning orange and then yellow.

'The railway,' said Maryse.

'I hope so,' said Arthur. He'd given instructions to Patrick only last night to begin attacking the railway lines. He was impressed with their efficiency.

That night when Arthur went to bed, he found it difficult to sleep as his mind kept wandering back to Maryse and how it had felt to hold her against him. When he finally drifted off to sleep, she even managed to filter into his dreams.

Arthur woke early the next morning and went out to the farm boundary that was fast becoming his regular spot. He liked to look out across the valley and take a moment to appreciate the vista, to pretend it wasn't infested with German soldiers.

The sun was already heating up the air and he wiped his brow with his sleeve. He could do with a proper wash. The fresh air only served as a reminder as to how stinky it was in the barn with Freddie. He looked over towards the river he'd heard when he'd come down here that first night. It was so inviting. Sod it. He was going in.

In a matter of seconds, he had stripped off, leaving his clothes on the grass. Surprisingly, it was colder than he imagined. He ducked under the water, surfaced and shook his head like a wet dog, droplets of water flying out around him. God, it felt good. In another time, another life, he'd be happy here, he thought, rubbing his eyes with his fingertips. He stood up and the water lapped just below his navel. It was then he heard some giggling. The soft giggle of a female. He dropped his hands and scanned the bank of the stream, spinning around a full 360 degrees.

It was then he spotted her, a little further upstream, standing under the branches of a willow tree. She had a large basket resting on her hip, her hands holding each of the handles. A white headscarf was tied back at the nape of her neck, keeping her rich brown hair at bay.

He raised a hand and then looked for his clothes but they had disappeared from the grass. He looked back at Maryse, whose grin spread wide across her face.

'I wash them,' she said in English.

Arthur didn't miss the mischievous glimmer in her eye.

'I can't stay in here though,' he protested. 'And I can't get out.' He probably could, he thought, but he didn't think that would be a wise move.

Maryse took some clothing from the basket. 'These are clean. There are some for your friend too.'

'*Merci*,' he said, giving a small nod of thanks.

She came down towards him and placed the clothes on the grass, together with half a bar of soap. 'It is mine, but you can keep that half.'

'That bad, am I?'

She laughed. 'I thought Hugo had brought some wild boar and was keeping them locked up.' She picked up the soap. 'I suppose you want me to throw this to you?'

Arthur gave a shrug. 'I could come and get it.' He threw his head back and laughed out loud at the look of horror on her face. He made a movement in the water, as if he was going to jump out right there and then, stark naked. Maryse leapt back, squealed and turned her head away, only to look slowly back at him.

Arthur realised it was the first time he had laughed in a long time. And then felt immediately guilty. He was in the middle of a bloody war. Stuck in the French countryside with his oppo close to death.

The reality of his situation slapped the smile from his face at the precise moment Hugo appeared at the top of the hill and bellowed at Maryse.

The smile disappeared from her face too and she turned to go back up the hill, stopping after a couple of strides to turn and throw the soap to him, before scurrying back up to her angry-looking brother. They exchanged words, heated words from what Arthur could tell, although he couldn't make out what they were saying. She didn't look back but hurried out of sight. Hugo gave Arthur a long hard stare. No words needed.

20

'There we go, Gramps,' said Maddy, her hand under his arm, guiding him into the chair. 'Shall I put some music on for you? I'll make a cup of tea once I've unpacked the shopping.'

'Tea? That will be nice,' said Gramps. His fingers pulled at the sleeves of his cardigan, adjusting the cuff and readjusting.

'Esther, be a sweetheart and take off Gramps's shoes. His slippers are there. Pop them on.' Maddy smiled at her daughter. She was proving such a help with the little things that went to making life with Gramps a bit easier.

As she went out to fetch the shopping from the car, Maddy could hear Esther instructing Gramps to lift his foot. It made Maddy feel both proud and sad at the same time. Age was such a stripper of dignity. The slippers being the tip of the iceberg. Yesterday, Maddy had needed to help Gramps get out of the shower cubicle. At least he'd been spared the indignity of an eleven-year-old responding to his cries of help when he couldn't open the shower door. Maddy had managed to reach the bathroom a few seconds ahead of Esther.

Maddy opened the rear door of the car where she had ended up putting the bags of shopping. She hadn't realised just how much space in the boot Gramps's wheelchair would take up. It had left no space for the weekly shop.

The whole shopping excursion had taken all morning, much longer than the usual hour Maddy was used to but negotiating a wheelchair and a trolley around the supermarket – even with Esther's help – hadn't been as straightforward as she had envisaged.

Maddy lifted two shopping bags out and lugged them up the drive, through the house and into the kitchen. It was surprising how much she had needed to buy. Not only food shopping but household items too – it turned out Hazel hadn't stocked up on anything and had been running down the provisions. Poor old Gramps had needed practically a whole set of toiletries, not to mention some new socks and underpants. So far, Maddy hadn't been able to find a matching pair of socks, let alone a pair that didn't have a hole in them. It was a minor thing, Maddy acknowledged, and although not essential to Gramps's basic human needs, she thought he'd had an air of neglect about him when she had first arrived. He had looked untidy, she thought – far removed from the smartly dressed and well-groomed man she remembered from her childhood.

Fifi wandered into the kitchen having already welcomed Gramps and Esther home and been let out into the garden. Maddy eyed the dog, trying to gauge what sort of mood she might be in. It was hard to say. Fifi paused, padded over to the shopping bags, had a little sniff and then sat herself down at Maddy's feet.

'Hello, Fifi,' said Maddy. She took a packet of dog treats from one of the bags. 'You want to know me now you can smell some treats, is that it?' She broke the seal. 'I don't care. I'm all for bribery.' The dog's ears twitched and Fifi cocked her head to one side as if understanding exactly what was being said. Maddy wasn't going to risk feeding Fifi by hand just yet, so instead dropped a treat onto the floor. Fifi didn't waste any time hoovering up the offering. She sat back down at Maddy's feet, looking up at her.

'Oh, it's like that, is it? You're so cheap!' Maddy took another treat and again dropped it onto the floor. Fifi was even faster this time. Maddy ventured to stroke the dog's head but the animal turned her back on Maddy and trotted out of the kitchen. 'Snubbed by a dog,' muttered Maddy, putting the treats away in the cupboard.

Maddy finished unpacking the two bags and fetched the last one from the car, deciding that perhaps it would be best if she shopped online in future and had it delivered. It would be much easier and instead of struggling around the supermarket with Gramps and Esther, she could use that time to do something nicer, such as take Gramps for a walk around the park and Esther could play on the equipment. She could even bring Fifi with them.

Her phone rang and she fished it out from the bottom of her handbag. It was a withheld number and she debated for a moment whether to answer it but deciding it could be the council or social services about the forms she had recently completed for Gramps, she answered the call.

'Can I speak to Mr Arthur Pettinger, please?' came a male voice Maddy didn't recognise.

'Who's calling?'

'I'm Conor Jones from the *Puff Daily*. Is Mr Pettinger there, please?'

Maddy racked her brains. The *Puff Daily* sounded familiar but she couldn't quite place it. Something made her err on the side of caution. 'I'm afraid he can't come to the phone.

I'm his granddaughter. Can I help at all?'

'Would it be possible to phone back?'

'What is it about, please?'

Conor Jones cleared his throat and lowered his voice. 'It's a personal matter, which I do need to speak to Mr Pettinger about.'

Maddy felt suddenly defensive about Gramps. This Conor Jones sounded a bit too cagey; she didn't like it at all. 'Well, as I said, Mr Pettinger can't come to the phone so you'll need to leave your number and give me some idea what's it about.'

A small silence followed before Conor Jones spoke. 'Do you know who the woman is that Mr Pettinger is trying to find?'

'What?' Had she missed something? It was the first she'd heard about it.

'Maryse. Do you know who she is?'

'I'm sorry but I don't know what you're talking about.' Maddy hung up the phone. She had taken an inexplicable dislike to the man and every sense was telling her she should protect Gramps from him. She didn't know what he was referring to and could only assume the caller had got his wires crossed somewhere along the line.

Maddy set about making the tea she had promised her grandfather and, although she tried, she couldn't shake off the phone call. She didn't know why, but she felt troubled by it.

'Nice cup of tea for you, Gramps,' she said carrying his cup into the living room. 'Squash for you, Esther.' She put down the drinks. 'Are you two OK?'

'I'm showing Gramps my YouTube channel,' said Esther. 'I've got over seven hundred likes.' She sounded excited and

Maddy was impressed. Esther had been working on her channel for about a year now.

'What was your last upload about?' asked Maddy.

Esther glanced at Gramps before answering. 'I made cheesecakes.'

'Wow! And over seven hundred likes in total. Your channel is going really well.'

'Not seven hundred in total,' said Esther. 'Seven hundred for the cheesecake vlog.'

'Just that one video?' asked Maddy, for clarification. She wasn't up on what was a good number of 'thumbs up' but even she knew seven hundred for one video for Esther was pretty amazing – and all for a cheesecake video.

'Can I watch it?' She had meant to look before, as she always liked to surreptitiously monitor the channel for content and comments. Technically, Esther wasn't old enough for her own YouTube account, so they'd set it up using Maddy's details and monitoring it had been one of the conditions Maddy had insisted on.

'Oh, I've just closed it,' said Esther. 'I'll show you later.'

The house phone rang out, making everyone in the room jump. Maddy looked at the caller ID. It was a mobile number but apart from that she had no idea who would be calling the landline. 'Hello.'

'Oh, hi. I'm trying to get hold of Arthur Pettinger or his granddaughter, Esther. Have I got the right number?'

Instantly, Maddy was on her guard. This sounded far too similar to the previous call and this woman was asking for Esther by name. 'I'm Mr Pettinger's granddaughter,' she said, making her way out of the room. 'Who is this, please? I'm Esther's mother. My daughter is a minor so unless you tell me straight away what this is about, I'm going to hang up and report you to the police.' She hoped she sounded far more confident than she felt.

'I'm sorry, please don't hang up. I'm Chrissy Thomas from County News. We saw your daughter's YouTube video and we'd like to help. Perhaps we could come over? We think it's such an interesting story and coming at it from a local angle, we could raise more awareness. Of course, it would have to be with the stipulation that it was an exclusive and you wouldn't be able to give the story to anyone else. I've—'

'Wait! Stop right there,' said Maddy, interrupting the woman whilst simultaneously trying to process everything she'd just heard. 'I don't understand why you're so interested in a cheesecake vlog and how this relates to my grandfather is beyond me.'

'Mrs... Maddy... please. I have it on the screen in front of me. It has over seven hundred thumbs up; it's been viewed over fifteen thousand times. It's being shared on social media. Twitter is going mad for it.'

'But a cheesecake video?'

'You haven't seen it, have you?'

'Well... no, not yet. I've been busy.' Maddy suddenly felt like the worst parent in the world.

'You need to watch it. Your grandfather's plight has touched the hearts of thousands. It's getting bigger by the second. Now, if you give your verbal agreement not to speak to anyone else, I can be with you by six o'clock tonight.'

'I'm not sure. I need to look at this first.'

'I don't want to pressure you, but I need to know. I need a verbal commitment now.'

'I'm sorry,' said Maddy, although not feeling the sentiment in the slightest. She could tell when she was being hassled and

Chrissy was definitely going for the hard sale. 'I need to see the channel first.'

'OK. As you wish, but I'll tell you what,' persisted Chrissy, as if she was doing Maddy a huge favour, 'you have a think about it. Don't sign with anyone before you've seen me. I'll still come over as planned and we can chat about the details then.'

Chrissy hung up before Maddy could protest any further. She definitely felt she had been outmanoeuvred there. The last thing she wanted was someone turning up. She needed to look at that vlog and see what all the fuss was about.

She had made it no further than the end of the hall, when her mobile rang. She looked at the caller ID and her heart missed at least two beats.

Joe Finch's name blinked on the screen.

Maddy was rooted to the spot, unable to move as she stared at the phone. She'd never got around to deleting his number from her contacts and it appeared he'd never deleted her contact number either. She should have changed her number – that would have been the sensible thing to do. The call cut out and went to voicemail. Almost immediately it rang again. Still Maddy gaped at the screen as the shock left her but indecision took its place.

When it stopped ringing, a text message came through straight away. It was from Joe.

Hi Maddy, I've rung a couple of times but it went to voicemail. Sorry if this has taken you by surprise but I need to talk to you. I wouldn't bother you if it wasn't important. It's about Esther and Gramps. Thanks. Joe.

Maddy read the text several times as she stood in the hall. It couldn't be a coincidence that Joe was ringing about Esther and Gramps when she'd just received two phone calls back to back about them. And as for speaking to Joe, it wasn't high on her wish list.

As she read the text message yet again, she realised that Joe must have the 'read message' facility on his phone as it showed she'd opened his message. Damn it. There was no pretending she hadn't seen it. When her phone rang again, she knew without looking it would be Joe. Whatever it was, it must be important. She looked at the living room door where Esther and Gramps were sitting, enjoying each other's company as the music played in the background. An avalanche of love, and the need to protect them, hit her and before she knew it, she was accepting the call.

'Hello.'

'Hi, Maddy. It's me… Joe.' His voice was soft with a touch of uncertainty about it.

'I know,' she replied, attempting to match her tone with his, but she could feel her stomach rolling over and there was a waver in her voice. She walked back down the hall to the kitchen out of earshot from the living room.

'I'm sorry to pounce on you like that,' Joe was saying. There was a pause. 'Are you OK?'

She swallowed hard before answering. 'If you're asking in general, then yes. If you're asking at this precise moment, then, I'm not sure.'

'Sorry, but it's important and too much to say over a text.'

'You kept my number, then?' She could have kicked herself as she said that.

'You kept mine,' he replied and there was a touch of amusement in his voice.

She'd asked for that. She attempted to sound more business-like to cover her embarrassment. 'You said it was important. That it was about Esther and Gramps.'

'Yeah, sure. Right.' Maddy imagined Joe composing himself in response to her brittleness. 'I've seen the YouTube vlog Esther made.'

'Go on,' replied Maddy, managing to contain her surprise and stop herself exclaiming *what the hell* down the phone.

'I thought maybe I could help you find the woman your grandfather is looking for.'

'Gramps isn't actually looking for anyone,' she heard herself say. 'It was a misunderstanding on Esther's part. There is no woman to be found.'

'It didn't sound like that to me.'

'And what would you know? You've not been about for the last few years, in case it had slipped your mind.' She knew she was being particularly scathing but she couldn't help herself as the memories of rejection surfaced like an Icelandic geyser.

'Ouch,' said Joe. 'I see the old adage of time being a healer isn't applicable here.'

Maddy could tell from his gentle tones that he wasn't intending to be antagonistic; it was just Joe's way of attempting to de-escalate confrontation. Humour had often been his best form of defence but the anger she was experiencing right now pushed her to ignore the potential olive branch. 'Look, Joe, I would say I appreciate your concern but I don't know if I do. Let's just leave it that I don't need or want your help.'

'Maddy, please, don't be like that.'

'I'm not being like anything. I'm simply looking out for my family.'

'OK, I understand but I'm here if you need me.'

Oh, the irony of those words! 'Need you?' she said and then managed to stop herself taking that comment any further. 'Thank you but we'll be fine. Goodbye, Joe.'

She hung up hoping to feel a certain amount of satisfaction but it was absent. Instead all she felt was an overwhelming sadness. *Damn you, Joe Finch.*

21

'So, that was me told,' said Joe, as he finished recounting the conversation he'd had with Maddy from the privacy of his car a short while ago. He took a sip of his pint and rather than meet the eyes of Kay and Matt sitting opposite him, he took a slow look around the pub. It was its usual busy Friday lunchtime and they'd been fortunate enough to grab a table almost as soon as they walked in.

'Look, I'm going to be honest with you,' said Kay. 'You need to do this as much for yourself as for Maddy.'

Joe raised his eyebrows in question. Kay glanced at her husband, who gave a resigned sigh.

'What Kay means,' began Matt before being interrupted by a dig in the ribs from Kay. 'What *we* mean is that... well... you've been moping around far too much lately. You need something to do, to keep your mind busy. Something to bring that spark back.'

'What we mean,' said Kay, 'is that we're worried about you. We have been for a while. It's time to stop wallowing in self-pity. Forget about Lisa. She's gone. History. She's not coming back. You've got to move on.'

'Since when did you become my counsellors?' asked

Joe, slightly irritated by his friends, despite knowing their intentions were well-meaning.

'Don't go getting all sulky,' continued Kay. 'Just because we've hit a nerve. We're not at home to Mr Sulky-Pants.'

Joe nearly choked on his beer. He wiped his mouth with the back of his hand. 'Mr Sulky-Pants?'

'If the cap fits... or in this case, if the pants fit...' replied Kay.

'She's got a point,' said Matt.

'Thanks for the support.' Joe shot his friend a look.

'Mate, it's only because we care about you.'

Kay took up the baton again. 'What better things have you got to do with your time? You go to work, come home, bung a ready meal in the microwave, slump out in front of the TV for half the night watching some crappy box-set, drink beer and eventually haul your backside up to bed.'

'Jesus! It's like living next door to MI6,' muttered Joe.

'Thin walls,' said Matt with a shrug.

'It's because we love you,' said Kay.

'Steady on,' cut in Matt. 'Who said anything about love? Like, I can do. As in, I like you a lot.' He gave Joe a slap on the back. 'In a mate sort of way, of course.'

'Of course,' said Joe, letting out a sigh.

Kay hadn't finished. 'Anyway, the point is, this is so your thing. I can't understand why you're not chomping at the bit to get involved.'

Joe gave yet another sigh. He was doing that a lot lately. 'Because it's Maddy and she doesn't want anything to do with me.'

'I'd say all the more reason to get involved,' said Kay. 'Trouble is, Maddy doesn't know it yet either.'

'Look, I'll be honest, last night, I did do a little bit of research and, yes, it did interest me but Maddy is particularly hostile to the whole thing, including to me. I wouldn't be surprised if she didn't really want to find this mysterious Maryse.'

'How do you know that? You barely spoke to her,' asked Kay.

'For a minute, just forget about any history between me and Maddy.' Kay and Matt shrugged their agreement and Joe continued. 'It's simply some romantic idea an eleven-year-old kid has got that her great-grandfather wants to see a woman he once met in France during the war. Esther's got some crazy idea it's all going to end happily ever after, which it won't.'

'You don't know that,' persisted Kay as she tapped at the screen of her iPad. 'Look, the video is getting hundreds and hundreds of likes. It's going viral.'

'Technically, you can't say it's going viral until you're into the millions of likes,' corrected Joe, even though he knew he was being pedantic. 'At the moment, it's just popular.'

'Whatever,' said Kay, ignoring him. 'They need someone on their side who is honest and can help them.'

'I'm not the Lone Ranger or some cyber vigilante. And, just for the record, I'm well over Lisa,' said Joe. He really was getting tired of the conversation now. Much as he loved Kay, he wished she'd drop the subject. 'Anyway, I hate to break up the party, but I need to get back to work.'

'I'm not giving up yet,' said Kay as the trio headed out of the pub and regrouped on the pavement to say their goodbyes. 'Please phone Maddy again, Joe. Honestly, you need to help her before someone takes advantage of them.'

By the time Joe arrived back in his office, he was feeling a little guilty for writing off Esther's vlog so quickly. If he was honest with himself, Kay's words had stung. They had hit home. He knew she was right about his behaviour but it was easy to wallow in his own self-pity. It wasn't that he was mourning the end of his relationship with Lisa – no, that had come to a natural end – but he had been fed up with never feeling completely satisfied with any of the relationships he had embarked upon. A little voice added 'since Maddy' but he knew that wasn't strictly true. It had been different with Maddy. It wasn't that he had been bored or not cared about her, it had in fact been the opposite and it had frightened him.

He'd witnessed first-hand that even after twenty-five years of marriage and two children, you couldn't bank on anything lasting. After the break-up of his parents' marriage, he'd decided prevention was better than cure, where matters of the heart were concerned. He shook his head at himself – of course, back then, he saw things very much in black and white. It was a shame the awareness of grey came a bit too late.

To bat away Kay and Matt's comments and his depressing self-analysis, he transferred his thoughts to Arthur Pettinger and his apparent plight to find Maryse.

The truth was, the story had intrigued him and he was just as keen to find out who the woman in the photo was as he'd been last night.

Going into the office, Joe was aware of the excitement in the air. There was a buzz of anticipation that usually accompanied the scent of a new case.

'Hey, what's up?' he asked Caz as she tapped away at her keyboard.

She held up a hand, while she called out to the boss, 'Over twenty k views and I've just seen it on Twitter!' She glanced at Joe. 'Some kid on the internet trying to trace an old girlfriend of her great-grandfather's. Something to do with when he was in the war. The love story of the year if we can find her.'

'Really?' said Joe, trying to disguise his knowledge and connection with the story. He was aware of the prickle of annoyance that his firm was already onto it. 'Are we going for it?' he asked, hoping to pitch an equal amount of interest as disinterest.

'It's up to the boss but it all depends if there's any money in it.'

'Is he dead, then? The old man?' asked Joe, continuing his act of innocence.

'No but he's ninety-six so could be by the time all this excitement reaches home.'

'Charming.' Joe bit down the urge to say anything else at the distasteful remark.

'You know how it is,' said Caz. 'Anyway, there's PI work in it. We can make some money tracking down the woman.'

'Presuming they have money to pay us and, of course, if they want us to.' Joe was growing increasingly uneasy with the approach Caz was adopting.

'Have you got a number yet?' called out the boss.

'Just getting it now,' called back Caz.

Joe sat down at his desk and kept one eye on his colleague, while pretending to be accessing some files on his computer. He found himself hoping Caz would get the same brush-off that he had received. Suddenly, it mattered to him that she didn't persuade Maddy to sign with the firm. They wouldn't have Maddy or Arthur's best interests at heart; they were far more mercenary. It just helped if you liked tracking people down, which Joe did. He always found people's history a fascinating subject.

He listened as Caz began to speak. She had barely finished

introducing herself when she was interrupted. Joe's hopes rose as his colleague was clearly on the back foot and trying to win Maddy over, who wasn't having any of it.

'Please, Miss Pettinger...' Caz was saying. She stopped abruptly, her mouth open. She looked up at the boss. 'The bloody cow hung up on me!'

Joe smothered a grin with his hand and avoided looking at either Caz or the boss.

'Phone her back,' instructed Southerton.

Caz didn't look too happy at the prospect but she dialled the number all the same. 'It's ringing out. She's not picking up.'

'Try again later,' ordered Southerton, going back into his office.

Caz turned in her chair to look at Joe. 'He can think again. I'm not ringing her back. Stuck-up cow.' She got up and went over to the coffee machine.

Joe took out his mobile and tapped out a quick message to Kay and Matt on their group chat.

> OK. You win. Meet me after work. Five-thirty at the car park. We're going house-calling.

22

Arthur finished his cup of tea and looked around the living room. He felt a little agitated and he didn't know why. The child was sitting on the sofa sharing a biscuit with the dog.

'I hope that's not my favourite biscuit you're giving the dog,' he said and then when the child looked up in alarm, he gave her a wink.

The child smiled. 'Fifi loves digestives. They're her favourites but don't tell Mum.' She put her finger to her lips.

'Mum's the word,' said Arthur with a knowing nod. 'We won't tell the boss.' He noticed the child was looking at a book. 'What's that you're reading?'

She held up the hardback book, which had botanical flowers drawn on the front. Arthur squinted to read the title but the words didn't make sense. What on earth did it say?

'Mum said I could have a little bit of the garden to put plants in and grow things.'

'Gardening, eh?' That was the word he had been trying to read. Yes, he knew it now. 'I used to grow things. In a big field. I had a tractor.'

'On your farm?'

'That's right. I wanted to grow flowers but my mum said I had to grow things to eat. Beans. Potatoes. Cabbages. Peas.'

'I've got some pepper plants to put in. Do you want to help me?' The child looked at him eagerly.

'Help you? That would be good,' said Arthur. He would like to help her. He tried to remember when he last did some gardening but couldn't think when that might have been. He frowned trying to locate the memory but all he could see was a field of wheat waiting to be harvested.

'Shall we do it now?' The child was up on her feet and at his side.

'Yes. Why not?'

After a little effort, Arthur got to his feet and with the help of his walking stick he made his way down the hallway following the child.

'Oh, where are you two off to?' His granddaughter – the nice one – came out of the kitchen. He didn't know where Moaning Minnie had gone. She wasn't here anymore and he was pleased about that.

'We're going into the garden,' said the child. 'Gramps is going to help me plant the peppers.'

'Oh, that will be nice. Here, Gramps, let me help you outside. Be careful, won't you? There we go.'

It was lovely out in the garden; Arthur surveyed the outside area. His potting shed was on the right-hand side and a brick-paved path gently curled its way along the edge of the grass. There was a plum tree and an apple tree in the middle of the lawn and deep flower beds either side. Joan had liked her flowers. He had a sudden image of her kneeling on a cushion as she weeded the flower beds. She was wearing a blue button-up dress and had an apron over the top to protect her clothes.

She never wore gloves, he remembered. Said she liked to feel the earth.

'We're going to the end of the garden where the vegetable patch is,' said the child, walking on ahead. The dog trotted down the steps after her. With the help of his granddaughter, he negotiated the three steps from the patio area down to the path.

'Thank you, duck,' he said.

'I'll come with you.'

'No. No. Not at all. I'll be fine. I'm only going to the veg patch.' He could manage it himself. He knew he could. As long as he took it slowly, he'd be fine. Blast his doddering old legs, though. Blast his doddering old body come to think of it.

Taking small steps he followed the path, past the crowded beds of agapanthus, lupins and foxgloves. Joan had loved all the bright colours and haphazard planting of the summer flowers. As he reached the end of the flower beds, the path took a left turn, cutting across the breadth of the garden, and then a right turn down to the veg patch and washing line. An old Anderson shelter was at the bottom. Left over from the war, it now served as a shed where he kept his tools. A charred incinerator was to the side and beyond that a compost heap.

The child was kneeling down in the dirt, digging a hole for the plants. She had half a dozen pepper plants about ten centimetres in height.

'Dig the holes a bit bigger,' said Gramps. 'Wet them with a drop of water before you put the plants in.'

'There's a seat over there,' said the child jumping up. 'I'll bring it over and you can sit down.'

'Thank you.' He was touched by her thoughtfulness and also grateful to sit. It was awkward resting all his weight on his one good arm. Damn the bad arm! He sank down into the canvas chair and watched as the child dug the holes a bit deeper, before going over to the water butt and filling up the green watering can. It looked quite heavy for her and Gramps wished he could help.

'Do you want to do one?' asked the child.

'I would but I don't know if I can reach.'

She brought the tray of plants over. 'You can take them out of the pots for me.'

Arthur picked up the first pot and studied it. He turned it around in his hand, looking at it from all angles. He used his fingertips from his injured arm to help steady the pot. Then, he wasn't sure why, but he felt he needed to squeeze the pot gently. The earth inside loosened from around the edges. Yes, that's what he was supposed to do. He did it several more times and, again, without considering what he was doing, he tipped the pot over and the little black container came away. He discarded the pot onto the ground and picked up the root ball of the plant. The damp compost sifted through his fingers and fell onto his lap.

'Thank you, Gramps,' said the child, coming over and holding out her hand.

Arthur looked at the child's muddy fingers, dirt sitting in the palm of her hand. He looked back at the plant in his own hand and hesitantly passed it over. She smiled and took the plant over to the hole she'd made, placing it in the ground and covering it back up with soil.

'Push down with your hand,' said Gramps. 'That's it. Well done, duck.'

He took another plant pot and repeated the process. His hands knew exactly what to do, even if he couldn't quite understand how or even what they were doing.

Arthur rubbed his fingertips with the tips of his thumbs,

feeling the cold damp earth roll between his skin. He brought his hands to his face and sniffed the soil.

His stomach gave a flutter and his heart beat a little faster. He sniffed again, this time deeper and longer. It reminded him of another time, another place, another life and that memory was becoming clearer with each second as he continued to rub the soil between his hands. A tear trickled down his cheek.

23

May 1944

Arthur wiped the tears from his face. It wouldn't do to cry. It wouldn't help and it wouldn't bring Freddie back.

He had known a couple of days ago that Freddie wasn't going to make it. The smell had told him so. Gangrene had set in his leg from his injury and sepsis had followed swiftly. The only saving grace was Freddie had known little about it. He had been too weak to stay conscious for long and when he was, the fever had too strong a grip for him to be aware of what was happening.

The only time Arthur had been concerned was right at the end, when Freddie had called for his mother. Arthur had heard it told that grown men cried for their mothers on their deathbeds and he'd been sceptical – now he knew it was true.

Hugo had fetched the village priest, an ally, an active member of the resistance. He'd given Freddie the last rites and although Arthur had no idea whether Freddie was a religious man, or indeed of what persuasion, he didn't care. As Arthur's mother was fond of saying, if it didn't do any good, it didn't do any harm.

Now he felt the burden of guilt. He should have taken Freddie in the night, carried him to the village and asked for help, then no one would suspect they'd been protected by the Duponts. His sensible head knew that was too dangerous. He'd heard what the fascists did to whole villages; they would punish them until someone confessed who had been hiding the British soldiers. The blame would come right back to the Duponts. One death on his conscience was bad enough, but a whole family – Maryse included? No, that would be too much for one soul to bear.

Arthur held his cap in his hands and stared at the newly dug grave. Hugo had wanted to do it, but Arthur had marched across the land to the far end of the field that overlooked the valley and the village of Sérent, snatching the shovel from the Frenchman's hands. He'd shouted at him to go. He'd shouted at another man not to help.

The two Frenchmen had stepped back and watched for several minutes as Arthur had attacked the ground, fast and furious, his grief giving him the energy he didn't have to bulldoze his way through the hardened soil.

And then, without saying anything, Hugo had taken a pickaxe and began swinging it into the ground, breaking through the earth. The other man had joined in too and Arthur hadn't protested. It had taken nearly an hour, but they had finally dug a grave deep enough for Freddie.

Maryse and her mother had wrapped Freddie's body in a sheet and tied it up with string, then the three men, together with the village priest, had laid Freddie to rest on the French hillside under the shade of a pine tree.

The excess soil had been transferred to the vegetable patch and the ground where Freddie's body was buried had been flattened out and covered with twigs and foliage to match the surroundings. If anyone visited, they would have a job to know this part of the ground had been freshly dug.

The Duponts and the priest had retreated some time ago, leaving Arthur alone at the side of the grave. He sat down on the ground, his arms around his bent knees and his head bowed.

He didn't hear her approach but he sensed her before she sat down next to him.

'I'm sorry,' said Maryse, in a whisper. She put her arm around Arthur's shoulder and he allowed himself to lean against her, just as she'd leant against him the other night when her heart was a burden. Under normal circumstances, he didn't like to show his emotions but these weren't ordinary times and to hell with the stiff upper lip.

Maryse stroked his hair and rested her cheek against his head. It was comforting. He'd missed the touch of another human. He didn't have a girlfriend back home. He'd been quite friendly with one of the girls in the village but that had amounted to nothing more than a chaste kiss goodnight on the eve of his departure. There'd been a couple of girls during training but they weren't the sort you'd want to take home to your mother. In fact, they seemed to want even more of a good time than some of the lads. So to feel real warmth and empathy from a woman was something of a novelty, despite Arthur barely knowing Maryse. Arthur stayed there for a long time, waiting for the wave of grief, the spike of anger and the rumble of frustration to pass.

He sat up and faced Maryse, cupping her face in his hand. 'Thank you. *Merci*,' he said.

She turned her head and whispered into the palm of his hand. 'You do not need to thank me. I don't like to see you so sad.'

'You've helped take away some of the pain,' he replied, honestly. If this war had taught him nothing other than to make the most of each day, each hour, each minute, then for that Arthur was grateful.

Maryse smiled and pulled away from him. 'I'm sorry,' she said, getting to her feet and brushing down her skirt.

Arthur jumped up, not wanting her to leave, but realising he might have frightened her off. 'I'm sorry. Please don't go. I didn't mean to…' He searched for the words in French but came up with a blank. He held his palms upwards and sighed.

'*C'est bon*. It's OK,' she replied, before turning and hurrying back towards the house.

Arthur watched her disappear through the gateway into the courtyard with a growing sense of disappointment. He lit a cigarette, annoyed he'd let his emotions get the better of him. He was in the middle of a war, he'd just buried his mate and here, in a small patch of tranquillity, he'd allowed himself to be blinkered from what was really going on by foolish fantasies of romance.

24

By the time Sheila turned up late afternoon, Maddy had switched off her mobile phone completely and unplugged the house phone. She'd had several more phone calls about Esther's YouTube channel.

'I had no idea this was on it,' confessed Maddy as she watched Esther's video with Sheila. 'What do you think?'

'I can't pretend I'm up on all this technology that the kids are into today,' said Sheila, 'but I have a small understanding.'

'I mean what do you think about the content?'

Sheila patted Maddy's hand. 'I know, dear.' She paused and gave Maddy a sympathetic smile, before casting a look towards Esther who was sitting on the footstool by Gramps's chair, awaiting the verdict of the adults. 'I think,' began Sheila. 'I think it's a very sweet and touching thing to do. It was all done with the right intent, from a place of love.'

Maddy raised her eyebrows a fraction. She was surprised by Sheila's response. For some reason, she thought Sheila would frown upon it, much like she had herself. 'Don't you think it's a bit irresponsible considering the repercussions?'

Sheila tipped her head from one side to the other. 'Hmm, maybe but what real harm has it done?'

Maddy went to protest but took a moment to think about

what Sheila had said. What harm had it done? None, other than send Maddy up the wall fending off phone calls and, of course, Joe trying to get involved.

'I think I wasn't prepared for all the fuss,' said Maddy. She looked at her daughter. 'I would have liked to have known before you posted this.'

'I didn't think,' said Esther. 'I didn't plan it, it just happened. I didn't know everyone would ring you up.'

'No. To be honest, I wouldn't have thought that would happen either.'

'See, no real harm done.' Sheila put a hand on Maddy's knee. 'You can't put an old head on young shoulders. They don't rationalise things like we do as cynical adults.'

Maddy gave a small smile. Sheila did have a point. 'I think we should take the video down though,' she said, choosing to let Esther's comment drop. 'Just to stop other people ringing me up.'

Esther jumped to her feet. 'No! Don't. Please don't. It's my best video. Look at the comments. People are interested. They love it. They want to help.'

'But I don't want people ringing me up constantly. I don't even know how they got my phone number.'

'You can find out on the internet,' said Esther.

'I still think we should take it down.'

'But what if someone knows who the lady is? How will they know we're looking for her?'

'We're not though, darling,' said Maddy. She looked at Gramps who had somehow managed to nod off amongst all of this. She lowered her voice. 'Did Gramps ask you to find this lady? I mean, who even is she? We don't know anything about her or the circumstances in which they met.'

Esther twiddled her fingers in the way she did when she was anxious. 'Gramps loves her. He wants to tell her he's sorry. He talked about her children. We must find her.'

'What do you mean? How do you know that?'

'He told me. Sort of. When he looked at the picture he said he was sorry. He also said something in French.'

'French?'

'He said he loved her with all of his heart,' said Esther.

'How do you know that?'

'I used an app on the tablet,' said Esther. 'You speak into it and it translates it.'

'My word. Well, I never,' said Sheila.

'Gramps was upset. He cried,' said Esther softly. 'I wanted to help him.'

'Oh, sweetheart,' said Maddy, going over to her daughter and wrapping her arms around her. 'That's so kind of you but I think you should have spoken to me first. The thing is, Gramps doesn't always remember everything and sometimes gets muddled up. We can't just go rushing headlong into things without finding out the facts first.'

'I'm sorry,' said Esther.

'It's OK.' Maddy took her daughter over to the sofa and sat down next to her. 'I think what you did was a loving and caring thing, but I'm not sure it was the right thing to do and I still think we need to take the video down.'

Once again, Esther leapt to her feet. 'No! You can't!' This time her voice was fierce and loud. 'We must find this lady.' With that, she snatched up the tablet where Maddy had left it on the arm of the sofa and ran out of the room. Her feet thundered up the stairs and her bedroom door slammed behind her.

'I'm not having that,' said Maddy, springing to her feet.

Sheila rose and put her hand on Maddy's arm. 'She's only a child. Everything is simple when you're eleven years old.'

The words were spoken without malice and Maddy felt immediately ashamed of her reaction, her temper quelled instantly by the older woman's wisdom. She let out a sigh. 'You're right. It's just, well, I'm not sure what Esther's done. It could open a whole can of worms. I don't even know who this woman is she's trying to find. It's not my grandmother – the woman Gramps married. So who is she? And what if she doesn't want to be found? What if Gramps isn't even remembering everything properly?'

'Of course, I know that; you know that, but we've got a few years of experience behind us,' said Sheila. 'Look, I'll pop the kettle on. You have a chat with Esther.'

Maddy was grateful for Sheila's calming approach and by the time she tapped on Esther's bedroom door, she felt much more composed.

'Can I come in?' she asked softly.

There was a moment's silence before Esther responded. 'If you want.'

Maddy smiled at Esther. 'You OK?'

Esther shrugged. 'Don't know.'

Maddy sat down on the bed beside her daughter and put her arms around her shoulders. Esther stiffened but Maddy ignored the resistance. 'I'm sorry we argued,' she began. 'I may have over-reacted. I was just so fed up with the phone calls today and then the video, which I knew nothing about. It all took me by surprise.'

'I'm sorry too,' said Esther. 'For shouting.'

Maddy acknowledged that Esther hadn't apologised for what she did. She obviously felt strongly about it and didn't believe she'd done anything wrong. And, if Maddy took a step back, took a moment to look logically at the events and ask herself exactly what had upset her about it so much, if she was honest, then she'd say she was more fed up with the phone calls and in particular the call from Joe. Putting it like that, she felt quite embarrassed at her reaction.

She dropped a kiss on the top of Esther's head. 'Why don't we go downstairs and have a proper talk about it. You can show me the photo. We can look through Gramps's scrapbook. Maybe even see if Gramps can tell us anything about it. We'll discuss it and decide the best way forward. How does that sound?'

'But you'll still want me to take the video down?' Esther wasn't going to be so easily pacified.

'How about if we make it private for now... just while we talk and then, if we still think it's a good idea, we make it public again?'

'You're not just saying that?'

'No. I promise you. We'll ask Sheila what she thinks too.'

'OK,' said Esther. Her fingers fidgeted in her lap. 'There's something else.'

'What's that?' Maddy managed to rein in her alarm.

'I wrote—'

Before Esther could reply, there was an almighty crash from downstairs followed by a loud groan.

Maddy leaped to her feet and hurtled down the stairs. She almost swung around the newel post and dived into the living room. Sheila was kneeling down next to Gramps who was sprawled out across the carpet.

'Shit!' cried Maddy, rushing to her grandfather's aid.

'I don't know what happened,' Sheila was saying. 'I was about to bring in the tea, when I heard a loud bang.' She reached out and picked up one of Gramps's shoes. 'I think he was trying to get up and might have tripped over this.'

'Is he all right?' came Esther's voice from behind them.

Maddy looked over her shoulder at her daughter standing in the doorway, her fingers anxiously winding themselves around each other. 'Wait there,' she said.

'It's my fault,' said Esther, her face draining of colour. 'I left his shoes there when I put his slippers on.'

'It's not your fault at all,' Maddy reassured her. She wanted to comfort Esther, but Gramps was her priority. 'Don't cry, darling. Run upstairs and get a blanket for Gramps.' It was the first thing she could think of to both occupy Esther and to get her out of the room for a moment. Maddy turned her attention back to Gramps. He was conscious – always a good sign. She couldn't see any blood – another good sign. 'Do you hurt anywhere?' she asked, her words slower and louder, in a bid to make herself understood.

She wished she knew some sort of first aid. Gramps gave a small grunt. At least it wasn't a groan of pain.

'Does your head hurt, Arthur?' asked Sheila, gently touching his head. 'What about your arms? Or your legs?' She touched each body part as she spoke.

Gramps gave a small groan. Definitely a groan this time and tapped his arm. 'Ooh, painful,' he said.

At this point Esther reappeared with the blanket, her face now pink and her eyes wet. 'Will Gramps be OK?'

Maddy took the blanket. 'He may have hurt his arm,' she said. 'I think we need to get someone to check him over.' She was about to place the blanket over Gramps, when he shifted position and tried to sit up. 'Don't move,' said Maddy. 'Stay where you are. You might hurt yourself more.'

Either Gramps wasn't listening or didn't understand, but

he continued to manoeuvre himself towards a sitting position. By now, alerted by all the commotion, Fifi had hopped out of her basket and was trying to wedge herself between Maddy and Gramps.

The doorbell buzzed suddenly and at the same time, Gramps gave a small cry of pain. Maddy was aware of Esther going out of the room and voices at the door, but she was so concerned about Gramps and trying to decipher what he was saying above the groans and moans, she was distracted for a moment.

Maddy glanced over her shoulder as she heard Esther come back into the room. For a split second she thought he was a paramedic and wondered how he'd got there without being called but immediately she realised her mistake. For a start he wasn't even dressed in the usual green overall of a paramedic. In fact, he was in a suit. She did a double take and almost wobbled over such was the shock. It was Joe! He didn't look any different to how he did when she'd last seen him three years ago. He still had the same dark blond hair, maybe cut a little closer than she remembered, his face was sun-kissed and there was a hint of shadow on his jaw.

Joe took one look at the scene in front of him and immediately came to kneel down next to Maddy. Sheila moved out of the way and with her arm around Esther, stood back to give the man some room.

'I'm a first responder,' Joe reminded Maddy. 'What happened?'

'He fell. Tripped over the shoe,' said Maddy, still shocked to see Joe. She felt dazed and yet relieved at the same time. Joe had always been good in an emergency. Always able to keep a clear head when others went into a panic. 'I can't see any blood or a cut but he said his arm hurts.'

'Hello, Arthur. It's me, Joe Finch. I'm just going to check you over.'

Maddy sat back and watched as Joe carefully took Gramps's head in his hands and checked all around his skull, all the time looking back at Gramps. She didn't bother to mention that Gramps probably couldn't remember Joe, but it didn't matter, her grandfather was calm and responsive as if he trusted Joe already.

'Should I call an ambulance?' she ventured as Joe ran his hands down Gramps's limbs. Gramps winced as Joe touched his forearm.

'I would. Just to be on the safe side, especially as he looks in pain with his arm. Does it hurt anywhere else, Arthur?'

'He's a little bit confused,' said Maddy when Gramps didn't answer. 'He doesn't always understand what's being said to him.'

Maddy made the call in the hall, while Joe continued to talk to Gramps. She came back into the room. 'They said it would be at least an hour.'

'An hour!' exclaimed Sheila. 'That's terrible.'

'Apparently, they're busy. There's been an accident on the motorway and they have a high volume of calls. Gramps isn't in imminent danger.' She closed her eyes and blew out a breath.

Joe stood up. 'Do you have a car?'

'Yes.'

'You could drive him to the hospital. If he can get into the car, it will be quicker than waiting for an ambulance.'

Maddy was hesitant. 'I don't know if I can manage him on my own. It would be best to wait.'

'But you said yourself it could be over an hour,' said Sheila. 'I'll stay here and look after Esther and Fifi.'

'I could drive you,' said Joe. 'You could sit in the back with him.'

Maddy was torn between waiting for a paramedic and taking Gramps to the hospital by car. 'I don't know.'

'I would say wait until Kay and Matt get here,' said Joe. 'Kay being a nurse, she might be in a better position to advise.'

'Kay and Matt?' Maddy shook her head in disbelief. 'Why are they on their way over?'

'Don't worry about that now,' said Joe. 'I don't know how long they'll be. If there's been an accident, they may get caught up in it.'

'Just go,' said Sheila.

Reluctantly, Maddy agreed. 'You drive and I'll sit in the back with Gramps. There's a local hospital that has a small A&E. It closes at seven. If we hurry we can get there and not have to go to the main hospital, which could be busy.'

'Have you got a T-shirt that we can make a temporary sling from, just to keep his arm in place while we're on the move?' asked Joe.

Maddy turned to Esther. 'Top drawer, my room. There's a white T-shirt. Fetch that down, sweetheart.' Esther ran off and returned almost immediately with the item of clothing.

With a great deal of care, Joe manoeuvred Gramps's arm into the T-shirt cum sling. Gramps winced. 'Sorry, Arthur. There, that will be a bit more comfortable for you.'

'It's his bad arm,' said Maddy. 'He was injured during the war and never regained full mobility in it.'

'I know,' said Joe.

Of course he'd know. It wasn't like he didn't know Gramps. 'Sorry,' said Maddy.

'I'll be extra careful.'

Between them they helped Gramps to his feet. He didn't

protest at being moved, but he winced and groaned in pain when he was on his feet and shuffling towards the car.

'I don't think it's broken,' said Joe.

'I'm still not convinced this is a good idea,' said Maddy.

'It's your call,' said Joe. 'If you want to wait, we can.'

Maddy looked at Gramps. He was agitated and waiting around in pain would only trigger more of the same emotions in him. Who knew how long the ambulance would take to get here? 'OK. We'll take him,' she said, hoping it was the right decision.

After some effort and a lot of patience, they managed to get Gramps into the car and Maddy settled herself in beside him, placing the blanket over his knees. Fifi had followed them out, refusing to go back in when Esther called her and had promptly hopped up into the car, placing herself between Gramps and Maddy. 'Out you get,' ordered Maddy but Fifi stubbornly refused to move.

'Looks like we've got a stowaway,' said Joe, as he slid into the driver's seat.

'As long as she doesn't think she's coming into the hospital,' remarked Maddy.

Joe stretched his arm back and stroked the dog behind the ears. 'She's lovely. Come on, girl. Come here in the front.' He patted the seat next to him and the dog jumped over the centre and plonked herself down on the seat.

'Traitor,' muttered Maddy, as Fifi then settled herself down and curled up in the front.

Sheila took Esther inside, distracting her with promises of making some rock cakes for when Gramps got back. Maddy felt a pang of gratitude for Sheila.

Joe reversed the car off the drive and onto the road. 'Which way? Left or right?'

'Err... right and then right at the end of the road,' said Maddy. She sat back next to Gramps wondering how much more surreal it could be. Here she was sitting in the back of Joe Finch's car, with a French bulldog on the front seat riding shotgun.

As Joe turned the car out onto the next road, he had to swerve to avoid an oncoming driver, who had decided overtaking on a bend was a good idea. 'Bloody idiot,' Joe muttered yanking on the steering wheel and braking.

As he did so, the bag on the back seat slid forwards, sending some of the contents onto the floor. Maddy leant down and began to gather up the ejected items – a notebook, a couple of pens and an envelope. She paused at the sight of the envelope face up in her hand. There was no mistaking her daughter's handwriting on the front and the spelling mistake, which she'd seen many times before in Esther's writing, confirmed it.

Private and confidentshall
To Joe Finch

She sat upright and met Joe's gaze in the rear-view mirror.
'I can explain,' he said, glancing at the road and then back to her.
'I bloody hope you can.'

25

'I had a letter from Esther.'

'I can see that.'

'Open it. Go on, read it.' Joe silently cursed himself for not mentioning the letter before but he genuinely didn't want to betray Esther's trust. She wasn't supposed to get in contact with him at all. It had been a bumpy end to his and Maddy's relationship and Esther had found it difficult to cut ties as readily as the adults had. Esther had phoned Joe on several occasions using Maddy's phone and the house phone and even sent him a birthday card, despite being told not to by her mother. In the end, Maddy had made Joe promise not to respond to any communication from Esther and although it had been hard, ultimately it had done the trick and Esther had stopped contacting him. Despite all this, knowing it was for the best, Joe had always felt a bit of a shit for ignoring Esther.

He glanced in the mirror again as Maddy read the letter. 'Was this before or after the phone call?' she asked.

'Before. It came the other day. I was going to tell you this evening; that was one of the reasons for coming over.'

'I'll have to speak to Esther again. I'm sorry she contacted you.'

'It's no big deal.'

'It is! And you know it.'

Shit. He was getting this all wrong. 'I know you said on the phone you weren't interested in finding this Frenchwoman, but there have been some developments since then.'

'If it wasn't for the fact that I need to get my grandfather to hospital I would make you stop the car and piss off right now.' Maddy glared even harder at him.

'Technically, I wouldn't be able to piss off. It's my car,' quipped Joe. He looked for the smile but Maddy wasn't having any of it. They were approaching another junction. 'Left or right?'

Maddy tutted. 'Left. I'm not sure now. I can't remember. Let me check my phone.'

Joe slowed while she tapped away at the device. 'I'll go left and wait for you to get your bearings.'

'OK. I've got the satnav up.'

Proceed west along Great North Road. At the roundabout take the second exit onto St Cuthman's Way, came the robotic-voiced instructions.

'So, what are these developments?' asked Maddy, as she held the phone between the two front seats.

'The YouTube video Esther posted has attracted lots of attention and you're going to get all sorts of people ringing you up, doorstepping you, offering help. Some will be genuine and some won't.'

'And no doubt you're genuine,' said Maddy without trying to disguise her disdain.

'I am actually,' said Joe, feeling put out by her manner. 'Not just because it's you and Esther and I want to help but, you know, I'm a historian. And I'll admit, initially, I didn't think it was a good idea but my work is all over this and want to sign you.'

'Really?' Maddy's tone was laced with sarcasm. 'No doubt you'll want a fee. I mean, who does these things out of the goodness of their heart?'

'Huh! Aren't you the precious one?' Joe couldn't help himself.

'And aren't you the presumptuous one,' she snapped back. There was an awkward silence, filled only with the directions from the satnav.

In fifty metres, turn right onto Centurion Way. Your destination is on your left.

Joe pulled the car into a parking space. Maddy nearly jumped out before they had even stopped, such was her eagerness to get her grandfather examined.

'I can do it,' she said, placing her body between her grandfather and Joe. 'Come on, Gramps. That's it. Mind yourself now.'

Seeing her struggle to get him onto his feet, Joe stepped in. 'Here, let me help. Please?'

She paused and he thought for a moment she was going to refuse his offer but she moved aside. Joe leaned into the car and hooked his left elbow under Arthur's left armpit and, using the door as leverage, he hauled Arthur to his feet. 'Try to keep his right arm in one place,' said Joe. The makeshift sling had a little too much stretch in it. 'That's it, Arthur. Let's get you into the wheelchair.'

Arthur took some persuading as he didn't understand what was being asked of him. 'What's this? A pram? I can walk, you know,' he was saying.

'This is easier. We can go quicker if you sit in the wheelchair,' Maddy coaxed.

Once safely in position, Joe took the handles. 'I'll push. I'm sure you can, but I'm taller so it will be easier. Not implying just because you're a woman, you can't.'

'I didn't think for one minute you were,' she said, still with a haughty tone. They had walked only a few steps when she stopped and let out a long sigh. She turned to Joe. 'I'm sorry, I'm being an ungracious cow. I'm actually quite grateful that you're pushing. I find it difficult to control these things. They're worse than shopping trolleys.'

He smiled back, relieved the tension had broken and a truce appeared to have been drawn.

'Do you want me to wait with you?' asked Joe, as he eased on the brake of the wheelchair in the A&E waiting room. 'I can wait outside if you prefer?'

'Stay if you don't mind. Besides I haven't finished interrogating you yet.'

'Go easy on me. I'm simply a lowly historian.'

'Now we both know that is a serious understatement.' She grinned at him. 'You OK, Gramps? Hopefully we won't have to wait too long.'

'Where are we? I'd sooner be at home.'

'I know. We're just at hospital. The nurses are going to look at your arm in a minute. You fell over. In the living room. Do you remember?'

Arthur looked confused. He tugged at the T-shirt on his arm. 'What's this? I don't like it.'

'Keep your arm in there for now, Gramps. You hurt your arm and someone needs to look at it.'

'Arthur,' said Joe, trying to distract the man from the object of his agitation. He took his mobile phone from his pocket and opened his photo app, located the folder he was looking for and showed it to Arthur. 'Look, these are some pictures from my archive collection of war photos.' He slid his finger across the screen. 'Here's one of soldiers marching along.'

Arthur looked at the screen. 'Oh, yes. My regiment.'

'Maybe?' said Joe, moving on to the next photo. 'Here's another.'

Arthur squinted at the phone. He nodded. 'Yes. That's right.'

As they made their way through the pictures, Arthur became less and less agitated with the sling and concentrated on the images Joe was showing him. Joe exchanged a look with Maddy who whispered a thank you to him.

Eventually, a nurse came out to the waiting room and called out Arthur's name. Maddy rose to her feet. Joe did too. 'Do you want me to push him through? Then I'll come back here and wait until you're done.'

Maddy hesitated for a moment. 'If you don't mind. And perhaps you could stay. It's just that I'm worried Gramps might get a bit anxious again.'

'Sure,' said Joe, with a sympathetic smile. 'OK, Arthur, time for you to see this lovely nurse who's waiting for you.'

He wheeled Arthur through to the assessment room where the nurse carried out an initial visual observation and made some notes on the file. 'I'll try to get your grandfather seen as quickly as possible,' she said.

They were shown through to another room where the nurse said it was quieter and might help Arthur to remain calm. Joe could see the relief in Maddy's face.

'You look tired,' he commented as they sat themselves down.

'It's been a tough day,' she admitted. 'I took Gramps and Esther out on a shopping trip earlier. I didn't realise how difficult it was pushing a wheelchair and trying to help an eleven-year-old marshal a shopping trolley. I think I'll be shopping online from now on. And then this afternoon the whole vlog thing erupted.' She let out a groan. 'Oh no. I forgot to change the privacy settings on the vlog.'

'What were you doing that for?'

'Honestly, the number of phone calls I've had…' She trailed off.

'Ah, yes. Me being one of those to add to your misery.' He did actually feel a bit embarrassed now. 'I'm sorry. I didn't mean to hassle you.'

'Forget it. To be honest, it's the least of my worries now. I didn't see the vlog before it went live. I hadn't had time. I usually check what Esther is doing, you know, just to make sure everything is OK and of course, the one time I don't – all hell breaks loose.' She looked at her grandfather and rested her hand on his. Arthur had nodded off and looked peaceful.

'Do you want to log onto your YouTube channel and change the privacy settings now?' He held out his mobile to her.

'I can't remember them. I know I should but we have an automatic log-in on the tablet.'

'Could you phone Esther and ask her to do it?'

'To be honest, I think the damage, if that's the right word, has already been done. It's been shared all over social media and I don't think I can stop that now.'

'There are ways,' said Joe.

'Maybe I'll look at it tomorrow.'

'Let me know if you need any help.'

'Thanks.'

They sat in silence and Joe was relieved the tension between them had ceased. He wasn't one for confrontation and least of all with people he cared about. Almost as soon as the thought passed through his mind, he kicked it into touch.

People he cared about – of course he'd still care about them but not any more than he cared about his other friends.

Before he could spend any more time picking apart his subconscious, the nurse came back with a doctor. With great care, the doctor carried out an examination of Gramps's arm and said that while she didn't think anything was broken, she'd like an x-ray.

Fortunately, there was a lull in the small hospital at that time of the day and Arthur was taken down and brought back within half an hour.

'I've had a look at the x-ray now,' said the doctor, coming back into the room. 'And I'm pleased to say there's nothing broken.'

'Thank goodness,' said Maddy. 'I'll ring Esther and let her know – she'll be worried.' The call only took a minute and Joe could see the dark shadow of worry had lifted from Maddy's face. 'I don't know what I would have done if he'd broken his arm,' she said. 'I'd have social services around, wondering why I'm not looking after him properly.'

'Stop worrying,' said Joe, with a smile. 'These things happen. Give me a minute, I just want to call Kay and Matt.'

'Oh, God, I forgot about them.'

'They went home in the end; the traffic was still heavy and there wasn't any point them coming since we're at A&E.'

'But what were they coming for?'

'Moral support.'

'For you, I assume. To try to win me over.' She gave a raise of her eyebrows.

'Something like that but it's all academic now. See you in a minute.'

He popped outside to make the call, opting to call Matt, rather than Kay.

'You all right, mate?' asked Matt.

'Yeah. All good. We're just about to leave the hospital. No broken bones.'

'Great. What are you doing now?'

'I'm going to take Maddy and her grandfather home and make sure they're all settled before heading home myself.'

'That sounds very cosy.' There was a note of amusement in Matt's voice.

'Piss off,' said Joe, but was smiling as he said it.

'Hang on, Kay wants to know if you're going to help find the missing woman now you're on such good terms with Maddy?'

'I don't know yet. I haven't asked her.'

'What?!'

He laughed at Kay's cry of disbelief and hung up before she could question him further.

As he walked back into the hospital, he pondered the question himself. Did he want to help find this mystery woman? He was, without a doubt, intrigued by the story and tempted by the challenge but there was something else too. Seeing Maddy again had kicked up some feelings he thought were well and truly out of play.

The last thought stopped him in his tracks. He pushed the idea away. He wasn't going there at all.

26

May 1944

In the days following Freddie's death, Maryse came to visit Arthur more often and they got into the habit of taking a walk alongside the river.

She had opened up to him a bit more about her brother, recounting stories from their childhood and how they'd always looked out for each other. It was something Arthur was able to relate to and found himself exchanging tales of his adventures with John before his brother had signed up.

In a way he hadn't been expecting, it brought him comfort to talk about John. Arthur didn't want to dwell on John's death – that was still too raw to deal with – but talking about their childhood and happier days was a good way to cope with his grief. He sensed that Maryse was experiencing the same sort of cathartic feeling and it was an equal comfort to them both.

'Here, I have something for you,' said Maryse, as they walked down to the river that evening. From her pocket she pulled out something wrapped in brown paper. She held it out to him with a warning not to squash it.

Arthur took the package and carefully unwrapped it. 'Cake!' he exclaimed. 'Well, this is luxury.'

'It is a special recipe my mother devised because we cannot spare eggs for it. There's a little fruit in it. I hope you enjoy it,' said Maryse.

'And what have I done to deserve this?' Arthur admired the fruit cake.

'It is my birthday.'

'Today? Then it should be me giving you a gift, not the other way around.'

'It is my pleasure,' reassured Maryse. 'Please, eat the cake. Tell me what you think of it.'

Arthur bit into the cake. It had a sponge-like texture, denser than one of the Victoria sponges his mother would make at home, but it was just as tasty. 'It's beautiful.' Arthur meant it. He couldn't remember the last time he had something so sweet. He offered her a bite of the cake but she shook her head and smiled as she watched him polish it off. 'Thank you so much,' said Arthur. 'That was very kind of you. One day, I hope I can repay your kindness.'

'I won't let you forget that,' she replied softly.

Maryse was so close to him, he would only have to lean in a few inches and… He took a deep and calming breath. Every instinct in his body was urging him to make the move and to kiss her. She smelt of rose water, a sweet and intoxicating fragrance, just like Maryse herself.

He reached for her hand, rubbing his thumb along her knuckles. He felt the pressure of her fingers as they closed around his. Before he had time to reconsider his actions, Arthur took a half step closer to her, lowered his head and tentatively kissed her. Just a small fleeting brush of her lips with his. 'Thank you and happy birthday,' he murmured not entirely certain if he was thanking her for the cake or the kiss.

'You are always welcome,' she replied, her voice a little breathless.

The sound of Hugo's voice booming out across the evening air, calling Maryse, broke the spell between them and Arthur jumped back as if he'd received an electric shock and then promptly stumbled backwards over a tree root, ending up on his backside.

Maryse burst out laughing, her hand going to her mouth to stifle the ensuing giggles. 'Are you OK? Have you hurt yourself?'

'Only my pride,' muttered Arthur.

Hugo's voice grew louder as he bellowed out for Maryse again. She glanced over her shoulder. 'I had better go.'

'Yes, please do. Leave me to my embarrassment.'

Maryse hesitated and then dropped to her knees beside Arthur and to his surprise, planted a kiss on his lips. She paused and looked him dead in the eye, before getting to her feet and giving him a final look over her shoulder before she disappeared from view.

Arthur sat on the ground, both delighted and dismayed with the turn of events. Maryse had left him in no doubt how she felt about him but he had to remind himself that it wasn't exactly professional to get involved with a local farm girl. That was most definitely not in the briefing.

27

'Thank you so much for everything,' said Maddy, genuinely grateful for Joe's help. He'd driven them home and then taken time to help her get Gramps indoors and up to his room. He'd even helped her get him undressed and into his pyjamas. Poor Gramps was shattered and had dropped off to sleep almost immediately, but not before Esther had sneaked out of her room to give Gramps a kiss and cuddle goodnight.

'Back to bed now, sweetheart,' said Maddy. 'I'll come and see you in a minute.'

Esther had hesitated on the landing before giving Joe a quick hug. 'Night, Joe,' she said before scampering off to her room.

At the foot of the stairs, Sheila was fastening the buttons on her coat.

'Would you like a lift home?' asked Joe. 'It's quite late. Or I could call you a taxi.'

'Thank you, that's very kind, but I've already sorted out a taxi. It's waiting outside,' said Sheila.

Maddy was touched by Joe's thoughtfulness. She gave Sheila a hug goodbye, promising to call her tomorrow to let her know how Gramps was. It was then she was struck by the realisation that she was alone in the house with Joe.

'I'll get off too,' said Joe as he stood in the doorway and watched Sheila get into her taxi and wave as it pulled away.

'Thank you again for everything this evening.' Maddy heard herself saying. She felt self-conscious being alone with Joe and wasn't sure why or if she liked the effect it was having on her.

'No problem. Don't forget to sort out that vlog. At least change the settings.'

'Oh, yes. I'll do that in a minute.'

'Look, I know this is the wrong time to bring it up... but if you'd like me to help you find Maryse, I'd like to do what I can. Genuine offer. No strings. Simply me helping out an... old friend.'

She ignored the old friend tag he'd applied to their relationship. She was too tired to argue the point. 'I'm not sure,' she replied forcing her mind back to Gramps. 'Part of me is quite interested, but part of me is wary. I don't know what I'd be getting us into.'

'True. But we could, at any time you're not comfortable with the search, call a halt to it.'

'I need time to think.'

'You might not have too much time, not with all the interest it's garnering.'

'If I just say no to everyone, they'll get bored and go away,' said Maddy.

'Or you could say, you've already signed with someone to look for her. That's more likely to keep any tracing agents off your back. If there's no money in it for them, then they will go away. As for the media, they will calm down and find another story in a day or two.'

'I feel overwhelmed by it all,' admitted Maddy. 'I've only been looking after Gramps for a short time; moved here, had to make lots of changes in my life and now all this blows up.' Her words caught in her throat.

'Hey, it's OK,' said Joe. He went to move towards her and then stopped awkwardly. 'It's been a long day. Get some rest. Maybe I can call you tomorrow? Once you've had a good night's sleep. Then if you want me to help you with anything, I can. And I don't mean just looking for the woman. If you need any help fending off unwanted callers and the media, I'm more than happy to help.'

'Thank you,' said Maddy. She met his eyes and looked thoughtfully at him. 'Why do you want to help me?'

He looked embarrassed and gave a shrug. 'You seem like you could do with some help.'

'I'm not a damsel in distress,' she replied, keen for him to understand she had her shit together. 'I'm just tired and emotional.'

'I know. I didn't mean it to sound patronising.' Joe gave a heavy sigh. 'Kay thinks I need to get my life back together. She's on some sort of rescue mission. I don't need rescuing.'

'Don't you?'

'No.'

'It's good to have friends who care about you,' replied Maddy, her gaze still locked with his. 'You should listen to them.'

'What about you and your friends?'

'They're busy doing their own thing. None of them are local.' It was a bit too painful to admit that she didn't have many friends in the true sense of the word. One or two but the rest had mostly been people from work and since being made redundant, contact with them had waned. 'Anyway,' she said more brightly. 'I'm here now. Fresh start and all that.' She forced a wide smile, silently pleading that Joe wouldn't press her about her reasons for being here.

'Yeah. New beginnings, eh?' he said, much to her relief, although there was an empathy in his eyes she hadn't seen before.

There followed another silence before Maddy spoke. 'Sorry, I don't mean to kick you out... but...'

'Oh, God, sorry. No. It's me. Loitering when I should be going. And yes, you do mean to kick me out. You absolutely should kick me out.'

They both laughed, maybe a little more heartily than the occasion demanded but it broke the tension. Maddy opened the door for him. 'Thanks again for tonight.'

'No bother. Shall I call you tomorrow?'

'Yes, do. That would be nice.'

The next morning Maddy woke with a start. Standing at the end of her bed was Gramps. He had been unsettled in the night, getting out of bed several times and padding around the house, mumbling incoherently. Each time Maddy had got up and persuaded him to go back to bed. His arm was tender to the touch and he winced every now and again. The visit to the hospital had obviously distressed him and he was particularly confused. She glanced at the alarm clock on the bedside table. It was only six-thirty.

Gramps was pulling at the cuff of his pyjama top. 'I can't find her,' he said. 'Where is she?'

'Where is who?' Maddy pulled on her dressing gown.

'She's not here. I've looked everywhere. Not in her bed.'

Maddy's heart gave a little leap of fear. Although her

rational thought countered Gramps was just confused, it didn't stop her having a moment's panic that Esther might be the subject of his distress. She hurried out onto the landing and slowly opened Esther's bedroom door. She let out a small sigh of relief to see her daughter sleeping peacefully in her bed.

She closed the door and almost jumped out of her skin, as Gramps was standing right behind her.

'Is she there?' He looked worried.

'Shall we go downstairs and have a cup of tea?' suggested Maddy, defaulting to one of the few things that pacified her grandfather. 'Then you can tell me who you're looking for.'

She coaxed Gramps down to the kitchen and seated him at the table, before switching on the radio and tuning in to the Days Gone By station. Sheila had told her about this station. It played music and songs from the 40s and 50s. Maddy had read on the Alzheimer's website that music was good for people with memory loss, that it ignited some sort of connection in their brains.

The Glenn Miller Band played out softly in the kitchen and as she went about making the tea, she could see Gramps begin to relax a little. He stopped fidgeting with the cuff of his pyjamas and every now and then hummed a little as if he recognised the tune.

She placed the cup of tea in front of him.

'Thank you, duck,' said Gramps and for a moment he looked at peace. However, a few minutes later he was worrying again. 'Do you know where she is? I was supposed to meet them. Do you think they're all right?'

Maddy placed her hand on his arm. 'Who are you supposed to meet? Who are you looking for?' she asked softly.

'Maryse and the children,' he replied. He gave a sniff and

Maddy was alarmed to see tears fill his eyes. 'I'm supposed to meet them.'

From the breast pocket of his paisley pyjamas, Gramps took out a now-crumpled photograph. Maddy recognised it from the scrapbook. It was of Gramps and Maryse standing outside a remote-looking farmhouse. Gramps dressed like a local.

'That's a lovely photograph,' said Maddy. 'Gramps must have had his camera with him. He loved taking photos. I guess someone took that one for him.'

'*Je suis désolé. Je t'aime avec tout mon coeur.*' Gramps shook his head and looked at Maddy. He was saying he was sorry and he loved her with all of his heart. Maddy squeezed his hand but he continued, reverting back to English. 'I must find her. She's waiting for me.'

28

May 1944

The past week, Arthur had been busy every day, working in the fields with Hugo and helping Andre with deliveries while, all the time, gathering intel on the movements of the German troops and distributing instructions to the local Maquis through Patrick. There was a certain amount of satisfaction that he was doing this right under the noses of the Germans and now he understood what Maryse had meant when she had paraded by the soldiers in the square that day.

He wouldn't say he was confident at a checkpoint now – he couldn't afford to be that complacent – but his face was becoming a regular for the German soldiers on duty, which coupled with the odd bottle of wine Andre passed their way, was making moving around the area a lot easier.

He'd had a particularly tough day in the forest with Hugo, thinning out some of the trees and shrubs, chopping up tree trunks and branches for firewood and stacking it onto the back of the cart. They had some guns to move the following day, which were to be hidden at the bottom of a woodpile on the cart. Arthur wasn't particularly keen on this idea but Hugo assured him it was an effective way to move a stash of arms around the area.

Back at the farm now, Arthur made his way down to the river. The dust and dirt from the woodland had stuck to the sweat on his skin. It was a relief to peel off his shirt and let the air get to his body. Dirt had drilled its way under his fingernails and he was sure he had blisters on his blisters where he'd been using the bandsaw!

Every bone and muscle in his body was protesting at the hard labour it had endured. Arthur stretched back his shoulders and moved them around in circular motions. He rolled his head across his chest to try to ease the crick in his neck and free up the muscles that were in danger of seizing up.

He sensed someone behind and spun around to see Maryse approaching, wheeling a bicycle, and she looked particularly beautiful today. The afternoon sun was highlighting her well-defined cheekbones and picked up the red tones in her dark brown hair that he hadn't noticed before. She was wearing a pretty floral button-up dress with a collar and short sleeves.

'*Salut*,' he said, finding himself smiling broadly like the proverbial Cheshire cat. What an idiot he was! He brought his smile under control and at that point remembered he was shirtless. He didn't miss her eyes discreetly scan his body. She noticed him looking at her but didn't flinch.

It was then he saw the basket on the front of the bike laden with eggs, bread and what he assumed was cheese wrapped in wax paper.

'What have you got there?'

'Exactly what it looks like,' she replied, while adjusting a cloth to cover the goods.

Arthur gave her an appraising look. 'Where are you going?'

'I'm running an errand for my mother.'

Arthur pulled on his shirt and stood in front of her. He

went to lift the cloth, but she clamped her hand over his. He was too strong for her to remove his hand from the basket, but he didn't want to fight her, he just wanted her to know he wasn't going to take his hand away until he had inspected the contents. He wanted to know what she was doing. An unexpected fear that she might be putting herself in some sort of danger gnawed at his stomach.

Maryse locked eyes with him but eventually let out a sigh and the tension in her arms disappeared as she removed her hand from his.

'*Merci*,' said Arthur.

'You must not let anyone know I have shown you. I will get into a lot of trouble.'

Arthur removed the provisions. He knew there was something far more sinister than just eggs, bread and cheese. A red and white checked cloth hid something metal and as Arthur lifted the fabric, the sun caught the steel barrel of a gun. There were three handguns nestled in the bottom of the basket. There were also several rounds of ammunition next to the weapons. He wasn't sure what he was expecting to find, maybe a note or a map – something to help the resistance, but certainly not guns.

'Where are you taking these?' Arthur hurriedly replaced the cloth to hide the dangerous cargo. 'How come I don't know anything about this?'

'It is not for you to know.'

'It is.' The gnawing in his stomach increased.

'It's something one of the men asked for. Hugo said not to bother you with it, that you have bigger things to worry about.'

Although there was some truth in Hugo's thought process, Arthur couldn't confess to liking the idea that Maryse was carrying weapons. If she was caught, she'd be… he didn't like to think of the outcome.

'I'm coming with you,' he said.

'No!' She almost shouted the words and then checked herself as she glanced furtively around and continued in a more controlled manner. 'I should go alone.'

'I don't like it.'

'This is nothing. It's the least I can do to fight against the German bastards. Others are far braver than I am. Others have endured far worse things.'

Arthur held her look. She didn't need to expand. He'd seen the reports, seen first-hand how others had paid dearly for their fight against the German occupation.

Without thinking, he pulled her towards him and held her in his arms. She was tense and awkward against him for a moment, before her body relaxed and she wrapped her free arm around him. He held her tighter, trying to squash his fears before finally dropping a kiss on top of her head. 'I'm coming with you,' he said softly, ignoring her protests. 'We can get a drink at the café. Nothing wrong with that and perfectly normal.'

She made a huffing noise and pushed him away with her free hand. 'There's a bike in the barn. Hurry up. *Dépêche-toi!*'

Arthur hadn't ridden a bike since he was a child and despite the danger of the situation, he allowed himself a few minutes of enjoyment as they free wheeled down the track that led to the main road.

The checkpoint guard let them through without any issues, thanks to Maryse's gentle flirting with the young soldier that she apparently knew by name, distracting him with a giggle and flutter of her eyelashes as she inspected a small tear in her stockings higher up her leg. The soldier was clearly distracted at the glimpse of a stocking top and waved her through. Arthur rolled his eyes as if in despair of his friend as the guard inspected his papers, including the bicycle permit SOE headquarters had issued him.

Safely through the checkpoint, he drew alongside her on his bike. 'You look like you've done that before.'

She scowled. 'They make my skin crawl.'

'You should be careful.'

'I know what I'm doing. Anyway, it's a small sacrifice compared to others.'

'Where do you draw the line?' Arthur heard himself asking, wondering what lengths Maryse would go to in order to win her small personal battles.

She stopped her bike and planted her feet on the ground. 'Death.' The word was simple and clear. 'The same as you.' With that, she was peddling away again, leaving Arthur to catch up.

After trailing their way through the main square and turning left, Maryse stopped opposite the *Mairie* – the town hall – adjacent to a small hotel that was now occupied by General Weber. Arthur was uneasy about the whole situation. He was all for mingling in with the locals and village life, but this was brazen. Foolhardy, in fact.

He took Maryse's bike and leant it against his leg while he still straddled his own and, as nonchalantly as possible, he lit a cigarette. All the time he scoped the street from under the brim of his hat.

Maryse was already entering the house with her basket of goods and it was several painstaking and sweat-inducing minutes before she reappeared, calling a cheery goodbye to an elderly man in the doorway and hopping onto her bike.

It was then she stopped in her tracks with an expression

of horror on her face as she looked down the road. Arthur was alert immediately and followed her gaze. 'What is it?' he asked quietly.

As Maryse gathered herself together and set off pedalling down the street, Arthur had no option but to follow once again. As they cycled past the schoolhouse, it was then Arthur realised what the problem was.

The familiar and threatening sight of a black Citroën four-door saloon, the calling card of the local Gestapo, was parked outside the schoolhouse. Two uniformed soldiers stood at the gates with rifles in their hands. At that moment, Monsieur Rochelle appeared through the front door, flanked either side by two plain-clothed men. One of the men had his handgun drawn with the barrel poking at the head teacher's ribs. There was a look of terror on Monsieur Rochelle's face and a thin stream of blood trickled down from his eyebrow.

Maryse gave a small gasp, stopping abruptly.

'Don't even think about it,' hissed Arthur, already anticipating her move. He grabbed at her arm and held her fast.

'But the children!' Maryse's hand went to her mouth. 'Where are the children?'

'Just wait,' said Arthur.

Keeping well back on the other side of the road, they watched as the black saloon drove away with their victim. At once, Maryse rushed across the road and, practically throwing her bike against the stone wall, she raced into the house, calling out for the children.

Arthur waited outside, keeping alert for any soldiers who may either come back or take an interest in what was going on at the schoolhouse.

Maryse came outside about five minutes later. 'I'm going

to take the children back to the farm. They can't stay here on their own and their cook has got enough mouths to feed at her own house. She doesn't need two more.'

'How are you going to do that?' asked Arthur.

'Yvette can sit on the crossbar of your bike and the boy – he's only little – he can sit on the back of mine.'

Before Arthur had time to argue that he didn't think this was a good idea, Maryse was gone again, disappearing into the house. He sighed at her impulsive reaction and yet at the same time admired the compassion she had once again shown. She was an extraordinary young woman.

29

Maddy checked her reflection in the mirror and smoothed down her hair. She tipped her head from side to side and considered whether to apply her dusky pink lipstick, then scolded herself for being so vain. When was the last time she'd worn lipstick? When she wanted to look good for a man. Those days were long gone. Was she trying to look good for Joe? She didn't like the idea that it mattered to her what he thought. Christ, he'd seen her yesterday when she was ragged – why did it matter to her now?

Purposefully, she dropped the lipstick back into her makeup bag.

Joe had called her earlier that morning and had been delighted when Maddy had accepted his help in finding Maryse. It wasn't something she was entirely comfortable with but Gramps's distressed state last night had swung the balance for her. As for it being Joe who was helping, this was both reassuring and unnerving at the same time. She knew she was in capable hands when it came to tracking down missing persons and if anyone could find out what happened to Maryse, then he was the guy. However, having Joe around was throwing her a little off-balance as she tried to swerve out of the path of her conflicting emotions about seeing him again.

'What time is Joe coming?' asked Esther, standing in the doorway to the bedroom.

'In about half an hour.'

'You look pretty.'

Maddy blushed a little. It was silly, but she felt like she'd been caught out by her daughter. Getting dressed up for Joe's arrival. Honestly, it was no better than considering splashing on her lipstick. She looked at the floral dress she was wearing. 'Is it too much? Should I wear my jeans?'

'No. You look nice. I like it when you wear a dress. You always wore jeans when we lived at the flat.' Esther gave a smile and disappeared down the stairs.

Maddy took a moment to contemplate her daughter's observation. She was sure a psychologist would have a field day with that one. Giving herself another look in the mirror, she swished her skirt from side to side, pleased with what she saw. Who cared whether she was doing it for Joe or not, she thought as she trotted downstairs. It made her happy and that was something she hadn't felt often enough lately.

'Everyone OK?' she asked, walking into the living room. 'How is your arm, Gramps?'

Gramps was still a little on the confused side but nodded all the same. 'Very well, thank you.' He gave the sling a small tug. 'Don't like this thing.'

'You just have to keep it on for a few days,' said Maddy, gently holding his hand so he couldn't pull at the fabric. 'You fell over yesterday. You've got a few bumps and bruises so you need to rest. And your arm needs to rest too.'

Gramps gave her a sceptical look. 'Fell over? Hmm. I don't know.'

'Don't worry, Gramps, we'll look after you,' said Esther, passing him a biscuit.

'Oh, digestive. My favourite. Thank you.'

As he munched on the much-loved biscuit, Maddy and Esther exchanged a smile. Maddy was touched by her daughter's subtlety and impressed that she had picked up on this little trick already.

The doorbell sounded out, making both Maddy and Esther jump. 'It will be Joe, but I'll just check.' Maddy got up and looked through the window, pleased to see it was him. She had been doorstepped earlier that morning by the reporter from the local TV station, but once Maddy had told her she had signed a contract with a private investigator, the reporter had left.

'Hi,' she said, suddenly feeling self-conscious in her dress as Joe was unable to tame a look of surprise.

'Good afternoon,' he said with a big smile. 'Well, I must say you look a lot less worried today than you did last night.'

She held the door open wide to let him in. 'Sorry if I was a bit stressed yesterday but it was all happening at once. I could barely keep up with things.'

'Any more nuisance phone calls?'

'A couple but I haven't been answering them. I've been letting them go to voicemail or answerphone and then blocking the number.'

'I like your style.' Joe once again took in Maddy's appearance and she wasn't sure exactly what he was referring to.

'Gramps is in the living room,' she said, indicating to the

door and then realising that of course, Joe would know where that was. 'Can I get you a drink? Tea? Coffee?'

'Erm, yes, tea will be good, thanks.'

As Maddy prepared the tea for everyone, she heard Joe talking to Gramps. She liked the way he spoke to him, respectful but friendly and without any hint of a patronising tone. He treated Gramps as an equal, even when Gramps wasn't always answering the questions properly. However, Gramps seemed to be engaged and Maddy couldn't help wondering if it was because Joe, being another male, made it easier for Gramps to relate to.

Joe was chatting away with such ease, she was almost certain Gramps was keeping up with the conversation. She decided to find out about any more local groups for the elderly, in addition to the one Sheila took him to from time to time in the village hall. Perhaps she could take Gramps to a get-together where he could interact with other people and possibly other men. He had been in the army after all so maybe it was something he liked, maybe it felt comfortable to him. Or, and she allowed herself the indulgent thought that maybe, just maybe, Gramps remembered Joe or at least felt familiar with him.

As she busied herself making the drinks, she realised this idea that Gramps was aware of a connection with Joe, was a comforting thought and acknowledged that it was possibly her subconscious way of giving herself permission to allow Joe back into their lives, albeit briefly.

Going back into the living room with a drink for everyone, she found Joe leafing through Gramps's scrapbook, which Maddy had left on the table.

'Oh, I hope you don't mind,' he said, 'but I was just taking a look.'

'Not at all,' said Maddy. 'In fact, that's why I left it out.'

'I'm just going to have a flick through here to see if there's anything else I can glean and then I'll probably have some questions.'

'Sure.'

'You are still happy about this, aren't you?'

'Of course. It feels more the right thing to do than the wrong thing. I must admit, I am a little nervous about what you might find out, but if it can bring any comfort to Gramps, then I'm all for it.'

'And you're happy for me to try to find Maryse, Arthur?'

Maddy liked that he was consulting her grandfather, including him in the conversation. Not just ignoring him, even though they were both aware that Gramps's understanding was limited.

'Maryse,' said Gramps, with a frown. 'Dear sweet Maryse.'

'We're going to see if we can find out what happened to her, Arthur, but it was a long time ago so I'm not sure what I'll discover.'

Gramps's hand shook a little as he reached out. Maddy wasn't sure what he wanted but then realised he was pointing to the scrapbook. Joe held it out to him and her grandfather, somewhat shakily, turned the pages. He appeared to be looking for a particular page.

'What are you trying to find?' asked Maddy, motioning to get up from her chair, but Joe made a small stop gesture. She sat back down.

'We'll just give him a moment.'

Finally, Gramps settled on a page and everyone looked with anticipation. He was pointing to a picture of the farmhouse with the French countryside sprawling out behind.

Maddy exchanged a look with Joe, who looked equally uncertain as to the relevance.

Gramps gave a sigh. 'Couldn't come back. He couldn't come back with me.'

Maddy reached over and placed her hand on her grandfather's, gently holding the bony, tanned fingers. 'Who couldn't come back with you?'

He looked up at her, confusion resting on his face. 'A long time ago?' He looked back at the photograph. 'I don't know. I don't know when it was.'

'This was during the war, Arthur,' said Joe. 'When you were a young man.'

Gramps nodded. 'I suppose you're right.' He took a hanky from his pocket and dabbed at his face and blew his nose. 'I'm a silly old man.'

'No you're not!' exclaimed Maddy, giving him a hug. 'You're not at all. You're a wonderful, intelligent man.'

'I'm not what I used to be.'

'None of us are,' said Joe, removing the scrapbook from Gramps's lap.

Gramps leaned back in his chair and closed his eyes.

'Freddie was my friend,' he said into the silence.

'Freddie?' Maddy asked, giving Joe a shrug in answer to his questioning look. 'Was he your friend in the army?'

'That's right. My friend. Freddie... erm... Freddie Travers. Yes, that's right.' His jaw tightened and he clenched his lips together for a moment. 'We did what we could. Tried to fix his leg. Bloody thing.' Gramps opened his eyes and pointed towards the scrapbook on Joe's lap. 'Had to leave him there. He's still there. Looking down over the valley.' Once again, he dabbed at his face with his handkerchief.

'Oh, Gramps,' sighed Maddy, now understanding what her grandfather was telling her. 'I'm so sorry.' Maddy looked at Esther who had remained quiet. She was sitting on the chair next to Gramps, with Fifi alongside her. Normally, Maddy would have told the dog to get off the furniture, but it looked like Fifi was offering some sort of comfort to Esther. She'd speak to Esther later and make sure she understood what was going on and that it wasn't upsetting her.

Joe was scribbling a few notes in his pad. 'I'll see what I can find out,' he said quietly to Maddy. 'I don't suppose you have any idea where in France this might be?'

'Sorry, I've no idea. You could try asking Gramps?'

Joe gave Gramps an appraising look. 'Maybe not right now.' He opened the book and looked at the photograph again. 'I know the British Army was in Brittany and Normandy regions ahead of the D-Day landings to make contact with the French resistance and coordinate attacks. I may be able to pin it down a bit further. I'll have a look through all the photos and see if I can find any clues, but I wouldn't be too hopeful. It looks pretty remote wherever they are.'

'Lizio,' said Gramps.

Maddy and Joe looked at Gramps. 'Say that again,' said Maddy.

'Lizio,' repeated Gramps. 'Across the valley. Picked up in the night. Twenty-two hundred hours. The next moon.' Gramps mumbled something else that was unintelligible.

'Did you get that?' asked Maddy to Joe.

He tapped his page with his pen. 'Yep. That's a great help, Arthur,' he said. 'Really great. Thank you.'

Gramps gave one nod at Joe and then the faraway look

returned to his face. 'I left them both. I promised I'd come back.'

'Don't go upsetting yourself, Gramps,' said Maddy. 'I think maybe that's enough for one day. Why don't we go for a walk? Some fresh air would do us all good.' The dog gave a whine, as if understanding her. 'And I suppose you'd better come too.' Maddy put her hand out to stroke Fifi but the French bulldog jumped down from the chair and trotted out to the hall. 'That dog hates me so much.'

The fresh air was indeed what they all needed. Maddy could feel the tension from earlier slipping away. Joe had gallantly insisted he push the wheelchair for which Maddy was grateful, and Esther was skipping ahead with Fifi trotting along beside her, apparently happy to be off the lead but not feeling the need to scamper off as Maddy had feared.

'Are you warm enough, Gramps?' asked Maddy, adjusting the blanket over his knees.

'Yes. Yes, very warm, thank you.'

'And your arm's not hurting you too much?' Fortunately, the path around the park was smooth tarmac and a flat walk. Ideal for wheelchairs, bikes and pushchairs. They were overtaken by a couple of joggers who were also enjoying the benefit of the outdoor area.

Gramps pulled a face at her question. 'Don't like this thing.' He jabbed his forefinger at the sling.

'Only for a few more days,' explained Maddy patiently, as she had done several times already that day.

'Did they get the bullet out?' asked Gramps.

'The bullet?' questioned Joe.

'Yes, damn thing.'

Maddy clicked what her grandfather was referring to. 'Yes, the bullet is out, Gramps.'

'So, do you think you'll stay here permanently?' asked Joe as they continued their walk.

There was a casual note to his voice but his eyes betrayed his faux nonchalance, something Maddy had always been able to see through. She was certain Joe had been thinking about their time together and was, like her, trying to dislodge the memory from taking root. How ironic, they were shunning those memories while Gramps was trying to hold on to his.

'I think so,' she said. 'I wouldn't want to leave Gramps in the care of anybody else. There's a good chance there will come a time when I can't manage him on my own or at home, but I'll cross that bridge when I get to it. I want to spend as much time with him as possible.'

'Who'd been looking after him before?'

'Hazel. She lived in for the past six months but she's had enough now.'

'That's decent of her. The living-in part, I mean, seeing as she's not related.'

'And not of me, seeing as I'm related by blood.'

'I didn't say that.'

'But you were thinking it.'

'Give me a break, Maddy,' said Joe, tagging a frown onto the end of the sentence.

Maddy wanted to sulk but she knew it was only because Joe had hit a nerve. 'I'm sorry. Touchy subject,' she confessed. 'And long, so I won't bore you with the details.'

'I'm not easily bored.'

Maddy looked on as Esther was now throwing a ball for Fifi who was doing an excellent impression of a retriever by chasing the toy and bringing it straight back for Esther to repeat the process. She looked back at Joe, who smiled encouragingly. 'Don't say I didn't warn you.'

'Disclaimer accepted.'

'Hazel isn't a blood relative of Gramps; she's from my mum's second marriage. You know that, right?'

'Yeah, sure. I don't think of her as your half-sister though.'

'No and, to be fair, I don't think anyone does. We were both treated the same. Gramps didn't treat us differently.'

'He's a decent man,' commented Joe.

'He is. And Hazel, of course, is fond of Gramps and it suited her to move in with him at the time. And in all honesty, it suited me. Mum finally sold her house in the UK so Hazel, who had been living in it, was going to be homeless. Mum suggested she move in with Gramps and be his carer. Hazel did get paid an allowance – which is only fair.'

'Ah, I didn't realise it was an official thing.'

'Like I said, it suited Mum and Hazel. As it turned out, Gramps needed more care than Hazel anticipated and it got too much for her.'

'She resigned basically.'

'I guess so. I think she thought it would be an easy gig, but it doesn't suit her now and it's perfectly fine. Gramps is my grandfather and I should be looking after him. I'm truly grateful to Hazel for stepping in when I couldn't.'

'Why was that?'

Maddy looked across the park as people walked their dogs, played football with their kids, chatted to other parents – all enjoying the simple aspects of family life. A breeze tickled the back of her neck and she hooked a strand of hair behind her ear. 'I needed to reassess my life. I was stuck in a bit of a rut. My flat was OK but the area wasn't a great place to bring Esther up, not as she got older and wanted more freedom. I'd also come out of a relationship I shouldn't have been in.' She noted the look of alarm on Joe's face. 'Oh, it wasn't anything like that. He was a nice enough guy but his lifestyle didn't fit in with me having an eleven-year-old. He had a good job – solicitor and a respectable salary, a nice apartment – note I didn't say flat.' She attempted a smile to lighten the mood.

'It's all right having the fundamental needs, you know, the first layer in Maslow's theory of hierarchy, but you need all the layers to complete the pyramid.'

Maddy gave a snort of laughter. 'That's very profound.'

'I can do profound when I need to.'

'Sometimes I wonder if I'm aiming too high. Maybe I should settle for steady and reliable.'

'Never sell yourself short,' said Joe firmly. 'Don't stay in a relationship that's not right for you.'

Bloody hell, that comment stung and to come from Joe, it hurt doubly. 'Is that why you didn't want me and Esther to move in with you?' She couldn't help herself. The words were out and they sounded bitter. Maddy ground to a halt and Joe stopped walking too. She looked up at him and could see the stunned look on his face. She immediately felt remorseful. 'I'm sorry. That was uncalled for. I shouldn't have said that.'

'You're entitled to say what you like. You know, Maddy, people change. They grow up. Not everyone is a complete dick all their life.'

Maddy studied him hard, unsure what to read into that

statement. Was that an admission? A confession? An apology? 'Do you include yourself in that?'

'I'd like to think so.'

They continued their walk, both lost in their own thoughts once again. It was Joe who broke the deadlock first.

'Maddy, about what happened...'

She held up her hand to cut him off. 'Don't. What's the point in going over all that again?'

'There's every point. I need to say something. To tell you something. Please, hear me out.'

'So you can wipe your conscience clean?'

'No. So I can explain. There were things then I didn't understand but do now. I wish I knew then what I do now.'

'Don't we all.' Maddy fixed her gaze ahead of her. 'Honestly, Joe, raking all that hurt up again isn't going to help anyone.'

'You don't know what I have to say. Give me a minute. One minute, that's all.'

She shrugged and looked at her watch. 'Starting now.'

'I was an idiot back then. I was immature. I handled it all wrong.'

'A bit like now.' Maddy couldn't help herself. She knew she wasn't making this easy for him but she was scared how she might react. She didn't want to break down in front of Joe.

'Yeah, a bit like now. What I'm trying to say, is that I'm sorry I hurt you. I'm sorry I wasn't ready for the commitment. I'm sorry I made a hash of everything.'

She stopped walking and looked at him. 'Is that it?'

Joe shrugged. 'I guess so. No. Maybe. I don't know.'

'If you want me to forgive you, then, yes. Consider yourself forgiven.' Maddy knew she didn't sound particularly generous in her forgiveness.

'Can we call a truce?'

'I wasn't aware we were in battle.'

'Why are you being like this?'

Maddy walked on again. 'Being like what, exactly? Being truthful? You brought the subject up, Joe. Not me.'

'Why don't you tell me what you feel then? Instead of being so cold and immune.'

'Let me refresh you of the facts.' Her pace increased as she battled with her anger. 'I loved you, Joe. I thought you loved me too. My daughter loved you. I let you into our lives. Not something I did lightly. We were together for over three years. I thought we were solid. So when the lease came up for renewal on your flat and I suggested you move in with us, it wasn't without foundation. It wasn't a surprise question. It was the natural progression of a serious relationship.'

'I know,' he said keeping up with her.

'You know and yet within a month you'd ended our relationship. Oh, sorry, technicality there – I ended it. I ended it because it was so obvious it wasn't what you wanted. You changed in that one sentence. You became distant, hostile even. Started making all sorts of excuses not to see me. It was pretty obvious what was going on in your head and when I walked, you never once tried to change my mind.'

'I'm sorry, Maddy. I was an idiot.'

Once again she stopped walking and closed her eyes for a moment to regain her composure. 'You don't have to apologise. I'm over it. It wasn't exactly a new experience for me. I don't know what it is, but I clearly can't do relationships. I haven't got a good track record if you consider you, my mum, Hazel, friends and a couple of other failed relationships along the way. The only difference with you was I genuinely thought I'd broken the curse. Clearly I hadn't.'

'It's nothing to do with you,' he said. 'Nothing. It's other people.'

Maddy laughed. 'The it's not you, it's me syndrome.'

'I can't speak for your mum or your sister but I can speak for me and it most definitely wasn't you. I take full responsibility for that. I fucked up. I was the fuck-up.'

Maddy took a moment to weigh him up. He looked and sounded so sincere and she desperately wanted to believe him, but as she'd said herself, she was pretty rotten at judging people. How could she be certain she'd get it right this time? 'Look, forget it,' she said finally. 'We shouldn't have had this conversation. It all happened three years ago; we should let it go. Water under the bridge and all that.'

'Sure, but just let me say one thing,' said Joe. 'You are not the one who's bad at relationships. I've seen you with Esther and your grandfather and you have a wonderful and amazing bond with them both. No fault lines there.'

Maddy couldn't helping smiling at the compliment. 'Thanks. I appreciate that.'

They walked on, this time at a steady pace and with an easy companionship.

'Does Esther still see her dad?' asked Joe.

'When it suits him. It's supposed to be every other weekend but you know what he's like. He's currently on a month-long trip to Australia. He's thinking of emigrating.'

'That will be tough on Esther if he does.'

'Maybe. She's not too bothered, if I'm honest. It's him who's missing out on all the great things there are to being a dad. Some people will always be dicks.' She gave a small laugh at the borrowed phrase.

'Some people don't know how lucky they are.'

Maddy glanced at Joe yet again, trying to detect any sign that he was joking, but he appeared genuine in his sentiment. 'You're right and before I came here, I'd count myself as one of those. I took having Gramps about for granted and now I'm losing him I've got to make the most of the time that's left.'

'Life has a way of distracting us,' said Joe.

'To my shame, I got too caught up in my own life and forgot about being the good granddaughter. Hazel's email about not being able to look after Gramps anymore made me take a long hard look at myself. I knew where I needed to be. Here with Gramps and Esther.' Maddy forced herself to look away and focused on Esther who was throwing a ball for Fifi. 'And a French bulldog who hates me.'

'Ah, that dog doesn't hate you, she's just messing with you,' said Joe affably. 'Animals can sense tension.'

'I'm not tense.' She gave a small self-effacing laugh. 'Well, maybe a little but I'm still working on not being uptight and this whole YouTube business hasn't helped much.'

'No, I don't suppose it has but hopefully that will all settle down now. You did change the settings, didn't you?'

'Oh yes, I made sure I did that this morning. Although, I can't control what's happened to the content since then and I appreciate that's out of my hands but with any luck, no real harm done.'

They carried on their stroll around the park, the conversation turning to safer subjects such as the weather and holiday destinations. Maddy was tempted to ask Joe about his personal life, but the opportunity never arose and by the time she'd got home she decided to leave it for another day. She was still reconciling with herself for being so open with Joe. Not to mention Joe kind of saying he regretted his behaviour and how their relationship had ended. Or was she reading too much into it all? Was it possible he had changed?

30

May 1944

The Rochelle children had been at the farm for two days now and each day Maryse had taken them with her to school, stepping in for the headmaster who was still being questioned at the local police headquarters.

Arthur could do nothing to ease her worry, which grew with each passing day. For the first time in his life, he felt utterly helpless. He hated feeling so damn useless. In another first for him, he now truly understood what it was to be under the rule of occupied France.

'I wish there was something I could do,' he said to Maryse on the second evening as she walked with him back to the barn. Since Freddie's death, on the insistence of Maryse and with the blessing of Madame Dupont, he had been invited to eat with them at the house. A gesture he appreciated and acknowledged as a small act of acceptance by his hosts.

'I know. But you are, even if indirectly,' she replied, slipping her hand into the crook of his arm as if it was the most natural thing in the world and although it was a gesture they had done before as a show for the Germans, tonight it felt so much more than that. 'Sometimes an individual has to make a sacrifice for the greater good and I know that is how

Monsieur Rochelle feels, but I cannot stop thinking about the children. Jean-Paul has cried himself to sleep every night and Yvette has barely said a word. Some of the other children at school have been saying things to him. Asking what his father did wrong. One of them even called Jean-Paul a Jew boy. Imagine that, at their age.'

'It obviously hasn't come from the child. Someone's said that at home,' replied Arthur.

'You can't trust anyone. Everyone is so scared; they are willing to turn in their neighbour to save themselves.'

'One day, when all this is over, if we make it, then we will all have to hold ourselves to account and be able to live with what we have done.' Arthur turned to Maryse. 'I don't want any regrets.'

She looked straight back into his eyes. 'Neither do I.'

He swept her cheek with the tips of his fingers and then cupped her face. He could feel himself being drawn towards her and he was sure she felt it too. A small voice at the back of his mind began to make itself known. This wasn't a good idea. He couldn't afford to get involved with Maryse. How could they when their lives could be torn apart at any moment but how could he not? How could he pass up this moment and live the rest of his life regretting it?

'No regrets,' he whispered.

'No regrets,' she echoed.

The sound of the floorboards creaking woke Arthur with a start and he sat bolt upright, nearly clonking his head on the wooden beam. From the light of the moon shining through the circular window he could see Maryse at the top of the ladder.

'I didn't mean to wake you,' she said. 'I have to go. My mother will not tolerate me being out all night.'

Arthur scrambled over to her. 'Are you sure that's why you're going?'

She leaned over and kissed him. 'My mother is not someone to cross.' She smiled. 'It's Sunday. I have to accompany her to church.'

'Say a prayer for me.'

'If I thought it was worth it, I would,' said Maryse as she began her descent of the ladder. 'If there was a God who answered prayers, then we wouldn't be having this conversation.'

Arthur couldn't argue with that and after watching her from the window as she scurried back across the courtyard, he tried to settle back down to sleep. However, his mind had come alive and although this usually meant he would be going over operational tactics and instructions from London, tonight, he could only think of Maryse.

Needless to say, when he woke the next morning, he felt as if he was suffering with a hangover. He smiled as he splashed cold water over his face and thought of Maryse again – it was, of course, all worth it.

Arthur spent the morning in the woods at the back of the farm, sorting the chopped firewood into stacks ready for the winter. Despite his concerns about the transportation of weapons on the back of the cart, it had proved an efficient method of moving arms around.

Once he'd completed his task, he began to make his way back through the forest towards the farm. He could hear voices as he neared the river and on the farm side bank, he could see Maryse with the Rochelle children. Jean-Paul was high in the apple tree, shaking the branches while Maryse and

Yvette scurried to duck out of the way of the falling fruit and then scramble to collect their winnings in the basket.

He remained where he was, watching them for a while, glad to see the children smiling for a change. Maryse looked up and caught his eye, waving to him from across the river. 'We're going to make *tarte aux pommes*!'

Arthur heard the engine a split second before Maryse did. It wasn't the deep rumble of an army truck but to his attuned ear, he was pretty certain it was two smaller vehicles, one a car and one possibly a jeep. He and Maryse exchanged a look of concern. Were the Germans here for the children or for him?

'Stay there,' she hissed across the water to him and then ordered Jean-Paul from the tree, before telling the siblings to stay out of sight. Arthur knew she didn't want to appear to be hiding the children: that would only cause suspicion if they were discovered and weren't the actual targets. She sat them at the edge of the river with an apple each. Picking up the basket, she hurried back towards the farm.

Arthur crouched down behind a bush, watching the children and keeping an eye on the track back to the farm. He was desperate to know what was going on, but knew he had to stay put.

After a few minutes, Jean-Paul got to his feet and wandered closer to the riverbank. Arthur watched on anxiously. There had been a lot of rain the past few days and the river had swollen, lapping the sides of the sodden embankment. He could see Jean-Paul walking closer and closer to the edge.

He took a gamble and moved from behind the bush, softly calling to the boy to sit back down with his sister. Seconds later, he wished he hadn't. Surprised to see Arthur, the boy lost his balance and, slipping on the saturated grass, he slid into the water.

Yvette leapt to her feet. '*Au secours! Il ne sait pas nager!*' She shouted to him to help, that her brother couldn't swim.

Arthur could see Jean-Paul disappearing under the water, before reappearing a little further downstream. His cries were swallowed up by the water as the undercurrent dragged him down again.

Arthur didn't have time to think; he ran along the bank, getting ahead of where he anticipated the boy to be. He yanked off his boots and dived into the water. It wasn't particularly deep for his six feet height but for the boy, there was no way he could touch the riverbed.

The water was murky from the mud that had seeped in with the rain and Arthur was blind in the water, grabbing out, hoping to catch the boy. Surfacing, he caught a glimpse of him and by some miracle he was in the direct line of Jean-Paul. Trying to get a foothold while keeping his head above the water, Arthur braced himself. The little boy's body slammed into him, knocking him from his feet, but no way was Arthur going to let go. He found his footing again and got a better hold on the boy, hoisting him under his arms and propelling him upwards so his head was out of the water. Fortunately, Jean-Paul had been swept alongside the bank and with one final push, Arthur was able to dump the boy onto the grass where his sister, almost hysterical now, was there to hold on to him.

Arthur was aware of other people running towards them and gathering around the boy. As he went to clamber out of the river himself, a hand was thrust towards him. He took hold of it and he was yanked out of the water where, on his hands and knees, he coughed and spluttered out the river water he'd ingested. Still trying to catch his breath he raised his head to thank his helper. The sight of army boots and the barrel of a rifle pointing right between his eyes told him all he needed to know.

He turned his head towards the boy and was relieved to see him now coughing up water, with Maryse at his side. He looked around for Hugo but he was nowhere to be seen.

Two officers stood watching the proceedings as the soldier ordered Arthur to his feet. One of the officers approached him.

'Papers.' It wasn't a request; it was an order and he held out his hand.

Arthur motioned to his trouser pocket and slowly moved his hand to retrieve the sodden identity papers. Bugger. He was going to have to request duplicates from London, assuming he got out of this mess, that was.

The officer regarded the sodden mass of paper in Arthur's hand. 'Name?'

'Christophe Martin.'

'You live here?'

'I'm a farmhand.'

The officer nodded and then gesturing to the children he addressed Maryse. 'Are these your children?'

'No. I'm their teacher. They came to collect apples,' she replied, pointing towards the basket of fruit.

'Why was a farmhand here with the children?'

Arthur interjected. 'It was a coincidence. I had just finished logging. Look, my cart is over there.' As they all looked across the river, there was Hugo emerging from the forest.

Hugo led the horse over the small wooden footbridge, the cart rumbling across the planks behind them. He drew to a stop, strategically placing the horse and cart between Maryse and the German officers.

'Is this true?' asked the officer. 'You've just finished work?'

'*Oui*,' replied Hugo, his face and tone neutral, certainly not belying any nerves. Arthur was impressed.

'And did you see anyone in the forest?' The German continued with his questioning, turning back to Arthur. 'No one hiding out there?' There was suspicion in his tone now.

'No one,' replied Arthur, giving his best Gallic shrug.

'These children, what are their names?' The officer was switching from one line of questioning to another, obviously hoping to catch them out.

Maryse got to her feet and moved closer to the horse. 'They are from the village. From Sérent.'

'I didn't ask where they were from,' snapped the German. 'I asked what were their names? Where are their papers?'

Before anyone could answer, the usually docile horse suddenly reared and neighed in alarm, its legs flying in the air. Everyone took a step back. Hugo who was holding the head collar, nearly had his arm wrenched from its socket but somehow managed to keep hold of the animal.

The horse then tried to bolt as Hugo attempted to calm it.

There was pandemonium as the German soldier who had his rifle trained on Arthur had to jump out of the way, as did the two officers.

Everyone was shouting at once as Hugo tried to calm the horse who seemed to relax and then suddenly start up again. It was then Arthur realised Maryse was poking the animal in the ribs with a stick.

The diversion worked. The officers, clearly not used to being around horses, demanded Hugo get it under control and that it should be locked away if they came back again otherwise they would personally shoot the thing.

As the Germans marched back to their vehicles, Hugo followed on behind with what Arthur was certain was now a calm horse but Hugo was continuing the pretence of keeping it under control. It wasn't until the cars had left the farm, that he stopped to pat the horse, congratulating it on its performance.

'That was close,' said Arthur as he helped Jean-Paul to his feet. 'Ça va?'

The little boy nodded.

'Thank you,' said Maryse, hugging Arthur. 'Thank you for what you did.'

'No, thank you,' said Arthur. 'I think you just saved all our lives.'

3 1

O ver the next few days, Maddy was relieved the attention from social media was dying down. She was grateful for Sheila putting out a discreet tweet saying she had signed up with a company to look into Gramps's story. She was also grateful that Esther hadn't put any details out on her vlog either. Maddy shuddered at the thought of someone getting hold of the photograph with the address on the back.

As she busied herself in the garden, cutting the grass while Esther and Gramps were sitting on the patio having a bite to eat, her mind turned to the photograph. She was sure the address on the back held the key but she couldn't work out why or how. Joe was looking into the electoral register for that address to see who was living there during the war.

Joe had phoned her every evening for the past four days to keep her up to date with what he was doing. It wasn't necessary, Maddy knew that, but all the same she was beginning to look forward to his calls. Last night's call had drifted from the subject of Gramps and they had ended up speaking at length about a variety of things, from what music they were currently into, the films they had seen and holiday destinations they'd been to – all this since they had separated. Finding out their tastes were still similar was comforting in a way Maddy hadn't expected. She felt some sort of reassurance and even a touch of excitement in the knowledge they still had so much in common. It was like putting on a favourite well-worn jumper or curling up on a comfortable sofa, wrapped in a blanket with a mug of hot chocolate in one hand and a book in the other.

So far, they had avoided talking any more about their relationship, either past or present, or the circumstances of their break-up. Maddy felt they'd come to some sort of understanding, having navigated the emotional terrain of their relationship, and neither wanted to dig the past up again.

Maddy enjoyed talking to Joe, albeit on a superficial level. She had to admit since coming to live with Gramps she had started to feel a little lonely. It was difficult to have a proper conversation with her grandfather due to his Alzheimer's. She was grateful for Esther being there but it still wasn't adult conversation. Sheila was lovely and had called in regularly but apart from that, Maddy was pretty much on her own. Maddy didn't like to burden Sheila too much with any of the difficult moments she had with Gramps.

She didn't regret her decision to come here. She'd done the right thing and for the right reasons she reminded herself, as she turned the mower around to make the final trip down the lawn. She was quite impressed with her grass-cutting skills. She remembered how Gramps had mowed in lines and she had stood at the top of the steps and admired the alternating dark and pale green stripes in the grass.

She finished the last strip and switched off the mower, before putting it away in the shed and going to join Gramps and Esther on the patio where they were playing a card game.

'We're playing patience,' said Esther.

'Oh, I used to play this all the time when I came to Gramps for the holidays.'

'How long did you stay when you came here?' asked Esther, turning a card over and placing it in the correct position.

'Two weeks at Easter, a week at Christmas and three weeks in the summer,' replied Maddy. 'I often came on my own when I got older as Hazel preferred staying with Carol or seeing her dad.'

'Carol said I could go and stay with her in Spain,' said Esther, using her grandmother's Christian name as she had been taught to do from day one. The day Maddy had found out she was pregnant, Carol's immediate reaction was that she was too old to be a grandmother. From the day Esther had been born, Carol had insisted on being called by her first name. 'Do you think I will one day?'

Maddy hesitated before answering. Would the truth be too brutal? She was sure it had been a throwaway comment from her mother. Carol was always good at making promises to get her out of an awkward situation but then never following up on them. She'd said much the same to Maddy, but the invite had never materialised. 'I'm not sure. I think Carol is quite busy over there. She's got a new boyfriend and I don't think there's much room at the house.'

Esther appeared to be considering Maddy's reply before finally speaking. 'It would be a bit weird going to stay with Carol on my own. I'd miss you. Anyway, I like it here.'

'I used to hate having to go back home after visiting,' said Maddy, steering the conversation away from her absent mother, who was equally happy at letting relations with her granddaughter slide in much the same way as her relationship with her own daughter. Maddy couldn't ever imagine treating

Esther like that. 'Do you remember, Gramps, I used to cry when I left you in the holidays?'

'Don't be crying,' said Gramps. 'We don't want any tears.'

'Not now. I was talking about when I was little and I used to leave you to go home.'

'You're not going are you? Can't you stay a bit longer?' A look of concern settled on Gramps's face.

'Oh, we're not going,' Maddy reassured him. 'I promise you. We're staying right here with you.' She reached out with her other hand and placed it on her grandfather's arm. 'The three of us. We're like the Musketeers.'

'One for all,' began Esther.

'And all for one,' finished Gramps, looking up at them with a smile.

'Ooh, did someone mention Musketeers?' came a voice from behind the garden gate. The handle rattled and in came Sheila. 'Can I be the fourth Musketeer? D'Artagnan?'

'You can indeed,' said Maddy, smiling as Sheila came into the garden and, rising, went to fetch the other garden chair. Fifi stretched and got to her feet, greeting Sheila enthusiastically. Maddy was sure the dog thought she should be the other Musketeer rather than Maddy.

'So, who needs challenging to a duel, then?' asked Sheila, sitting down.

'No one,' said Maddy. 'I was just reassuring Gramps that we're not going back to London. We love living here.'

'Oh, that is good news,' said Sheila. 'I'd have to kidnap Esther if you decided to whisk her away.'

'No kidnapping required,' confirmed Maddy.

'What's this? Patience?' asked Sheila, turning her head to see the cards in front of Gramps. 'I used to play this game when I was a child. Right, Arthur, let's see... what about putting that Queen there?'

Maddy sat back and watched as the older generation contemplated the card game along with Esther. It was a warming sight and she felt a surge of happiness in her chest. It had been a long time since she'd felt that and she could only imagine it was similar to a shot of adrenaline. She put her head back, closed her eyes and enjoyed the warmth of the sun on her face.

32

'Hi, Gramps.' The child walked into the room with the little dog at her heel. She parked herself on the sofa next to his armchair.

'Hello, duck,' he replied, noting she was holding that rectangle television thing in her hands. She had that with her quite a lot. 'What are you doing with that today?'

'I thought I might make another vlog,' she replied. 'Do you want to help me?'

Arthur wasn't sure if he should or not. He had a feeling they caused a bit of trouble when they were in the kitchen. He couldn't remember the detail but he eyed the contraption with suspicion. 'What does your mum say?' he asked.

The child shrugged. 'I can't upload them until she has approved them.'

Arthur wasn't sure he understood the answer but the glum expression on her face wasn't encouraging. He looked around the room for something else to distract her with and he spotted his album. 'What about we look at my book?'

The child didn't look particularly excited by the idea

but she went over to the shelf and brought the book back. Arthur turned the pages and looked at the photos, his emotions churning from happy to sad and back again with the passing images. He wished he could capture one of those memories properly. It was so frustrating. He couldn't explain it to anyone; he wasn't even sure he understood his own reactions or thoughts. Everything raced past him far too quickly to hold on to. It was like trying to catch the wind in your hands as it whistled through the tiniest of gaps between your fingers.

'Who is this?' the child was asking.

Arthur turned his attention back to the book. It was a photograph of a girl and a boy sitting by a campfire.

He recognised them but their names were elusive, as was the context of this knowledge. They were snuggled up together with a blanket draped around their shoulders, their eyes full of bemusement. A sense of sadness overcame Arthur and he didn't know why. 'Rochelle.' He heard himself say the name. 'Rochelle,' he repeated it.

'Is that the girl's name?' asked the child.

'Yes. Rochelle.'

'What is the boy called? Is that her brother?'

Arthur looked intently at the photograph as distant memories began to push their way through the fog in his mind. 'Rochelle. That's right, Rochelle.'

The child looked doubtful. 'They are both called Rochelle?'

'They lived in England,' said Arthur. 'On their own. Evacuated.'

'We learnt about evacuees in school,' said the child. 'We all had to dress up in old clothes and make a box for a gas mask. Did you have a gas mask?'

Arthur closed his eyes for a few seconds. So many images and thoughts swirling around in his head, moving so fast, not giving him enough time to concentrate on one. He opened his eyes. 'Gas masks?' he said, focusing on the child's face. 'Smelly things. Didn't like them.'

The child was looking at the photograph again. 'Did they have to leave their home?'

From nowhere, a surge of sadness welled up inside Arthur's chest, engulfing him, shutting out all other thoughts and emotions. 'Yes,' he stuttered, feeling for his handkerchief in his pocket. 'Yes, they had to leave their father. Poor man. Maryse was so sad. They took him, you know.' He mopped at his face again. 'They were brutal.'

'Everything OK?' It was his granddaughter's voice. 'Oh, Gramps, what's wrong?' Maddy came over to his side. She went to take the album but Arthur didn't want to let it go. He gripped the side of it tightly.

'I didn't mean to upset him,' said the child. She looked concerned.

'It's OK,' said Maddy. 'I know you didn't do anything on purpose. Sometimes Gramps remembers things and they upset him.' She tried to ease the book again but still Arthur clung to it.

'They were so young,' he said. He wanted to explain to them about the children, but the words weren't coming out properly. In his mind, he knew what he wanted to say, but he didn't know the right words to use.

'Do you know who they are?' asked Maddy.

'Gramps said the girl was called Rochelle,' replied the child. 'He said that about the boy as well, so I don't know really.' The child reached over and took the handkerchief from Arthur, dabbing his eyes. 'Don't cry, Gramps.'

Arthur was shocked. He was crying and this poor child was wiping his eyes. He looked at her and for a moment thought she was the child from the picture. He was confused. He knew it couldn't be. It wasn't possible. How could she be here? 'Yvette?' Everything was hazy in his mind and through his eyes. He blinked hard. 'Yvette?' he asked again.

'No, it's Esther,' said the child. 'It's me, Esther.'

'Where's Jean-Paul?' Arthur frowned. Something wasn't right but he didn't know what. He was anxious. He was frightened. He needed to know if the children were OK. 'Where are they? Tell me. Where are they?'

'Gramps. Gramps. Everything is all right,' said Maddy.

He felt her slide the book from his hands but he didn't care. He just wanted to know what had happened to the children. He looked at the child in front of him. Was she a friend of the children? He grasped her hand. '*Gardez les enfants! Où sont-ils?*'

'Gramps, stop. You're frightening Esther.' Maddy took his hand from the child's. 'It's Esther. She doesn't know where they are. *C'est Esther. Elle ne sait pas où ils sont.*'

Arthur looked from the child to his granddaughter and back again. She looked frightened. He looked down at his hand clasped around hers. What was happening? What was wrong with him? He released his fingers and patted her hand with the other one. 'It's OK, duck. I'm sorry.' He wasn't quite sure what he'd done wrong but he'd caused a fuss and now they looked worried. He patted her hand again. The child gave a small but uncertain smile, glancing at her mother for reassurance.

'Gramps was just a bit confused,' said Maddy, gently. 'You're all right now, aren't you, Gramps?'

'Yes. Yes, I am.' Arthur forced a smile to cover his embarrassment and frustration. 'Don't mind me. I'm a silly old man.'

33

Now in dry and clean clothing, Arthur sat on the upturned crate that he used as a chair in the loft room, reflecting on the eventful past hour. It troubled him the Germans had paid a visit and he was sure he hadn't seen the last of them. He reasoned that if they had any evidence that something was amiss at the farm, then they would have acted on it. He was sure there was some ulterior motive behind the visit – maybe it was to scare the Duponts.

With this in mind, he had come to the decision to move out of the farm. He couldn't put the Duponts at any further risk, especially not Maryse. He couldn't bear the thought of anything bad happening to her. No matter what she said about being prepared to die for the cause, he wasn't so prepared and would do whatever it took to keep her safe.

It was going to be one heck of a wrench not seeing her every day. He looked forward to her visits and the time they spent together was special. If there was one good thing to come out of this whole bloody war, then it was Maryse.

He turned his thoughts back to keeping her and the family safe. He'd have to get Hugo to set up a meeting with Patrick so he could pave the way for Arthur moving out to the forest near Saint-Marcel where there were currently about 1800 men and women hiding out as they prepared for the return of the Allied troops.

Arthur had been to the forest several times over the past few weeks to discuss tactics and operations with Patrick and the other commanders, so they could, in turn, organise the destruction of telephone lines, blowing up of bridges and railway lines in readiness for the big event next month.

Arthur hadn't been able to pass on all the details of Operation Overlord. He didn't even know it all himself. It was purely on a need-to-know basis and his task was to prepare the resistance for the event.

As he mulled over what he needed to do, he heard the latch of the barn door lift and the now familiar footsteps of Maryse as she entered the building and climbed up into the loft space.

Tonight there was no smile on her face as she stepped off the ladder and onto the floorboards. She rushed over to him and held him tightly.

As he held onto her, pulling her against his body, Arthur knew she'd already come to the same conclusion as he had. She raised her head to look at him.

'I can't come with you,' she said. 'I can't leave the children.'

'I know, *ma chérie*, I know,' consoled Arthur. He raked his hand through her hair, pulling the band free so her locks fell down her back.

'It's not just the Rochelle children,' she carried on, her voice wobbling as she spoke. 'It's all the other children at the school. I have to look after them. I'm sorry. So sorry.'

'It's OK. *C'est bon. C'est bon.*'

He kissed her tenderly at first but the desire, fuelled with love and heartbreak, overtook all conscious thought between them.

That night, Maryse didn't return to the farmhouse; she stayed in his arms. Arthur held on to her like his life depended on it. How was he going to manage without her? He knew there wasn't much time before Allied troops landed and who knew what would happen after that. Would they get through it? The future was so uncertain and much as he wanted to promise Maryse everything would be OK and once the war was over, they could be together forever, he knew it wasn't realistic.

When dawn finally broke, Maryse had to return to the farmhouse to get the children ready for school and herself for work. She kissed him hard. 'Don't go before I get back.'

'I'll wait for you,' said Arthur.

'Promise?'

'I promise.' He kissed her again and held her one last time, knowing they wouldn't have this privacy once he was living in the forest.

Arthur helped around the farm that morning while Hugo went off to make contact with Patrick and to put arrangements in place for Arthur to move to the forest as soon as possible.

When Hugo finally returned that afternoon, the expression on his face was grim.

'What's the matter?' asked Arthur, wiping his hands on a rag where he had been fiddling with the engine of Andre's truck, which hadn't been running well all week.

'Good and bad news,' said Hugo.

'Let's have the good news.'

'Monsieur Rochelle was released this morning.'

'That's brilliant news,' said Arthur, knowing Maryse would be delighted to welcome the head teacher back. 'How is he?'

'He's been knocked about a fair bit but he'll live.' Hugo dabbed at his forehead with a cloth from his pocket.

'And the bad news?' prompted Arthur.

'You can't go to the forest tonight,' said Hugo. 'Patrick has gone missing. We can't find him. No one knows where he is. The men in the forest are worried. They don't want you there, not yet. When things have settled down and we know what has happened to Patrick, then we can move you but for now, you stay here.'

Arthur mulled over the news. 'What do you think has happened to Patrick?'

'I don't know and I wouldn't like to speculate. For now we sit tight.'

'You think that's wise?'

'What choice do we have?' Hugo swore at no one in particular. 'If only the boy hadn't fallen in the water. If only you hadn't jumped in to save him.'

'Oh, come on, you can't mean that, surely?' said Arthur in surprise. 'You think I should have let the boy drown?'

'I didn't say that.' Hugo glared at him. 'You should have stayed where you were and let one of us go in after him.'

'Well, no one was there,' snapped back Arthur. He went back to looking at Andre's truck engine. He didn't particularly want to get into an argument with Hugo. It was pointless. What was done, was done. They had to deal with that. What was more worrying, was Patrick disappearing. He hoped to God, he hadn't been arrested. Patrick was key to liaising with the resistance who, by and large, weren't too impressed taking orders from an Englishman, albeit half French. That apparently counted for nothing.

*

'Don't let him get to you,' Maryse said to him that evening as he recounted the conversation he'd had with Hugo. They were sitting up in the hayloft having made love. Maryse had brought a blanket with her and they were snuggled naked underneath. 'I know it's dangerous you being here but I can't help being thankful, not just for Monsieur Rochelle being home but because we have a few more days together.'

'I can't argue with that,' said Arthur, kissing her.

It was a touch of bravado on both their parts – he was aware of that. They both knew how much danger not only he was in, but also the whole Dupont family if the Gestapo somehow found out his true identity.

For now though, Arthur was content with indulging himself in the fantasy that he and Maryse would one day see this war out and spend the rest of their lives together. It was a far better notion than the reality.

34

Joe had been home for an hour and had been so engrossed in finding out more about Maryse that he hadn't even made himself a drink.

With the refreshment issue finally resolved, he went back to the computer, refreshing the tab for access to the electoral register. Strictly speaking, this was meant to be for work purposes only. Sussex PI and other tracing agencies had access to certain records that weren't necessarily readily available to the general public.

Joe logged onto the site, hoping Southerton wouldn't check his digital footprint. His boss had been known to check up on his employees to see what they were doing but Joe didn't think it was something Southerton did regularly. Joe was willing to take the chance and anyway, he'd pass it off as a trace for another case. No one at work knew about the letter Esther had sent. No one knew the address was a connection to Arthur and Maryse.

It took some digging and two cups of coffee, but eventually Joe's persistence paid off. The address had been used as a guest house between 1934 and 1948, owned and run by a Mrs Amelie Cohen. He checked for a Mr Cohen but there wasn't anyone by that name listed. Joe flicked the pen around his fingers.

What connection would Maryse have with Amelie Cohen? The Christian name was possibly French and the surname was Jewish. Was there the possibility that Amelie Cohen was originally from France and had relocated before or soon after the German occupation? Had she fled the country as the restrictions and persecutions of the Jewish population increased? It was a possibility.

He logged onto the French record system, again via his work portal, and searched for Amelie Cohen. Unsurprisingly, there were a number of Amelie Cohens and Joe needed some specific information to conduct a proper and fruitful search; still he began methodically going through the names and ruling out those from areas other than Brittany and Normandy. It left five names.

One of those remaining five was fifteen in 1934 so he scrubbed out her name on the basis of being too young. The other four were split evenly between Brittany and Normandy. He decided to look at the Bretagne women first.

Amelie Cohen, forty-four, and Amelie Cohen, thirty-two, at that time. Both could easily have been married and fled to England.

Joe spent the next couple of hours trying to find out some more information about these two women. Did either of them have a connection with England beforehand? Were there any records of either of the women in France after 1934? It was going to be a long night.

He checked his watch and was surprised to see it was already eight o'clock. He had been so engrossed in his research that he hadn't remembered to call Maddy. He picked up his phone and saw he had a text message from her and a missed call.

'Shit,' he cursed out loud when he realised his phone was still on silent mode from when he was at work. He opened the text message.

Hi. Can you give me a call when you get a minute? Not urgent. Thanks. x

He noted the kiss at the end of the text and realised he was smiling. However, he sensed there was an unease in the message, which concerned him enough to call back straight away.

She answered on the second ring, her voice low as if she was trying not to disturb anyone.

'Oh, thank you for ringing,' she said. 'Sorry to be a pain.'

'You're not a pain at all. What's up?'

'I'm a bit worried about Gramps and what we're doing.'

'OK,' said Joe slowly, trying to gauge just how worried she sounded. 'I'm all ears.'

'It's been bothering me all night,' began Maddy. 'Yesterday, Gramps got upset by a photograph he and Esther were looking at in that album of his. He was really confused. At one point, he thought Esther was the girl in the photograph.'

'The poor man,' said Joe, thinking not for the first time, how the disease had taken hold of Arthur so rapidly in the past three years. He was a different man to the one Joe had known and it saddened him greatly. 'What photo was that?' he asked trying not to dwell on the heartbreak of the situation.

'A photo of two children about Esther's age. I don't know who they are. Gramps told Esther they were evacuees.'

'I suppose we can't totally rely on what your grandfather is saying,' said Joe, carefully, not wanting to upset Maddy.

'I know that.'

There was a prickle in her voice and Joe winced at the thought of causing her distress. 'Sorry.'

He could hear Maddy exhale slowly. 'No, I'm sorry. It's me. I'm being tetchy and you're one of the last people I should be taking it out on. I just hate to see what's happening to Gramps.'

'I wish there was something I could say or do to help,' said Joe with genuine remorse.

'It's awful seeing him slip away,' replied Maddy, her voice cracking. 'It's like grieving for him while he's still alive. I feel like I'm losing him and yet being tortured as he's still here.'

'Hey, Maddy, come on, sweetheart. Your grandfather is still there. He may not be aware of everything but he's still there in snatches of time. Hold on to those moments, relish them. Whatever he may say or not say, may remember or not, he knows you love him and he loves you too. I've seen it in his eyes when he looks at you. He *knows* you love him and he might not be able to completely process that in the same way we can, but he *feels* that love. Hang on to that.'

Maddy let out a sob and Joe could hear her crying softly. He murmured soothing words of what he hoped would be comfort down the phone. Maddy was a strong and resilient woman but she was also in touch with her emotions and not afraid to lean on people she trusted. He hoped she could dredge up some of that trust they'd once shared and allow herself to be comforted.

After a minute, the crying eased. 'Oh God, sorry, Joe. I didn't mean to get all emotional.' She sniffed and blew her nose.

'You don't have to apologise,' replied Joe. 'Are you OK? I can come over if you need me to. I could be there in a little over an hour.'

'Thank you. That's very kind, but I'm OK now. Honest.' She sounded more composed. 'Sometimes, I need to let it all out. It's hard keeping up a brave face.'

'You know where I am if you ever need me for a shoulder to cry on. Any time.'

'Thanks, Joe. I appreciate that.'

'Right, well, back to business,' said Joe, hoping to boost her morale. 'I might have some news.'

'News?! Really?'

'Don't get too excited. It may be nothing and if you don't want to go ahead, then I can forget all this now.'

'Ignore me. I'm just tired and sad,' confessed Maddy. 'I do want to help Gramps. I hate seeing him upset.'

'I'll tell you what I've found out and then you can have a think about what you want to do. You may feel differently once you've had a good night's sleep.'

'Oh, don't keep me in suspense, what is it?'

Joe was glad to hear she sounded more upbeat now. 'I might have some news on Maryse. It's proving quite hard to track down anything definite, but I'm working on it.'

'What have you found out exactly?'

'I'm not sure yet.' Joe looked at his computer screen. 'To quickly summarise, the address on the back of the photograph used to be a guest house owned by a woman called Amelie Cohen. It's only a hunch but I think she might be from France, so I've tracked down a couple of women with that name who might have been her. Of course, they wouldn't be alive anymore but both had children and they might be able to tell us some more.'

'Wow you've been busy. Imagine if we find Maryse! Do you think she's still alive? It would be amazing if she was.'

'It may all lead to nothing. I'm working on pure speculation, which isn't ever the best thing. Anyway, hopefully I'll have more to tell you tomorrow.'

'I suddenly feel all excited about it now,' said Maddy.

'Yeah, it can get to you like that.'

'Maybe if it's not too late, I could ask Sheila to come and sit with Gramps and Esther for an hour and we could go down the pub and talk.'

'Are you asking me out on a date?' said Joe, his broad grin sounding clearly in his words. Well that was a turnaround and he was pleased the thought of good news had tamped down the doubts she'd had.

'No! I mean, not a date as in a date *date*,' said Maddy. 'I mean, a drink... you know... just a drink, not a date.'

'Oh, you really know how to crush a guy,' replied Joe, attempting to sound dejected.

'It's not that I wouldn't, it's just that... oh, stop! You know what I mean.' Maddy laughed.

'So it is a date, then,' Joe quipped. 'It's all right, you don't have to deny it. We'll keep it on the down-low.'

'Honestly, you're incorrigible,' said Maddy.

'I'll see you tomorrow at six-thirty for our date-not-date.'

He ended the call and sat back in the sofa, the grin on his face wider than he thought possible and unbelievably hard to control. He was looking forward to seeing Maddy tomorrow and it reminded him of how he used to feel when they were dating. It also served as a reminder that he hadn't felt that buzz of anticipation with anyone since they'd split up.

He then frowned and brought himself to heel. This wasn't a date. Not a real one. He'd had a bit of banter with Maddy, albeit flirty banter, and they were simply going for a drink to talk about her grandfather. He needed to remember this was business, not pleasure.

The following day, Joe had managed to get away from work early, using a house call to a client as a good excuse. He'd only needed to check a few details with the Benson family and could have done that over the phone but calling in to see them was good cover. He'd wanted to go home to get washed and changed before heading over to Maddy's.

Matt had been coming in from work at the same time and Joe had given his friend an update.

'Kay won't forgive me if I don't keep her informed,' said Matt. 'She's so excited about it all. It's like some sort of mini reality show she's created and now she's doing the whole Big Brother thing and wanting to know all the detail.'

Joe laughed at the description. 'She does make me laugh,' he said, good-naturedly. 'But to be honest, and don't tell Kay this, I'm quite enjoying it. I'm off there in a minute. Me and Maddy are going for a drink so I can update her.'

'A drink, eh?'

'Just a drink. As…' Joe searched around for the elusive word.

'Friends?' Matt supplied with a look that clearly meant he didn't believe it. 'Next you'll be telling me you're just good friends.'

'You're as bad as your wife,' called Joe as he headed indoors.

'I'm simply observant!' came the retort.

★

Joe found himself arriving at Maddy's early and spent at least ten minutes checking and rechecking his appearance in the rear-view mirror. God, why did he feel so nervous? This wasn't a date. Maddy had made that clear and yet here he was getting himself all wound up like he was a teenager about to take the hottest girl in the school out for the night.

Finally, it was six-thirty and Joe hopped out of his car and rang the doorbell. He could hear voices calling out to each other inside the house and Sheila opened the door.

'Ah, Joe, come in,' she said opening the door wider. 'Maddy won't be a moment. Wardrobe crisis.' She whispered the last two words.

'How are you?' asked Joe as he followed Sheila into the living room. 'Hello, Arthur.'

Arthur looked up and gave Joe a nod of acknowledgement, before returning his attention to the television where some sort of Last Night at the Proms type of show was playing.

'We're watching a DVD I found in the charity shop this week,' said Sheila. 'We like all the old songs, don't we?'

'Oh yes,' agreed Arthur and began humming along to the music, his fingers tapping on the arms of the chair. Joe wasn't entirely convinced Arthur was humming the same tune as was being played on the DVD but he was enjoying himself, nevertheless.

'Mum won't be a minute,' came Esther's voice from the doorway. 'She's just putting on a different skirt.'

'Are there no secrets in this house?' Maddy appeared behind her daughter. 'Hello, Joe. Sorry to keep you.' She smiled and smoothed her hair with her hand.

'Right, you two youngsters get off, then,' said Sheila. 'And don't worry about us. We're all fine, aren't we?'

'We are indeed,' agreed Arthur.

'Oh, this is one of my favourite songs,' said Sheila. She settled herself on the sofa, next to Arthur's chair, with Esther on her other side. Taking their hands in hers, Sheila swayed in time to the music.

Maddy and Joe left the house to the sounds of singing and humming, agreeing that the unlikely trio were in their element.

The pub wasn't busy and being early, they were able to get a table easily.

'Have you eaten?' asked Maddy, picking up a menu.

'No. I didn't have time.'

'Good. That makes two of us. Shall we eat?'

'Does that make it a date – you know, a romantic meal for two?' asked Joe, plucking a menu from the next table.

'No, it doesn't,' said Maddy firmly, not looking up at him.

'Oh, well, worth a try,' said Joe.

They ordered their meals and while they were waiting for it to be prepared, Maddy once again apologised for getting upset the night before.

'Honestly, Maddy, you need to stop apologising. It's OK to get upset now and again. It's not a sign of weakness.'

She smiled and rummaged in her bag, checking her phone. Joe felt it was more for something to do than necessity. He couldn't quite put his finger on it, but Maddy was a little distracted tonight. He wondered if it was still to do with Gramps. 'Is everything all right?'

'Just an alert on a stupid dating app thing I briefly considered joining.'

He managed to swallow his mouthful of beer and avoid spluttering it out all over the table. 'A dating app?' She threw him a defensive look, as if daring him to laugh. He wasn't that brave. 'OK. Right. A dating app.' He attempted to sound casual despite the roll his gut gave at this idea.

'I've not signed up. I was just thinking about it.' She said the words slowly, her gaze now fixed on him.

'Hey, you don't have to explain anything to me,' replied Joe, which was of course the polar opposite to how he felt about it. He briefly acknowledged that the sensation he was experiencing did in fact have a name. Jealousy. He had no right to feel jealous. He'd been the one to turn Maddy away, the one to let her and Esther down. And now, what the hell was he thinking of?

'It's more of an app for single people to meet up. Not really dating, just company.'

'Cool,' said Joe. Cool? What the hell? He never said cool. He was so trying to overcompensate for his private admission of jealousy.

Maddy raised her eyebrows. 'Cool?' she repeated. 'When did you start saying that?'

'About two seconds ago.' Joe looked up at her and they both burst out laughing.

'Heart on your sleeve as always,' said Maddy good-humouredly once they'd stopped laughing.

'Guilty as charged.'

'I don't think I'll bother just yet though. I've got too much going on with settling into life at Hemingford Grey. You never know, I might meet some local bachelor when I'm least expecting it and live happily ever after.'

Joe was heartened by the fact Maddy wasn't joining a dating app or whatever the hell it was, but he wasn't entirely on board with her meeting-the-local-bachelor aspirations. He swallowed down his beer. 'Fancy another?' He tilted the empty bottle in her direction.

'Sure, then you can tell me what you found out about Maryse.'

Joe returned with their drinks as the waitress was bringing over their meals. 'Perfect timing,' he said, sitting down and raising his glass. 'Cheers.'

'Cheers. So, what have you found out today?' asked Maddy, clinking glasses with him.

Joe went over in more detail this time what he'd discovered about the guest house and how he had narrowed the Amelie Cohens down to the two most probable. 'It's a long shot but if one of them was the Amelie Cohen from Peterborough, she might have mentioned or spoken about Maryse or your grandfather to her family. If they can provide us with the missing information, we might know where to start looking for Maryse.'

'Have you got a phone number for the families?'

'Haven't been able to get hold of that but it would be tricky on the phone. I don't speak French, well, only schoolboy stuff. *Je m'appelle Joe. Je jouer au foot. Je viens d'Angleterre.*'

Maddy giggled at his decidedly dodgy French accent. 'Not much use in reality,' she concluded.

'No. It would be easier face to face. But then again, it's all right preparing what you're going to say – it's when they talk back that's the problem.' Joe looked up at Maddy, who was smiling in a smug sort of way. 'What?' he asked.

'What you need,' she said slowly, 'is someone who can speak French fluently or near enough fluently.'

'Yeah, that's what I was thinking.' He grinned at her. 'Someone whose grandfather spoke French, who had taught their son and their granddaughter to speak the language would be perfect.'

'I haven't spoken it for ages though,' admitted Maddy. 'If you don't use it, you lose it.'

'I'm sure it's still all up there,' said Joe, tapping his head with his finger. 'You could come with me. You could speak to these families. It would be perfect.'

'Me? Come with you to France?'

'Yes. Who or what else did you think I meant?'

Maddy, however, didn't look so enthusiastic. 'I couldn't go to France. I'd have to leave Gramps and Esther. I couldn't do that.'

35

'Are you sure there's no way you could come? It would be ideal. You could do all the translating. We could achieve so much more.'

'I can't leave Gramps and Esther overnight. It's simply not possible. I could take Esther with us, but I'm not sure it would be a good idea taking Gramps,' replied Maddy. It wasn't that she resented her daughter or her grandfather but she was being pragmatic. It would be difficult taking Gramps over to France, taking his wheelchair, finding suitable accommodation and not only that, it could be confusing for him if he was having a bad day.

'You couldn't ask Sheila to stay overnight?' suggested Joe.

She considered the idea for a moment, then shook her head. 'It's not ideal. What if something happened in the night? To either Gramps or Esther? I don't think it would be fair asking Sheila to deal with any emergency. She doesn't drive,' she said. 'You do know she's in her eighties?'

'Really? Wow, she looks good for her age. I know she's no spring chicken but I would have said seventies.'

'She used to drive for the army,' continued Maddy.

They fell into a small silence, each lost in their own thoughts for a while. It was Joe who spoke first. 'I have an idea.'

'I'm all ears.'

'Why don't we ask Kay to come over and look after them. She is a qualified nurse, after all. She's a ward sister now – but you probably know that anyway.'

Maddy was startled by the suggestion. Her knee-jerk reaction was to say no but for some reason she found herself stopping the words coming out. 'I'm not sure,' she said instead.

'Not sure is good,' said Joe. 'It means there's room for me to persuade you.'

'You don't even know if Kay would want to do it. I haven't spoken to her in a while.'

'Oh, she would. Besides, she's the one who convinced me to come and see you in the first place. I don't think I would have done, if she hadn't been so determined.'

'Yes, but that's still different. It's a big favour asking her to look after a ninety-six-year-old and an eleven-year-old. Anyway, how long are we talking about? I wouldn't be happy leaving them for long.'

'We could be there and back in two days. Or if you think you could stretch to a long weekend, we could take the ferry. It will be cheaper.' Joe pushed his glass to one side and rested his forearms on the table, leaning towards her.

'You make it sound simple. And yes, I'd prefer the ferry if it's cheaper.' Maddy considered his plans. If it was that easy, then maybe just maybe she could be convinced. 'I'm not ruling it out but I don't know if it would be fair for Gramps to have a stranger in the house. He might find it confusing or even frightening.'

Joe looked crestfallen. 'Yeah, I see what you mean. I hadn't thought of that. Sorry, I was getting carried away there for a moment.'

Another silence stretched out as once again they contemplated the predicament.

'Wait! There is a way round this,' said Maddy suddenly. 'I could ask Sheila if she would stay over as well. That way there is someone Gramps knows, as well as someone in a professional capacity. I'd be a lot happier if they were both there. And I'd pay Kay. I wouldn't want her to do this for nothing.'

'I'm sure she wouldn't want paying,' said Joe. 'And, to be honest, it might make things more complicated. You know a bit like if you pay someone to look after your child but they're not a registered childminder.'

Maddy was impressed with his knowledge in this area. 'I didn't think of that.'

'I only know because my ex was a nursery nurse,' said Joe.

Maddy noticed he didn't look at her when he spoke and wondered if there was still more pain there than he was letting on. 'Why is she your ex?' Maddy couldn't help herself asking.

'We were like chalk and cheese. I'm not sure how we lasted as long as we did.'

'Which was how long precisely?' Please don't let it be a long time, Maddy found herself silently saying.

'Six months. A record. Present company excepted.'

'Any regrets?' Maddy heard herself asking this out loud, as a small sense of satisfaction ran through her that their relationship had lasted far longer – two and a half years longer.

'No regrets. It wasn't going anywhere for either of us.'

Maddy was aware of the little flutter of relief that Joe had not only had a brief relationship but that he appeared to have absolutely no regrets about it whatsoever. 'So you're not too bruised that you're sworn off women?' she heard herself asking. Bloody hell! What was wrong with her? That was supposed to have been a thought. She felt herself blush. 'Sorry. That's being too nosy. I shouldn't have asked.'

He gave a chuckle. 'I like that you asked.'

She couldn't look at him and inwardly winced at her lack of tact and sophistication. 'Please, forget I said anything,' she mumbled.

He leaned across the table and peered closely at her. 'I'm not sworn off relationships,' he said. 'We can't always get it right the first time. We're human and we make mistakes.'

Maddy's heart hammered against her chest. She hadn't missed the inference of what he had said.

'That makes two of us, then,' she replied softly.

Joe opened his mouth to speak but whatever he was going to say was interrupted by the waitress appearing at the table and clearing their plates away.

'Hold that thought,' said Joe.

'I'd better get back,' said Maddy, checking her watch. 'I didn't realise but it's getting late. Sheila will be wanting to go home.'

'I'll give her a lift,' said Joe, standing up.

As they drove back to Maddy's house, she pondered the idea of going to France. If Kay could come and look after Gramps, then it was a possibility. In fact, the more she thought about it, the more she warmed to the idea.

'Supposing, I did ask Kay to look after Gramps and she agreed, I'd have to treat her in some way if I can't pay her and that way it would be Kay just doing me a favour,' said Maddy as they pulled up onto her driveway.

Joe smiled like a kid at Christmas. 'Sounds good. I'll quickly text her now. She's probably at work. I don't think her shift finishes for a while but I'll ask her to call me and I can talk to her properly.' He quickly tapped out a message, before returning his phone to his jacket pocket. 'Now, all we have to do is ask Sheila, book the ferry, book accommodation, find the two women and hope they'll agree to speak to us.'

Maddy laughed. 'Yeah, that's all. Do you think we should phone ahead so the Amelies know we're coming?'

'I'll see if I can get a phone number for the ladies but you'll have to ring. It's no good me trying to speak to them – they won't understand a word if they don't speak English.'

Maddy felt both excited and nervous at the same time. She wasn't quite sure what she was letting herself in for and whether the excitement was all down to the fact they might be meeting someone who could bring them closer to Maryse, or whether it was because she was going to be spending some time with Joe.

'You looked miles away there,' commented Joe.

'I'm fine. I was thinking about the trip. I hope one of these Amelies is the right one. Are you sure that the Amelie Cohen we're looking for went back to France?'

'I don't know for definite but seeing as there's no record of her after that date anywhere in the UK, my guess is she did go back. I'm going to check tomorrow for some sort of military service record for the husband. It could be he was killed in action. If so, there'd be no reason for her to stay in the UK.'

'Is there anything I can do in the meantime?' asked Maddy. 'I feel like a spare part.'

'I don't think so. You've got enough on your plate anyway.'

Some ten minutes later, as Joe helped Sheila into the car, Maddy couldn't help feeling disappointed their evening was already over.

'Let me know what you find out tomorrow,' she said needlessly.

'As soon as I know anything, I'll ring you,' said Joe. He closed the door on Sheila and walked around to the driver's side where Maddy was standing. 'I really enjoyed this evening.'

'So did I.'

He leaned forwards and gave her a peck on the cheek. 'That bit earlier where we said about making mistakes and second chances...'

'Yes,' she said, taking a deep steadying breath.

'We should revisit that conversation. If you'd like to, that is.'

'I would. Very much so,' she said with a reassuring confidence.

He smiled broadly, climbed into his car, started the engine and buzzed the window down. 'Goodnight, Maddy,' he said, slipping the car into gear and driving away.

Esther came to the door just as Maddy turned to come in. Maddy slipped her arm around Esther's shoulder and walked her back into the living room. 'There's something I need to talk to you about. Something important.'

36

May 1944

Arthur heard her before he saw her. Maryse was screaming his name and she came hurtling into the courtyard on her pushbike. Arthur dropped the broom and rushed over to her.

'Maryse, what is wrong?'

'Quick! Hide. You must hide. Come with me!'

'What?'

'Just do as I say. The Gestapo know about you!'

Hugo was now out in the courtyard. He exchanged a look with his sister. 'How?'

'Jean-Paul. He didn't mean to. He saw his father all beaten up. He was scared. The Gestapo came to the school this morning. They were talking to the children. Tricking them into talking. When you grabbed Jean-Paul from the river, you spoke English to him.'

'I did?' Arthur was mortified but had no recollection of doing so. 'Oh, God, I must have said something without realising it.'

'Monsieur Rochelle warned me,' explained Maryse.

'You idiot,' snapped Hugo.

'There's no time for this,' urged Maryse. 'We have to go.'

She was pulling Arthur across the courtyard.

'My stuff?'

'Hugo will deal with that. Come on!'

Immediately, Hugo was running across to the barn, shouting over his shoulder that he'd throw Arthur's bag down to them. Arthur had always made sure he packed his belongings in his bag, ready for a quick exit.

He caught the bag as Hugo hurled it down from the loft room and then without hesitating, he broke into a run, following Maryse as she ran out the back of the farm, towards the river, across the bridge and on into the forest beyond. He covered the ground swiftly, soon catching up with her. It was no point asking her where they were going. He would have to trust her on this.

They ran deeper into the woods, following an unmarked route, weaving through the trees, which blocked out the light and the heat of the day. The ground was spongy under foot and the bracken was almost up to Arthur's thighs.

Eventually, Maryse slowed to a walk and breathing heavily she pointed ahead of her towards a small wooden shack no bigger than a garden shed. 'There,' she said. 'We can shelter in there. Hugo uses it if he's out hunting at night.' She pulled open the wooden door, which creaked in protest.

Inside, a wooden bench ran the length of each side and on a shelf above were a couple of tin cups and plates with two knives, two forks and two spoons. A heavy pot and a ladle were beside them. Apart from that it was empty.

'I hope your mother will be all right,' said Arthur, wondering what was happening back at the farm.

'My mother is a strong woman,' replied Maryse.

'Like you.'

'I don't have any choice. As a woman I have even less choice.'

Arthur felt a rise of anger in his chest at the implications of her words. 'I'm sorry...' he began, but she held up her hand to stop him mid-sentence.

'You have nothing to be sorry about. One day, these soldiers will have to go home and face their wives, their girlfriends, their sisters, their mothers and they will have to live with the knowledge of what they have done to other wives, girlfriends, sisters, mothers. They will have to take that knowledge to their graves.'

'And you?' asked Arthur gently, hoping to God he was wrong. 'Do you have to bear anything?'

She offered a small smile. 'No. I don't but that is not to say I wouldn't. We all have to do things to stay alive. For some, it's a matter of survival.' Maryse sat down on the bench. 'But don't tell Hugo that. He cannot understand that and calls all women who liaise with the Germans filthy whores who are traitors to the country.'

Arthur was indignant on behalf of the women. He might not approve of their behaviour but he was unable to summon up the hatred Hugo clearly harboured. 'Everyone must do what they have to,' he said. 'It's not for us to judge.'

'I agree. Sometimes I'm scared I might have to put my views to the test,' replied Maryse.

Arthur felt an overwhelming sense of protection towards her. He put his arm around her shoulder and pulled her close to his body. 'I promise, all the time I am here and while there is breath in my lungs, I will do whatever it takes to protect you.'

37

Sitting in the passenger seat of Joe's car, Maddy gave one last look over her shoulder as they reversed off the driveway and out on to the road. Esther, Sheila, Kay and Gramps were all on the path waving them off like some sort of wedding party. Wedding? Where did that idea come from?

'They'll be fine,' reassured Joe. 'Kay is brilliant. She'll be in her element.'

'I know, but I can't help worrying,' replied Maddy, relieved he had no notion what she had just been thinking. 'Kay said she'd ring but only in an emergency.'

'Kay is one of the most competent people I know.'

It was true, Kay was indeed brilliant at her job and was a highly valued member of the hospital nursing staff. Since enlisting her help, Kay had been over every evening for the past three days to get to know Esther and Gramps and to learn the routine of the house. Kay was efficient and professional but above all, charming and easy to warm to. Maddy remembered Kay being exactly the same when they'd first been introduced through Joe. In fact, both Kay and Matt were welcoming and although she and Maddy had kept in touch, it hadn't been that often. Maddy realised how much she'd missed having Kay as a friend.

'Look, we'll be back in a few days. If there's any emergency, Kay will deal with it and let us know and I can get you on the first flight home.'

Joe was reassuring her for the one hundredth time and Maddy appreciated his patience. She made a conscious decision to try not to think about home while she was gone.

Joe was an easy travelling companion; he was relaxed and also had everything organised. The conversation was easy and when they lulled into a comfortable silence, Joe had put on a CD and the familiar sounds of Van Morrison filled the car.

'Oh we used to play this all the time.' Maddy smiled.

'I know.' Joe winked.

Maddy settled back in her seat, the smile still on her face as she focused on the music, rather than the memories – that would be far too dangerous.

They arrived at the ferry port a couple of hours later and were soon on board, climbing up the metal staircase from the car deck to the main passenger part of the vessel.

'There is the posh restaurant upstairs if you prefer,' Joe suggested when they reached the main deck.

'I'm happy with cheap and cheerful self-service café,' replied Maddy, looking down at her jeans, which were hardly suitable for fine dining.

'A girl after my own heart.' Joe put a hand on her elbow and guided her between the passengers waiting in the main reception area. 'Let's beat the crowds.'

As they wandered out of the café an hour later, Maddy couldn't help thinking of times gone by when she and Joe had done this as a couple. She smiled as she remembered the short break they had taken in Cornwall.

'What are you smiling at?' Joe asked, hooking his overnight bag onto his shoulder and taking hers.

'Oh, I was just remembering that time we went on a romantic break to Cornwall.'

'You had to bring it up, didn't you?' said Joe, shaking his head in mock despair.

'I've never recovered from the experience.'

'It wasn't that bad, surely?'

'The romantic break that turned out to be a weekend in a caravan on top of a cliff.'

'It had a beautiful view,' countered Joe.

'Yes, but not when it was pouring with rain and a gale blowing.'

'I couldn't help the weather.'

'And the restaurant you booked?'

'It was an easy mistake to make… Polruan and Polperro – they sound practically identical.' Joe held the door open for her and they went out onto the deck.

The moon was shining from a cloudless night sky, reflecting like a glitter ball on the sea. Maddy scooped her hair into her hand and brought it over her shoulder to stop the breeze from swirling it around her face. 'And we couldn't get in anywhere as we'd left it too late because there was some book festival going on in Fowey.'

'But you didn't go hungry though, did you? Lamb kofta overlooking a moonlit harbour.'

'A kebab sitting on a bench outside the public toilets,' corrected Maddy.

'You can't say it wasn't a memorable night.'

Maddy laughed and her face softened. 'Unforgettable,' she said with more tenderness than she intended.

They had a couple of drinks at the bar and watched the on-board cabaret act belt out some 80s power ballads. The conversation between them wasn't quite as easy-going as earlier. Maddy wondered if it was just her who was painfully aware of the other and confused by the mix of emotions it was throwing up. She needed to take a step back, she reminded herself. She'd been rejected by Joe three years ago and she couldn't afford to let history repeat itself. That would be far too humiliating.

'I think I'll turn in now,' said Maddy as she finished her drink. It was at that point she realised they hadn't discussed sleeping arrangements.

'I'll do the same,' replied Joe. He gave her another of his looks as if deciding on what he was about to say. 'We're in the same cabin but of course it's just bunks. Why don't you go and get ready for bed now and I'll come along in ten minutes once you're sorted.'

Maddy headed back to the cabin, relieved Joe wasn't even considering he suggest anything other than separate bunks.

'We should be down to Sérent in about three hours, depending on traffic,' said Joe, as they came through the small passport control area the next morning. 'What do you want to do… stop on the way for lunch at a café or shall we grab a sandwich at a motorway service station and eat on the go?'

'Eat on the go works for me,' said Maddy. 'It will save us time and we're not exactly here on a jolly.'

Within thirty minutes they were bombing their way along the motorway, the satnav set for the village of Sérent.

Maddy looked at the folder Joe had put together on Gramps's story. The first Amelie Cohen had been found on the French record system and lived in an old people's home, her husband having died some twenty years ago and Amelie herself passing away five years later. They were survived by a daughter and two sons. The name Collette Beaufort was underlined, followed by an address and telephone number.

'What's the approach then?' asked Maddy. She was leaving this to Joe – it was something he did day in day out.

'Well, I thought we'd get down to the village where Collette lives and then you could call her. I can coach you on what to say. Hopefully, she'll either talk to us on the phone or in person, especially if we say we're in the village.'

'You sound optimistic about this.'

'It's how I usually work.'

She nodded, as much to herself as to Joe. 'Let's hope I can sound as charming and persuasive as you do.'

'So, you admit that I'm charming?' he said, giving her a sideways look.

'Maybe a little. Don't let it go to your head though.'

It was another couple of hours before they found themselves in the little village of Sérent. There was a market on in the square, which was overlooked by an impressive church, its spire reaching high above the skyline of the village, the shingle roof tiles and shuttered windows, typical of the Breton region. The market stalls were food stalls – vegetables, fish, fruit, with another selling crepes. Next to that, a rotisserie with several spits filled with roasting chicken and the smell of onion and the gravy soaking in the juices made Maddy's stomach rumble. In the end, neither had been that hungry on the drive down and they hadn't bothered stopping.

'Do you want to eat here?' asked Joe, as he circled the car one more time around the car park.

'We should call Collette first,' replied Maddy. 'Chances are, she'll be at home having her lunch and we can persuade her to meet us.'

'OK, I'll park here and we'll ring her. Well, when I say, we, I mean you.'

'*Bien sûr*,' replied Maddy. Her stomach was fluttering with nerves. It had been a long time since she'd had to use her French and as she explained to Joe, it was somewhat rusty. She had tried to brush up on it over the last couple of days in a bid to give her a little more confidence.

Joe parked the car, fortunate to take a space under a tree that another car was vacating. It was late July and the temperature although just a few degrees hotter than the UK was high enough to make them both sweat.

'All set?' he asked as he tapped in the phone number, switched it to speaker and hovered his finger over the call button.

'Go for it,' she replied with more confidence than she felt.

The call was answered promptly. '*Oui, hello*,' came the voice of a middle-aged woman.

'*Madame Beaufort?*' enquired Maddy.

'*Oui*,' the reply was more guarded.

Maddy had the script Joe had given her and began her opener; glad she'd had time to rehearse this. 'My name is Maddy Pettinger from England and I'm trying to locate a person for my grandfather. He is in his nineties and would love to be back in touch with them. As we understand it, your mother, Amelie Cohen, might know this other person. We wondered if we could come and talk to you. We're in Sérent now.'

'My mother passed away. I'm sorry I can't help you.'

'Please, Madame Beaufort, it won't take much time. If we could ask you a few questions.'

There was a long pause and for a moment Maddy thought the connection had gone but eventually the Frenchwoman spoke.

'It's for your grandfather, you say?'

'Yes, he was here in France during the war but we believe your mother to be the connection to him and this other person when she was in England.'

'I don't know a great deal about that time. My mother didn't speak much of the war.'

'No, I appreciate that, but perhaps we could meet just to ask a few questions. Please?'

'I'm not sure. I will need to speak to my son.'

'Would that be today? We're in the village and we can wait.'

'If I meet you it will be this evening. Seven o'clock at the restaurant St Pierre opposite the church.'

'Thank you so much. I hope we see you then,' said Maddy. '*Merci, beaucoup, madame.*'

'I don't know why I bothered listening,' said Joe. 'I didn't understand a word of that. Is it good news?'

'She's going to speak to her son first. It sounds hopeful though and we're to go to a restaurant opposite the church this evening to meet her and, fingers crossed, she'll turn up.'

'OK, it wasn't a straight no, so that's good,' said Joe. 'How about we try to get in touch with the other Cohen family and see if we can arrange a meeting with them this afternoon?'

'OK. How far away are they?'

'According to the map, about an hour's drive. We have enough time if they're willing to meet today.'

'I'll phone now,' said Maddy, flicking the page to the next Cohen family and diligently dialled their number. The response this time was less guarded. In fact, the family was very interested in the backstory leading up to Maddy and Joe's visit and many of the details of the story seemed to match. Maddy felt confident they had the right Amelie Cohen's family.

'Please, come over,' said the woman, Madame Petit. 'My sister lives with me. We would be interested to find out more about our mother.'

They agreed a time and Maddy ended the call.

'I might not be able to translate, but that sounded positive,' said Joe, starting the car engine.

'They want us to come over now. It's two sisters, daughters of Amelie Cohen.'

'Great. What time?'

'Three-thirty.'

'Even better. We have time to stop for some proper lunch.'

'Honestly, Joe, a sandwich or a baguette would do me fine,' said Maddy.

'My treat. I insist.'

Joe sounded like he'd made his mind up and wouldn't take no for an answer, so Maddy didn't bother trying to protest. 'Where to?' she asked.

'According to my research, there's a creperie around the corner here,' said Joe, steering the car down a narrow street. Old stone town houses lined the way, with wooden doors, shutters at the windows and practically every other house had a window box of red geraniums. 'Everywhere looks dead,' commented Joe, looking up at the shuttered windows.

'Keeps the heat out in the summer,' explained Maddy. 'And

apparently, the geraniums deter the flies. And yes, I am full of useless information.'

'Not useless if I wanted to buy a house in France,' said Joe. He pulled up outside the creperie. 'Do you feel any connection with France? I mean, you speak the language and you know all about shutters and geraniums.'

'Watch it or I'll tell you all about how many times you kiss someone depending on how well you know them and which side to go to first so as to avoid that awkward nose bumping,' said Maddy, with a laugh as she got out of the car.

'Now that sounds far more interesting!'

Maddy laughed again, unsure how to answer that.

The creperie was busy, which in a small town Maddy decided was a good thing. It meant the locals liked to dine here so the food must be up to a high standard. They were seated by the window and left with the menus while the waitress went off to fetch their drinks.

'So, do you feel any connection with France now that you're here?' Joe asked again, once they had ordered.

'I don't know if I do. I suppose the romantic answer is to say yes, but honestly, not a connection. I feel comfortable here but that's probably because we used to holiday in France a lot when we were kids and speaking the language does make it feel less alien.' Maddy realised that this was something neither of them had discussed before.

'But it's not in your blood?'

'I don't think so because I suppose it isn't actually in my blood – unlike you. You were born in Ireland and lived there for a couple of years, but I don't ever remember you feeling particularly Irish.'

'True,' conceded Joe. 'I hold an Irish passport but I'm not sure that makes me feel Irish. I don't get that distinct sense of roots or heritage and, to be fair, I haven't been back since I was about sixteen when my Aunt Marie got married.'

'What do you feel though? Do you feel English then?'

'I feel like I belong and yet, don't belong in England or in Ireland. Sort of somewhere in between.'

'Does it bother you?'

'Not really.'

Maddy looked thoughtfully at Joe for a while. She sensed there was more to that statement than he was letting on. She took a punt. 'So, your lack of roots or belonging, you say it doesn't bother you but has it bothered anyone else?'

'What makes you ask that?'

'Just curious.'

'You know what they say about curiosity and the cat.'

'I'm assuming I'm right, then? It has been an issue for someone.'

Joe took a long slug of his beer and looked out onto the square, before putting down the glass and adjusting his position in the chair. 'OK, my ex-girlfriend thought it made me restless. That I didn't have any roots and as a result was emotionally detached. Apparently, when she was psychoanalysing me during one particularly heated argument, she told me that's why I'd joined the police – because I wanted to belong somewhere – and that's why I did the PI job – because I wanted to be involved in something I didn't have. You know, after my parents divorced after twenty-odd years of marriage.'

'Wow. That all sounds deep but I can see her angle.' Alarm bells were ringing in Maddy's head that she was stepping into dangerous territory, but she couldn't stop herself. The ex-girlfriend had summed Joe up to a tee.

A muscle in Joe's jaw flicked and his shoulders tightened.

She'd struck a nerve and now Maddy regretted it. She had no right to do this to Joe and it annoyed her that she'd clearly overstepped the line in the sand they'd drawn before.

The waitress brought over their meals, both having chosen pizza, but neither made any attempt to start. 'This looks delicious,' said Maddy, trying to restore the easy atmosphere between them. 'I'm starving.' She picked up her cutlery and overenthusiastically tucked into her food.

38

May 1944

They'd stayed hiding in the shed for another two hours before Hugo came to give them the all clear but Arthur hadn't minded at all.

He'd held Maryse in his arms for the whole time, enjoying the sensation of her body close to his, to luxuriate in the shared comfort of human contact, one with no fears and no demands. Those few hours were an oasis of calm and solace as the war in Europe raged around them.

'Is everyone all right?' asked Arthur, knowing Maryse had been worrying about her mother.

'They had a good look round the farm,' said Hugo. 'But found nothing, of course. They were persistent with their questioning but they didn't get anything out of us. They have no proof, only the word of a young boy who was so scared for his father, he was willing to make up all sorts of stories.'

'Is that what they believe?' asked Maryse.

Hugo shrugged. 'Who knows what they really think. They play with us like a cat plays with a mouse. They keep us frightened. It amuses them. We just have to hope they remain that way for a little longer. I had word from Patrick. He's lying low until the fuss dies down.' Hugo gestured towards

Arthur. 'The sooner we can get you out of here the better. You're drawing too much attention to us.'

'Fine by me,' said Arthur. 'I don't want to stay here either.'

Hugo eyed him speculatively, then thrust something towards him. It was a gun, wrapped in a piece of grey cloth. 'You'd better keep that on you,' he said before turning and making his way back through the forest.

Arthur weighed the gun in the palm of his hand, checked the barrel and was pleased to see it was loaded. Making sure it was safe, he slipped it into his jacket pocket.

Once at the edge of the farm, Maryse turned on him, her expression one of hurt and anger. 'Did you mean what you said? About not wanting to stay here?'

Arthur groaned. He had meant it on the one hand, but on the other he hadn't. He reached out for Maryse but she shrugged him away. 'Maryse, please,' he began.

'Leave me alone,' she snapped and once again brushed his touch away, before breaking into a run. Arthur watched her disappear through the gate and into the courtyard.

'Bugger,' he sighed. He realised then he was at Freddie's resting place. 'That didn't go well, did it?'

Arthur trudged back to the barn where by now his blanket and flask with some fresh water had been returned. It rankled him that he'd upset Maryse. It was the last thing he wanted to do. But it was unlike her to over-react like that; she was usually much more rational. He put it down to the strain of the situation and hoped he'd be able to talk to her soon and smooth things over.

Not able to get comfortable or to relegate thoughts of Maryse from his mind, Arthur went for a walk around the farm. He wandered out of the barn and across the cobbles. It was a quiet and still evening, where the sounds were amplified and carried in the air. His booted footsteps echoed around the courtyard, bouncing off the stone buildings and somewhere down the hillside a dog was barking. The air was damp and although the day had been bright and warm, he noticed a shift in the weather. As he walked down towards the river, he could see the clouds on the horizon beginning to make their way towards the farm. They were going to be in for some rain that night. As sure as eggs is eggs, his father would have said.

He reached the riverbank and was about to take out a cigarette to light it when he sensed movement behind him. He spun around, not sure who or what to expect, drawing his gun as he did so and pointing it in front of him, ready to fire.

Maryse let out a yelp of fright and flung her hands in the air. 'Don't shoot! It's me!'

'Shit!' Arthur sighed and lowered his gun. After making sure the safety catch was on, he pushed it into his belt. 'Don't ever creep up on me like that.' He didn't mean to sound cross and felt immediately remorseful when he saw her face drop. 'Sorry, you scared me – that was all.'

'I wanted to say I was sorry for being angry earlier. I had no right to behave like that.'

Arthur found himself apologising again. 'I didn't think what I was saying,' he tried to explain.

'It's fine. I just don't want you to go,' confessed Maryse. 'I know it's right that you should. I think I was over-reacting.' Maryse took something from her pocket and offered it to Arthur. 'For you.'

It was a white handkerchief. Arthur took the gift and it was then he saw the letter M had been embroidered in the corner. He ran his thumb over the red thread. 'You did this?'

'Yes, this afternoon.'

'It's beautiful,' said Arthur. He lifted the handkerchief to his nose and took in the soft scent of rose water.

'To remind you of me,' Maryse said.

'Thank you, so much,' he said, stepping towards her. She didn't wait for him to reach her before moving towards him. He enveloped her in his arms, their mouths hungrily seeking one another.

39

Arthur felt restless and yet at the same time tired. He liked the nurse who was looking after them and she had been kind to him and the child. He couldn't recall her name but she didn't seem to mind him calling her nurse. She said he had been up in the night walking around a lot and that was why he was tired. He'd heard her saying to his friend Sheila that he was disorientated because Maddy wasn't there. He missed Maddy. He liked it when she was here; it made him feel safe.

The child was sitting next to him looking at the little television screen thingy bob she carried around with her. She was watching something that made her laugh out loud every now and again. He liked to hear her laugh and he enjoyed her company. Even when they didn't talk much, he just liked her being there.

'Shall we see what's on the telly?' asked Sheila, coming into the room. 'I think that show where they find long-lost relatives is on. I like that. Always makes me cry but in a good way.'

'Oh, you don't want to be crying,' said Arthur.

'It's happy crying,' said Sheila. 'So lovely when they find someone they've been looking for after so many years.'

The child put the screen thingy bob down, her attention

caught by what Sheila was saying. 'Long-lost families?' she asked. 'That's what Joe does. He finds people.'

'That's right,' replied Sheila who glanced at Arthur. 'Hopefully he will have good news when he comes back from France with your mother.'

Arthur watched the TV show with Sheila and the child. He wasn't entirely sure what was going on but he was getting the general idea. And yes, people did cry but it was because they were happy to see each other again.

'Oh, look at this one, Gramps,' said the child tapping his arm. He might have nodded off, he wasn't sure, but the child had caught his attention now. 'They are looking for someone who was evacuated during the war.'

He peered at the television, concentrating hard on what the presenter was saying but he couldn't keep up. He needed them to speak slower so he had more time to consider the words and translate them into something more meaningful. He was able to catch snatches of the conversation and, yes, the child was right, they were indeed talking about being evacuated.

He leaned forward in his chair, intent on listening carefully. 'Is it Yvette they're talking about?' he asked.

'No, Arthur, it's someone else,' said Sheila. 'It's a boy who was evacuated to Kent during the war. This woman here...' She pointed at the screen. 'She's his sister. They were separated in the war and their mother was killed so they had to be adopted.'

Arthur looked to the child. 'It's not Yvette?'

'No, Gramps. Do you know where Yvette was evacuated?'

'Come on, Esther,' interrupted Sheila. 'Don't be pestering Gramps now. Remember what your mum said.'

Arthur really was lost with the conversation now. What

had his mother said? He looked back at the child. 'I just want to know that she's safe.'

'She's safe.' Sheila reached over and patted his arm. 'Why don't we watch something else?'

'But it might help Gramps remember things,' protested the child. 'Please, Sheila.'

Sheila cocked her head to one side and let out a sigh. 'Oh, all right. It is one of my favourite programmes.' She settled back in her chair and concentrated on the television.

The child smiled at Arthur and he squeezed her hand. She was a good ally to have.

Arthur spent the rest of the programme trying to fathom out what was going on and watching the child who, every now and then was typing things into the thingy bob on her lap.

'Oh, look, Gramps! They've found the boy who was evacuated!' cried the child.

Arthur looked at the screen and was expecting to see a young boy but was surprised to see an old man. 'Who's that?'

'That's the boy. Well, he's not a boy now, he's seventy-nine but he was a boy when he was evacuated. Look, his sister is so happy to see him.'

'Was he at Hickory Farm too?' Arthur frowned. 'Were they together? Was Yvette at the farm?'

'Hickory Farm? Are you saying that's where the children in the photo were?' asked the child.

'What children? What photo?' Arthur could feel the anxiety building up within him. He didn't know what the child was asking.

'That's enough now,' said Shelia. 'Don't be quizzing your grandfather like that.'

Arthur drummed his fingers on the arm of his chair. He

was confused and he knew he shouldn't be. He felt a wave of anger wash over him. He hated being like this. Hated it! And then the feeling was gone, replaced by a sadness that had been edging its way forward since the programme had begun. It was to do with Yvette, the child and the television programme but it was all muddled up in his mind like a heap of spaghetti and he didn't know where the strands of thought started. They were a jumbled mess of words and images, fragments of memory and snatches of thought – all knotted up together.

He put his head back against the chair and closed his eyes. Trying to unravel his thoughts was tiring. He just wanted to sleep. He felt the hand of the child slide over the top of his and she gently closed her fingers over his knuckles. Her hands were soft and smooth – a contrast to his bony and wrinkly old skin.

Then her hand moved away and although his eyelids were heavy, he inched them open and watched as the child took the blanket from the foot stool, opened it out, and then placed it over his knees. His eyelids drooped and, feeling content and calm, Arthur allowed himself to succumb to the tiredness.

'Gramps. Gramps, are you awake?'

Arthur was already stirring from his catnap when the child's voice penetrated his half-conscious state. He blinked a few times and squinted his eyes into focus. 'Hello, duck. Where's the fire?'

He looked around the room but no one else was there.

'There's no fire,' replied the child earnestly and then lowering her voice, said, 'I have to tell you something before Sheila comes back.'

Arthur shuffled himself back in his chair and looked attentively at the child. 'What is it?'

'I know how we can find Yvette.' She looked pleased with herself. 'If we can find Yvette, then we might be able to find Maryse.'

Arthur sat up even further. Yvette! The child knew how to find Yvette. This was good news indeed. 'How?'

'You can't tell anyone, not even Sheila.'

Arthur grew concerned. He wasn't sure he liked the idea of keeping secrets but he nodded all the same. 'Scout's honour,' he said, tapping his forehead with his fingers.

'You said earlier about Hickory Farm…' She paused.

'Hickory Farm. Yes, that's right.' A solid memory was beginning to form in his mind. 'Yvette. Hickory Farm. She lived at Hickory Farm. The teacher took her, with lots of other children. The teacher said they were being billeted in Cambridgeshire. I didn't see her again.' The sadness crept back into his heart. 'I need to know she was safe.'

The child grinned at him. 'I know how to find out.' She held up the thingy bob she had in her hands – the little television screen that was beyond Arthur's understanding. 'When the programme was on earlier, I made some notes on how to find an evacuee. I've googled Hickory Farm and I know how to find it. I looked up how far away it is and it's only twenty-five miles.'

Googled? Arthur had no idea what the child was talking about but she was excited and was saying she knew where Hickory Farm was. 'Is Yvette still there?'

The child's expression dropped a fraction. 'I don't think she'll still be there now, Gramps, because she will be very old now but…' she paused and the excited look returned '…but we can go there. Me and you. We can go and find out what happened to her. I looked at the village website and it says stuff about the history and the evacuees. It says that the vicar kept a record. We can go there and ask him... or whoever is there now.'

It took a while for Arthur to process everything the child was saying and he needed her to repeat herself but this afternoon his mind was firing on all cylinders and boy was that a relief, especially if there was ever a time for him to think straight, then it was now. 'Are we going to call them?' he asked.

'We're going to do better than that. We're going to go there. Me and you. It's going to be our secret mission, just like when you were in the war.'

Arthur beamed at the child. A secret mission. Yes, he was up for that. He saluted the child – some things you never forgot – pushed his shoulders back and jutted out his chin. 'Yes, sir.' It was an unexpected turn of events, but a good soldier was able to adapt to new orders with ease.

40

May 1944

Maryse stayed with Arthur that night, stating she had every intention of making the most of her time with him. Arthur wasn't going to argue with that one. As they emerged from the barn, the sound of someone shouting urgently and feet pounding across the courtyard of the farmhouse had Arthur and Maryse spinning around.

'It's Claude!' gasped Maryse as a young boy of about ten came hurtling towards them. He only stopped as Arthur caught him up in his arms.

'*Calme-toi. Calme-toi*,' said Arthur, as he released the boy.

'What's wrong, Claude?' asked Maryse, kneeling down in front of the red-faced child.

A flurry of words spilled from the boy and Arthur wasn't sure if he was translating it correctly. It was hard to understand the local dialect the boy was speaking. He could tell from the look on Maryse's face that it wasn't good. She looked up at Arthur.

'The Rochelle's house is being commandeered by the Germans. They have two hours to vacate the property. All the staff are to leave as well. Monsieur Rochelle is scared he is going to be taken away again.'

'What can we do?' asked Arthur urgently.

By this time Hugo had joined them from the house, after hearing all the commotion. 'There is nothing we can do,' he said gravely.

Maryse looked down at the child and held him close to her body. 'I am not going to let the Germans take the children.'

'Are you crazy?' demanded Hugo.

This was one of the few times Arthur agreed with Hugo, but at the same time he knew he couldn't stand by and let the children be deported. He'd heard dreadful stories of what the Germans were doing to the Jews. He stepped to Maryse's side and laid his hand on the boy's shoulder. 'We have to do something.'

'I am not going to stand by and let these children go,' said Maryse, with a determination Arthur hadn't heard before.

'You are asking for trouble. What are you going to do with two Jewish children?'

'Hide them. Keep them safe,' she retorted.

Brother and sister glared at each other for a few moments, before Hugo huffed and shook his head. 'Very well, but you have to go now.' He looked at Arthur. 'You stay here.'

'Wait a minute,' said Arthur. 'I'm not just going to sit here while Maryse goes off on her own.'

'My brother is right. You can't come. It will be too dangerous. If we're stopped, we'll both...' She paused as she glanced down at Claude. 'Well, you know what I'm saying. If I'm on my own it will be safer and I'll draw less attention to myself.'

'You can't just walk up to the house, take the kids and wander back as if you're out for a stroll,' countered Arthur. 'Once the Germans realise the children are gone, they will be looking for them and you. What if one of the staff tell them? No, I'll come with you. I'll go in and get the children. I'll bring them to you. That way, no one will know who has them.'

'Just do it. We haven't got time to argue. I agree with you. It's better you are in danger than my sister. Stay off the roads. Now, go!' barked Hugo. 'I'll take Claude back home.'

Maryse led the way, darting in and out of the trees, which to Arthur all looked pretty much the same. On any normal day, if the country wasn't occupied by the Germans, Arthur would have taken time to admire the trees, the bushes and the scenery around him. The light filtered through the branches like sparkling moonlight on a pond, dancing and shimmering as they wound their way along the path. But he couldn't indulge in the spectacular nature; he had to keep his wits about him. Any minute now they could run into trouble.

He kept a few paces behind Maryse and after about twenty minutes they came to the edge of the woods and the terrain sloped down towards a large imposing house.

'That's the Rochelle's house,' said Maryse. 'I don't know where the children are likely to be.'

'Don't worry. I'll find them.'

'I'm going to come with you,' said Maryse. 'The children will be frightened of you. They will trust me and come quietly.'

'But...' began Arthur, then realising it wouldn't make any difference to argue with Maryse, he closed his mouth. Besides, she was right. He just felt the extra responsibility now to keep Maryse safe. He wasn't sure what London would make of this escapade, but he didn't have time to ponder it. 'OK, I'll lead now. Stay close behind me and do what I say when I say it. Understand?'

'*Oui.*'

Keeping low, they scrambled down the hillside and slunk

their way to the back of the house. The double doors, which overlooked the rear of the garden, were open and ensuring no one was watching they slid into the sitting room.

The door on the other side was ajar, filtering through the sounds of urgent voices and hurried footsteps as the staff rushed around. No doubt collecting, sorting and hiding family artefacts.

It was then as Arthur looked around the room, he noticed that there was a blank space and an empty hook on the wall where a picture had been removed. A side table now stood empty except for a small lamp. The sort of table that would proudly display family photographs. It looked like this room had already been cleared.

They walked carefully across the wooden floor to the doorway. Arthur waited for the sound of footsteps to scurry past and then poked his head out. 'Come on,' he whispered and they hurried out of the room and up the main staircase. At the top of the landing, Arthur thought their luck had run out.

A tall man, with a moustache and greying hair, dressed in shirt and trousers stepped out of a room. Arthur recognised him as the man he'd seen being marched out of the house by the Gestapo. He started at the sight of Arthur, shock and alarm registering on his face.

Maryse moved in front of Arthur. 'Monsieur Rochelle, it's OK,' she said in hushed tones.

'Oh, Maryse. I've been praying you would come,' he said. 'I sent Claude to get you. He made it, then?'

'Yes, he did. He's with my brother now. Hugo is going to take him home. We've come to get Yvette and Jean-Paul.'

'Yes, come this way. They're in Yvette's room.'

They followed the man along the landing, coming to stop

outside a door at the end of the corridor. Monsieur Rochelle paused with his hand on the doorknob. He looked gravely at Maryse and then Arthur.

'You do know the probability of me returning is slim?'

Maryse lightly touched the older man's arm. 'I promise I will do everything I can to keep your children safe.'

Monsieur Rochelle patted her arm, tears gathering in his eyes. 'That will be the only thing that will keep me alive. Knowing they are safe and that one day...' His voice broke and he swallowed hard. 'That one day, I may see them again.'

It was an emotional moment, but Arthur was anxious not to stay any longer than necessary. 'Please, Monsieur,' he said softly. 'We need to get the children to safety as soon as possible.'

Monsieur Rochelle drew a deep breath and stood upright, his head held high. 'Of course.' He opened the door and Arthur and Maryse slipped inside after him.

The children were momentarily excited to see their schoolteacher and rushed to give Maryse a hug. Arthur hung back near the doorway, giving them space, not wanting to scare them but at the same time mentally urging them to hurry up.

'Now, children,' said Monsieur Rochelle. 'Maryse is here to take you back to her farm where she'll look after you until I've finished my business trip in Paris.'

'Hooray! We get to stay with you,' sang the girl. However, Arthur noticed her younger brother didn't share the enthusiasm. He remembered Maryse saying, the boy had been subdued and sad, that he was much more in tune with what was going on than his sister was.

Monsieur Rochelle hugged and kissed his children fiercely and Arthur couldn't imagine what was going through the man's mind. Stoically, Monsieur Rochelle managed to keep his voice light as he told his children how much he loved them and that they were to be good for Maryse while he was gone. The little lad clung to his father. Unable to stifle the sob that escaped from his throat, he buried his head into his father's shoulder.

Arthur felt a lump in his own throat. This was hard. The injustice of it all slammed around in his head. The inhumanity of it was incomprehensible. No man should have to say goodbye to his children under these circumstances.

The sound of car tyres on the gravel driveway and raised voices from outside broke up the farewell hugs. Maryse rushed to the window and with her back to the wall, sneaked a look out.

'They're here!' She dashed back across the room as Monsieur Rochelle hugged his children for the final time, telling them he loved them.

'Is there another way out of here?' asked Arthur, already opening the door and checking the hallway.

'There's a back staircase,' replied Monsieur Rochelle. 'It's hardly used. This way.'

They followed the Frenchman down the hallway and into another bedroom. 'It's here. It's the way the servants used to take the chamber pots so they didn't walk them through the main house. It hasn't been used for many years. Help me push it open.'

Arthur rushed over and leant against what looked like wood panelling. He could hear the German soldiers shouting orders and hammering on the main door downstairs. He groaned as he leaned into the hidden door, the pain in his shoulder shooting right up to his neck. After another effort, he felt the door give and then, finally free, it whipped open, causing Arthur to stumble with the momentum. 'Where does it come out?' he asked.

'At the back of the kitchen. It's a storeroom now,' said Monsieur Rochelle. 'The door opens onto the rear gardens. You can escape that way.' He turned to his children. 'You must be very quiet and very brave now.'

'But, Papa, I don't want to leave you,' said Jean-Paul.

Even Yvette looked concerned now. 'Why can't you come with us, Papa?'

'I will come as soon as I can. I promise.'

'I'm sorry but we have to go,' said Arthur. The voices of the soldiers were now echoing up the main stairwell. He suspected they had little more than seconds to escape. 'Monsieur, you must go downstairs and greet your guests,' he said. 'Try to remain as calm as possible. Delay them if you can from coming upstairs for the children. We need as much time as we can possibly get.'

Monsieur Rochelle passed Arthur a candle and lit it with a lighter from his pocket. He then held out his hand to Arthur. 'Thank you. May God be with you.'

Arthur shook the man's hand. He didn't believe in God but he recognised the hope in some divine being when there was nothing more a man could do.

Arthur refocused and led the way down the narrow staircase as it twisted its way down the turret of the house. They rounded the first corner, where it became even darker as the door to the bedroom was closed behind them. As they carefully made their way down, he could hear more footsteps and shouting from inside the house.

Reaching the bottom of the staircase, Arthur paused and rested his ear to the wooden door and listened. The room beyond the door sounded empty of life and, lifting the latch, he prepared to heave against the door but was relieved when it opened without so much as a creak of disapproval at being disturbed after all this time.

The storeroom was empty and he beckoned the children and Maryse out. The back door was opposite and after again checking there were no Germans about, he unlocked the door and shepherded his charges out into the fresh air.

Suddenly, there was a shout from within the house and as Arthur turned, he could see a German soldier, drawing his rifle in their direction.

'Halt!' the soldier shouted again.

41

They pulled up outside a traditional stone-built Bretagne house, picturesque enough to be on a postcard in a souvenir shop with its grey slate roof, walls rendered on the outside with exposed stonework around the doors and windows. Net curtains hung from a rail halfway down the window, depicting chickens. It was so twee and Maddy felt like they had stepped back in time.

She couldn't help thinking of Gramps and wondered if this was the sort of sight he was greeted with during the war. Joe had told her this part of Brittany hadn't been heavily bombed during the war, as the D-Day landings had stretched along the coast and further inland towards the east.

'All OK?' asked Joe, bringing her from her thoughts.

Maddy nodded. 'Yes, sorry, I was thinking of Gramps and wondering if I was treading in his footsteps – literally walking the path he had once walked.' She smiled despite herself. 'It's a far-fetched notion, I know.'

Joe smiled back in a soft and sympathetic way. 'Shall we?' he asked after a moment.

'Yes, let's do this,' said Maddy, rustling up her best gung-ho attitude.

Before they reached the door, it was opened and they were

greeted by an elderly lady, who Maddy estimated to be in her early seventies.

'*Bonjour,*' she said. '*Vous êtes Madeline Pettinger?*'

She said Maddy's surname slowly but successfully wrapped her tongue around the unfamiliar language construction. '*Oui. Bonjour, Madame Petit.*' Maddy stepped forward and held out her hand. '*C'est mon ami, Joseph.*' She used Joe's full name as she introduced him as her friend, thinking it would be more familiar for the older woman, in the same way as saying Madeline instead of Maddy.

'*Arlette.*' She shook Maddy's hand and then beckoned them inside.

They followed Arlette inside the house, which was darker than Maddy had expected due to the shutters being closed, but it was cool and made a refreshing contrast to the ever-warming afternoon. She remembered from holidays that it was often hotter in the afternoon despite the closing of the day.

'*Ma sœur, Cybille,*' said Arlette as they followed her into the living room.

Cybille was sitting in an armchair beside the fireplace with a crocheted blanket over her knees. There was a faint smell of cigarette smoke and Maddy noticed the dog-ends of hand-rolled cigarettes in the hearth of the fire. A walking stick was hooked onto the arm of the chair and Cybille raised a bony hand in their direction and nodded. '*Bonjour,*' she said, her voice husky, suggesting many years of smoking.

They undertook the greetings and Maddy introduced Joe again, who was suitably deferent to the older women and Maddy was reminded of his ability to put people at their ease, to somehow make them warm to him without him saying a word.

Arlette offered them coffee, which both Maddy and Joe accepted out of politeness more than desire, but she didn't want to offend their hosts. Twenty minutes passed before they were all sitting down with their drinks and the two sisters looked expectantly at their guests.

Maddy began by explaining about Gramps and how he was stationed in France for part of the war and how they were trying to trace a woman who was close to Gramps but had lost touch.

'Ah, so often the case in the war and afterwards,' said Arlette.

'Do you think our mother is that woman?' asked Cybille.

Maddy didn't miss the slight indignation in her voice. 'No, not that woman, but Maryse – the lady we are looking for – we believe may have stayed or was planning to stay in a guest house in England, which your mother owned or ran in Peterborough.'

'Our mother didn't own a guest house,' replied Cybille. She exchanged a look with her younger sister. 'Do you know anything about this, Arlette?'

'There was talk of a guest house,' insisted Arlette. 'Mother often spoke about it.'

Cybille tutted impatiently. 'Yes, but she didn't own it. She went on holiday to England with Mémé but that was in the fifties. We went with her.'

Maddy followed this exchange and could see confusion on Arlette's face as she tried to put all the facts into order and on Joe's face as he didn't understand what was being said but had no doubt picked up on the disagreement. He looked at Maddy for some sort of clarification but she gave a slight shake of her head as she tried to follow the sisters' conversation. They had lapsed into the Breton patois and she could only pick out a few words here and there but enough to get the general gist of their exchange.

Cybille finished with a humph and folded her hands on her lap in an act of finality, giving her sister a stern look. There was an uncomfortable silence before Arlette turned to Maddy.

'There appears to be some confusion as to whether you are looking for our mother or not,' she said. 'My sister may be older than me but she has a very good memory and perhaps I should have checked with her first, but the guest house I thought my mother owned, actually belonged to a family friend. An Englishwoman.'

Maddy leafed through the file that Joe had put together. 'Was your mother Amelie Cohen?'

'Yes, she was,' confirmed Cybille.

'And your father was called Jack?'

'That's right.'

'He was English?'

Arlette shook her head and Cybille raised her eyebrows in an exasperated way as if she knew all along this would end badly. Arlette spoke. 'Our father was French. Not English.'

'Jack Cohen?' Maddy repeated for clarity.

'Yes. That's right,' replied Arlette. She rattled off in Breton again and Cybille rose and from the cupboard, she retrieved a box containing official-looking papers which were slightly yellowing at the edges. She flipped through them and pulled out an envelope, which she then removed a slip of paper from. 'Here is his birth certificate.'

Maddy opened the document, examined the information and then silently passed it over to Joe as realisation dawned on her. She waited for him to absorb the contents.

'Shit,' he muttered to himself.

Both ladies looked expectantly at Maddy. 'I'm sorry we bothered you,' she said. 'There has been a mix-up. We're looking for Amelie Cohen who was married to Jack Cohen, spelt J A C K. Your father's name sounds the same but is spelt differently in French J A C Q U E S.'

Arlette tapped her heart with the palm of her hand. 'The same name. Both married to an Amelie? How can that be?'

'It's an amazing coincidence.' Maddy looked at Joe. 'Is there any way it could be the same man? He just used different spelling depending what country he was in?'

'I suppose it's possible.' He looked at the document again. 'Ask when their father married and when he died?'

Maddy relayed the question to Arlette and translated the answer to Joe. 'He died 10th June 1944 soon after the D-Day landings.'

'Our Jack Cohen died 15th July 1944,' said Joe.

'Oh no,' Maddy groaned, the comprehension of what had happened hitting her like a body blow. When she was on the phone confirming the details, had she muddled up June with July?

'I'm so sorry.' She looked at Joe and then at the sisters. 'We are really sorry. The dates of death are similar. It's my mistake. So sorry to have bothered you.'

A few minutes later after more grovelling apologies Maddy followed Joe back to the car. The silence filled the space, heavy and pressurised.

'I'm really sorry,' she said for the umpteenth time.

'It's OK. These things happen all the time.'

'But I've wasted the afternoon. I don't remember what I said but I can only imagine I got the months muddled up. And I think I only quoted the month and not the actual date of death.'

'I should have double-checked the French database. I'd have seen the names were spelt differently and it would have made me check everything else again. I would have found the dates of death were different.'

'You're being very gracious about it,' said Maddy.

'I'm being realistic.'

'And very chilled out.'

'No point getting upset over a little mistake.' Joe tapped in the address for Sérent on the satnav and they headed back for their second meeting of the day.

At some point Maddy must have nodded off on the journey. She awoke to the sound of Joe gently calling her name and tapping her forearm. 'Hey, sleepyhead,' he said. 'We're here.'

Maddy blinked and sat up with a start. 'I'm a lousy travelling companion, aren't I?'

'Fine by me.'

'Just hope I didn't snore or dribble.' She checked her reflection in the vanity mirror on the sun visor.

'Well, I can neither confirm nor deny any of that,' said Joe. He grinned at her as she looked in horror at him. 'I didn't notice any dribble and I turned the volume up on the radio.'

'You're joking. Please say you're joking.'

He got out of the car without answering and Maddy followed him, slightly concerned that he might not be joking. Wonderful!

The café they were meeting Amelie Cohen's daughter in was more traditional than the crêperie they had eaten in earlier. The heavy dark wood furniture was typical of the Breton style. There were about ten tables and roughly half of them occupied. The stone walls and tiled floor made the room feel refreshingly cool after being out in the heat of the day.

They were shown to a table by the window and brought water and bread while they browsed the menus.

Maddy's stomach gave a rumble. She clasped her hand to it and glanced over the top of the menu at Joe. Great, she sure knew how to make an impression on someone.

'Did you hear that?' said Joe, still looking at the menu. 'Sounded like thunder.'

'Oh, don't. Sorry. I didn't think I was hungry until I started looking at the options.'

He flashed her a smile. 'Could be worse.'

Maddy felt herself blush and shook her head at him. 'Enough,' she said. 'Back to the menu and decide what you want to eat. This is on me, by the way.'

'We can argue about that later,' said Joe. Maddy went to protest but Joe didn't give her a chance. 'Anyway, you're going to have to translate for me – it's all in French. I've just about made out ham and pizza but that's it.'

'What sort of thing do you fancy?' When he didn't reply, she glanced up at him and the smile at the corner of his mouth, and his raised eyebrows, had her blushing and burying her face behind the menu where she read out some options.

'I tell you what,' said Joe after she'd finished. 'You choose. Surprise me.'

'What? You might not like it.'

'Let me worry about that.'

'At least give me a clue.'

'Just go with your instinct.' He closed the menu, placed it on the table and sat back with his arms folded.

Maddy looked at him for a moment. 'Are you sure about this?'

'Absolutely.'

'You really want me to order you something?'

'One hundred per cent.'

'OK, if you're sure.'

'Totally.'

The waitress came over and Maddy placed their orders, speaking in French. 'Right, that's that done. I'm not going to tell you what I've ordered. It will be a surprise. You can guess what it is.'

'I'm suddenly wondering if this was a good idea. You've got a mischievous glint in your eye,' said Joe, breaking a piece of bread.

'It was your idea,' said Maddy.

After about twenty minutes, the waitress appeared at the table with their food.

'Madame,' said the waitress placing a salmon salad down in front of Maddy. And then to Joe. 'Monsieur.' A silver domed food cover hid his order.

'*Merci*,' said Maddy.

'I don't know if I dare look,' said Joe, eyeing up the dish in front of him. He glanced around the restaurant. 'Why is everyone watching?'

'I think they are simply interested in what you are having for dinner.'

Joe reached over and, with fingers poised on the ring handle on top of the dome, looked at Maddy. 'Me and my bright ideas.' He lifted the lid with a flourish and then yelled in surprise, nearly falling back off his chair. 'Urgh! What the f…?'

The restaurant erupted in laughter, Maddy included.

'Would Monsieur like some salt?' asked the waitress, somehow managing to keep a straight face.

Joe looked pleadingly at Maddy. 'What have you ordered?'

'*Langue de Boeuf*,' Maddy finally managed to say. 'Beef tongue.'

'What? I'm sorry, all bets are off. That is hideous. I can't eat it.' He pushed the plate away and dropped the lid back down to cover the food.

'Chicken,' said Maddy through more laughter.

'I'd sooner have chicken,' retorted Joe.

'So you're not going to eat it?' asked Maddy. She looked up at the waitress and grinned before looking back at Joe. 'Just as well I ordered you a Boeuf Lasagne.'

The waitress now grinning too, turned and took another dish from the side and presented it to Joe. And much to his relief, took the *Langue de Boeuf* away.

'Thank you, God,' said Joe, clasping his hands as if in prayer and looking up to the ceiling. 'Thank you.'

'Sorry, I couldn't resist that one,' said Maddy as she managed to get her laughter under control. 'Honestly, your face…'

Joe shook his head. 'I owe you now – you do realise that, don't you?'

'Ah, I see I'll have to be on my guard.'

They chatted over their meal, going over the misunderstanding of earlier yet again and discussing the way forward, both hoping Madame Beaufort would turn up and save the day.

Every now and then, one of them would glance up at the door or out of the window to see if Madame Beaufort was there but with it now being ten minutes past seven, Maddy was beginning to doubt the lady would turn up.

'Do you think she's going to come?'

At that moment a man, dressed casually in an open-necked

shirt and jeans came into the restaurant. He scanned the tables, his gaze coming to rest on Maddy and Joe. He strode over.

'Are you the woman who telephoned my mother this morning?' he asked in heavily accented English.

'Erm, yes. Madame Beaufort,' replied Maddy.

'I am her son. My mother is not coming. She does not want to speak to you. Please do not contact her again.' His manner was abrupt and firm, almost as if he was cross with her.

'Not coming?' Maddy broke into French, to ensure there was no misunderstanding.

'No.'

'But why? Why has she changed her mind? Did she tell you why we wanted to talk to her? It's important – it's my grandfather.'

The man held up his hand. 'No. Enough.' He too spoke in French. 'Please do not pursue this any further. I will call the police if you do. This is harassment. I forbid you to talk to her again.'

'Please, Monsieur, if I could just explain to you,' pleaded Maddy.

'I said no.' The man's voice rose in volume and a hush settled in the restaurant.

Joe got to his feet. 'Monsieur, please don't speak to Miss Pettinger like that. I don't know what's being said, but whatever it is, you're coming across as aggressive.'

Joe's tone was calm but his words were firm.

Maddy jumped to her feet. 'It's OK, Joe, I've got this.'

'Doesn't look like it,' said Joe, his eyes still locked onto the man.

'Joe. I can handle this,' she insisted.

'There is nothing to discuss,' said the man, in English. 'This is the end of the matter. Do not bother my mother again.' He turned and marched out of the restaurant, slamming the door behind him.

Aware they were now the sideshow for the evening, Maddy grabbed her handbag, found her purse and pulled out a bunch of notes. She left more than enough to cover the meal.

'Thanks for that,' she said, glaring at Joe.

'What have I done?'

'Butted in when I was dealing with it. I could have got him to change his mind.'

'Didn't look like you were doing a very good job,' retorted Joe. He picked up the notes and shoved them back at Maddy, before replacing them with his own.

Maddy threw her money back down. 'I don't need you to pay either. In fact, I'm not sure why I agreed to come on this stupid fool's errand. I should have told you to forget the whole thing in the first place.'

She rushed out of the restaurant, ignoring Joe calling her name.

42

May 1944

Arthur sped across the courtyard. 'Run! Take the children and run!' Maryse briefly glanced back but didn't falter as she grabbed the children by their hands and raced across the terrace and onto the lawn beyond, cutting through the treelined privy for shelter. Arthur darted behind a pillar, his handgun drawn, held up against his chest. He listened to the sound of the soldier's boots clatter across the flagstones as he pursued his target. Arthur held his nerve. Timing was key. His instincts were telling him to jump out now, but he managed to control the urge and then as the footsteps sounded right on top of him, the soldier ran past and with the butt of his handgun, Arthur thumped the German on the back of the neck.

The soldier dropped like a stone, his rifle clattering on the terrace. Arthur didn't have time to see if the German was alive or not. Any second now the area would be swamped with other soldiers. He dragged the lifeless body to the edge of the terrace and rolled him under the shrubs. At least he'd be out of sight for a while and it might buy him enough time to get Maryse and the children to safety. He picked up the rifle though and took it with him as he made his escape out of the grounds.

He was dismayed to see Maryse waiting on the other side of the rise, huddled with the children against a tree. 'Why didn't you carry on?'

'You don't know the way,' she protested, clearly annoyed at his questioning.

'I would have found the farm,' he replied, trying to keep his own annoyance at bay. They shouldn't have stopped. The children couldn't cover the terrain as quickly as he could and could have done with a head start. No point arguing about it now; it was all academic. 'Right, well, let's get moving.'

Maryse led the way, running through the trees, holding Yvette's hand while Arthur took hold of Jean-Paul's. They could hear more shouting in the distance coming from the house.

Maryse looked around at Arthur but he shook his head to silence her. He didn't want to frighten the children any more than they already were. Sobbing children could give them away to any outlying soldiers.

Maryse appeared to understand and, picking up the pace, continued their escape. When Yvette complained her legs were aching, Arthur gave her a piggy-back. 'We need to keep moving,' he said. He passed the boy's hand from his to Maryse's. 'Make sure Maryse keeps up the pace,' he said, looking earnestly at the ten-year-old.

Jean-Paul nodded and whether he knew Arthur was patronising him or not, it was hard to tell, but he did as he was told. Maybe it was to disguise his own feelings of fear, thought Arthur.

The voices from the house faded with each step the escape party made and it wasn't until they had been moving for fifteen minutes that Arthur began to relax and believe they had managed to avoid capture.

It was then he heard the low and distinctive rumble of an engine. Too deep to be a car, more like a small truck. One that transported troops around. It grew louder as it drew nearer, travelling along the road that ran parallel with the woods they were navigating.

'Stop,' said Arthur in a hushed voice. He had to repeat himself for Maryse to hear. She turned and there was genuine fear in her eyes.

'We're only ten minutes away from the farm,' she whispered. 'Can't we keep going?'

'Not just yet.' The truck was coming along the road. He could make out the dark grey shape of the vehicle from his position in the trees. It rumbled past them, but then came to a stop about fifty metres ahead.

Almost immediately, German soldiers disembarked from the back of the lorry. Arthur counted six as they lined up in the road and a sergeant began issuing orders. Arthur swore under his breath.

'Are they looking for us?' asked Yvette. Her voice trembled as she spoke.

'I think they are,' replied Arthur. 'But don't worry, we'll get out of here before they find us.' He exchanged a look with Maryse but said nothing. He was sure she was aware of the extreme danger they were in. 'Now what I want you two to do,' said Arthur turning to look at the two frightened siblings, 'is to go with Maryse. She will take you to safety and I'll stay here to make sure they don't follow you.'

'No!' hissed Maryse. 'You can't stay. You must come with us.'

'I'm better alone. I can move faster, hide better, take care of myself better if I don't have to worry about where you three are.' He patted Maryse's bag she had slung across her body, which housed the handgun he knew she had with her. 'You must protect yourself too.'

Maryse eyed him for a moment and he thought she might argue but she leaned across and kissed him. 'Make sure you come back,' she whispered.

Before she could turn to leave there was a crunch of feet on twigs behind them and Arthur spun around, pointing the rifle and simultaneously releasing the safety catch.

'*Merde!* What are you doing?' It was Hugo.

'What the hell are you doing?' retorted Arthur, lowering the weapon. 'You nearly got your bloody head blown off!'

Hugo gave a sceptical look. 'And you nearly got your throat slit.'

The two men glared at each other. It was only Maryse's intervention that broke the deadlock. 'There are German soldiers down there. They're looking for us.'

Hugo nodded. 'Come, quickly.'

They began to move in a crouching position deeper in amongst the trees, and it was only then that Arthur noticed several more men with Hugo. He recognised one from the farm and assumed the others were part of the local resistance. He couldn't help feeling both relieved they now had backup and annoyed that Hugo felt he wasn't able to deal with the evacuation of a couple of kids. His ego was slightly bruised but he knew that now was an inappropriate time to worry about male pride.

Keeping close to Maryse and the children, ready at a moment's notice to protect them, Arthur kept a keen eye on the trees ahead and those to the roadside. Again, the sound of orders being issued and booted feet pounding on the road filtered through the woods ahead of them. Arthur feared they were running straight into trouble.

'Shouldn't we move further into the woods?' he asked in a low voice to Hugo, which only earned him a scowl in reply.

A few minutes later, there was a shout from ahead. It was the soldiers.

'*HALT! ARRETEZ-VOUS!*' came a heavy-accented German voice.

Arthur pushed Maryse and the children behind a large fallen tree, shielding them with his body as he peered over the top of the log. Maryse appeared beside him. He was about to tell her to duck down when he changed his mind. It would be pointless; he could see a look of determination in her eyes. She wasn't going to shrink away.

A gunshot rang out. It had come from one of the resistance fighters. Immediate retaliation began as the Germans fired off a rally of shots, sending Arthur and Maryse ducking for cover behind the tree. Yvette let out a whimper and Maryse put her arms around the girl's shoulder.

'Stay calm,' she instructed. 'You need to be ready to run when I tell you to. Do exactly what I say. Understand?'

'*Oui*,' came the fragile reply.

More shots were exchanged between the two groups, Arthur using the rifle he had acquired at the house. It fired off to the right and it took a couple of shots for Arthur to get his eye in. The next few minutes passed in a haze of bullets as both sides took casualties.

'We need to get out of here!' shouted Arthur to Hugo who was several metres away, pinning his back to the trunk of a large pine tree for cover.

It was not without a begrudging acknowledgement that Hugo ordered his men to retreat back to where Maryse and the children were. He issued firing cover to allow them the chance to escape. 'You go with them,' he told Arthur. 'Hurry!'

Arthur's heart was pumping hard with adrenaline. He didn't feel frightened. He didn't have time to feel anything other than a sense of purpose. At whatever cost, he would give his life to make sure Maryse and the children got out of this unscathed.

As they ran, keeping low, through the trees, shots still rang out. He felt something whiz past his shoulder and the bark of the tree in front of him exploded as a bullet lodged itself in the wood.

'Faster!' he shouted. Another bullet shot past. Yvette let out a cry and clasping her hands to her ears, her eyes scrunched tightly closed, she dropped to her knees. Arthur scooped her up. 'Run!' he shouted. 'Keep running. *Allez! Allez!*'

They didn't have time to slow down. The bullets had come far too close for his liking. The Germans must have somehow outflanked Hugo and his men.

Without warning, they came to a rise in the terrain and Maryse, who was leading the way, stopped in her tracks. She was breathing hard as she surveyed the steep slope before her. It was about twenty feet, Arthur estimated. It looked clear of any rocks, just a ragged mossy, grass slope.

'Is this the quickest way?' he asked.

'Once we're down there, we can cross the stream and there's a drainage ditch we can run along. We won't be seen from up here.' She eyed the drop. 'It's very steep.'

'We don't have a choice,' replied Arthur. 'Now, children, I want you to lie flat on your stomachs, and slide down the hill with your feet first.'

Yvette shook her head. 'I'm scared.'

'It will be OK. I promise,' said Arthur.

'I'll go first,' said Maryse. 'I'll wait at the bottom to catch you. Watch how I do it.'

'I don't want to.' Yvette began to cry.

'You have to,' said Jean-Paul. 'Papa said you had to be brave. Stop crying.'

Arthur gave Jean-Paul's shoulder a gentle pat. He may only be ten years old but he had a wise head on his shoulders.

'Now, Yvette. I won't allow you to argue with me,' said Maryse, her voice taking on an authoritative tone. Her schoolteacher voice, Arthur guessed. It had the right effect as Yvette looked up at her teacher, with a slightly stunned expression, but she sniffed and managed to stifle another sob. 'Very good,' continued Maryse. 'Now, I'm going down first. You next and Jean-Paul afterwards. Christophe will follow us. Do you understand?'

'*Oui, madame*,' replied Yvette.

With that Maryse dropped to her stomach and with her feet and hands stretched out, allowed herself to slide down the bank. If there were any stones or small rocks, grazing her body as she went down, she didn't let it show on her face. She kept her eyes firmly fixed on Yvette's. Dust, dirt and leaves scuffed up as Maryse made her descent and Arthur realised that this trail would easily be spotted by the Germans if they came here. Speed was of the essence.

'Right, Yvette and Jean-Paul, why don't you go down together, side by side? You can make sure each other is safe then?'

Yvette was more cheered by this suggestion and within seconds, after making Yvette promise not to cry out, Arthur was watching the two children bump and slide their way down the embankment. He was relieved when Maryse sweep them up.

As he turned he saw a streak of grey storm through the trees. There was a flash of a gun muzzle and next a searing hot pain pierced his shoulder, the velocity spinning him around and sending him plummeting into thin air as he fell. The wind was knocked out of him as he hit the ground and unable to do anything to stop himself, his body tumbled and twisted as it sped to the bottom of the embankment. He vaguely registered a shriek but then everything went black.

43

Joe muttered a hurried apology at the other diners, albeit in English, threw in a couple of *pardons* in his best French accent and finished off with an *au revoir* before hurrying out after Maddy.

That had escalated fast and he wasn't entirely sure where from. He was still trying to fathom out exactly what he'd done wrong. He looked up and down the pavement left and right. He caught sight of her disappearing around the corner of the church, which stood in the middle of the square.

'Maddy! Wait!' he called, breaking into a jog.

'Go away!' She didn't turn but her words were clear and bounced off the walls of the surrounding buildings.

'Maddy, please!' He was at her side now. He skipped around in front of her, now literally on the back foot and half-walking half-jogging to stop her ploughing into him. 'I'm sorry,' he said. 'Can we talk about this? Please, Maddy?'

She stopped walking and he let out a sigh of relief, but she performed a sharp ninety-degree turn and started marching off again. 'I don't want to talk to you,' she said.

Once again, Joe placed himself in her path. 'You can't just walk off like this. You're not being fair. I don't entirely know what I've done to piss you off – I can make a guess and apologise but I want to talk about this like adults, not a couple of stroppy teenagers.'

Joe winced inwardly at the anger that washed over Maddy's face. Not the right thing to say.

'Stroppy teenager! Huh!'

'Well, you're not exactly being adult about it.' In for a penny in for a pound.

This time she did stop. Her arms folded across her chest, her mouth set in a firm line and her eyebrows knitting together, creasing her forehead. 'If you must know,' she began, 'I am quite capable of looking after myself. I don't need you or anyone else for that matter stepping in like something out of *The Bodyguard*.'

Joe raised his hands in surrender. 'OK. OK. I misjudged the situation. I was only trying to help. I apologise.'

'I could have talked him round. I didn't need you butting in. Now we're never going to find Maryse. We don't have any other leads.'

'Again, I apologise,' said Joe. He was getting a better idea on what was making Maddy so cross and it wasn't necessarily just his actions. Her hopes of finding Maryse had taken a knock and the desperation was manifesting itself in anger directed at him for... for what? For sticking up for her? Why did he do that? 'Look, Maddy, I didn't think. It was an automatic reaction. I would have done the same if it had been Kay, Matt or any one of my friends. It wasn't some display of macho ownership or playing the hero and defending your honour as a woman; it wasn't a slight or an insult at your ability to look after yourself; it was just me looking out for a friend.'

Her shoulders slumped and she looked away. Her anger sapped and extinguished. She looked back at him, down at her feet. 'I may have over-reacted a little,' she finally admitted. She looked up at him and grimaced. 'A lot. I'm sorry.'

'Apology accepted.' He pushed his hands into the pockets of his jeans. He had this urge to wrap his arms around her and tell her it was all right, but he wasn't sure of the reception he'd receive.

'I mean it,' she said.

'I know. So do I.'

There was a small pause. 'So… are we OK?'

'I am if you are.'

'You're far too easy-going,' she said.

'Despite that little display of male preening back there, I'm not really into confrontation.'

'It wasn't until that moment, when the opportunity to find Maryse and to complete the puzzle, to perhaps give Gramps some kind of resolution was denied, that I realised how badly I wanted it. And now…' she gave a despondent shake of her head '…and now, our only lead has gone. I feel gutted.'

'It's not the end of the road. It's a disappointment, I know, but there are other ways and means.'

'Legal?'

'Best not to ask. But I promise you, Maddy, I'll do everything I possibly can, call in every favour I'm owed and rack up a few in the process, to find Maryse.' He tipped his head down and looked up under her fringe. 'Want a hug?'

She stepped forward and put her arms around his waist, resting her head against his chest. He was surprised she'd taken him up on the offer, but he knew that despite the strong independent woman exterior, there was also a tender woman who was used to doing the hugging mostly. He closed his arms around her back and rested his chin on her head. Then unexpectedly, probably surprising Maddy as much as he did himself, he moved his chin and dropped a kiss on her head.

She pulled back only enough to lift her head.

Joe returned the look. A thousand thoughts swirled around in his head. Right at this moment, things could go either one way or the other. He surprised himself again when he found himself wishing for a particular outcome.

'*Monsieur! Madame!*' A voice from across the road broke the moment and both Joe and Maddy's attention was drawn sharply to the restaurant owner hurrying across the street to them. She was waving some euros in her hand.

Joe groaned at the interruption. 'It's your change,' he said to Maddy. '*Merci, madame.*' He smiled at the older woman. She didn't smile back but her frown deepened. She spoke quickly to Maddy as she pushed the ten-euro note into her hand. And then she was gone as abruptly as she had arrived. 'What was that all about?'

Maddy had a stunned look on her face. 'I can't believe it.'

Joe wasn't sure if she was speaking to him or to herself. 'What did she say? What can't you believe?'

44

'All is not lost,' said Maddy, turning to Joe, a look of excitement now taking residence on her face. 'The lady from the restaurant, she just had a phone call from Amelie Cohen's daughter.'

'What, the one who doesn't want to see us?'

Maddy grabbed Joe's arm. 'That's just it, she does want to see us. It was her son who didn't want her to. She couldn't say anything to her son, but she wants to meet us tomorrow.'

'Wow! That's brilliant!' Her delight was contagious, and he found himself grinning madly at her. 'Did she say when?'

'We have to wait here while Mass is on and she'll slip out of the church to speak to us.'

'You know what this must mean?' He paused, waiting for Maddy's train of thought to catch up with his.

'She must have something to tell us. There must be some sort of secret or something. Oh, God, Joe, wouldn't it be wonderful if we can find Maryse?' She flung her arms around him, laughing as she did so.

Instinctively, Joe lifted her up and swung her around. 'Woohoo!' He joined in with her mini celebration, giving her one more twirl before returning her to terra firma. 'That would explain why the son was so against us speaking to her.'

There must be some connection and one he doesn't want us to find out, even after all this time.'

'I have no idea what it could be. Even when Gramps was younger and, you know, his memory was better, he never spoke in any detail about the war.'

'People didn't. Still don't. It was such a horrific thing to endure and I think those who went to war – the servicemen – they saw the worst of it. But they didn't have the support then like they do now. No one recognised PTSD. It was a case of suck it up and don't talk about it.'

Maddy looked thoughtful. 'I hope Gramps hasn't suffered in silence all these years.'

'Don't go getting yourself all depressed about it,' said Joe. 'There's nothing you can do to change what's happened. Your grandfather was loving and kind – still is. I'd like to wager he's been OK. The only thing that has troubled him is Maryse.'

'Exactly. Which is why it's so important we find out what happened.'

'And I'm going to do everything and anything in my power to see we do.' Joe wasn't sure he had been so sincere about anything in a long time.

'You know what, Joe Finch?'

He raised his eyebrows. 'What's that?'

'I'm so glad you convinced me this would be a good idea. And I can't thank you enough for agreeing to help, even when I can only pay your expenses. I do appreciate it.' There was a deep sincerity in not only her voice but in her eyes too – eyes he couldn't stop looking at, transfixed by their intensity.

'I'm so glad as well,' he said. There was an awkward silence, neither apparently capable of speech. Joe gave himself a mental shake and broke the deadlock first. 'Heard from home?'

'No, but that's a timely reminder to call them.' Maddy looked a little flushed as she delved into her bag for her phone.

The evening temperature was still warm as they strolled along the riverbank, and the tranquillity and serenity slowly began to suck away the tension between them. A motorboat passed them, the gentle hum of the engine easing its way through the water, while in the distance, the church bell rang out the hour.

Maddy spoke to Kay and then to Esther. From what Joe could hear of her side of the conversation, it sounded like everyone was fine and had had a great day.

'They've all been to the park and fed the ducks,' said Maddy as she slipped her phone back into her bag. 'Esther and Sheila have made some rock cakes and now they're playing scrabble. Kay and Gramps against Esther and Sheila.'

'Perfect,' said Joe, feeling they were back on an even footing. 'I told you Kay was great. You can stop worrying now.'

'Apparently, though, Gramps has been talking about the children in the picture a lot.'

'Really? What's he been saying?'

'The same sort of thing. He's been asking Esther if she knows the little girl. If they were friends and does she know what happened to her?'

Joe grimaced. 'Whatever the connection is, it's obviously bothering him.'

'The same way Maryse has been bothering him.'

'Esther's been keeping him company, which is lovely, but I do hope when she starts her new school in September that she makes some friends. At the moment she hasn't got anyone her own age.'

'I'm sure she'll be fine. She's a lovely kid. Very sociable.'

'Thanks. You know she thought a lot of you. Still does, as it happens.'

'Not sure I deserve that loyalty,' said Joe honestly. It hadn't been only Maddy he'd hurt in the past; Esther had been a casualty too. Something he'd never been able to reconcile.

'I don't want her getting hurt again, Joe.' Maddy ground to a halt and looked out at the river, her arms folded against her body.

'It's the last thing I want.'

'She's only a child. She has no coping mechanisms. She hasn't got the experience to know when to protect her heart.'

'Unlike you. Is that what you're saying?' Joe dug his hands into his pockets. It was the safest thing to do with them. Putting them around Maddy wasn't on the list of options right now.

'Yeah. Unlike me,' replied Maddy with a note of sadness. 'Although, some things are easier said than done.'

Crickey! He wanted to tell her she didn't need to protect herself against him but he knew it wasn't as simple as that. He needed to be patient and take this slowly. 'I've always been honest with you,' he said. 'And that won't change. I promise.'

'Come on, let's get back. I don't know about you but I'm shattered and we've an early start in the morning,' replied Maddy, almost dismissing what he had said. Had he hit a nerve? Had he rushed it already? She began walking back the way they'd come but paused and turned to look at him. 'And, Joe, don't make promises you can't keep.'

'That's promise number two,' he called after her before jogging to catch up.

45

A rthur was sitting in the garden with the child and the dog, as they watched the birds dart out of the bushes to land on the bird feeder for a few seconds, peck at the seeds the child had put there earlier, before shooting back to the safety of the foliage.

'There's a robin,' said Arthur. 'He's a bit of a bully. Likes to scare the other birds away.'

The child had a book of garden birds open on her lap and a pair of small binoculars held to her eyes. 'There's another bird now with a black crown.' She lowered the binoculars and checked in the book. 'I think it's a great tit.'

'Very good,' commented Arthur, following the flight of the robin who was now sitting in the apple tree surveying the goings-on. He was reminded of a song. He wasn't quite sure where the recollection had come from, but he began singing the words. '*Alouette, gentille Alouette, Alouette je te plumerai…*'

'I know that song,' said the child and joined in with him.

At the end of the verse, the sound of someone clapping made both Arthur and the child turn around. It was the nurse.

'*Bravo!*' she declared. 'You'd win one of those TV talent shows with that. You'd melt everyone's hearts.'

'We could record it for my vlog,' said the child enthusiastically. 'Mum can't complain about that.'

'You should check with her first,' warned the nurse and then to Arthur: 'Now, I've got to go down to the pharmacy and collect a prescription for you. I've just been checking the medication and we're short on one thing.'

'Where's Sheila? Is she going with you?' asked the child.

'No, she's going to stay here.'

'We would be all right on our own,' replied the child.

'I'm sure you will but your mum would prefer someone else stayed with you. I won't be long.'

'Maybe we should get Gramps his coat. It's getting a bit chilly,' suggested the child and with that hopped up and disappeared indoors.

Arthur wasn't sure if he had said he was cold and he didn't think he was, but the child had made up her mind and here she was back now with his big overcoat.

'I'm not sure Gramps needs his big coat,' remarked the nurse.

'It's his favourite,' insisted the child and was already slipping Arthur's arm through the sleeve. He went along with her and soon had another layer of clothing on. It was a bit bulky but Arthur did like this coat. He noticed the child push a bag under her chair and was now putting on a jacket herself.

'Are you cold too?' asked the nurse. 'Perhaps you should both go inside.'

'No, we want to watch the birds, don't we, Gramps?'

Arthur nodded. It seemed the right response.

Sheila came outside to sit with them. 'Ooh, I didn't think it was coat-wearing weather.'

'Neither did I,' said the nurse. 'But who am I to argue?' She smiled as she spoke. 'Right, I'll head off now. I shouldn't be any longer than thirty or forty minutes. Ring me on my mobile if you need me.' She handed Sheila the house phone. 'My number is on speed dial; you just have to press the on button here and then press number two and that will call me.'

'Perfect,' said Sheila.

'Sheila,' began the child after the nurse had left. 'I think me and Gramps will go inside now. We could have some cake. I made it this morning.'

'Oh, that would be nice.'

The child helped Arthur up from his chair and they made their way indoors. 'Shall I take my coat off?' asked Arthur, fiddling with buttons.

'No. Leave it on for now,' instructed the child.

It seemed odd to Arthur that he should keep his coat on indoors, but he did as she wanted and soon they were sitting in the living room. The child flicked the small heater on before Sheila came back in with the tea and cake.

'Oh, this is cosy,' said Sheila as she settled into the armchair.

'Let's listen to some music,' said the child, going over to the radio and turning it on. She sat back down on the sofa near Gramps with the dog making itself comfortable on the rug near the heater.

Arthur must have nodded off. The next thing he knew the child was gently shaking his arm and whispering to him to wake up. He went to speak, but she put her finger to her lips. 'Sheila is asleep,' she said. 'Come on, we're going out on an adventure. We're going to find out about Yvette.'

Yvette! They were going to see Yvette? Arthur certainly wasn't going to protest. He liked the sound of an adventure and the child's eyes were wide with excitement. He wondered if they should wake Sheila and take her with them but the child was hurrying him out of the room, down the hall and out through the front door.

'Stay there, Fifi,' she said to the dog, giving her a biscuit. 'Good girl.'

'Where to now?' asked Gramps.

'Into the taxi,' replied the child. She guided him down the path and opened the door of a waiting saloon car. Arthur shuffled himself in and the child climbed in next to him. 'Little Paxton, please.'

'Just the two of you?' asked the driver.

'Yes. My dad is waiting for us at Little Paxton,' replied the child.

'If you're sure.' The driver looked at Arthur in the rear-view mirror.

'Yes, we're sure,' said Arthur.

The driver took a look at the house and then back at Arthur. 'OK. Little Paxton it is.'

Arthur settled back and although the seat belt was uncomfortable as it pressed against his sore shoulder, he did his best to ignore it. He'd experienced far worse discomfort in his time, he thought as he looked out of the window.

46

May 1944

The pain burned into his shoulder. He screamed out loud. Tried to move. Hands held him tight. Forcing him back down on the hard surface. Voices he didn't recognise gabbled away all around him. He couldn't understand what they were saying. The pain came again. Hands tightened even more so this time he couldn't move. He screamed. Someone stuffed something hard in his mouth and he bit down, tasting wood.

Arthur's eyes pinged open and a blur of faces looked over him. Who were these men? What were they doing to him?

Someone removed the wood from his mouth and he felt the cold glass neck of a bottle being pushed up against his lips and then the liquid hitting the back of his throat. He swallowed. A reflex reaction. Whisky.

He took greedy gulps.

Coughed.

Spluttered.

And then allowed himself to slip back into the blackness.

Until the next stab of pain.

The cycle repeated itself several more times and when Arthur next became conscious, he was first aware of the silence around him. There was no stinging, burning pain, just a constant throb.

Tentatively he opened his eyes. It took a moment to clear his vision and when he was able to see properly, he was rewarded with the sight of Maryse. She was asleep in a chair on the other side of the room. She looked so peaceful and content.

He tried to sit himself up but as he did so, pain shot through his shoulder. He let out an acute groan.

Maryse woke with a start and jumped to her feet. Two strides and she was next to him.

'Are you all right? Look at me? Are you all right?'

'I'm right as rain,' he said sarcastically. 'Chipper. Just chipper.'

He flopped back on whatever the hell he was lying on. His hands felt the sides of the surface. It was thick heavy oak. He turned his head to take in the rest of the room and realised he was in the dining room of Maryse's farmhouse. He raised his eyebrows at the observation. Promotion, eh? No longer shoved out in the barn.

Then the events of the past few hours came crashing to his mind. He looked down at his shoulder and raised his opposite hand to feel the wound. He winced as he did so.

'Don't touch it,' ordered Maryse, leaning over and taking his hand away. 'I've dressed it but I don't want you to get it infected. We need to keep it as sterile as possible.'

'What happened? Are the children all right?' asked Arthur.

'The children are safe,' Maryse reassured him. 'They are upstairs playing quietly.'

'And everyone else?'

'Hugo is safe. We lost one man. Another injured and yourself.'

'I'm sorry,' he said.

She bowed her head. 'Thank you but he died fighting for his country. No one will forget him for that.'

Fragments of memories like still frames began to invade Arthur's thoughts. He remembered the German soldiers and he remembered the children sliding down the embankment. Where were they going? Oh, yes, that's right: Maryse had mentioned a drainage ditch. Then the image of Hugo and some of the other resistance fighters emerging from the trees, their guns in their hands. The Germans must have been hot on their heels. Then he remembered the flash of light from one of the rifles. He remembered spinning around and falling. After that it was all still a blank. 'How did I get here?'

'My brother and some of the men. They carried you.'

Arthur gave a hollow laugh. 'I bet that pained him.' Maryse gave him a reproachful look, but there was the faintest of smiles at the corners of her mouth. 'Must remember to thank him,' finished Arthur.

'Best not to. He was less than impressed at having to carry you.' Maryse leant over further and her lips brushed his own. 'I'm glad they did though.'

'Must get shot more often,' murmured Arthur as they broke their embrace for a moment. 'Although, must make sure it's purely superficial. Nothing fatal. Bit pointless otherwise.'

'Stop,' said Maryse. 'You had me very frightened.'

The numbing effects of the alcohol were beginning to wear

off and the unmistakable deep-rooted pain was firing up now. 'How bad is it?' asked Arthur.

'I'm not a nurse,' said Maryse avoiding eye contact with him.

'In your opinion... how bad? Is it as bad as it bloody well feels?'

'The doctor who came – he said...'

'Just say it.'

Maryse hesitated a fraction before she replied. 'He said you're lucky to still have your arm...'

'And what else?'

She hesitated only for a moment, blinking back tears that had gathered in her eyes. 'Your arm will be of little or no use to you.'

Arthur let out a low whistle. Not for any particular reason other than to stop himself shouting or screaming at the prognosis. What sort of doctor was this man anyway? What would he know about these types of injuries? 'I'll get a proper medical opinion from the army.'

This time she let the tears fall freely and leaned her head on his good shoulder. 'I'm so sorry. So sorry.'

He stroked her hair and kissed her head. 'Hey, don't feel sorry for me. It could have been worse.' His words sounded empty and in all honesty, they probably were. He had never imagined himself as a war casualty. What bloody use was he now?

'They're talking about flying you out of here with the next moon,' said Maryse. She sobbed harder this time and it was then that Arthur realised the implications of what she was saying.

'They're sending me home?'

'*Oui*. Back to England. I won't see you again.'

'Oh, Maryse, my darling Maryse. That's not true. We will see each other again. I promise. I will come back for you. I will find you. I'll never stop looking for you. All you have to do is survive the war and I will find you.'

47

The ride in the car was pleasant and Arthur sat back in his seat and enjoyed watching the streets lined with houses gradually disappear as they left behind the village, zooming along a main road heading for somewhere the child was excited about. He tried to catch a glimpse of the road signs as they sped along at a steady speed but he didn't have enough time to decipher the coding of the alphabet.

'So, what are you going to Little Paxton for?' asked the taxi driver.

'Visiting my dad,' replied the child.

'And to see Yvette,' added Arthur. They were going to see her, weren't they? Isn't that what the child had said?

'Oh, right. Is she your daughter?' asked the driver.

'Yes,' put in the child before Arthur could answer. Was Yvette his daughter? He didn't think so, but he could be wrong. The child was now tapping his arm and distracting him from his thoughts. She was showing him something on that TV screen thingy bob she carried around with her a lot. Oh, there were their faces. It was like a camera.

'Just taking a selfie,' she said. 'Smile, Gramps.'

Arthur wasn't sure how long they'd been in the car for,

but they were now pulling off the busy road onto a smaller, quieter one.

'Where in the village do you want to go?' asked the driver.

'To the church,' replied the child. She checked something on the thingy bob. 'It's St James's Church.'

A few minutes later, the taxi pulled up outside a church that reminded Arthur of the one he used to attend when he was a boy. It was a sand-coloured stone building with a bell tower at one end. A weathervane fixed at the top of the tower wavered in the breeze.

The driver was speaking to him, asking for some money. Arthur wasn't sure how much he was asking for but the child was looking in her purse. She pulled out a note and handed it over to the driver.

'Do you want the change?' he asked.

The child shook her head and hopped out of the car, coming around to Arthur's side and helped him climb out.

'I'm glad we're not in that car anymore,' said Arthur as the white saloon pulled away. 'It was too cramped. Now, where are we off to? Who are we visiting? Are we going to church?'

'Yes. We're going to see Reverend Jenny Jones,' replied the child. 'She's the vicar. She should be out of the service in about ten minutes. We can wait here on the bench.'

'Jenny? Is that the vicar?' asked Arthur. He wasn't sure he was understanding this right. 'That's a lady.'

The child grinned at him. 'That's right, Gramps. The vicar is a lady.'

Arthur raised his eyebrows. 'Well, I never.' He wasn't quite sure when that had become a thing but he hadn't heard of it before. Oh well, he was sure she was nice. Her name sounded nice anyway.

They sat down on the bench at the side of the path that

threaded its way through the graveyard. It didn't look a big graveyard and Arthur wondered where they put everyone these days. He was glad of his coat as although the sun was shining, the wind was a little on the chilly side. The child slid along the bench next to him and fixed her eyes on the wooden church doors.

'Did Sheila come with us?' asked Arthur, looking around. He couldn't see his friend anywhere and he was sure she was with them earlier.

The child shifted on the bench. 'Erm, no, Sheila stayed at home to look after Fifi,' she said eventually, not meeting his gaze.

Arthur was puzzled by the child. He couldn't put his finger on what it was exactly but he got the sensation she felt uneasy about something.

The church bell chimed and shortly afterwards the Sunday morning congregation began to emerge. Arthur surveyed the people spilling out. Most of them were hurrying along their way and a few stood talking in small groups, buttoning up their coats against the chill that was now in the air.

The child got to her feet and was trying to see over the heads of the villagers. He could tell by the look on her face she had spotted something or someone of interest. She turned excitedly to him. 'Up you get, Gramps. The vicar is over there. Let's go and talk to her.'

'The vicar? Yes, let's go,' agreed Arthur, getting to his feet with the help of his walking stick. He followed the child along the path and they waited patiently for the remaining group of people to disperse.

A kindly-looking woman turned and smiled at them. 'Hello. I don't think we've met,' she said, holding out her hand.

The child shook hands and Arthur did the same, noticing then the dog collar around the woman's neck. She was a vicar! He frowned to himself. Had he been told that? It wasn't entirely a surprise.

'I'm Esther Pettinger-Shaw and this is my great-grandfather, Arthur Pettinger.'

'Very pleased to meet you both,' replied the vicar. 'Do you have relatives in the village? Are you visiting?' The vicar looked at Arthur as she spoke but it was the child who took up the conversation.

'No, we don't,' she replied. 'We're trying to find out about some evacuees from the war who were here and we looked on the website and it said there were church records.'

'Indeed, there are.' The vicar remained smiling. 'They aren't kept here at the church though. They're back at the vicarage.'

'Can we see them?' asked the child. 'We're only here for a day visit.'

The vicar considered the request and checked her watch. 'I don't see why not,' she said eventually. 'I have a home visit but that's not for another couple of hours.'

'Thank you!' exclaimed the child. 'Gramps, we can go back to the vicar's house and look at the records.'

'Oh, that is good,' replied Gramps.

'Is it just the two of you?' asked the vicar as she locked the church door.

'Yes. Just me and Gramps.'

The vicar began walking along the path that wove through the graveyard to the rear of the premises where a small wooden gate was located. 'Through here.' She held the gate open as Arthur followed the child through. 'Have you come far?'

'Hemingford Grey. We got a taxi,' replied the child.

The gate opened into a cottage garden that reminded Arthur of his own back home. He had a sudden pang of homesickness and a small panic welled inside his chest. This wasn't his home. What was he doing here? Where was he? Where was Maddy?

'Are you OK, Mr Pettinger?' enquired the vicar as they reached the house. 'You look a bit pale. Come inside.' She turned to the child. 'Do you think we should maybe call someone? Your mother or father, perhaps?'

'Gramps is all right,' said the child. 'He just needs to sit down.'

The vicar gave Arthur a long look, her lips pursed. 'Right, I'll take your word for that. Let's go into the living room – you'll be more comfortable there.'

Arthur did indeed feel more at ease once he was sitting in the winged armchair by the fireside. It was much like his own at home. Ideally, he'd like to take his coat off but that would mean standing up again and he wasn't sure he had the energy for that right now.

'Can we see the evacuee records?' asked the child.

'Yes, of course. I'll make a cup of tea for Mr Pettinger and bring the records back with me.'

It was a long time before the vicar returned but Arthur was mighty pleased to see a hot cup of tea and plate of biscuits. Not his favourites, but a shortcake would do the trick.

The vicar opened the records book. 'So, who are you looking for and when exactly?'

'We're not sure of the date but probably around 1944 and the name is Yvette Rochelle. She would have been about twelve years old.' The child looked confidently at the vicar, who began flicking through the pages until she came to a list of names. She scrolled down with her forefinger, stopping about three-quarters of the way down the page.

'Here we go. We're lucky that the vicar, a Reverend Howard Milton, kept an excellent account of the evacuees. He also kept a diary during the war years. We don't have it here – it's in the local museum but it's fascinating reading.'

'Have you found Yvette Rochelle?' asked the child.

Before the vicar could answer, the sound of the telephone ringing in the hallway broke up the conversation. The vicar placed the book on the coffee table. 'I'll just take that call.'

She left the room, pulling the door behind her. Arthur could hear her talking, but he couldn't make out the words. The child rose and crept over to the door, listening at the crack. Her brows furrowed and she raced back to her seat.

'She's talking to someone about us,' whispered the child. She looked anxious, her hands clenching her bag tightly.

'About us? Why?'

'Shhh,' hushed the child. She took the screen thingy bob from her bag, fiddled with it for a moment and then with a quick glance over her shoulder, she knelt down at the coffee table and opened the leather-bound book the vicar had been looking at.

Arthur watched as the child rifled through the pages, every now and then glancing back towards the door. He could sense the tension but there was also excitement too. He could feel the danger crackle in the air like rapid-fire gunshot. The child found the page she was looking for and took several pictures of it with her device.

Fleeting and disjointed images rushed to the fore of Arthur's mind. Snapshots of events he wasn't sure he'd been part of or just witnessed from his time in the army. The memories flared and then receded to be replaced by others. If only he had time to study them, but no sooner had they appeared than they were gone again. However, the sensation was constant – one of fear, excitement, danger and relief all marching straight through him.

The vicar was coming back into the room and the child was now sitting on the sofa, with her hands over the bag on her knee and the book on the coffee table was closed.

The vicar gave a small cough to clear her throat. 'That was a lady named Kay, your carer for the weekend, I believe. It seems you two runaways have caused quite a stir.'

48

May 1944

The pain in Arthur's shoulder where they had dug the bullet out was considerably worse now all effects of the alcohol had worn off. So acute was it, Arthur couldn't sleep properly. After a heated discussion between Hugo and Maryse, he had been allowed to stay in the house and Maryse moved him to the sofa. Arthur had heard them arguing out in the kitchen – Maryse defending his need for comfort after being shot while Hugo countered that it wasn't safe for him to be in the house.

To be fair, Arthur did think Hugo had a point and was on the verge of getting up to say so, when Hugo finally relented. Even then Arthur had offered to go back out to the barn, but Maryse wouldn't hear of it. Besides, she was going to sleep in the armchair next to him all night to make sure he was OK.

'You'll be far better off in your own bed,' said Arthur, as Maryse came in and dumped some blankets onto the chair.

'The children are in my room,' she replied.

'What are you going to do with them? The Germans will be looking for them.'

'I know.' She hesitated and he could see something was troubling her.

'What is it?'

'They are looking for you too. General Weber is not happy that they have disappeared. He suspects you took them.'

'Well, he's not exactly wrong there, is he? It's best he's allowed to think that.'

'He's also sure that someone is keeping you and the children safe.'

Her expression was one of fear and worry. Arthur reached out with his good hand. 'Come here. You know what this means, don't you?'

She nodded. 'It's just happening so fast.'

'What did you expect?'

'I don't know, but I had to rescue those children.'

He stroked her hair. 'You did the right thing. Don't let anyone tell you any different. Who could be so heartless as not to help those kiddies?'

'But I've put you in danger and…' Another sob came. 'And there might be reprisals.'

There wasn't a lot Arthur could say to this last statement. It was true, the Germans could well take revenge on the locals but what was done was done. There was nothing they could do to change that now. 'Look, it's out of our hands,' he said. 'General Weber, he's not as bad as some of the others. Hopefully, he won't let the disappearance of two children cause so much fuss that he draws attention to the fact that he has been outwitted.'

'But the price for you… that's something worth making a fuss for,' said Maryse, raising her head to meet his gaze.

Arthur cupped her face with his hand. 'I can't stay here,' he said at last. 'It's too dangerous for you all. The next moon is in two days. I'll have to leave then.'

'And the children?'

'Oh, Maryse, my darling, I know what you're asking but I'd have to get clearance.'

'Can't you just take them?'

'They wouldn't be allowed on the plane with me.'

'But if they were there, with you... and you put them on the plane... the pilots couldn't say no, could they?'

Arthur churned over the suggestion. It was true, if the children were there, on the plane, then what could they do? They wouldn't throw them out. 'London would have my guts for garters,' he said finally.

'Better than leaving two defenceless Jewish children to their fate.'

A sudden idea entered Arthur's head. With some difficulty and pain, he managed to shuffle himself into a more upright position. 'Listen, Maryse, this is going to sound like a crazy idea but... but I'm going to say it anyway.' She looked at him questioningly, waiting for him to speak. 'Come to England with me. Don't stay here – come in the plane with me. If I'm going to get my knuckles rapped for two children, then I might as well get them properly rapped for you as well.'

Her face lit up with excitement. 'Me? Come to England with you? But then what?'

Arthur let out a laugh. 'Then marry me, of course!' He frowned. 'Damn it! That wasn't a very romantic proposal. Bloody hell, I can't even get down on one knee. What I should have said—' But his words were stolen as Maryse kissed him and squeezed him tightly. Arthur let out a cry of pain and Maryse jumped back, apologising again and again.

'I'm so sorry, I was just so happy,' she said with a broad grin on her face.

'I take it, that's a yes?'

'*Bien sûr! Oui! Oui! Oui! Oui!*'

'So, come with me to England. In two nights' time.'

'But what about my family? Hugo – he won't be happy.'

'Don't tell them.' Arthur knew he was asking a lot of her but as he had so often thought, these days of war were not normal times and normal rules did not apply. 'When the war is over, we can come back and visit them and explain everything.' At least this way she would be safe, Arthur reasoned with himself. She was far safer in England than she was here, bar the bombings, but if she was in the countryside rather than a city, he was sure no harm would come to her. He simply wanted her out of danger. He was certain he'd go out of his mind with worry if he went back home and left her here. He would spend every waking moment wondering if she was safe. It would be unbearable.

Over the next couple of days, Arthur was unable to do much, other than sit around and hope his shoulder healed soon. He was able to move it around but use of the arm was limited. Maryse had fashioned him a sling made from an old tablecloth she had found in the back of the laundry cupboard.

'I hope your mother won't mind,' said Arthur as she fastened it at the back of his neck.

'She's happy to see it go,' said Maryse. 'She said it's ugly but at least it's gone to good use.'

Arthur gave a laugh. Maryse's mother was a quiet woman who said little to her family he'd noticed, never mind much to him at all. But she was a kind woman and he was grateful of her hospitality.

'Why is your mother so quiet?' he asked that evening as he and Maryse had gone out to sit by the river.

'She's always been that way. My father, he was killed in the first war and she's never got over it.'

'I'm sorry,' said Arthur. 'Do you remember your father?'

'No. I was only two months old. He never saw me. I was born while he was away fighting.'

Arthur put an arm around her shoulders.

The silence was broken by the sound of Hugo calling out their names.

Arthur got to his feet with the help of Maryse and they hurried up to the house. It was getting dark now and he could make out the shapes of several other men standing behind Hugo.

'What's going on?' asked Arthur. He sensed some sort of tension in Hugo and the other men looked concerned too.

'You need to leave now,' said Hugo. 'It's too dangerous for you to stay here. Too dangerous for you and too dangerous for us.'

'What do you mean?' demanded Maryse. 'Go where?'

'You will have to hide out in the woods with the men tonight,' continued Hugo, ignoring his sister. 'The Germans are looking for you. They are systematically going through the homes of the villagers. There's been talk.'

'What kind of talk?' Arthur felt Maryse move closer to him and for the first time in front of anyone else, she slipped her hand into his. He appreciated her act of solidarity but at the same time it broke his heart. If the Germans were looking for him and taking it out on the villagers, not only did he feel immensely guilty, but he also knew Hugo was right.

'Staff at the house. Someone saw you. Fortunately, for you and for us, you didn't kill that soldier. I think General Weber is making a point of looking for you.'

'What about the villagers?' asked Maryse. 'Are they safe?'

'He's just sending his men in to frighten people. No one has been made an example of yet,' replied Hugo.

Arthur was grateful that at least innocent villagers weren't being lined up in front of a firing squad in retaliation.

'Do you think they will come here?' asked Maryse.

'I am certain,' said Hugo. 'And it will be tonight or tomorrow.'

'If he goes then I must go too. And take the children with us,' said Maryse, a determined look settled on her face.

Arthur's initial reaction was to insist Maryse stay at the farmhouse but he knew her well enough by now to know that when she set her mind to do something, she did it. She was a determined woman – that was for sure. He watched as brother and sister eyed each other for a few moments and it was Hugo who relented.

'Very well. The plane will come tomorrow night to pick up our friend.'

Arthur didn't miss the emphasis on the last two words. He was in no doubt whatsoever that he was anything but a friend where Hugo was concerned. Arthur assumed it was because of his relationship with Maryse but there was nothing he could do about that so Hugo would simply have to put up with it. He allowed himself the pleasure of imagining Hugo's face once he found out that he and Maryse were married and they were now in-laws.

'What is so funny?' Hugo's voice jolted Arthur from his thoughts.

Arthur coughed, using his hand to mask his face as he wrestled to downgrade the smirk to poker face. 'Err, nothing,' said Arthur. 'I was just thinking of being back home in England.'

Hugo took a step closer to Arthur. 'It's easy for you, you can fly home away from all of this. We have to live with this every day of our lives. You wouldn't be smiling if we had left you for the Germans to find, would you?'

'Hugo!' It was Maryse. 'Stop.'

'Your brother has a point,' said Arthur. He looked at Hugo. 'You're quite right and I apologise for any offence. I am, of course, very grateful for all you've done for me.' It wasn't strictly how Arthur felt but the need to defuse the situation was greater than the need to punch Hugo on the nose and tell him to shut his mouth. Arthur wasn't here by choice and, yes, he was truly grateful they had found him and not the Germans but, bloody hell, they were all on the same side and fighting for the same thing. The British Army and Air Force had sustained more than their fair share of casualties already; it wasn't a one-sided sacrifice.

Hugo gave some sort of conciliatory grunt, before turning to his sister. 'You have one hour to get ready before you need to leave. Hurry.'

Arthur just needed to grab his bag, which was already packed. He hoisted it up onto his good shoulder, wincing slightly as his brain sent shooting reminders of the injury. Arthur hadn't been able to change the dressing yet and he was reluctant to do anything to it until they were back in England and an army doctor could have a look at it. He wasn't entirely sure what sort of butchery the local quack had performed on him. Saved his life, no doubt, but at what cost to his long-term recovery and the use of his limb? He pushed away the thought. He'd have plenty of time for that once he was back home.

He made his way down to the end of the field where Freddie had been laid to rest. The mound was invisible to the eye; the grass had already grown back. If it wasn't for the fact Arthur had made a mental note of where exactly Freddie was buried, he wouldn't have found it.

Kneeling down under the shade of the pine tree, Arthur resisted the urge to brush away some fallen pine needles. He didn't want to disturb anything in case it caught the attention of the Germans when they arrived. They would be looking for any kind of clue that he was hiding here.

'Well, my old mate,' said Arthur softly. 'Time for me to go. There's a taxi coming for me tomorrow. Going to spend the night in some top-notch accommodation though.' He paused and let out a long slow breath. 'I'll let Ivy know where you are.' He looked out across the valley. 'You've a cracking spot here. I'll be sure to tell her all about it and give her your love.' Arthur got to his feet and took one last look at Freddie's final resting place. 'I'll have one at The Feathers for you. Cheers, mate.'

He closed his eyes for a moment before walking back to the courtyard where Maryse was standing outside the main house with the two children by her side. Poor little mites. They looked terrified. He forced a smile and went over to them. 'All set? Done everything you need to do?'

Maryse nodded. 'Let's go. We haven't got much time. Hugo's men are waiting for us.'

A horse and cart were now in the yard to hasten their transportation to the forest. There were four apples and two slices of bread. 'These are for you to take into the forest,' said Hugo. 'It's not much but it will keep you going until tomorrow night. *Bonne chance*.' He tipped his hat at Arthur.

'*Et vous*,' Arthur replied as he climbed up onto the back of the cart to sit alongside Maryse with the children on the opposite side.

The farmer who Maryse knew, but who Hugo hadn't felt the need to introduce to Arthur, clicked his tongue between his teeth and flicked the reins in his hands. The grey shire horse moved on. It reminded Arthur of being home on the farm and for the first time in a long time, he thought of his parents and felt a small flutter of anticipation at the prospect of seeing them soon.

49

Maddy woke the next morning, excited at the prospect of meeting Madame Beaufort, the clandestine nature of their meeting only ramping up the flow of adrenaline. She had just finished drying her hair and getting dressed when there was a tap at the door.

'Maddy? You ready?'

She opened the door to Joe. 'All present and correct.' She gave a mock salute.

'Excellent. Let's move out. Quick march.'

They positioned themselves on a stone bench opposite the main doors of the Breton church. It was a cooler morning than the one before and Maddy pulled her body warmer tighter around her. The sky was a crisp clear blue, laying a hazy veil over the sun.

They people-watched as the locals turned up for Mass, parking around the square and entering by the north door. Both Maddy and Joe kept an eye out for Collette Beaufort. As the church bell tolled ten o'clock there was still no sign of her.

'Maybe she's changed her mind,' said Maddy. She bit her bottom lip as she scanned the cobbled square. Then from around the corner, a petite figure appeared. The woman glanced over at Maddy before hurrying into the church.

'Game on,' said Joe. 'We just have to sit and wait.'

'I always considered myself to be a patient person, but this is really putting that theory to the test,' commented Maddy, looking at her watch yet again and was discouraged to see only ten minutes had passed. 'I expect you're more used to this waiting-around lark.'

'Comes with the job,' replied Joe. Maddy couldn't help noting how appealing he looked as he relaxed on the bench, his elbows resting on the rung behind him, one leg crossed over the other, his ankle hooked on the opposite knee with his head tilted up towards the sunshine. 'I was thinking...' he began.

'You want to be careful about that,' said Maddy, feeling flustered he'd caught her looking.

'Ha-ha.' Joe sat forwards, uncrossing his leg and moving his elbows to his knees. 'I was thinking about your grandmother and how she figures in all this.'

'It has crossed my mind once or twice,' confessed Maddy. 'I don't doubt that Gramps loved her. From what I remember they always got on well. They're more from the generation who once married, stayed married. Apparently, when Mum and Dad were going through a bad patch, Nan told them that they'd said their vows and they needed to work things out and if they couldn't then they needed to come to a compromise. She said it was too easy to get divorced and it wasn't something she approved of.'

'Do you think she was speaking from experience?'

'Sounds that way. She was a good woman, but she wasn't one of those hands-on, cuddly grandmothers. She didn't fuss us much and was quite strict with us. Very much the opposite to Gramps.'

'Why do you think they married in the first place?'

'My grandmother was a widow when Gramps married her. They had known each other growing up, along with her first husband, who was killed during the war,' explained Maddy. 'I remember asking Nan once how she and Gramps had met and started seeing each other and it was one of the few times she showed her soft side. She said that Gramps had looked after her when she was widowed. That they were both lost souls and they'd been a comfort to each other.'

'So, when did they get married?'

'I don't know off the top of my head, but I think it was a couple of years after the war.'

'After Maryse,' said Joe.

'Yeah, I guess so. I suppose Nan and Gramps found each other when they were trying to get their lives back on track after the war.'

'And when they'd both lost a loved one, maybe?' suggested Joe.

Maddy considered the scenario, wondering why she'd never given it much thought before. 'I'm glad they were there for each other when they needed someone,' she said at last. 'They may not have been the burning first love, but I think they were the enduring second love.'

Joe ran his hand through his hair. 'What do you think is best? First love or second love?'

Maddy attempted a nonchalant shrug. 'Maybe first love is just a dry run.' She kept her eyes fixed on the church across the road. 'What about you?'

'Neither,' he replied without hesitation.

Maddy swallowed an unexpected lump in her throat. 'Neither? You don't believe in love at all?'

'I didn't say that.'

'What are you saying, then?' She looked at him now,

annoyed at his reply because it only served to highlight how off the mark she'd been in terms of the status of their relationship.

'Wait. Heads up,' he said, nodding towards the church. 'Here comes Collette Beaufort.'

Maddy saw Collette descend the church steps and then cross the square, heading to a small footpath that ran between the houses on the opposite side of the square.

Joe got to his feet and Maddy followed suit. 'I guess we follow her.'

As they crossed the square, Joe guided Maddy over the cobbled stones with his hand cupping her elbow. Collette by now had disappeared into the alleyway. As they reached the other side, Joe dipped his head so his mouth was at Maddy's ear. 'True love,' he said.

Maddy gave him a quizzical look while at the same time navigating the raised flower beds surrounding the square. 'What?'

'I believe in true love,' replied Joe.

The footpath ambled downhill and out onto a grass bank overlooking the village lake, where Collette was waiting underneath the drooping bows of a willow tree. There was a stillness to the air and a gentle mist rising from the water, giving the whole place an eerie atmosphere.

'*Bonjour, madame,*' said Maddy, holding out her hand, while attempting to push Joe's comment to the side. 'Thank you for agreeing to meet us.'

Collette shook Maddy's hand and then Joe's, the latter managing a passable greeting in French.

'I can't stay long,' said Collette. 'I'm sorry about my son if he was rude last night. He is not happy that all this is being brought up. He is of the generation that it should be laid to rest and kept in the past.'

Her voice was low as if she was scared of being overheard and she spoke quickly.

'We do appreciate it,' replied Maddy.

'We can speak English if it is easier,' said Collette, looking at Joe. 'I don't think your friend can understand us otherwise.'

Maddy was surprised at how good Collette's English was and grateful that Joe would be able to follow the conversation without her having to translate. 'Thank you, madame, that would be very helpful,' said Joe.

'Collette. You don't have to call me madame.' She turned back to Maddy. 'Now, tell me why you want to speak to me.'

Collette listened patiently as Maddy relayed the story of her grandfather and their quest to find the mysterious Maryse. 'So, we're trying to give my grandfather some sort of closure. Or as much as we can. His memory is failing him and it's not always easy to get the exact information.'

'It is difficult. My father was troubled in the same way,' she said. Her face softened as she looked at Maddy. 'My mother did indeed run a guest house in England during the war. She and my father – he was English which is why I am fluent in the language – they had connections with the war office… with SOE. You know what that is, don't you?'

'Special Operations Executive,' said Joe.

'Indeed,' carried on Collette. 'The guest house was a safe house too. It was a drop-off point, where messages could be left, meetings could take place – secret things were discussed.'

Maddy felt her eyes widen. 'Wow. And, your parents knew all this?'

'*Bien sûr*. They ran the operations there. I was a child at the time – a teenager – and although I wasn't supposed to know, I did. My mother swore me to secrecy. She told me lives were at risk and she and my father were doing what they could to help the war effort and to free France from occupation.' Collette stood a little taller as she spoke. There was a pride in her eyes, which danced fiercely from the memory.

'So, did my grandfather have any connection with the guest house?'

'I cannot say for certain if he did during the war,' said Collette. 'But, afterwards yes. And so did Maryse.'

'They did?' Maddy had to try to tamp down her excitement. This was their first positive lead. 'Were they there at the same time?' She took a deep breath to calm herself.

'In 1946, a year after the war ended, a young Frenchwoman came to the guest house. I remember because it was I who greeted her. She said she was looking for an English soldier she met during the war in France. His name was Arthur Pettinger and he lived on a farm but she didn't have an address – only that she knew it was in Cambridgeshire.'

'That's my grandfather,' said Maddy. She fished out the photograph of Maryse and showed it to Collette. 'I know it was a long time ago, but was it this woman?'

Collette took her glasses from her pocket and looked at the black and white photograph of Maryse standing outside a cottage. 'It's hard to tell but it could be,' she said at last.

'Do you know if the woman staying with you ever found the man she was looking for?' asked Joe.

Collette shook her head and a sadness entered her eyes. 'I do not think so. She stayed with us for two weeks and she went out every day and every evening she came back, each day looking more tired and dejected.'

'Oh no,' said Maddy, feeling an overwhelming sadness. 'What happened after the two weeks?'

'She said she had to go back to France. She didn't know where else to look. She had been given the address of the guest house by someone from the army who she had made contact with. I don't know who but they obviously didn't know anything about the man she was looking for either. I think the guest house was becoming more well known by this stage. However, before she returned to France, she gave my mother an envelope. I didn't know this at the time. My mother never spoke of it until a few years before she died. She told me I was to keep it in case Arthur ever came looking for it.'

'And do you have the envelope?' queried Joe. 'Do you know what was inside it?'

Collette opened her bag and withdrew an A4-sized padded envelope, the opening sealed. She held it in her hands for a moment as if deciding whether she was making the right decision before pushing it towards Maddy. 'I think it's time it was passed on to Arthur's family.'

Maddy's hands trembled as she took the brown envelope, its corners battered but still intact. She looked at the handwriting on the front.

Arthur Pettinger was written in blue fountain pen, which was faded now but still legible, the letters elegantly slanting to the right. She turned it over but there was no other writing. The contents were hard to make out by touch alone but the envelope felt packed with several different items, not sheets of paper, which would indicate a letter. 'You've never opened it?'

Collette shook her head. 'My mother respected the privacy of the contents and so have I. I think maybe my mother didn't want to know what was inside. You must remember she lived through difficult times and I, well, it is not my business. My son thinks it should stay that way and I could be causing trouble, but I have always felt this envelope contained as much love as it did sadness. There was a reason why a young woman would travel to England and spend two weeks searching for a man. It can only be love.'

Maddy pressed her lips together to steady her composure before speaking. 'Thank you,' she whispered. 'Thank you so much.'

'I'm glad you came,' said Collette. She reached out and patted Maddy's arm. 'I hope it brings what you are looking for. Now, I must go back before I am missed.'

'Thank you,' said Joe earnestly.

'Yes, thank you again,' said Maddy, hugging the envelope to her body.

They remained standing under the willow tree as Collette Beaufort made her way back up the pathway towards the main square of the village.

'Wow,' said Joe. 'I don't know what I was expecting, but I wasn't expecting a parcel that had been kept safe and sealed for over seventy years.'

Maddy looked down at the package and drew her hand across her grandfather's name. 'It feels wrong to open it when it's clearly for Gramps,' she said. 'But at the same time, I need to know what it contains. I don't want him to have any upsets. Who knows what sort of memories it might stir and how he might react?'

'I think that's a wise decision. Let's get back to the car. You can decide then where and when to open it.'

50

May 1944

It had been a bloody uncomfortable night, sleeping on the forest bed, and Arthur had been grateful when dawn had started to break through the trees. They'd arrived the night before under cover of darkness and had been hurried along to a part of the forest where they were bundled into some kind of makeshift shelter. It wasn't exactly the five-star accommodation he had blagged to Freddie about, but it was dry. It also had the added benefit that Maryse could snuggle up to him in the night once the children had gone to sleep. Arthur had woken with Maryse wrapped in one arm and something – or rather, someone – snuggled up against his legs. It was little Jean-Paul. Yvette had sought the comfort of the other side of Maryse in the night. Not for the first time his heart swelled with pity for these poor kids.

Arthur could now make out the sticks and branches that had been put together and the dried mud to make the shelter weatherproof. He was pretty impressed with the ingenuity and sophistication of the hut. When he had ventured out on the offer of breakfast, he had been even more surprised and no less impressed by the set-up of the camp. It was like its own little community. There was a campfire in the middle where women were preparing breakfast, baking bread and taking deliveries of supplies which, he assumed, were from the surrounding villages. There were several huts set up like an outer circle surrounding the campfire, much the same as the one they had slept in.

'Can I do anything to help?' Arthur asked one of the men who had come to sit beside him.

The man gave a shrug. 'You have to ask Jean-François. He's over there.'

Arthur noted the man dressed smarter than most of the others in the camp. He was wearing a tweed jacket, which notably was lacking in the darning and holes that was typical of the other men. His trousers were clean with no evidence of the forest on the cloth.

Jean-François turned to look around the camp and upon seeing Arthur, gave a nod of acknowledgement. He turned back to the man he was talking to and the map they appeared to be studying.

Arthur swallowed the last of the strong black coffee he'd been given and went over to Jean-François, introducing himself.

'I know who you are,' replied the man.

'Any news as to whether the farmhouse was visited by the Germans last night?' asked Arthur, aware that Maryse was worried about her family.

'They visited. Found nothing. No harm done,' said Jean-François.

'Good,' seemed a fitting reply. Jean-François appeared to be a man of few words. 'What do you want me to do today?'

Jean-François gave Arthur's shoulder a pointed look. 'Nothing. You rest. You are being picked up at ten o'clock tonight. Make sure you're ready to leave here at nine.'

Arthur trudged back to the shelter where Maryse and the children were now awake and huddled together; they cupped warm milk in mugs while Maryse nursed a coffee. They looked a sorry sight, Arthur had to admit as they ate the bread Maryse had brought with them.

'We just have to sit tight for today,' said Arthur. He didn't have a lot of choice and if he was entirely honest with himself, he was looking forward to getting across the Channel, fixed at the military hospital and then back into action. He estimated that he could be sidelined for about six to eight weeks and it was quite timely as it would give him the opportunity to make sure the children were safe and the time to introduce Maryse to his family and have her settled in the house with his parents before he was recalled. He smiled at the image of Maryse in the kitchen baking bread and preparing the meals, alongside his mother, both women speaking French. His mother would love that. She often said she missed speaking in her native language.

He stole a glance in Maryse's direction but she caught him and gave a small smile. There was a sadness there and he wondered if she was lamenting leaving her own mother behind. The notion lifted some of the rose-coloured tint from his imagination. He realised he was asking Maryse to leave so much behind her in such difficult circumstances. Had he been fair to ask her to marry him? Had it been a selfish request on his behalf?

As he went to sit on the chair at the table, he moved Maryse's coat out of the way. The weight didn't go unnoticed. It was heavier on one side and he knew it was because of the handgun her brother had given her.

'Ça va?' asked Maryse.

He hesitated a beat before replying. '*Oui. Ça va.*' It wasn't the truth. He was far from OK.

'Is your shoulder hurting you?' She put her empty coffee cup on the ground and rose, walking around to inspect his shoulder. She unfastened his shirt and slipped the fabric down his arm. The dressing was still in place but fresh blood had seeped through. 'You need a clean dressing.'

Arthur placed his hand over hers. 'It will be fine for now. I'll get it seen to as soon as I'm back in England.'

Maryse lifted his hand to her lips and kissed it softly, before easing his shirt sleeve back up and over his shoulder. 'It must be the first thing you do.' There was a catch in her voice and she glanced at the children. They had moved from the bed and were standing in the doorway of the shelter, the heavily darned blanket drawn back, allowing a shaft of light through.

'If I'm to run away with you to England, I should at least know your real name.'

It was strictly against rules to reveal his true identity but Arthur decided it was right that Maryse should at least know his name. 'This is for your ears only,' he said. Then putting his mouth to her ear, he whispered it to her.

Maryse appeared to consider this revelation and nod in approval. 'I will get used to it,' she said.

They spent the rest of the day at each other's side, taking the opportunity to nap in the privacy of the shelter, cuddled up together, not for warmth but for comfort. The children had been taken under the wing of one of the women from the camp and Arthur listened to the day as it unfolded and the occupants went about their daily tasks of gathering firewood, preparing meals, making plans for the next act of disruption they could inflict on the Germans.

Finally, the hours passed and it was nine o'clock. Together with the children, they followed the reception committee assigned to guiding in the British plane to a nearby field.

It was an agonisingly dangerous hour while they prepared the makeshift landing strip by placing lanterns in position, then hiding under cover of the woods until it was ten o'clock. The weather was on their side – it was a cloudless night and the full moon highlighted the open stretch of land.

A distant hum of a plane engine alerted them and then there was a flurry of activity as the landing strip lanterns were lit and the plane was guided in. The aircraft bumped its way across the grassy field, slowing right down before making its way to where Arthur was standing.

The door flew open and three metal steps unrolled from the hatch.

'Christophe Martin?' asked the RAF pilot.

'Good to see you,' said Arthur. He brought Yvette and Jean-Paul to the front. 'Extra passengers.'

'We've not been briefed about extra passengers,' said the co-pilot. 'Sorry, no can do.'

'Sorry,' said Arthur, picking up Yvette with his good arm and placing her in the plane. 'No can leave them here.' He turned and repeated the same with the boy. And then to the co-pilot. 'Jewish. Orphans. I'm not leaving them.'

There was a shout from the front of the plane to get a move on. 'The place is going to be swarming with Jerries!' called the pilot.

Arthur turned to Maryse, looking at her intently. She rushed forwards into his arms, kissing his cheek and then his mouth. 'Come back for me.'

It took a second for Arthur to realise what she was saying and his gut churned in anguish. 'No!' he yelled at her over the noise of the engines. 'I can't leave you!'

'I cannot go. I cannot abandon my country like this.' She tried to pull away from him but Arthur held her tightly.

'Come with me, please.' He didn't care he was begging her now.

There was the thud of a hand on his shoulder and the co-pilot shouting in his ear that they had to leave and leave now.

Arthur cradled Maryse's face in the palm of his hand. Maryse the gun-toting patriotic resistance fighter – how could she possibly settle down in rural England and be content with baking bread while her country was under siege?

The co-pilot yelled at him to get a move on.

Arthur knew he had to leave without her.

'Come back for me! When the war is over. Come and find me.' Tears streamed from her eyes.

'I will. I promise.' Arthur kissed her one more time before reluctantly climbing aboard. He turned and watched her, wanting to savour every last moment of her before the door was shut. His darling, beautiful, brave and loyal Maryse.

51

'Why don't we head over to Lizio. There's a nice spot by the lake where you could look at everything in the envelope in peace,' said Joe. He wasn't sure how Maddy was going to react to whatever was inside. She may need some privacy and in the middle of a square in a French village wasn't exactly ideal.

It was a peaceful area by the lake, with a picnic bench tucked away in a corner, shaded by the surrounding trees. A sign marked the trail for mountain bikes and another for walkers. Little water boatmen skidded around on the surface of the lake and every now and then a dragonfly darted in and out of the reeds.

Joe passed a bottle of water to Maddy. 'Look, I'll have a wander along the bank and leave you to look through the contents in private.' He wanted to give her some space, despite being desperate to see what had been kept sealed in the envelope for all these years. It was a historian's dream come true to be the first to open such an item but it wasn't for him to do. This was Maddy's prerogative.

'Joe! Wait!' He turned back towards the bench. 'Don't go,' she said. 'Open it with me. Please?'

'Are you sure?'

'Of course I am. I wouldn't even have this in my hands if it wasn't for you.'

Joe sat down opposite her and watched as she slipped her thumb under the seal and gently worked it across the edge of the paper.

Joe reached out his hand and rested it on hers. 'Just think,' he said. 'No one has seen the contents in over seventy years. No one knows what's in there other than Maryse herself. Imagine that. You're about to touch something that Maryse handled.'

'I know. I'm quite nervous but excited too,' replied Maddy. 'I hope it's worth the wait.'

Joe watched patiently as Maddy peered into the depths of the envelope before carefully sliding the contents out onto the wooden picnic table.

One by one, they picked up the items – several bus tickets, all returns to Peterborough, a map of Cambridgeshire with numerous villages circled in red pen, another ticket, this one a ferry ticket from Dover to Calais, a train ticket from Paris to Calais and another from Ploërmel to Paris.

'What are all these tickets about?' asked Maddy.

'I think it's a trail. I think Maryse has left a trail for your grandfather. For some reason she didn't want to give any specific information but she knew these would be significant to him.'

'So, we can piece together her journey?'

'Yes, so your grandfather would know she had been to England and was trying to find him. Perhaps she didn't know exactly where he lived. She's taken the bus out nearly every day to different locations.'

'But she never found him. Oh, that's so sad.'

'She left this envelope at the guest house as it was the only address they had in common or at least the only one she thought he might go to.'

'I can't help feeling a little disappointed,' said Maddy. 'I was hoping for a letter or a photograph. Something, I don't know, something more personal, I guess.'

Joe had to admit he too felt disappointed. He was hoping it would give them more clues as to where Maryse was now. Joe picked over the tickets, looking at the names and corresponding them to the map. Three of the bus tickets stood out from the others. He peered at them more closely, turning them over and back again in his hand, referring to the map to double-check the details.

'What is it?' Maddy had noticed his interest.

'I'm not sure.' He rummaged through the tickets again, eventually seizing on one. He laid them out beside each other. 'One ticket to Little Paxton and three tickets to St Neots.'

'She went to St Neots three times?'

'Maybe. Little Paxton is ringing a bell. I'm sure I've researched that quite recently on a job for work.'

'Never heard of it.'

Joe took out his phone and looked up the place. 'Yes, a little village in Cambridgeshire near St Neots.' He tapped away at his phone some more. 'Used to be in the county of Huntingdonshire in the war. Paxton Park Maternity Home was where a lot of pregnant women were evacuated to give birth.'

'Do you think Maryse went there for some reason?'

'Possibly, although I can't think why.'

'You don't think she was pregnant, do you?'

Joe met Maddy's gaze. 'With your grandfather's baby?'

'Wait, let's do the maths... No, it wouldn't be possible, not unless she had the gestation of an elephant.'

They both gave a small laugh at the idea but neither could hide their frustration. 'There must have been a reason that your grandfather would know but we don't.' Joe was back looking at his phone.

'And why three tickets?'

'I've no idea, but I think it's important.'

'There's a train station in St Neots. Are there any train tickets going from there to, say, London or Dover even?' They rummaged around some more but drew a blank. 'There must be a connection with St Neots and Little Paxton that we're missing.'

'But what?' Maddy's shoulders slumped. 'I wish Gramps could tell us more but I just don't think he can remember any of it.'

'Maybe some of this will trigger his memory?'

'It might do.'

'We need a surname for Maryse. It would help if we knew that.'

Maddy shook her head despondently and began gathering the items strewn across the table. 'It's a shame we didn't ask if there were any records for the guest house. They must have had a name for the booking. I don't suppose they've kept anything like that.'

'I doubt it and if it was used by British Intelligence then those records may have been destroyed or not accessible, you know, wanting to keep everything top secret.'

'Is there any way we could check?'

'I can make some inquiries, but don't get your hopes up.'

'What about Collette Beaufort? Do you think she might know?'

Joe checked his watch. 'If we hurry, we'll catch her coming out of Mass. She might speak to us and she might remember but, again, I doubt it.' He didn't want to give Maddy false hope.

He drove swiftly back to Sérent and had just enough time to park and climb out of the car before the church doors opened and the congregation began to disperse.

Collette Beaufort was one of the last to leave and whether it was some sixth sense, Joe didn't know, but as she made her way down the steps, she looked over and spotted him and Maddy standing there. She stopped for a moment to exchange a few words with the priest before crossing the square in their direction. Maddy made a move to intercept her, but Joe caught her arm.

'Just wait a moment,' he said, quietly. They watched as Collette stopped to look in a shop window. 'Go over there now and discreetly pose the question. I'll wait here.'

He watched in what he hoped was a casual manner as Maddy wandered over and, after browsing one shop window, went to look in the same one as Collette. He couldn't tell if they were talking to each other but less than a minute later, Collette was walking away from the shop and down a side street.

Joe joined Maddy at the shop window. 'You'd make a good spy.'

She made a scoffing sort of noise. 'All seems a bit ridiculous but I get it that Collette doesn't want anyone telling tales on her to her son.'

'What did she say?'

'She said it was Dupont. She remembered because she had an aunt with the same surname.'

Joe gave a groan. 'Dupont? Is that what she said?'

'Yep. I assume you already know that apparently Dupont is as common as, say, Johnson is in England.'

'Yep.' Joe rubbed the side of his face with his hand. 'On the bright side, at least now we have a surname but...'

'I know – don't get my hopes up. I also asked her if she knew why Maryse would be visiting St Neots or Little Paxton.'

'And?'

'She said she knew a lot of women and children were evacuated there but that was all.'

'Which is what we knew already.'

'She did say one thing though,' continued Maddy. 'She said that something had always stuck in her mind as strange about Maryse and she'd forgotten all about it until she was sitting in church and thinking of her. She said it suddenly came back to her.'

Joe felt a ripple of excitement in his stomach. 'Don't keep me in suspense.'

'She said it was probably nothing, but she went up to make the beds one day – that was her job at the guest house – and Maryse had left her case on the bed. Collette went to move it but it wasn't closed properly and some things fell out. Amongst the clothing were two teddy bears. One with a blue ribbon and one with a pink ribbon.'

'Teddy bears? Is that it?'

Maddy nodded. 'That's it. Odd, I know. What was she doing bringing two soft toys to England with her?'

'Comfort?' suggested Joe. Although in his mind he had to admit he didn't think Maryse would have two teddy bears to cuddle at night-time.

'I've no idea.' Maddy slipped her arm through his. 'Fancy a coffee?'

'Yeah that would be good. I need time to try to process all this. I suppose the important info is we now have a surname, albeit a common one. I'll work on that while we have a coffee.'

No sooner had they sat down and ordered their drinks in the café across the square than Maddy's phone rang. Taking it from her pocket she looked at the screen. 'It's Kay.'

'Right.'

'I told her to ring only if it was important, like an emergency.'

'You want me to answer it?'

Maddy stared at the screen for another second. 'No. I'd better.'

52

September 1946

9th September 1946

> Holly Tree Farm
> Dairy Lane
> Hemingford

Darling Maryse

I don't know if you are reading this but I hope to God you are – you have been in my every waking moment since I had to leave you that awful night in France. I am making enquiries as to where you are and so far been given very little information. The British Army are still being careful about revealing their contacts and their whereabouts even though the war is officially over.

I am sending this to your home in France and once more, I hope to God, this finds you and does not cause you any problems with your family. I have wondered if it is wise to make contact now we are in more peaceful times and whether what we shared was something too extraordinary for ordinary times. But, my love, I have spent many a night tossing and turning, trying to decide what is the best course of action and always… ALWAYS… I come back to this – I must find you. My love has not dwindled or faded – if anything, it has grown. So I hope with all my heart this letter finds you and you still feel the same way about me, for I am sure our feelings were mutual.

I am also going to Peterborough as I've heard mention of a guest house there where SOE(F) were often directed as a safe house and if you have come to England, maybe you have been there.

If no luck, my next plan is to come to France to try to find you but first I must put together some money for this trip and try to arrange travel, which isn't very easy at the moment, but I shall not give up.

All my love

Arthur

Arthur folded the letter and slid it into the envelope addressed to Maryse. He kissed the seal and held it to his heart. He couldn't give up looking for her, not yet. He had to know what had happened to her and that she was at least safe. He'd heard different reports from different people, which ranged from the local resistance group all being rounded up in the days that followed his exit from Brittany and then shot in the village square, to all resistance members escaped and went to hide out in the forest. Either way, he had no knowledge if Maryse was safe.

Once the letter was posted, Arthur walked down the hill to the bus stop, where the bus would take him into town and he'd be able to catch the ten-thirty train to Peterborough.

Settling himself on the train, Arthur took out the photograph of Maryse. The edges were thumbed from his hands, where he'd kept the photograph in his top pocket and taken it out many a time to gaze at his darling girl. His heart both sang and cried every time he did so. He turned the photograph over and read the address on the reverse for what must be the one hundredth time. It was the safe house in Peterborough used during the war, run by an Englishman and his French wife, the same one Arthur had stayed at before he'd been dropped into France. He hadn't been able to remember the address, but an army pal who worked in the Home Office now had done him a favour and found it out.

Arthur drummed his fingers impatiently on his leg as the train made its slow exit from the station. He needed to get to the guest house. It was his only clue so far as to what happened to her. His chest tightened as he drove away imagined scenarios of what the alternative might be.

He found the road with ease, thanks to the street map he had bought at the station. It was relatively new, having been built in the early 1930s. A tree-lined road, grass verges, semi-detached and detached properties on either side, all with the signature bay window and open arched porch. He crossed to the road to the odd numbers and was soon standing outside number 29, with its black glossed front door and black and white window frames. Net curtains hung in the individual panes of glass, which made up the bay, neatly drawn together in the middle with a ribbon. It looked well-kept and much as he remembered from his brief stay there.

Arthur knocked at the door of number 29, straightening his tie before removing his hat as the door was opened.

'Good afternoon,' said the young woman in front of him. She wore a half-apron over her skirt, a white blouse and a pale blue cardigan. 'Can I help you?'

Arthur didn't know what he had been expecting, but it wasn't this young woman who had a clear-cut English accent. She wasn't the Frenchwoman who had run the waiting house when he'd been there.

'I'm looking for Mrs Cohen,' said Arthur.

'Oh, Mrs Cohen, Madame Cohen?'

'Yes, that's right. Is she here?'

'I'm sorry but she doesn't live here anymore. We moved here a year ago. We were bombed out of our street during the war. Still hasn't been rebuilt.' Just then a little boy of about three years old appeared at the woman's side and she picked him up.

'And you don't know where Mrs Cohen is now?'

'No. Sorry. Look, I've got to go. I've got the potatoes on the boil.' She gave him a sympathetic look, before closing the door.

Disappointment flooded Arthur. What a fool he'd been to think it would be so simple to find Maryse.

53

'What?! Where are they now?' Maddy gripped the phone in her hand, shocked by what Kay had just told her. She glanced across the bistro table at Joe who had stopped mid-sip of his coffee and was studying her carefully. They were sitting outside the café overlooking the square, which was now busy with locals buying their fresh bread from the boulangerie, vegetables from a small market stall and their Sunday dinner from the chicken rotisserie van. Joe had been oblivious to their surroundings, tapping away at his phone as he tried to make progress with the contents of the envelope.

'They're here, the vicar has just brought them back. She kindly offered to drive them. I'm so sorry, Maddy, I had no idea they would do anything like this.' Kay sounded mortified. 'I didn't know whether to phone you now or not, but I was worried the police might contact you. I'd already called them by the time the taxi firm got in touch.'

'It's fine, Kay, I'm not cross at you at all. I'm the one who should be apologising. Thank goodness for the taxi driver.' Joe had put his phone down now and silently mouthed a 'you OK?' at her. She gave a brief nod, although aware of the ball of fury at Esther's reckless behaviour that was building up inside her.

'Yes. Apparently, he couldn't help feeling something wasn't right and when he got back decided to report it to his boss.'

'I should speak to Esther now, but I'm not sure I'll handle it right. I'm livid that she's pulled a stunt like this.' Maddy felt Joe's hand cover her own and almost instantly registered a soothing effect. He may not know exactly what was going on but he could tell from her side of the conversation something bad had happened.

'Esther is extremely remorseful,' said Kay. 'Gramps is fast asleep. I think the little adventure has worn him out. Esther's taken herself up to her room. And poor Sheila, I was worried she was going to hyperventilate at one point. She was in a complete panic when she realised what had happened. Absolutely horrified.'

'And she didn't hear a thing?'

'No. She had nodded off and Gramps and Esther crept out.'

'Poor Sheila. Please tell her not to get upset.' Joe's hand might be having a calming effect but every now and then a burst of anger would rise in her chest. 'And they said they were looking for a friend of Gramps's?'

'Yes, I can't remember the name now. The vicar did mention it, but I was all in a dither and didn't make a note of it.'

'It doesn't matter, I can always ask Esther or even the vicar,' replied Maddy.

'Apparently, it was an evacuee they were looking for,' said Kay. 'A young girl.'

'What? Hang on,' said Maddy. 'I wonder if that's the same child who Gramps kept talking about the other day. I can't remember the name now myself.' Maddy sighed. 'That's by the by. Whatever the reason, Esther should have known better than to pull something like that.'

'I'm just glad they're back home safely.'

'Yeah, me too. Look, Kay, as I say, don't worry. I'm not cross with you at all. I'll speak to Esther when I'm home.' They ended the call and Maddy held her head in her hands for a couple of seconds before looking up at Joe. 'I assume you got the gist of what happened?' She filled Joe in on the details. 'I can't believe Esther did that. And how on earth did she find out where to go? Book a taxi? Find the vicar? If I wasn't so cross, I'd be congratulating her on her resourcefulness and independence.'

Joe gave a wry smile. 'Skills that will help her through life.'

'Maybe so, but I'd sooner she didn't employ them until she's at least eighteen. Or older.' It was a lame attempt at humour. Maddy knew she wasn't at that point yet. She still needed to confront Esther about her actions but she was glad there was a distance between them right now, otherwise she might say something in the heat of the moment and then wish later she'd handled it better.

'Try not to brood over it,' said Joe.

'I'm not brooding.'

'If you say so.'

'I do.'

'Fine.'

Maddy scowled at Joe and impulsively, not to mention childishly, poked her tongue out at him, which only caused him to burst out laughing. Maddy sighed and gave a small self-depreciating laugh. 'All right. Maybe I am a bit. Ignore me. I just need a few minutes to let it go.'

'Sure,' said Joe affably and after a pause, returned to his phone and coffee.

Maddy concentrated hard on relaxing and pushing thoughts of Esther and Gramps galivanting all over the place from her thoughts but it wasn't as easy as that. Her mind kept veering back to what could have happened to them and what the future held for the three of them. How long would she be able to look after Gramps on her own? His condition could become static or deteriorate and as much as it broke her heart to think about it, she knew there might come a time when she couldn't leave Gramps on his own even for a few minutes. When that time would be, she had no idea as although a rough progression of the disease could be plotted by health professionals, in reality it advanced at different rates and developed in different ways individual to each sufferer. What if Gramps's health deteriorated so rapidly that by September, she wouldn't even be able to leave him alone while she took Esther to school?

Maddy let out a long, disheartened sigh at the bleakness of the future. It was so cruel, so painful this long goodbye, watching her grandfather slowly disappear in front of her, knowing there was nothing she could do to stop the disease from ravaging his mind, stealing his memories, his ability to communicate diminished – she couldn't bear the thought. An explosion of emotional pain pierced her heart as living grief attacked.

She was glad she had her sunglasses on to mask her eyes. Sometimes it was too painful to talk about how she felt she was already grieving for her grandfather, knowing she would have to grieve for him all over again.

'Hey, Mads. You OK?' Joe's gentle voice broke her

thoughts. She nodded, not daring herself to speak. She was aware of Joe putting down his phone and resting his arms on the circular bistro table as he leaned a little closer to her. 'I'm here if you want to talk about it.'

A tear leaked from her eye and Maddy brushed it away with her fingertips. 'I feel so helpless at times. I wish there was something I could do for Gramps.'

'You're doing everything you can.'

'But it doesn't feel enough.'

'Listen, you're an amazing woman. You're so strong, Mads. I don't know how you do it. Not only are you bringing up Esther but you're also caring for your grandfather and, like I said before, he may not be able to tell you in words but I've no doubt in his heart he knows how much you love him and appreciates what you're doing for him.'

The sympathy was too much for Maddy to take and the tears raced down her face. She grabbed at the napkin on the table. 'I'm sorry.'

Joe rose from his seat, shoving his phone into his pocket and dropping a ten-euro note onto the table before coming around to Maddy and, with his hand on her arm, encouraged her from her seat. 'Let's go for a walk.'

Maddy didn't argue and as Joe put a consoling arm around her shoulder she allowed herself to sink into his body, appreciating the comfort it offered.

A few minutes later they were by the lake where they had met Collette Beaufort and as they ground to a halt, Maddy thought how ironic it was they should be standing underneath the drooping branches of a weeping willow tree.

She went to speak, to apologise, but Joe shushed her and wrapping both arms around her, drew her into him, her face nestling in the fabric of his shirt. She inhaled the zingy freshness of his aftershave as she slipped her arms around him. Her heart was still hammering but now for entirely different reasons and when she felt Joe drop a kiss on top of her head, she wasn't sure her legs would hold her.

'Don't let go,' she whispered.

'I've no intention.' Joe's hand moved up and down her back as if soothing a child and he left another kiss on her head. 'Don't be scared by the strength of your emotions. It's good to know how you feel so you can make the most of what you've got. Some people don't appreciate what they had until it's too late.'

Maddy pulled away a fraction so she could tilt her head to look at him. 'How did you get to be so wise, Joe Finch?'

'Past experience.'

And then his head was tipping down and his mouth moving towards hers. Maddy briefly considered objecting but knew she had no intention of doing anything of the sort.

Maddy wasn't sure how long they would have stayed there under the willow tree, locked in a kiss but Joe's mobile phone bursting into life cut the moment short. Reluctantly, they pulled away.

'This is unfinished business,' said Joe, his voice unusually husky. He gave her another brief kiss, before retrieving his phone from his pocket. 'Here we go. A message from a contact I've been waiting to hear back from.'

'What about exactly?'

'I've been trying to see if I can get a lead on Maryse Dupont before we have to leave tonight.'

'What does your contact say?'

'He wants me to call him.'

'Is that good?'

'Probably means he's got something to say that's too long or complicated for a text message.'

'Oh, so that's good news, then?' Maddy felt her mood lift with the possibility of a lead.

'Not necessarily,' replied Joe. 'I put the name Maryse Dupont 1940 into the search engine and got a shedload of results back, but either they refer to the name Maryse or the name Dupont but none of them to Maryse Dupont. I've been wading through websites trying to pin down something more concrete that's connected to this area, the war, the resistance, that sort of thing, but no joy.'

'Have you been able to trace Maryse through her birth records?'

'For some reason, I can't log onto the French database via my work's portal.'

'Is that a problem?'

Joe rubbed his chin. 'Possibly. It could be a glitch or it could be I've had my permissions revoked.'

'Why would they do that?'

'Not sure. Maybe they've guessed I'm helping you, albeit as a friend. They were keen to sign you themselves.'

'I remember.'

'Anyway, I've put in a request via a friend who has access to the French database and this is where we're at now. If he's been able to find a birth record we might be able to find a marriage or, and you have to prepare yourself for this, a death record.'

'I know. The chances are she's passed away. She'd be in her nineties if she was still alive.'

'I won't give up though, not until every avenue has been exhausted.'

'I do appreciate it, thank you.' She smiled at him, relishing the thought that he was doing this for her, not because he wanted anything for himself out of this, simply because he was interested in the story and he wanted to help Gramps.

'Here we go,' said Joe, as he pressed the call button on his phone. 'Hey, Daniel, it's me Joe Finch.' Joe wandered over to the water's edge and back. He was doing a lot of listening and not much talking.

Maddy sat down on the grass bank and hugged her knees to her chest while she waited for Joe to finish his call. She couldn't tell from what he was saying whether it was good or bad news.

However, when Joe finished his call and came over to her, she could see excitement dancing in his eyes. She jumped to her feet, buoyed by the thought they had, at last, some sort of lead. 'What? What is it? Don't tell me you've found her!'

Joe folded his arms. 'OK. I won't. Your wish is my command.'

'No! You can't do that!' She gave him a playful tap on the arm. 'Tell me. What did you find out?'

Joe gave a chuckle and then looking at his phone, he opened an email and read from the screen.

'Maryse Anne Dupont. Born 4 April 1924. Place of birth Vannes Maternity Hospital. Occupation, schoolteacher. Married Gilbert Pavard. Three children – I don't have the names for those yet. Resided in Vannes. Side note – was thought to have helped the local French resistance during the Second World War where her brother Hugo Dupont was executed by the Nazis after helping Allied forces prior to the D-Day landings.'

'Wow!' Maddy was lost for words momentarily. 'And your friend was able to find all that out?'

'Him and a friend of his. Like I said, they have access to certain records I can't easily get to at the moment. I owe him now.'

'Is that OK?'

'Sure. We do each other favours from time to time.' The expression on his face shifted from being very pleased with himself to one Maddy couldn't quite read. 'There is something else, though.'

Maddy felt the excitement evaporate. 'Bad news. I can probably guess.'

'There's no record of death.'

'No record? Well, that's good news, surely? It must mean Maryse is still alive!'

'Not necessarily.' Joe gave a sympathetic smile. 'It could be they just haven't found a death record yet. It happens.'

'Damn.' Maddy's heart clutched at her chest. 'I know this is going to sound daft, but I feel as if I know Maryse, like I have a connection and some sort of bond with her. I know you'll think I'm being over-sentimental but she's the last living link with Gramps's past that no one ever spoke about. I feel like it's my only chance to bridge the gap.'

'I know this must be so difficult for you,' said Joe.

'I'm gradually losing Gramps and they say their long-term memory is one of the last things to go. I thought if I knew more about his past, I could keep him with me for longer.' She blinked at the tears once again gathering in her eyes. 'I know it's stupid but I don't want to lose him this way. It's so sad and unfair.'

'Look, now I've got some info on the rest of the family, we could speak to them. If Maryse is still alive, then they might even be able to set up a meeting.'

'That would be amazing.'

'Of course, it's up to them and ultimately up to Maryse. You have to prepare yourself for the fact that she might not still be alive and if she is, she might not want to talk to us.'

Maddy reflected on the warning, wondering if she was strong enough to face direct rejection like that. Wondering how awful it would be if Maryse hadn't felt the same way about Gramps after the war. 'Oh, I don't know, Joe. Is it a good idea? What if Maryse hasn't even told them about Gramps?'

'We could go in softly, just in case. We could say we're researching the time your grandfather spent here and he had talked about Maryse and Hugo.'

'That's not strictly true though.'

'No but it means we don't go in and upset anyone. If they know the story of your grandfather and Maryse, then it won't matter and equally, if they know nothing, it still won't matter and we won't have caused them any harm or upset.'

'Maybe we should just leave it.'

'It's your call.'

'What do you want to do?'

'Whatever you want to.'

'That's not helping.' Maddy folded her arms and looked out across the lake as if the answer would magically appear.

'OK, imagine this scenario. We do nothing. We call it a day and no more delving into your grandfather's past. We go back to England tonight and that's that. No more talk of Maryse. No more wondering what part she played in your grandfather's life. We draw a line under it all.' He paused before continuing. 'Do you think you're able to do that without ever wondering if there was more to the story?'

She took her time to answer as she considered the idea. 'I think I am. I think I can leave Gramps to his memories. To let his secrets remain secrets.'

54

Arthur didn't like to see the child look so glum; in fact, everyone in the house was in a sombre mood. He knew he'd been out in a car that day, but he wasn't entirely sure where he went or why. He had a vague recollection of the child being with him and when they got back to the house, she had to do a lot of talking to the nurse who in turn did a lot of frowning and sighing. Was there a vicar there? Every now and then he got flashes of a woman vicar sitting here in the living room but that couldn't be right, could it? After that the child had gone upstairs and, well, he didn't know what had happened after that. All he knew was that he was sitting in his chair and the room was empty but that wasn't what was wrong. It was the house. It didn't have the same feel it usually did. He tried to pinpoint what was missing or different but the answer was elusive.

The dog came in and sat in front of Arthur, her big doe-like eyes looking pleadingly at him. 'I haven't got any treats for you. No good looking at me like that. You have to be a good dog to get treats.' Arthur thought for a moment and looked at the packet of digestives on the table. 'I don't think I deserve any treats.'

A well of emotion filled his throat and he gulped hard as a clarity he hadn't experienced for a long time washed over him. He remembered what he and the child had been doing, how they'd taken a taxi to see the vicar. Yvette! They were trying to find out what happened to the children he'd brought back to England all those years ago on that noisy aircraft.

He wished he knew how his story ended and what had happened to those he loved. Whatever the outcome, he just wished he knew. He didn't want to end his days never knowing. It was the worst thing and for now it was the hope of some sort of closure that encouraged him to cling to life itself.

On the horizon of his mind, the fog began drifting in on his lucid thoughts and harboured memories. Damn his stupid brain.

55

June 1947

Arthur stepped off the ferry as it docked in St Malo and paused to take in his surroundings. It had been under much different circumstances he had last arrived in France and by a much less orthodox method. At least today he hadn't had to parachute out of a plane in the middle of the night with only the moon to light his way. He thought of Freddie and how they had been so excited to be on a mission behind enemy lines. God, they had been young and naïve, thinking they were going to make a difference and come back heroes.

'*Passport, Monsieur?*' The voice of the French official broke through his thoughts. He mustn't dwell too much on Freddie; it was never good for his mood. It was a little over two years since VE Day and Arthur had finally saved enough money to come back to France to fulfil his promise to Maryse. He hoped it wasn't too late but more than anything, he hoped he would find her. Just to know she was safe and nothing had happened to her when he'd left her on that airstrip.

Once through passport control, he took the piece of paper from his pocket, which had his itinerary for getting to Sérent. It was going to take several hours of bus rides but there was no other way. France's infrastructure may now be better than when the Germans had left, but in rural parts of the country it still had some way to go.

Arthur winced as he lifted his small suitcase up onto the luggage rack above his seat. The French doctor had done a good job of saving his arm and the army surgeon had done an even better job of piecing back together his shattered bones, but the bullet had done too much damage for it to ever be one hundred per cent back to how it was before. As he took his seat on the bus, he caught sight of his reflection in the window. A bit different to how he looked when he was last here. Now in civvy clothes, his hair cut neatly and his face clean-shaven, he momentarily wondered if Maryse would recognise him – if indeed he was able to find her.

He hadn't received a reply to his letter sent to the family home. He had waited early for the postman each day. At first with the expectation of receiving a letter postmarked France, but as the days slipped into weeks, his expectation shifted to hope. His excitement at hearing the letter box rattle and post fall onto the doormat was dashed with every delivery, thinning out and eventually disappearing as the hope dissolved. He could only assume one of two things – either she hadn't received his letter in the first place or, and it pained him to have to consider this option, she didn't want to reply to him. Whatever the reason, he had to know. He had made a promise to her and he was damned if he was going to break it.

Several hours later the third bus Arthur had needed to transfer onto finally trundled its way into Sérent. He stepped down from the vehicle outside the church. It was ten minutes past one and the quiet little village was asleep as locals took their leisurely lunch hour or two. The buildings looked in pretty good shape and had survived with little lasting effects of the war. From what Arthur had learned, Brittany was finally freed from the clutches of the Germans some forty days after the D-Day landings. Unfortunately for him, he'd never been back to France since he'd left Maryse that night, his injured arm meaning he was no longer fit to serve in an active role. He'd been able to carry out a desk job but it had never fulfilled him. He wasn't a man who liked to sit around and push a pen across a piece of paper but he'd had no choice in the matter.

It took more than half an hour to walk from the village to the farmhouse and the heat of the summer sun wasn't making it exactly easy for him. Arthur was tempted to take off his jacket but resisted the urge, wanting to look smart when he arrived at the farmhouse and saw Maryse.

The dusty track that led from the road to the farmhouse felt longer than Arthur remembered but as he rounded the corner, the building finally came into view.

It had only been a few years, but the farm was a different place to the one he had left. The gates were open, one only hanging on by a single hinge and the paint was faded even more than he recalled. He walked through the stone archway and his eyes immediately travelled to the barn across the courtyard where he and Freddie had hidden. The sag in the roofline and the broken window in the gable end made for a neglected and pitiful sight.

The farmhouse itself looked unloved as paint peeled from the wooden shutters, which were closed, covering the windows. He didn't need to venture up to the front door to know the house was empty, but his feet were moving before he realised and his hand was on the door handle. He turned the knob but it was either jammed or locked. There was no letter box here to look through but Arthur knocked on the door anyway – just to be sure. There was no answer. He hadn't expected one.

The shrubs, hedges and flower beds were all overgrown and unkempt, giving the whole place a deserted and scruffy appearance. It was clear no one had lived here for a long time and Arthur's heart dipped. It was more than likely his letter to Maryse had never reached her.

He caught sight of the mailbox hanging on the gate post at the beginning of the drive and jogged over to the battered metal box. The front was still intact and locked. Joe took a small penknife from his trouser pocket, something he'd always carried on him since he was a boy, opened one of the blades and pushed it into the lock. With some persuasion, he managed to prise the lock open. There were several letters inside and he immediately recognised the one lying on top. It was the one he'd sent to Maryse.

He took out the letters and flicked through them. They were all addressed to Hugo. None of them had Maryse's name or that of her parents. Arthur's hopes were dashed. He had nothing else to go on. His search for her had arrived at a dead end. He returned Hugo's letters to the box and pushed the door closed, while slipping his letter to Maryse into his pocket.

Slowly, he walked through the courtyard, his mind filled with the many memories of his weeks hiding out here during the war. He had never expected to come back and find the farm abandoned. Empty. Only the ghost of his mate Freddie left to look over the place. He walked down to where the ground sloped away to the right, greeting the edge of the forest. It may be a few years now, but he remembered exactly where Freddie was. How could he forget? It was etched in his mind forever.

Arthur counted the trees, marked the steps and came to a halt under one of the pine trees. From here there wasn't the slightest indication of what lay below. No cross to mark the final resting place of his oppo. Arthur dropped to his knees as he was transported back to the day he had taken out his anger and grief on the ground, hacking away at the hardened soil to make a grave for Freddie.

'Hello, Freddie, mate. You still here?' He swept his hand over the hardened earth, like one might comfort a child stirring from their sleep. 'Told you I'd come back.' He patted the ground gently. 'A bit different to how it was last time I was here. Damn sight quieter, that's for sure. Ivy and little Vera are doing fine last time I saw them. They miss you but they're all right.' Arthur lit a cigarette and took a moment to look out across the valley and village beyond. He followed the path of the river, which tracked its way along the boundary of the farm. A thousand impressions filled his mind of him and Maryse here – laughing together, loving together, crying together, simply being together – it had been their spot. Their place to get away from the horrors of war and pretend for a few precious moments that life wasn't so cruel.

Finishing his smoke, he ground the stub out against the bark of the tree and flicked it into the dirt. 'Look, mate, I've got to go. Sleep well, Freddie.'

He ran a hand through his hair, loosened his tie and undid his shirt collar. Where to start now the trail for Maryse had gone cold? He hoped to God his worst fear wasn't going to be realised. He banished the notion from his mind, like he always did. He couldn't allow himself to imagine something terrible had happened to her. He refused to entertain that idea.

Slipping off his jacket and throwing it over his arm, Arthur turned with renewed determination. The village might hold the answer. Someone there would know, surely. He'd start with the priest, he decided.

He turned and began to walk purposefully back up towards the farmhouse. As he crossed the courtyard, he realised someone was standing at the gate, waiting for him.

56

After coming to the decision not to pursue Maryse and her family further, the rest of the morning passed in a subdued state. Maddy couldn't shake the sadness that had settled around her like a heavy blanket. She knew she should be making the most of her time with Joe as, once they got home, it would be full-on back to looking after Gramps and Esther.

Joe was doing his best to cheer her up, but she could tell he was running out of ideas. It was unfair of her.

'Sorry, I'm not very good company,' she said, as they finished packing their bags and checking ferry times and tickets.

'Hey, we're all allowed to feel disappointed and sad sometimes.'

'I know. And my logical, sensible head is saying just the same thing.'

'But your illogical, crazy head is saying otherwise?'

'I keep thinking about what you said: could I go back to England and draw a line under it all now? Have I completed the puzzle?' She zipped her rucksack shut. 'I'm not sure I can forget about it all. I just feel there's something missing. Something we haven't yet discovered or looked at. I don't

389

know what it is, but this can't be the end of the story.'

Joe turned her around to face him and held her hands in his. 'Some might say that's wishful thinking.'

'They might. But what if I'm right?'

'What if you're wrong?'

'How will I know?'

They both looked at each other for a long moment. Joe was leaving it up to her. She liked the idea that he wasn't trying to persuade her one way or the other.

'As I said before, it's your call,' said Joe.

She swallowed hard to quench her dry mouth. 'How far away is Vannes in terms of time?'

'Thirty minutes tops.'

'And our ferry? What time do we have to check in?'

'Ten-thirty tonight. Allowing three hours to get there. We'd have to leave Vannes by seven-thirty at the latest.'

Maddy looked at her watch. 'If we left now, we could be in Vannes by one-fifteen?'

'Yep.'

'And you think you could find an address for one of her children?'

'Already got that.' He took his phone from his pocket and gave it a wiggle in the air.

'I'm impressed.'

'Just in case you had a change of heart.'

The drive down to Vannes was straightforward and they had missed the rush-hour traffic into the town.

'I have an address that's only the other side of town,' said Joe, as he navigated the car in accordance with the satnav directions. 'It's a small coastal village south-west of Vannes. I looked it up on the internet. It's popular with holiday makers apparently. There's a harbour with a man-made lagoon and sandy beach. If we get time, maybe we could go down there and have a look.'

'Sounds like a good idea. We can celebrate or commiserate, depending how the meeting goes. It's Thomas, her son, you said?'

'Yes, that's right.' Joe slowed the car and took the right turn. 'And this is the road.' They cruised slowly down the tree-lined street, looking for number 43. They came to a stop outside a detached property with a grey slate roof and whitewashed walls. Two dormer windows protruded from the roof like eyes looking down at them. There was a small flight of steps up to the front door, with a car port below.

'I suddenly feel nervous, like this isn't a good idea,' confessed Maddy.

'Do you want me to go up first and speak to him?'

'Probably best if I come with you. You seem to have forgotten your linguistic skills may not be quite up to the job.'

'Ah, yes, good point.'

They waited anxiously on the doorstep as Joe rang the bell and after a few moments they were greeted by an elderly man. She knew instantly this was Maryse's son – she could tell by the eyes, which were exactly the same as she had seen in the photographs of Maryse.

'*Monsieur Pavard? Thomas Pavard?*' enquired Maddy, smiling at the gentleman.

'*Oui,*' he replied, looking suspiciously from one to the other.

'*Bonjour, Monsieur Pavard,*' began Maddy. She went on to introduce herself and give a brief explanation. 'We're here because we believe my grandfather, Arthur Pettinger, was a good friend of your mother's during the war – Maryse Dupont as she was then.'

'Yes, that's right. Maryse Dupont latterly Maryse Pavard,' replied the man.

The man's tone was guarded and Maddy could sense his reticence at discussing his mother. 'It's rather delicate, but we believe my grandfather and your mother were close friends and my grandfather speaks of her often. He never knew what happened to her after the war and we are trying to find out. He's an elderly man now and I think it would bring him a lot of comfort to know.'

The man's face hardened further. 'I know nothing about this. Nothing.'

'Arthur Pettinger – has your mother ever mentioned him to you?' Maddy's heart began to sink. 'Does the name mean anything to you?'

'What happened here in the war is in the past now and it should stay there. It is not your business or mine.'

'What's happening?' asked Joe under his breath.

But before Maddy had time to translate, Thomas Pavard had closed the door. Maddy let out a frustrated grunt, spun on her heel and marched back to the car.

'I take it he doesn't want to talk,' said Joe, slipping into the driver's seat. 'You get that sometimes.'

'It's so frustrating,' sighed Maddy. 'And I hate how I can swing from dejection to hope and back to dejection again. I suppose in my head I have some romantic idea that Maryse is still alive and wants to see Gramps or at least her son would say how much she loved Gramps and it would be something I could take as some sort of comfort and closure.' She threw her head back against the rest and closed her eyes. 'I'm just a stupid romantic who needs to stop believing in fairy-tale endings. Look where that's got me.'

'It's got you here with me,' said Joe.

Maddy opened her eyes and looked at him, unsure if he was teasing, but for once he looked sincere. 'How's that a fairy-tale ending?'

'It can be if you'll trust me again. Look, I know I don't deserve it, don't deserve you, but remember when I promised not to make a promise I couldn't keep?'

Maddy nodded as her heart flipped in her chest. 'Yes.'

Joe cleared his throat. 'I promise I'll never let you down again, you or Esther.'

'Oh, Joe... I don't know what to say. I want to say yes, but I'm scared.'

'I know and I don't know how to make you not feel scared of trusting me. I thought if I hung around enough, kept showing up and being here for you, that I could start to win your trust again.'

'I think it's working.'

'That's all I need to hear right now,' replied Joe. 'We can just take things nice and easy. No rush. No pressure. Your pace.'

Maddy reached across and held Joe's hand. 'Thank you.'

They drove out of Vannes in silence. Maddy going over again what Joe had said. Alarm bells should be ringing, she should not even be entertaining the idea that she and Joe could get back together, but her heart was having none of that sensible talk whatsoever.

For no logical reason, she took her phone from her bag and holding it away from her, she snapped a selfie of her and Joe. He grinned into the camera lens as Maddy continued to take several more pictures.

As she looked back through them, she noticed a new photo on the iCloud stream she hadn't seen before. She peered at the photograph.

'What's that?' asked Joe taking a peek at the picture.

'My phone and Esther's iPad share the same cloud for our photographs, so we can see what each other has taken a picture of. I set it up like that for online safety, you know because Esther has her vlog.'

'OK, so that's something she's taken?'

'Yeah. It looks like a list of names.' Maddy gave a gasp.

'What's up?' asked Joe, having to make a quick adjustment to his road position. 'What's wrong? Maddy?'

'It's a register,' she said. 'A register of children evacuated to the parish of Little Paxton during the war. This must have been what Esther and Gramps were doing there. Esther must have somehow been able to take a photo of the page.' She scanned the names. 'This one!'

By now Joe was pulling the car over into a side street. 'What one?'

'This name. Yvette Rochelle. That's the name Gramps kept saying. The child he was concerned about and said he needed to know what happened to her!'

'Bloody hell,' muttered Joe. 'Esther's a proper Miss Marple. I'm going to have to get her working for me.'

'Oh my God, you are not going to believe this.' Maddy could hardly believe it herself. 'It says here that Yvette Rochelle was collected by Maryse Dupont and taken back to France. There's another name in brackets. Jean-Paul Rochelle.'

'Her brother,' said Joe. 'This is gold. Somehow Gramps is connected to these children. He must have brought them over to England and they were part of the evacuee programme. And then, after the war, Maryse comes and finds them and takes them back to France.'

'The tickets!' exclaimed Maddy. She pulled out the envelope

Collette had given them and rummaged through the contents until she found the bus tickets. She held them out to Joe.

'That's why there are three tickets from St Neots,' said Joe excitedly. 'They're tickets for her and the children.'

'We need to know what happened to those children,' said Maddy. 'If I can give Gramps some good news, then that might counter any bad news about Maryse.'

'I agree but please don't get carried away,' cautioned Joe. 'One step at a time.'

'I know but remember, I'm a hopeless romantic and I believe in fairy-tale endings.'

Joe smiled. 'I'll do my best. Now let me see if I can get an address or some sort of info on Yvette Rochelle.'

It took another phone call to his contact in France and an agonising wait of forty-five minutes, spent cruising around the area just to kill time, before they received the information they were hoping for.

Joe beamed at Maddy as he ended the call. 'Yvette Tresor, nee Rochelle, and her brother Jean-Paul were brought back to France in 1946 by Maryse Dupont, then a year later Maryse married a Gilbert Pavard and adopted Yvette and Jean-Paul.'

'Wow, that's amazing!' Maddy was full of admiration for what Maryse had done. 'But what about Thomas? Where does he fit into all this?'

'Right, let's quickly check this,' said Joe, scrolling through the document his contact had emailed. 'Here we are… oh, that's interesting.'

'What is?' Maddy could tell Joe had moved into historian mode and was lost in the research.

'Sorry,' he said. 'According to this, which I have no doubt not to trust, Maryse Dupont married Gilbert Pavard in September 1947, the same month Yvette and Jean-Paul Rochelle were adopted by the Pavards. Then, six months later Thomas Pavard was born.'

'So... Maryse would have been three months pregnant when she married Gilbert Pavard.'

'Exactly.'

Maddy was thoughtful for a few minutes before finally speaking again. 'I hope she was happy and married him for the right reasons. I hate to think she might have waited for Gramps had she not fallen pregnant.'

'Missed opportunities. Circumstances conspiring against them. It happens. People live with regrets. It doesn't mean they can't be happy and enjoy the rest of their lives but there will always be a part of them that secretly wondered what if.'

Maddy turned to Joe. 'I don't want to live in limbo, always wondering.'

'Neither do I.' He leaned across the car and kissed her softly on the lips. Then moving away, he was back to his business-like self. 'I owe my contact a drink when I next see him. He's come up trumps this time.'

'How come?' Maddy asked, trying to refocus and not be overwhelmed by her ever-resurfacing feelings for Joe and hopes for what might be.

'We've got an address for Yvette and... according to my satnav... it's fifteen minutes away, in Vannes itself. In fact... wow! In fact, it looks like it was the house where Maryse lived during her marriage.'

'So, she might be there! This gets even more amazing,' said Maddy. 'Just think, we're going to be at the house that Maryse herself lived in. Actually standing in her footsteps.'

'Ah, you've caught the bug,' said Joe with a grin.

'The bug?'

'The history bug. The thought of time travel – or as much as is possible. Reliving moments of a time long past albeit partly in your own mind.'

'Seems like a nice bug to catch.'

'There's no cure for it, you know.'

'I can live with that.' She grinned, so glad she'd come across that photograph on iCloud. Butterflies stirred in her stomach in anticipation. 'I think our meeting is going to be a good one,' she said as Joe reset the satnav.

The house they parked outside was a beautiful double-fronted detached property, with three floors. Pale blue shutters shouldered each of the windows and as was typical of the area, the outside of the house had been rendered and painted white. A driveway swept through double gates into a turning circle, the lawn in the centre occupied by a large monkey puzzle tree, whilst shrubs and bushes bordered the lawn on both sides. Huge blue hydrangeas grew either side of the pale blue front door.

Joe gave a low whistle. 'Important-looking house. Not bad for a schoolteacher.'

'It looks like it might have been a schoolhouse once upon a time,' commented Maddy.

'I'd say that Monsieur Pavard was a wealthy man.'

'Oh, look, someone's there,' said Maddy, as the door opened and a woman with grey hair tied back and wearing a floral dress appeared. She looked over at Maddy and Joe before beckoning them to come through the gates.

'You are Maddy Pettinger?' she asked as they got out of the car. Her English was perfect, with hardly a trace of French accent, but Maddy was more surprised by the welcome they were receiving. It was as if this was a prearranged visit.

'Er… yes, I am. And you are Madame Yvette Tresor?'

'Yes, that's right.' She looked at Joe.

'This is my friend, Joe Finch,' supplied Maddy.

Yvette smiled warmly. 'I'm so glad you came. My brother, Thomas, telephoned me to say you had been to see him. I thought you'd come here next.'

Maddy was unsure how this was all playing out. Thomas had been positively hostile to their visit, whereas Yvette was welcoming. 'He wasn't happy to see us.'

'No. I must apologise if he was rude to you. My brother and I… of course when I say brother, I don't mean by blood… my blood brother, Jean-Paul, and I were adopted by Thomas's parents, but you probably know that.'

Maddy nodded. 'We've only just made the connection though. We were originally going to see Thomas about your adoptive mother and then we found out about you. It's a bit complicated.'

'That's a matter of opinion,' replied Yvette. 'Once you know all the facts, then it is straightforward. Thomas and I have opposing views about discussing what happened during and after the war. We have experienced different things and Thomas may know what Jean-Paul and I went through but that is not the same as having lived it. Please, come in and we can talk some more.'

Maddy exchanged an excited look with Joe and they followed Yvette into the house where they were shown to a large reception room on the right. It was tastefully and modestly furnished with elegant antique furniture.

'What a beautiful room,' said Maddy, admiring the chandelier that hung from the ceiling and the open fireplace big enough to stand in. There were framed photographs dotted around the room.

'Thank you,' said Yvette. 'My mother had good taste.'

Maddy stopped in her tracks as she noted the past tense Yvette had used. 'Your mother, Maryse, is she… is she here?'

Yvette gave a small but diluted smile. 'I'm afraid not.'

Maddy felt Joe's hand rest on her back. 'Oh, I'm sorry,' said Maddy. 'I didn't know. I was hoping…' The words faded as her hopes of meeting the woman Gramps had once loved were extinguished. She felt a heaviness inside her akin to grief, knowing she'd never get the opportunity to connect directly with Gramps's past.

'She passed away five years ago,' replied Yvette. 'Please, sit down. I can see it is a disappointment for you.' She indicated towards the sofa while she went over to the sideboard and picked up a photo frame. She held it out for Maddy. It was a picture of a young dark-haired woman sitting on a five-bar gate laughing at the camera. 'This is Maryse. She would have been about twenty. Please, feel free to look at the others. I will make some coffee.'

Maddy didn't want to sit. She felt gutted at the news and instead wandered around the room, taking in the photographs, identifying which ones she thought were Maryse. Such a beautiful woman, it was no wonder she'd never left her grandfather's mind or his heart. He, of course, must only have known her when she was a young woman, but the photographs here showed her over the years as she grew older, married, had Thomas, and the family gatherings and occasions as her family grew into adults themselves. Always, always, she was smiling. She looked to have loved life.

A moment of sadness entered Maddy's heart. She didn't know what she had been expecting, but seeing Maryse look so happy, she wondered if she'd ever missed Gramps. Had she not thought of him in the way he had thought of her? Had Gramps just been someone who she'd enjoyed a brief relationship with?

'Stunning-looking woman,' said Joe, coming to stand beside her. He took the photograph of Maryse in old age from Maddy and replaced it on the dresser. 'You OK?'

'I will be. Right now, I'm so disappointed,' said Maddy. 'And now, I'm scared of what we're about to find out.'

'Because it may not be the ending you'd hoped for?'

'You're too wise for your own good – you know that?' She rested her head on his shoulder briefly. 'I hope whatever we find out now isn't going to be something I regret chasing.'

'Whatever the ending, at least you'll know and then you can decide what you do with that knowledge. Sometimes, the truth is too painful. Too hurtful. Too crushing. I've seen it with families I've worked with. The skeletons come hurtling out of the closet and turn people's lives upside down. Sometimes for the better but often for the worse.'

'Now you tell me.'

'Sorry. I'm only trying to prepare you.'

'I'll deal with it. As long as Gramps is protected, I'm quite prepared to be the last one to know any secret. Apart from you that is, but I trust you.'

'I'm honoured to have your trust.'

There was no teasing or banter in his voice, just genuine sincerity, and it gave Maddy yet another reason to be thankful he was there.

Yvette returned with a tray of coffee. Maddy knew from Joe that Yvette was in her late eighties. She was elegantly dressed, her hair neatly fashioned in a bob, a touch of makeup and manicured nails completed the sophisticated look.

'*Alors*,' began Yvette once they were settled with their

drinks. 'You are probably wondering why I was pleased to see you and why I was so excited.'

Maddy nodded. 'You didn't seem surprised. Nor did your brother.'

'No. I've been waiting for a long time.'

'But how? I don't understand,' asked Maddy.

'My father was a schoolteacher at the village school,' began Yvette. 'Maryse Dupont, as she was then, worked alongside him. She was training to be a teacher herself when the war broke out.'

'This was in Sérent?' queried Joe.

'That's right,' replied Yvette. 'The war had been going on for a couple of years and the area was under German occupation. At first it wasn't too bad but then things began to change as the Germans began to round up the Jews and, of course, we all know the barbaric things that happened. Now, my father was a Catholic and so am I but, my mother, she was Jewish. One day, she was there and the next day she was gone.' It was obviously still painful for her despite the passing of time. 'They took my mother one day when I was at school. My father was teaching and someone ran to the school to tell him. We raced back home but it was too late. My father got there just as she was being bundled into the back of a lorry. It was awful, so very awful. Unimaginable. My father tried to stop them, but he was hit with the butt of a rifle.'

Maddy moved to sit next to Yvette and put her arm around the woman's shoulders. 'I'm so sorry. Please, you don't have to talk about it if you don't want to.'

Yvette sat upright, a defiant expression settling on her face. 'I will never be silent about what happened. I would sooner die than to dishonour my mother's memory and those who suffered at the hands of the Nazis.'

'Of course,' said Maddy. 'I can only imagine how it was.'

The shoulders of the older woman relaxed a fraction and her voice was softer when she spoke. 'You see this is where Thomas and I differ. He didn't witness any of this but I experienced it all.'

'And we owe everyone who went through that and for speaking up so we never forget, a great debt,' said Joe. 'It's important that the world knows the truth.'

'*Exactement.*' Yvette gave Joe an almost military-like nod of acknowledgement. 'Now, as you can imagine, my father was terrified they would come for me and Jean-Paul, even though we had been baptised and brought up as Catholics. Soon after my mother was taken, the Germans requisitioned our home. He was scared for us. He had heard terrible things about what was happening to the Jewish people so he asked Maryse for help.'

'To hide you?' asked Joe.

'Yes. My brother and I were only young but we understood what was happening. We didn't want to leave Papa but he said there was no choice. That day, Maryse came for us; she had help from a British soldier who had been at their farmhouse. He'd been hiding there after being parachuted in. Anyway, this soldier was your grandfather, Arthur.'

'Wow,' whispered Maddy, as a tingling ran the length of her spine. 'Gramps helped you escape?'

'Yes. Exactly that. A few nights later, we were put on an aeroplane with your grandfather and flown to England.'

'What about Maryse?'

'She didn't come. She wanted to stay and fight with the resistance. I remember her crying as they closed the aircraft door. Your grandfather was upset too. He had been injured – shot in the shoulder. He had no choice but to return to England.'

'What happened to you after that?' asked Joe. Maddy guessed he was rapidly piecing together all the information and was probably already several steps ahead of her.

'We were placed in different homes of English families. My family were kind but I was sad and lonely in the middle of East Anglia. All I wanted was to go home and find Papa.'

'Your brother?'

'Not so good. His family were poor and didn't treat him well. I didn't see him for the whole of the time we were in England.'

'Oh, how upsetting for you both.'

'They thought it was best to keep us apart in case it made us feel even worse,' said Yvette. She shook her head and tutted. 'When the war ended, we stayed with our families for another six months. Every day I asked when we could go home and every day I was told soon. And then one day, it was like my prayers had been answered and this beautiful angel had been sent to save me.'

'Maryse?' Maddy asked softly.

'Yes. She had come to England to try to find your grandfather. You see she loved him dearly, but she couldn't find him anywhere.'

Maddy swallowed down a lump of empathy in her throat. This was tougher to hear than she had imagined. 'But she found you?'

'Yes. Me and my brother. She brought us back to France.'

'And your father?' asked Maddy.

Yvette's eyes welled up. 'He was not spared. He had been killed soon after the Germans took the house. I believe he gave his life to save ours, refusing to say where we were.'

'Oh, I'm so sorry,' said Maddy, reaching across to hold Yvette's hand.

'We came back to the farmhouse with Maryse. She had lost her brother. She took us in and looked after us. Then she received a letter to say that Arthur had died from his injuries.'

Maddy gasped. 'Who told her that?'

'I don't remember. A well-meaning army officer perhaps. I just remember her crying and crying for days and days. After everything she had been through, this hit her the hardest. I may have been young but I knew then how much she loved the British soldier.'

57

June 1947

At first Arthur thought it might be Maryse – the sun was shining in his eyes and it was hard to make out the figure. But as he shielded his face with his hand, he could see it was a man – a younger man, maybe around Arthur's own age.

'*Bonjour!*' called Arthur with a small wave.

The young man waited for Arthur to near him before replying. '*Bonjour.*' He looked at Arthur with suspicion, wanting to know what he was doing. '*Qu'est-ce que vous faites?*'

'I'm looking for a friend of mine,' explained Arthur. 'I know the Dupont family. I'm trying to find Maryse Dupont. Do you know where they are?'

The man viewed Arthur through narrowed eyes. 'Who are you?'

'Arthur Pettinger.' He extended his hand but the offer was not taken. 'I stayed here during the war.'

The young man's eyes relaxed a fraction. 'Here?'

'Yes. I was injured and the family looked after me.' Arthur wasn't quite sure how much to say but felt he was being tested in some way.

'Alone?'

'No. With my friend but, sadly, he didn't recover from his injuries.'

There was a long pause before the man spoke. 'Victor Bisset.' This time it was Victor who offered the handshake.

Arthur accepted the gesture. 'Do you know what happened to the family?'

'Madame Dupont, she lives with her sister in Malestroit.'

'And her son?'

Victor shook his head. 'Dead.'

A sombre note loitered in the air. 'The Germans?' asked Arthur.

'*Oui*. Together with three other villagers. They were caught soon after you left.'

'No!' Arthur heard himself say in disbelief. He didn't want it to be true.

'Hugo and the men, they were treated badly. Tortured. Beaten. After three weeks of imprisonment and torture, they were lined up in the square in Sérent and shot.'

'I had no idea. I'm so sorry,' said Arthur. His mind was racing. He hardly dared to ask the next question. 'Was it just the men?'

'If you mean was Maryse captured, the answer is no. She managed to escape.'

Arthur let out a long sigh of relief. 'Thank God.'

'She inherited this place but she hasn't been back. My wife tells me it's because she can't bear the pain of the loved ones she lost.'

Arthur's heart felt it might break on her behalf. He couldn't imagine how traumatic it must have been for Maryse. 'Do you know where she is now?'

'Vannes. She's a teacher at a school.'

'Do you know the name of the school?'

'Sorry but I think it is near the church St Suzanne. My wife remembered because there is a chapel not far from here with the same name.'

'Thank you,' said Arthur trying to contain his excitement. He had some positive information about where she was. He was one step closer to finding her. 'I appreciate your help.' As he shook hands with Victor again, he was already planning in his mind how he was going to get to Vannes and how he'd find Maryse.

Part 3

58

The night crossing back to the UK had been uneventful and Joe had lain awake a long time into the night as he watched Maddy sleeping on the bunk opposite him. It had been an emotional weekend and he was glad he'd been able to share it with her. She looked peaceful now as she slept and Joe felt a deep desire to protect her but he wasn't sure that's what she wanted.

No, Maddy wanted commitment from him, someone she could trust to show up every day and be there for her but in an equal relationship. She wanted someone to love her and to care for Esther too. He was pretty sure she wanted him to do all that and he was absolutely certain he wanted the exact same thing too. He just needed to prove to her that he had changed. Maybe changed was the wrong word – he felt he now knew what he wanted. He'd lost it once when he'd been frightened to commit and God knows what he was frightened of back then but whatever it was, it wasn't part of the equation now. He loved Maddy then, loved her while she was gone and loved her now she was back in his life. It was up to him to convince her he was the real deal.

As he agonised what he could do to prove himself, he must have eventually drifted off to sleep, because the next thing he knew it was morning and the ship's wake-up music was filtering out through the tannoy.

'Hey,' said Maddy, as he rolled over. She was sitting on the edge of her bunk, already dressed, with her phone in her hand. 'Did you want to grab a coffee?'

'Yeah, sure. Give me five minutes.' As he took a quick shower, Joe continued to torture himself with ways to convince Maddy she could count on him. He had woken with the exact same feeling for her as he'd acknowledged the night before but as the water cascaded over his shoulders he realised he would have to tread carefully and be patient. Not one of his better known attributes but the more he thought about his predicament the more he was certain he needed to let her work through things herself. It was no good backing her into a corner. If she still wanted to see him once all this business with her grandfather had died down, then he'd be there but he wasn't going to make life difficult for her and put pressure on her.

By the time they had disembarked and driven home, Joe was convinced this was the right thing to do. Maddy had spent the journey either dozing or looking out of the window. She looked to be deep in thought and Joe didn't want to pester her. This was all part of his back-off-give-her-space approach. He only hoped it would pay off.

Ten minutes out from Maddy's house and Joe reached out to give her a gentle nudge. 'Hey, sleepyhead, we're nearly there.'

Maddy sat up and rubbed her face with her hands. 'Sorry, what a rotten travelling companion I've been.'

'Asleep or awake, you've been the best companion,' said Joe and he meant it. He'd loved spending time with Maddy and already knew he was going to miss her tonight.

'I'm glad we've had this time together,' said Maddy.

'Me too.' Joe couldn't think of anything better to say.

'I don't mean this to sound all deep and meaningful or cheesy, but being with you has been such a stark difference to the other men I've dated.'

'In a good way, I hope.'

'I think for a long time, I was just grateful for anyone being remotely interested in me. I mean, who wants to take on someone with an eleven-year-old child? Not exactly ideal relationship material.'

'You shouldn't ever feel you're not good enough, that you need to be something you're not. If someone cares about you, they accept you for what you are and if that includes an eleven-year-old daughter then that shouldn't be a problem because being a mother is a fundamental part of you.'

'Yeah, I'm not sure I've met anyone who sees it like that. They all make out they're cool with it, but really they're not. The truth is they don't want to take on someone else's child. But I'm fine with that. I don't want to have to feel grateful anymore or be made to feel like a pity-party.'

'It's not the things we say or do or the material things we can offer – they're just the basic stuff. It's how we feel and how we make others feel that's important.'

'Helps complete Maslow's pyramid,' said Maddy with a smile.

'Absolutely. Being told by someone they love us is not enough; we need to feel it too,' said Joe as he turned into Maddy's road. 'And it has to work both ways.' He forced himself to shut up in case he said too much. It was up to Maddy to decide; much as he wanted another chance, he wasn't going to force her into it. She needed to feel it.

As Joe pulled onto the drive of Gramps's house, he saw the

curtain to the living room move. They'd been spotted. Any second now the welcoming committee would be upon them. He wanted to lean across and wrap her in his arms, to hold her close, to kiss her, but he knew he couldn't.

'I know we need to talk – me and you,' said Maddy. 'But I need to talk to Gramps.'

'OK.'

'So much has changed in the last few weeks and I need time to deal with it all.'

'Still OK.'

'Thank you, Joe, for everything. It means a lot.'

Joe wasn't quite sure he liked the sound of this signing off. It sounded almost terminal but before he had time to say anything else, Esther was running out of the front door, squealing in delight. 'Mum! Yay! You're home!'

Maddy was out of the car, enveloping her daughter in a big squashy hug. Kay appeared in the doorway and gave a wave in Joe's direction.

As Joe got out the car to fetch Maddy's bags from the boot, Esther pounced on him. It took him by surprise, but he was delighted to receive a fierce hug from her too. 'Whoa! I wasn't expecting such a welcome.' He laughed, looking over the roof of the car at Maddy.

'I'm glad you're back,' said Esther, looking up at him. Her face took on a serious expression. 'Are you coming in?'

'Only for a minute. I'll bring your mum's bags in.' Joe took the bags inside and was greeted by an excited French bulldog. He put the luggage at the foot of the stairs and crouched down to make a fuss of the dog.

'At least she's pleased to see someone,' said Maddy standing in the hall.

'Now, Fifi, you and I need a talk,' said Joe, ruffling the

dog's ears. 'Much as I love you, I'm not your master. You have a perfectly good mistress over there. You treat her right and she'll love you forever.' He gave Maddy a wink and stage-whispered into Fifi's ear. 'Top tip, she hates her feet being cold, snuggle up to them at night to keep them warm.'

Maddy gave a laugh. 'Who do you think you are, Doctor Dolittle?' It was at that point Fifi looked up at Maddy as if seeing her for the first time. To everyone's amazement the dog trotted over to her. 'Wow! What have I done to deserve this?' Maddy squatted down and stroked the dog.

'Looks like she's missed you,' said Joe. 'You've a new friend there.'

'About time.' Maddy and Joe both rose. 'Come on, Fifi.' Maddy patted her thigh and walked down the hall, with Fifi following her. 'Your little talk must have done the job.' She beamed at Joe before going into the living room to greet her grandfather. 'Hello, Gramps! How are you?' She leaned over and gave him a kiss and a hug. 'It's me, Maddy. I'm back now.'

'Hello, duck. Did you get everything you needed?'

Maddy looked confused and turned to Kay, who had followed in behind Joe. 'I told him you'd gone to the shops. He's been asking about you this morning.'

'Oh, has he?' A look of guilt crossed Maddy's face and Joe immediately felt a pang of sympathy for her. He wished she wouldn't give herself a hard time about leaving Gramps for a few days.

'Yes, but your grandfather has been fine,' said Kay reassuringly. 'He's had a good weekend. I'll give you a call later to go over everything in more detail, if you like. I'll just nip upstairs and get my things together.'

'I suppose that means you need to get off,' said Maddy, turning to Joe, while still cradling Gramps's hand in her own.

'Yeah, 'fraid so.'

'Oh, do you have to?' asked Esther, sticking out her bottom lip. 'Can't you stay?'

'Ah, sorry, sweetheart.' He wanted to say he'd see Esther again soon, but he bit back the words, not wanting to put the pressure on Maddy or to break his word to the eleven-year-old. He was done with all that. He looked to Maddy hoping for some reassurance from her but she just gave a weak smile.

Fortunately, Kay was coming back down the stairs and the awkward moment was broken. 'Right. Got everything?' asked Joe, turning to his friend.

'Yep.' Kay said her goodbyes to Arthur, Esther and Sheila before accompanying Joe out the door.

Maddy came to the door and called Joe back. 'Won't be a moment,' he said to Kay, before walking back up the driveway to where Maddy was standing. 'You OK?'

'Thanks for everything again,' she said. 'I do appreciate it.'

'You don't have to keep thanking me. I enjoyed it. A lot.'

She twiddled the pendant on her necklace. 'I'll give you a call.'

'Sure. I'd like that.'

'Next week maybe.' She sounded uncertain.

'I'll look forward to that.'

'Thanks, Joe.'

He hesitated. His brain was telling him to go but his heart wasn't on the same page. Finally, he managed a compromise. 'I don't mind waiting. For a while, anyway. I'm a patient man, but maybe not as patient as your grandfather.' He attempted a smile.

'I know,' replied Maddy. She ran her finger down the edge of his jacket. 'I don't want to end up like Maryse. You know

– missing the chance of happiness. Letting it go because of other things going on. I don't want to have those regrets.'

'Me neither.'

'I will call. I promise.'

'Remember what we said about promises.'

'I haven't forgotten.'

It took all Joe's willpower to turn and walk away from her. He hoped to God she didn't wake up in the morning to reality and bitterly regret what had gone on between them – whatever that was. He also hoped he wouldn't regret walking away from her and Esther so easily for a second time although this time it was for the right reasons.

59

Maddy sighed as she went back into the house after seeing Joe off. She knew she didn't have the right to keep Joe waiting even though he wasn't backing her into a corner or delivering an ultimatum. He wasn't forcing her hand but letting her deal with things in her own way. She was also aware that a weekend away in France wasn't the rock to anchor her heart to.

'Your grandfather wants to go up to bed,' said Sheila, as Maddy walked into the living room. Gramps was standing up, one hand resting on his walking stick and the other gripping on to Sheila's arm. Gramps didn't look particularly happy.

'I'm tired. Very tired,' he said, walking towards her. 'I think I'll go up for a nap.'

'Here, I'll help you,' said Maddy. 'Thank you, Sheila. You sit down there – I'm sure you could do with a rest. I'll take Gramps upstairs.'

They made their way up to Gramps's room, each step on the staircase seemingly taking a lot of effort on Gramps's part. Maddy wondered if now was the time to move Gramps downstairs to the other sitting room so he didn't have to navigate the staircase anymore.

Finally, they made it to Gramps's bedroom. 'Lift your chin

up.' Maddy fiddled around with the tie and slid the knot down, before slipping the tie away. 'Let's undo those top buttons on your shirt. There, all done.'

Before she could move her hand away, Gramps covered it with his own. 'Thank you, duck. I do love you and I am grateful.'

'Oh, Gramps, you don't have to thank me,' sighed Maddy, relishing the moment of clarity from her grandfather. 'I love you too and it makes me happy to help you.'

'Where's that nice young man?' asked Gramps.

Maddy was a little taken aback by the sudden turn in conversation, not to mention disappointed that the moment of real connection between her and Gramps appeared to have broken. 'Young man? Do you mean Joe?'

Gramps frowned. 'The nice one. The one who makes you smile.'

As if by magic, Maddy did indeed find herself smiling. 'Yes, Joe.'

'That's it. The one who makes you smile like that.'

'Joe's had to go home.' Maddy felt the smile downgrade itself at the thought of Joe not being here.

Gramps was still holding her hand. 'What's wrong, duck? You can tell me. I know I'm a silly old fool but you can tell me.'

'Oh, Gramps, you are not a silly old fool. Not at all.' She hugged him and he put his arms around her, his bony hand patting her back. She stayed there, enjoying the comfort she hadn't experienced for a long time from her grandfather.

'There, there, lovey,' he said. 'It can't be as bad as that. Come on, sit down.'

Maddy sat down on the bed next to Gramps. 'I'm scared,' she admitted. 'I'm scared of my feelings for Joe.'

'You mustn't be scared. We have to be brave in matters of the heart.'

Maddy looked at Gramps, studying his face. He looked back at her with a confidence and compassion that reminded her of when she was a young child and he used to comfort her. Although, today, she wasn't sure if it was as easy to solve her dilemma as it was a scraped knee, a falling out with a friend or a bicycle puncture. Nevertheless, she found herself opening up to Gramps, maybe because it felt like a safe place to do so, even if Gramps didn't fully understand what she was saying. She knew these lucid moments, these times when communication came easy for him, were few and far between and something inside her was urging her to seize the moment, hang on to it and make the most of it. 'Joe was the first person I loved, outside of the family that is. And I don't think I've ever got past that.'

'You don't forget your first love.'

Maddy rested her head on Gramps's shoulder. He wasn't wrong there. Joe had never been far from her mind. She thought of Gramps's own life and couldn't help comparing it with her own situation. Gramps had gone on to love her grandmother. They'd had a family together and he'd always said how much he loved her. She was reminded of what her grandmother had said about them looking after each other as they recovered from broken hearts. They didn't have the luxury of a second chance at first love.

Maddy sat up as the thought struck her. What if in some cases, like hers, first love could also be true love? And what if she stopped being scared and took the chance? If she didn't, she'd spend the rest of her life not knowing and possibly never loving like she felt she could.

'Thank you, Gramps!' she said and went to hug him but

she saw his head was bowed, his chin dipping down to his chest and his shoulders slumped. Gramps was nodding off. She leaned over and kissed his cheek, this time whispering her thanks. 'Lie down, Gramps. That's it. Rest your head on the pillow.' She slipped off his shoes and, lifting his feet, she swung his legs around onto the bed and pulled a blanket over him.

'Night, night, duck,' mumbled Gramps.

Of course it wasn't night-time, but Maddy didn't correct her grandfather. She closed the door softly to Gramps's bedroom and made her way back downstairs. Was it as simple as all that? She loved Joe but she had to take that leap of faith and trust him again.

60

In the few days Maddy had been home, she found herself waiting eagerly and sometimes desperately to see Joe again, who had unexpectedly been caught up with work. She'd phoned him the next day after arriving back and they had chatted for ages about the weekend and Joe had promised he'd call her as soon as he'd finalised a case he was working on. She hoped it wasn't a brush-off, but Joe had assured her it was nothing of the sort, reminding her of the promise he'd made to her. So, for three days, she'd had to patiently sit and wait.

As she slipped her feet out of bed and onto the floor, she let out a little yelp of fright as her feet touched something warm and furry.

'Bloody hell, Fifi,' she gasped. 'What on earth are you doing in here?' The dog opened one eye and looked up at her but stayed curled up on the floor. 'So, you like me now, is that it? My, I am going up in the world.' She reached down to stroke her, but then Fifi jumped up and trotted out of the door with her nose in the air. 'Playing hard to get now,' called Maddy. Oh, well, it was progress.

Gramps was in good form that morning, which Maddy was pleased about. She had so far held off speaking to Gramps about Maryse and Yvette. While he seemed happy they were back, she didn't want to risk the possibility of upsetting him as she was frightened of the finality it would bring. Gramps hadn't spoken about either of them and she wondered if they had finally slipped the grasp of his memory.

Gramps and Esther were now in the garden and she watched from the kitchen window as together they refilled the birdseed holders. Esther was taking pictures and recording some small scenes that she wanted to upload onto her YouTube channel later.

It warmed Maddy's heart to see them there and it reminded her of when she was a child and used to do the same with Gramps. They would then retreat to the old Anderson shelter at the bottom of the garden, where they would sit quietly with the door open and wait for the birds to come to the feeding station. Then he knew every garden bird there was and would point them out to Maddy as they darted back and forth from the hedgerow to the feeder. Afterwards, they would look at a book Gramps had of garden birds and they would try to find the ones they'd seen.

Maddy went into the living room and looked along the bookshelves until she found what she was looking for. She was pleased to see the book of garden birds was still intact, albeit battered around the edges. It was as she remembered, postcard-sized, a green softback cover with a picture of a goldfinch on the front. She flicked through the pages, unsettling the dust from the edges of the paper. It had a musty smell and she wondered how long it had been since anyone had opened it.

She smiled at the memory of sitting in this very room with Gramps going through the pages. They'd put little pencil crosses by the birds they'd seen in the garden. The crosses were still there and as she ran her finger over the pencil marks, she felt a wave of nostalgia, followed by a little smattering of sadness. Gramps wouldn't remember those times. What had once been a memory they would have shared and been able to recall together, was now something only she had the knowledge of. She placed the book on the arm of the sofa with some vague hope that if Gramps and Esther looked through the book, it might strike a chord with Gramps and trigger some sort of recollection.

She thought of Gramps and Maryse. There was no one to tell their story first-hand now. Sure, she and Joe had found out a lot of what happened, but it wasn't the same as someone recounting a personal experience, where they'd add the tiny details that made it their own story, details that couldn't be found anywhere else other than in their minds.

The doorbell broke her thoughts and she went to answer it, hoping it would be Joe. He'd texted her last night to say he'd be with her by mid-morning.

She was pleased to see it was him. 'Come on in then.' She paused as Joe hesitated.

Joe pinched his bottom lip between his finger and thumb and then rubbed at his forehead. 'Erm…'

'What is it?' Maddy felt her smile drop from her face. 'What's wrong?'

Joe held up his hands. 'Nothing really. I… erm…' He glanced back down the drive and Maddy followed his gaze where she saw a taxi idling at the roadside.

She looked and looked again, this time closer. Her hand flew to her mouth. 'Oh my God. What? Is that…? Joe! Is that who I think it is?'

61

June 1947

Another long bus ride and Arthur found himself in Vannes. He checked his watch. If he was lucky and could find the school where Maryse worked, he might just be able to catch her leaving for home.

He grabbed a map from one of the tabac stores, asking if they knew where St Suzanne school was.

'*Désolé, Monsieur,*' replied the man as he handed Arthur the change. 'I'm sorry I can't help you.'

'What are you looking for?' asked a woman who was behind Arthur in the queue.

'*L'ecole St Suzanne.*' Arthur unfolded the map and looked hopefully at the woman.

'*Oui...*' She ran her finger across the map. '*Alors... c'est la.*' She tapped at the map where a lake was shown. '*Près du lac.*'

Arthur thanked the woman profusely and headed off in the direction the woman had shown him. It was about a ten-minute walk. The anticipation and excitement of seeing Maryse urged him on and in no time at all, he was turning the corner and the school was in sight.

He paused and took a moment to catch his breath. He

smoothed down his hair, brushed the arms of his jacket and
fiddled with his collar to make sure it was flat. There, he was
all ready to see her.

Some children were still leaving the school but it looked
more like the tail end of the pupils; it was now four-thirty
and school would be over, thought Arthur. A couple of
parents looked to be waiting outside, talking to each other,
two women and a man, but they didn't look to be in any
particular hurry. One of the women was holding the hand of
a little girl and the other woman was keeping an eye on what
her son was doing. He looked about two years old and was
fascinated by something on the ground as he crouched down.

Arthur watched the main gate and the playground beyond.
Any minute now, she'd come out. He knew it.

And then, there she was.

Walking across the playground.

Arthur's heart missed a beat.

His breath caught in his throat.

She was as beautiful, if not more so, than he remembered.

Her hair was fashioned neatly away from her face, a stray
strand lifting in the gentle breeze. She was wearing a skirt
and blouse with a cardigan across her shoulders. In one arm
she held some books as she glided across the playground. She
looked his way. Arthur raised a hand but she was already
turning her head away. As she came through the gate, the man
who had been talking to the two women stepped towards her.
She was still smiling, in that beautiful warm way she did. He
remembered it so clearly from their time at the farm.

Two older children had come out with her and she placed
an arm on the girl's shoulder, dipping her head and laughing
at a shared joke. The boy said something, laughed and ran on
to greet the man on the other side of the school gate.

Arthur could barely take his eyes off Maryse but he took a moment to look at the children and the man. They were all at ease with each other and in that second, a realisation struck him.

Rooted to the spot, he watched the man put his hand out towards Maryse and greet her with a kiss on each cheek. It was then Arthur noticed the man was holding a bunch of flowers, which he presented to Maryse. She laughed, her hand going to her chest in surprise as she took the flowers and then kissed him. But this time it wasn't a kiss of friends greeting each other. Arthur recognised the kiss. It was one shared between lovers. The man slipped his arm around her waist and pulled her towards him, clearly revelling in the embrace.

And then the little boy who he thought was with the other woman appeared at Maryse's side, tugging at her skirt. She pulled away from the man, who took the books and flowers from her so she could bend down and scoop the small child up into her arms, before showering him with kisses. The boy giggled and Arthur recognised the smile on the boy – the same beautiful smile as his mother's.

He realised his hand had paused in mid-air as he had gone to wave to get her attention. He let his hand fall away. Arthur thought he was going to be sick. He shouldn't have come. How stupid of him to think he could simply turn up here and she would be waiting for him.

His whole body felt heavy and weary. It took all the effort he could summon to turn and walk away.

He barely heard the distant sound of a woman's voice calling out his name. He carried on walking. The calling stopped. Replaced by the sound of heeled feet pounding across the cobbled road. He rounded the corner. He couldn't bear to look back. He didn't want her to see him. She was happy. That was all he could wish for now.

'*Attendez! Arretez! Arretez!*'

The voice was behind him again, demanding he wait. It was as if a bubble around him had been burst and all of a sudden the sounds were no longer muffled. They were crisp and clear. He spun around and there was Maryse standing just a few feet away from him.

'Maryse,' he heard himself whisper.

She was breathing hard where she'd run after him and now there was an uncertainty in her eyes as they raked his body from head to toe. '*C'est toi. C'est vraiment toi.*' She took three uncertain steps towards him.

Arthur didn't move. He didn't know what to do. He wanted to swamp her in her arms but he was immobile. He was confused. Hurt. Wounded all over again, except this time the damage was to his heart.

She was standing right in front of him now. Slowly, she reached up a hand and touched his face, holding the palm of her hand to his cheek. 'They told me you were dead.' Her voice was laden with a disbelief.

'They were wrong,' said Arthur, gently.

The tears spilled from her eyes and she flung her arms around his neck. Arthur held her with equal strength with his good arm. Oh God, it felt so good to have her close to him again. He had dreamed of this moment for so long. It had been the one thought that had kept him going through those long nights in the hospital as he recovered from the surgery he'd needed on his shoulder. He had agonised about her every minute of the day, worrying about her, wondering if she was safe. Planning how he'd go back for her. And now, after all this time, he'd found her but she hadn't waited for him. He couldn't blame her. How could he? She thought he was dead. She was young and beautiful. Why would she still be single?

It was a sobering thought and he gently eased himself from her embrace. Maryse was crying and he pulled a handkerchief from his pocket, flapped it open and offered it to her.

She took it, dabbed her eyes and then paused as she noticed the embroidered letter M in the corner. 'You kept it.'

'Of course.'

She passed the handkerchief back to him, their fingertips only a hair's breadth apart. 'I tried to find you,' she said. 'I went to England. I didn't know where to start but someone put me in touch with someone else from the British Army. They gave me an address in...' She hesitated as she tried to recall the name.

'Peterborough,' put in Arthur. 'A guest house in Peterborough.'

'You know? You went there?'

'I did but only last week. It's closed up now. No longer a guest house.'

Her face fell as more disappointment settled on her. 'I didn't know where else to look. I tried to find your farm but I had no address. I scoured the villages all over Cambridgeshire but I couldn't find you.' An anguished sob escaped.

'It's OK,' said Arthur. 'I'm so sorry.'

'I had to come back. I had no money and no more clues as to where you were. And then... when I got home about a week later, I received a letter to say you hadn't survived your injuries and all that time I had been looking for you, I thought it was all in vain. For no reason, for you were already...' She couldn't finish the sentence.

'Oh my darling Maryse,' said Arthur, pulling her towards him once again. He didn't care she wasn't his to hold like this anymore. He didn't care that her husband and child were just around the corner. All he cared about was her. He wanted to take away her pain. It was easier to deal with someone else's heartache than his own. He kissed the top of her head, stroked her hair and murmured soothing sounds.

He didn't know how long they stood like that, neither wanting to pull away as he knew that once they did, they would have to confront the awful truth of reality. He wanted to make the most of every single second, as he knew he would never be able to hold her again after this.

'Maryse! Maryse?' It was the voice of a man behind them that finally broke their embrace. Arthur knew it was her husband and he let his arms fall away from her.

Maryse took a step back and looked at the man who was standing there with the child in his arms. 'Gilbert... this is...' her words faltered.

Gilbert nodded. 'I know.' He looked at Arthur. 'You're the English soldier.'

'Yes.' Arthur didn't know what else to say.

Gilbert studied Arthur and then Maryse before speaking again. 'It's obviously a shock for my wife.' He held up his hand to quell whatever Maryse was about to say. 'I'll wait by the lake for a while.' He looked at Arthur again. 'You have my trust.'

'Thank you,' replied Arthur. He couldn't help but admire Gilbert's dignified response to the situation as the Frenchman walked off carrying his son with him.

'He's a good man,' said Maryse, turning to Arthur.

'I can see that. And the boy?'

Her face lit up for a moment. 'Mine and Gilbert's son. Thomas. He's eighteen months.'

'He has your eyes and your smile.'

They stood looking at each other, neither speaking. Arthur

just watched her, wanting to take in every contour of her body, every line on her face, every hair on her head. He wanted to remember her this way, with that small smile and look of love on her face as she thought of her son – oh, so beautiful. But not his. She never would be.

'What about you?' she asked breaking the moment. 'Have you…' She stumbled over the words.

'No. No wife. No children,' he replied. It was true. He had returned from war and hadn't been able to settle. He hadn't been able to contemplate another woman. And now, it was too late. His heart ached so much, he could feel it beginning to fracture.

Maryse took his left hand in hers and gently ran her other hand up his arm to his shoulder. 'They fixed you.'

He slipped his hand over hers, noting the wedding band on her finger, before covering it with his own. Out of sight and out of mind, just for a few moments. 'Yes. Arm's not much use though. They did their best.'

She rested her head on his shoulder and Arthur moved his hand around to cup the nape of her neck. He rested his cheek on her head and closed his eyes. His darling Maryse.

'Are you happy?' she asked, not moving away.

'Are you?' he replied.

'At this moment in time, I am the happiest I have been since you left but I am also the saddest I've been.'

And wasn't that the truth? Arthur couldn't have said it better himself. 'If you're happy then so am I. Just think of now, this moment. Don't think of what's been before or what's to come. Just this precise moment.'

She sighed deeply and held him tightly. 'You were and still are the love of my life,' she whispered.

'And you mine.'

Dear God, he didn't want this moment to end. If he could freeze time and stay like this forever then he knew he absolutely would. He would never let her go again. Not ever.

Arthur had no concept of time, but eventually Maryse raised her head. 'I have to go.' The tears were falling freely down her face.

'I know,' replied Arthur, wiping the tears away with his fingertips. He lowered his mouth onto hers. One last kiss. One he would cherish all his life.

And then she was moving away from him, her hand sliding back down his arm, the fingers entwining, pausing for a moment to look at each other, before breaking contact.

Arthur stood fixed to the spot as he watched her walk quickly away, her head bowed. She stopped at the corner of the street, took one last look back at him, her face crumpling with emotion before fleeing out of sight.

He looked at the empty space for a long time. A small part of him hoping she'd come back but he knew she wouldn't and he had no right to expect her to. He'd lost her but he knew his time with her was a precious memory he would cherish forever.

62

Maddy watched as Joe went back to the car and helped Yvette Tresor out and guided her up to the front door.

'Yvette, I had no idea,' began Maddy.

Yvette kissed Maddy on each side of the face. 'I'm sorry to surprise you like this. I didn't tell anyone we were coming. I only contacted Joe last night when we were already here. I had the business card he left with me.'

'We? You said we were coming?' Maddy looked beyond her visitor where Joe was now accompanying a smartly dressed man about Yvette's age. Maddy looked at Yvette in amazement as she rapidly tried to process what was happening. 'Your brother?'

'Yes. Jean-Paul. He wanted to come as well. We both want to see your grandfather. I have something for him.'

'OK, you'd better come inside.' Maddy took her guests through to the living room where she was formerly introduced to Jean-Paul.

'Sorry for the unexpected visit,' said Jean-Paul, his French accent more pronounced than his sister's.

'No, it's fine. I mean, it's great. I just need to prepare Gramps for this as much as possible,' she explained. 'I'm sure Yvette told you my grandfather's memory is failing. I hope you won't be disappointed if he doesn't recognise you, especially after all this time.' Although as she spoke the words she was aware of the bubble of excitement inside her at the thought Gramps might remember them. That would be amazing.

'We understand,' replied Yvette. 'Have you told him about Maryse?'

Maddy fiddled with her necklace. 'I haven't been able to bring myself to tell him yet.'

'Again, we understand,' came Yvette's reassuring reply.

'Just give me a minute to speak to him,' said Maddy, gathering her emotions together as she went to bring Gramps and Esther in from the garden.

Gramps was relaxing in his deckchair while Esther sat beside him sketching some of the garden birds they had been watching earlier that morning.

'Oh, hello,' said Gramps as she approached.

'We have some visitors,' said Maddy, sitting down next to him. 'Two people to see you.'

'Me? That's nice.'

'It's a French lady and her brother. You met them when they were children. When you were in France.' Maddy watched carefully to see if there was any recognition from her grandfather. 'It's Yvette. Yvette Rochelle. And her brother Jean-Paul.' Still there was no sign Gramps knew who she was talking about. 'Shall we go inside and meet them?'

'Yes. Meet them. Good idea.'

Maddy took Gramps into the living room and seated him in his usual chair by the window, before going to the dining room where their guests were waiting. 'I've told him you're here but I don't think he really understands what I'm saying.'

Yvette gave a sympathetic smile. 'Do not worry. Maybe when he sees us, he will remember.'

Maddy wasn't sure that would be the case and could already feel the disappointment welling up inside her. Nevertheless, she took the sister and brother into the living room.

'Gramps. It's Yvette and Jean-Paul. They've come from France to see you.'

She saw the love and emotion on the Frenchwoman's face as she stepped forward. 'Arthur. It's me, Yvette.' She took Gramps's hand and sat on the chair next to him. 'How are you?'

Gramps looked at Yvette for a long moment. 'Hello, duck. How are you?'

Maddy was sure this was Gramps's stock answer, one he employed when he didn't know who he was talking to. Her heart felt a little heavier. 'Yvette who you rescued in France,' she put in, trying to tap into his memory. 'You and Maryse rescued Yvette and her brother.' She indicated for Jean-Paul to go over to Gramps.

'Arthur,' said the Frenchman in his native language. 'It's me, Jean-Paul Rochelle. How are you? It is nice to see you again.' He held out his hand and Gramps shook hands.

'Nice to see you too.'

Another bland response, one born out of good manners and a habit decades old. Maddy was disheartened and silently remonstrated with herself for hoping otherwise. Why would Gramps recognise Yvette and her brother after all these years? In his mind they were still young children. He couldn't identify with them as adults and it was heart-breaking to acknowledge. How would he ever find the peace she so longed for him to have?

'Don't upset yourself,' said Yvette. 'Under normal circumstances it would be difficult to think of me and my brother, now in our eighties, as two terrified young children.'

'We are glad we came to see him,' said Jean-Paul. 'But we prepared ourselves for this... erm... this outcome.'

Maddy retreated to the dining room where Esther was showing Joe some of her YouTube videos. She smiled to herself as she watched unnoticed for a few moments, finding comfort in the sight of them together, knowing how much Esther was enjoying being with Joe again where he could fulfil all her ambitions of what a father was supposed to be like.

Joe looked up. 'Hey. How's it going?'

Maddy shook her head and gave a sigh. 'He doesn't recognise them.'

'Give him time.'

Later when they were all gathered in the living room, where Maddy had managed to rustle up enough sandwiches and refreshments for everyone, she looked around and could feel a sense of unity and belonging between them. They were all bonded together through their love for Gramps and for each other. Gramps looked happy and although he didn't appear to consciously acknowledge who their visitors were, she hoped he could sense the love that swamped the room.

'Thank you so much for coming,' she said to Yvette and Jean-Paul. 'I can't tell you how much it means to us.'

'It was the right thing to do. We have come with our families and their blessings,' replied Yvette. 'Even our brother, Thomas, agreed we should come. Unfortunately, the story of Maryse and your grandfather has not been one we have talked much about with Thomas. It never felt appropriate, so he didn't fully understand the circumstances.'

'The last thing we wanted was to cause upset to anyone.'

Yvette gave a philosophical shrug. 'There is nothing for

any of us to fear from the truth. In fact, that is what made us come. There is something I need to tell you. Something that I didn't tell you before.'

Maddy exchanged a look with Joe but he shrugged, seemingly as in the dark as she was. 'What's that?' asked Maddy gently.

Yvette smoothed out her skirt across her knees. She glanced at Esther but Maddy nodded. Esther was as much a part of this story as they all were and Maddy knew she could trust Yvette's judgement in what was appropriate to say in front of her. Yvette returned the nod before speaking. 'After you had been to see me, I spoke with both my brothers and, as you know, Thomas disagreed with talking about the past. He was frightened how it might affect the way people thought of his mother and father.'

'In what way?' asked Maddy.

'He didn't want people to think that his mother didn't love his father. He didn't want her name… er… tarnished.'

'He wanted to protect his parents,' explained Jean-Paul.

'I can understand that,' said Maddy. 'I feel the same about Gramps and my grandmother but I've come to the conclusion that both relationships my grandfather had were real and genuine, but different because of the circumstances and that Gramps loved them both.'

Yvette clapped her hands together. '*Exactement!* Exactly!' She turned to Gramps. 'Arthur, my brave hero, Maryse loved you dearly. You filled her heart with hope, love and compassion when all around there was despair, hate and fear. You were her first love and always in her heart. Dear Maryse had a big heart – big enough to love not just her own son, but me and my brother and of course to love the father of her son.'

Maddy watched Gramps carefully for any flicker of understanding and although he was looking intently at Yvette as she spoke, first in English and then repeated it in French, he was expressionless. She moved over to sit on the footstool in front of him.

'Gramps,' she said, gaining his attention. 'Maryse loved you very much and if she could, I'm sure she would be here to tell you herself.' An unexpected lump lodged itself in her throat and it took her two attempts to continue speaking. 'Maryse can't be here because she isn't with us anymore... She's passed away.' Still no indication of comprehension. It was brutal but Maddy felt it necessary. 'Gramps... Maryse is dead.'

The silence in the room was suffocating and filled every space around them.

'Arthur,' said Yvette breaking the tension. 'I have a letter from Maryse. She left it for you.'

'What?' Maddy tried to hide her shock at this announcement.

'I'm sorry, I should have given it to you before,' said Yvette. 'But although I was happy to see you and I firmly believe we should not bury the past, I too was scared. You see, Maryse didn't tell anyone about this letter. It was found after she passed away. It was in another envelope with instructions to pass on if Arthur or his family ever came looking for her.' She bowed her head. 'I needed to be sure your intentions were...' She waved her hand as if fishing for the word. 'Your intentions were genuine. I needed time to think if I could leave things as they were or if there was a final part of the story.'

'And I take it you decided there was?' It upset Maddy to see the anxiety in the older woman's eyes.

'Yes. After you left, I opened the letter and read it. I

showed it to my brothers and we decided your grandfather had a right to know the contents and that it was unfair of us not to let you know either. Most of all, it would be going against Maryse's wishes and none of us, despite our concerns or personal thoughts, believed this was right.'

'So, here we are,' said Jean-Paul. 'To bring the letter and to give everyone closure.' From the inside pocket of his jacket he produced a folded piece of paper and held it out to Maddy.

Maddy eyed the letter with a sense of longing that this would indeed be the final piece to join up the dots of Gramps's love affair with Maryse. She took the letter and carefully unfolded it. The hand-scripted words flowed across the page but as Maddy began reading it, her eyes blurred with tears and she had to swipe them away before they landed on the paper and smudged the writing. She felt Joe's arm around her shoulders but it was Esther's hand that eased the letter from her fingers.

'You read it,' said Esther, passing it to Yvette. 'Please?'

Yvette hesitated. 'Do you want me to?' She looked at Maddy for the answer.

'Oh, I don't know,' said Maddy. 'I'm not sure that's a good idea.'

'Why not?' Esther squared her shoulders. 'Gramps might understand it more from Yvette. It might jog his memory.'

'I'm not sure it's as easy as that,' replied Maddy, wiping her nose with the tissue Joe had produced from somewhere.

'I think it's a good idea,' said Joe. 'What harm will it do? If Gramps doesn't understand then he is in no better or worse place than he is now.'

'And if he does?' Maddy hated the way they were talking about Gramps as if he wasn't there but he hadn't shown any sign of recognition when Yvette and Jean-Paul had arrived and was now gazing out of the window, talking about the birds in the garden.

'I'm happy to read the letter,' said Yvette.

Maddy fiddled with the cuffs of her cardigan as she argued with herself whether this was a good idea or not. She looked around at the hopeful faces in the room and then at Gramps. She didn't have the right to deny him this last chance. She nodded. 'Thank you, Yvette. That would be kind of you.'

All eyes were fixed on Yvette as with one hand holding the paper and the other Gramps's hand, she read the letter out loud. It was written in French and Yvette carefully translated the words into English.

Arthur, mon amour

I don't know if you will ever read this but if you are, then it means you, or someone who cares for you, came to find how our story ended and although I may know how it ended, I've always worried you have not had the same privilege. I'm only sorry I didn't get the chance to tell you that day in Vannes.

The brother and sister, Yvette and Jean-Paul – those two terrified children you so willingly took back to England with you – I went back for them.

I made a promise that I would look after them and I wasn't going to break that promise. I brought them home with me to France where they were welcomed into my family and I was able to keep my promise to their father. But just as importantly, through them, I somehow felt closer to you. They were the connection that was never broken – a constant reminder of what we had sacrificed. Every time I look at them, I think of you.

I wish we could have met in another life, another time, mon amour. But we met at the wrong time, when our stars were unable to align, when there was so much turbulence in the world and so much for us still to do before we were able to freely love one another.

That's not to say I have not had a good life and spent many happy years with my family, for whom I would never have known such joy had things been different. So I cannot regret how my life turned out but at the same time, I cannot forget you and only dream of how it might have been. I have loved as I am sure you have loved, but it has been unlike anything I experienced with you. You were, always have been and always will be the love of my life.

My darling Arthur, always in my heart and soul. xxx

Everyone was watching Gramps for a reaction and although he had been looking at Yvette, there was not a shred of understanding.

'Read it again,' said Maddy.

Yvette did so. This time the words were more fluent in their translation but, again, Gramps did not react. He looked at Yvette, tipping his head to one side and Maddy found herself gripping Joe's hand tightly as she waited for him to recognise the lady before him but her hopes were dashed as he returned his gaze to the window.

'Read it in French,' said Esther. 'Please, read it in French to him.' She sounded desperate and Maddy's heart went out to her daughter.

'*D'accord*,' agreed Yvette. Reading in her native tongue was like someone sprinkling fairy dust in the air. The flow, the rhythm, the pattern of the speech, the emphasis on words was magical and sounded so much more sincere. There was far more emotion in Yvette's tone now, as if she was saying the words from her own heart.

By the time she had finished, both Maddy and Yvette were in tears. Maddy yearned for Gramps to say something, anything, even the slightest flicker of understanding, but his eyes showed no comprehension.

Yvette was talking softly to him in French now, her words filling the silence in the room. She was talking about when she was a child and how Maryse would teach them handwriting skills in the classroom. She was recounting a story where Yvette had been having great difficulty learning a particular poem for a school play and how Maryse had spent time after school helping her learn the lines.

'She was very kind,' Yvette said. 'She always had time for everybody. She always championed the underdog and helped people whenever she could. She would stand up for the weaker ones and challenge the stronger ones. I'm so glad she came and found us in England and took us back to France. Just before we were bundled on to the plane that night, she hugged me and whispered in my ear that I was to stay strong and she would come and find me one day and take me home. She promised she would not forget me. She always kept her promises.'

Gramps smiled and looked at Yvette. 'That's nice, duck.'

Maddy sighed. She felt disappointed not just for Gramps, not just for herself but for everyone in the room, for they had all played a part in making this moment happen and sadly there was no reward for any of them. 'Thank you,' she said to Yvette and then to Jean-Paul. 'I'm sorry...' Her voice trailed away.

'Please, do not worry,' said Yvette. 'If he doesn't remember then I hope he has some inner peace in his subconscious.'

Soon afterwards, the guests were gathering their coats and saying their goodbyes with promises to keep in touch. 'My son is waiting at our hotel in London,' explained Yvette. 'He wanted to travel with us but he didn't want to intrude by coming here.'

'He would have been more than welcome. When are you returning to France?' asked Maddy.

'We have a flight tomorrow. I'm glad we came and I'm very happy to have seen your grandfather again.' Yvette went back into the living room where Gramps was listening to a compilation of wartime tunes. Maddy watched from the doorway as Yvette knelt down in front of Gramps. 'Arthur, we are going now. Thank you for everything you did for us when we were children. I shall never forget your kindness and bravery.'

Gramps looked at Yvette. 'I wasn't brave. Maryse was the brave one,' he said.

Maddy stifled a gasp of surprise at this moment of lucidity. Yvette shot her a glance before returning to Gramps. 'She was indeed a brave woman. She sacrificed so much for those she loved.'

Maddy was aware of Joe now standing at her shoulder as she watched the exchange between her grandfather and the woman he'd rescued.

Gramps reached for Yvette's hand and held it tightly with both of his. '*Merci de m'avoir dit que ma chère Maryse a été heureuse. Cela m'a fait beaucoup de bien. Je suis content que tu sois en sécurité. Je n'ai plus lieu de m'inquiéter, ma petite.*'

'What did he say?' whispered Joe.

It took a moment before Maddy could compose herself as she watched Yvette crumple, her forehead resting on

Gramps's hands, who then slid one hand out and stroked the top of Yvette's head. 'Don't cry, duck.'

Maddy wiped her own tears away. 'He said, "I'm glad my darling Maryse was happy. Thank you for telling me. I'm glad you're safe. I have no need to worry anymore, my dear child."'

'Amazing,' murmured Joe. 'Simply amazing.'

Joe stayed with Maddy after Yvette and Jean-Paul had left and helped her get Gramps to bed. The events of the day had taken their toll and Gramps had been tired that evening.

After Esther had also gone to bed, Maddy finally felt she was able to relax and snuggled up to Joe on the sofa with a glass of wine.

'Wow, what a day,' she said.

'I know, right,' replied Joe, pulling her into him and kissing the top of her head.

'Love is an amazing thing,' said Maddy as she sipped her wine. 'It's such a powerful emotion that it can both transcend and endure time. And after all that happened, it triumphs over everything.'

'That's what true love does,' said Joe.

'You sound very certain.'

'I am. I can say that with authority.' Joe turned Maddy around to face him. 'Look, I know I got it wrong before. It's not an excuse, but I was frightened of the strength of emotion. The strength of how much I loved you.'

Maddy nodded. 'I think we've both come a long way since then. I think we were both frightened of love.'

'It's just I'd seen what it did to my mum and how the breakdown of a twenty-five-year marriage crippled her.

I never wanted to feel so vulnerable.'

'And I felt I was being rejected again and to be honest, I thought that for a long time but now I realise it wasn't my fault.'

'It wasn't your fault and I'm sorry if I added to the list of rejecters and contributed to you feeling like that.' Joe put his glass on the table. 'I'm telling you now, Maddy, I was a complete arse. I'd like to think I'm not anymore. If your grandfather's story has taught me anything, then it's not to waste my life running.'

Maddy swallowed hard. She knew this was the second chance for them and Joe was right, not everyone got that second chance. And not only that, but she knew Joe wanted to be part of not just her life, but part of Esther's and Gramps's lives too. He wanted the whole shebang. 'That makes two of us.'

'And so there's no doubt,' carried on Joe. 'I love you, Maddy.'

Her heart raced at his words. Oh, how many times had she longed to hear Joe Finch say that to her? Her heart was fit to explode with happiness. 'I love you too.'

63

He knew his name was Arthur Pettinger and he knew he was old. He couldn't remember how old but he was over ninety, he was sure.

'Hi, Gramps.'

Arthur turned as the child came into the room. 'Ah, there you are, duck,' he said. He remembered they were playing a game. He looked at the board in front of him. Snakes and Ladders. Yes, that was it. He congratulated himself for remembering the name.

'Are you ready for another game?' she asked, sitting down on the footstool on the other side of the table.

'I think so,' replied Arthur. He picked up the dice and put it in a little red plastic cup. 'Shall I go first?'

'Ooh, what's this? Snakes and Ladders? Can I come in?'

Arthur looked up and there was his friend, Sheila. He smiled at her. He liked Sheila being here. She would often tell him stories of when she was younger and she liked to sing songs with him. He liked that very much indeed. 'You can only come in if you know the password,' said Arthur with a chuckle.

'Tea and digestive biscuits!' replied Sheila, carrying a tray laden with said goodies.

'You'd better come and make yourself at home in that case.' The door opened again and this time it was Maddy. 'It's like Piccadilly Circus,' said Arthur good-humouredly. He was always pleased to see his granddaughter; she was like a beacon radiating happiness and love wherever she went. He couldn't see it but he could feel it and that's what mattered.

'Everyone OK?' asked Maddy. She walked over to the fireplace and checked herself in the mirror. She was wearing a posh-looking frock, Arthur noted as she looked at her reflection to apply her lipstick.

'You off out dancing?' he asked.

The child laughed. 'Mummy can't dance.'

'I'm sure your mother is a lovely dancer,' said Sheila.

'I'm afraid Esther is right,' said Maddy. 'I've two left feet.'

Arthur danced his feet around on the floor. 'I reckon I could still trip the light fantastic.' He began to hum a tune. He couldn't remember the name of it, but he didn't care. 'Hmm, hmm... meet again... don't know where... hmm, hmm... sunny day.'

Maddy smiled but this time not at Arthur, at someone else. It was another visitor. Another one that Arthur liked.

'Evening, young man,' said Arthur. Blast, he couldn't remember his name.

'Good evening, Arthur.'

'You look smart,' commented Arthur, noting the young man's freshly pressed shirt and trousers.

'Me and Joe are off out for dinner, Gramps,' said Maddy. 'It's our wedding anniversary.'

'Oh, is that right?' said Arthur. He frowned. Was he supposed to know this? When did Maddy get married?

'You came to the wedding,' said Maddy. She took a photo frame from the side and showed it to him. 'That's me. That's Joe. There's Esther as bridesmaid and Matt as best man.

Here's Kay, you know, your nurse. Sheila's next to her. And there's you. You gave me away?'

'Oh, yes,' replied Arthur with relief as a vague memory of that day drifted into his mind. 'You looked beautiful.' He patted Maddy's hand and as she replaced the photo frame above the fire, he felt the memory slipping away. He closed his eyes, trying to catch the last fragments before they fizzled into nothing.

'You OK, Gramps?' asked Maddy.

'Yes. I'm just a little tired now.'

'He'll be fine,' reassured Sheila. 'Esther and I will keep an eye on him.'

Maddy kissed him on the cheek. 'Behave yourself now.'

'Oh, I will,' replied Arthur. He nodded in the young man's direction. 'Don't do anything I wouldn't do.'

Maddy laughed and her and the young man who obviously made her so happy, waltzed out of the room.

'I'll see them out and wash these cups up,' said Sheila, getting up from the chair.

Arthur felt extremely tired again. It was an overwhelming fatigue.

'Shall I put some music on, Gramps?' asked the child. Arthur could hear her getting up and going over to the thingy bob that played the songs he liked. 'What do you want on?'

'Oh, I don't know. Surprise me.'

The gentle notes and soothing voice of Doris Day singing 'Dream A Little Dream' filled the room and Arthur hummed softly along.

'You've got your slippers on the wrong feet, Gramps,' said the child. Her voice sounded thin and far away. 'I'll swap them for you.'

She was such a sweet child, thought Arthur as she took his slippers from his feet and then put them on again.

The song finished and another began. He knew this one well. 'Bye Bye Blackbird'. His heart missed a beat as an image of Maryse filled his mind. He was back in France and he was standing by the river, the secluded spot away from prying eyes. Where he kissed her. Made love to her. Where he told her he would always love her.

She was smiling at him, beckoning him over. She laughed and her eyes sparkled with happiness. Then she was in the water. Calling him again. This time more urgently. Arthur stripped off his shirt, took off his boots and then his trousers.

The thin voice of the child drifted into his thoughts. She was calling him too. 'Gramps? Gramps? Are you OK?' He could feel her tugging at his arm. He didn't know which way to go; he didn't want to leave the child but… but Maryse was still calling him. The child's voice sounded even further away now. She was calling for her mother. Should he wait for her or should he go to Maryse?

And then there was the calm voice of someone else. Close to him, whispering in his ear. 'Gramps, it's me Maddy. It's OK. Everything is OK.' He could feel the touch of her fingertips as they softly stroked his hair. He felt something wet drop on his face. She was crying. Arthur was confused. He didn't want Maddy to cry. 'I love you, Gramps. It's OK. It really is.' He tried to open his eyes but they were so tired and too heavy and yet his body felt weightless.

Another hand slid into his, holding on to him as if he might slip away on a breeze. He knew it was the child. His heart expanded with love and he took one more deep breath, which rattled his lungs.

Maryse was calling again and he knew it was time to fulfil his promise and go back to her.

Acknowledgements

First on my list of thanks has to be to my fabulous agent, Hattie Grünewald, who believed in not only me, but this story when it was a mere idea on paper and who has championed both myself and this book without question. For the many hours Hattie, together with her assistant Sarah Conkerton, have read and reread this story, offering advice and insightful feedback.

A big thank you to my editor, Hannah Smith, for her love and enthusiasm for this story, which meant an awful lot to me. For all Hannah's fantastic feedback and advice in helping shape this book into the best version of itself.

Of course, writing a story is only a small part of getting it to publication so I want to thank the whole of the Aria Fiction team who have worked on this book – you are all wonderful!

Merci to fellow author, Carol Cooper, for her advice on the French language – usual disclaimer that any mistakes are very much mine.

I must also pay tribute to my youngest daughter whose relationship with my dad was one of great love and friendship and, although this book is not my dad's story, they were both the inspiration behind it.

SUZANNE FORTIN

My whole family and close writing friends have continually supported me with this book and I cannot express how much I appreciate this. The idea of the book came about a long time before it was written and my family have never faltered in their encouragement, showing incredible patience and belief. Much love to you all.

A huge thank you to the book blogging community for their wonderful support and for generously giving their time to read, review and spread the love of books.

Biggest thanks must go to my lovely readers, those who have found me through this book, together with those who know me from my suspense books and have come along with me as I step into another genre. Without you all, I wouldn't be able to do what I love doing.

About the Author

SUZANNE FORTIN writes women's fiction dual-timeline novels where she loves to bring the present and the past together, exploring relationships and adding a touch of mystery and suspense. Suzanne also writes as Sue Fortin where she is a USA Today bestseller, Amazon UK #1 and Amazon US #3 bestseller. She has sold over a million copies of her books and been translated into multiple languages.

Hello from Aria

We hope you enjoyed this book! If you did let us know, we'd love to hear from you.

We are Aria, a dynamic digital-first fiction imprint from award-winning independent publishers Head of Zeus. At heart, we're committed to publishing fantastic commercial fiction – from romance and sagas to crime, thrillers and historical fiction. Visit us online and discover a community of like-minded fiction fans!

We're also on the look out for tomorrow's superstar authors. So, if you're a budding writer looking for a publisher, we'd love to hear from you.
You can submit your book online at ariafiction.com/we-want-read-your-book

You can find us at:
Email: aria@headofzeus.com
Website: www.ariafiction.com
Submissions: www.ariafiction.com/we-want-read-your-book

   @ariafiction
   @Aria_Fiction
   @ariafiction